HATCHED
BY
JASON R. DAVIS

FoF PUBLISHING

Published by
FoF Publishing
1526 Kenilworth Ct.
Suite #1
Stoughton, WI 60115

Please visit us online at http://fofpublishing.com
Jason Davis website can be found at http://jasonrdavis.net

Cover Illustration by
SnS-Photo (Jim Sorfleet)
Cover Model: Kat McGill Mayer
Special Effects Makeup: Anthony Glenn Jaskulski
Copyright 2013
Cover Design by
Willy Adkins

Dedicated to my mother,
You have always supported me
in writing and in life…
Thank You

PROLOGUE

Jaime looked around the room. It was dark, barely lit by the twelve black candles that flickered and danced, sending shadows and around the room. While she stood by herself in the center, kneeling in front of the little makeshift altar before her, the shadows dancing around her electrified her with the sensation that she had more people, more like her, and they were all with her and around her. They were there to be a part of her and to feed her

The shadow people danced and along the walls, their images flickering over her bookcase partially full with some Stephen King, some Dean Koontz and the occasional John Grisham, early ones before he became a full-fledged novelist and just another word machine. Those weren't the books the shadow people danced over; those weren't the ones that called to her. It was what was on the bottom shelf that had them dancing. Those were her other books. Some were books on Wicca religion, but then there were others with actual spells. The other books concerned voodoo and witchcraft. There was a book on how to channel demons and an older book on how to trap and steal spirits. Most of the books were old and withered where only partial titles could be read.

All the books were well-used and marked with the Hammond Public Library seal, both on their visible sides and on their inside covers. They were all well past overdue, but she had no plans on returning them.

They were hers now. The books had told her that.

They had called out to her, had pulled her to them back when she used to go there every week and check out the latest new releases. Something about that back area, the hidden corner, the place in the library that seemed like the sun could never reach, had spoken to her. It told her to take those books home. She wouldn't need them then but, someday, there would be a time.

Jaimie looked up from the boiling pot and around at the dancing shadows. Something was happening. She could feel it. The night was alive; it had a presence and it was there with her. Something alive was in the room with her. It caressed her; she could feel its dark hands on her body, kneading her, feeling along her flesh. She could feel it as it moved along her, and then she let out a joyful gasp as she felt it slip inside of her.

It seemed to infuse her with an energy. She could feel the moon outside speaking to her. It was telling her what to do, and that it was time to finish this. The spell was ready to be made. It was time to pull them all together. All those books, so many thoughts, theories and beliefs but the moon and the shadows had showed her the common thread. That there was magic between the pages. That there was power by taking a little part from here and an incantation from there.

She had a way to use all those different books and religions, to use the pieces, because it wasn't so much the parts that made it work. It was how she made it whole. The true power in the magic came from her hate.

Wait, no, that wasn't right. She didn't hate him; she loved him. She didn't want to truly hurt him. She just wanted him to know how much he had hurt her. She just wanted him to come back to her.

He was hers, he should want to come back. He should know that death couldn't keep him from her, that they were eternally together.

But he was such an asshole. He deserved to hurt the way she hurt. He tore out her heart and left her on the floor crying. He has to know how that feels. He needed to feel how it felt to have your heart go numb and die in your chest. That pain of knowing that you were never going to truly be alive anymore because someone had crushed your essence and walked all over it like you were nothing.

Yeah. He needed to know. It was time for him to know.
It was time for that bastard to pay. But no-
No, that wasn't right. It was time for him to come back
to her.
It was time.

CHAPTER 1

"This is the screamin' demon heading westbound on I-80. I need a bacon check, come back," Bruce said into his radio. The road seemed clear ahead of him but it was a dark night, hard to see past the overpasses where there might be a pig hiding back in its sty waiting to write him up on some paper. The last thing he needed on this last leg would be a damned ticket.

He had already been on the road steady for thirteen straight days and was ready to take a hot shower and sleep in his own bed. He had four days off coming up on his return leg and was itching to spend almost all of that time in his own bed. His ice box had been acting up for the last couple of days, costing him a lot of time with having to make additional stops to check on his load. A couple of the times, he had to work on the unit to make sure it stayed cool and kept the meat he was hauling from going bad.

His CB crackled to life. "Hey, Demon. This is the Cat Scratch Express just coming from that way. You're all clear to exit 93. Smooth sailing."

"10-4, Cat Scratch. Keep an eye out as there is a bear sitting in that rest stop just past 112. He's perched and ready to pounce."

"10-4. Put the hammer down and catch you on the flip side."

"Stay safe."

"Same. Cat Scratch out."

Well, at least the road would be clear. That was one less thing to weigh on his mind. He would be able to make his way into that little truck stop outside of Ottawa, fill his tank and bed in for the night. Come morning, he would be able to carry on south towards Bloomington-Normal and, by mid-day, he would be home.

Something in the back sleeper area was starting to smell. There was part of that locker room smell of old gym socks which had been growing stronger throughout the cab, but something else also wreaked back there. He would have to clean out the whole truck to find out just what it was.. He should have pulled off and done his clothes along the way, but he had been itching just to get home, see his wife, and maybe even have a tea party with his little girl. His wife had been telling him about how his little girl had thrown a tea party the other day for her and her stuffed animals. He missed it, just like he missed other things, but he hoped he could still get some of that special time.

Maybe, over the weekend, he would get the energy to pull himself out of bed and take her to Build-a-Bear. It wasn't a special occasion, but he wanted to make it special. After all, this was his last long haul and, after this run, he was officially done with his contract. He would now be driving only five days a week and be home every night. His truck was now paid for. It was his. Which meant his life was back in his hands again. No more big companies to pull his strings, as it was now his truck and his rules.

He let out a long yawn and scanned the road ahead of him. Nothing had changed. A long stretch of interstate lay in the glow of the headlights as the road stretched off endlessly into darkness. His eyelids were heavy and his body was growing stiff.

These long hauls, the cross-country runs, were nice at first, got him out to see much of the countryside, allowed him to see places that he otherwise probably would have never seen. He had traveled from the Grand Canyon up to Maine and every mountain road and back again. There wasn't much to the great U.S. that he hadn't seen, and he had decided that it was time to hang up the saddle. His ride was over, or at least this part of it. Hell, it had been fun when he was a new driver, but that had been over ten years ago. He wasn't that young man anymore. He had a family and they missed him as much as he missed them. He needed to get home.

Two weeks after his contract ended, he would be starting up with another company that was based out of his hometown. Smaller company, pay wasn't as much, but he would be home every night and his weekends would be free and clear. He would be with his own truck and good or bad, if it didn't work out, he could always go somewhere else. His contract was over. He was no longer tied by the shackles of a lease. He was free and, as he tried to wipe the sleep out of his eyes, he couldn't think of anything better. There wasn't anything that he wanted more.

Up ahead, he could see the one mile warning for exit 98. The Clock Tower, that was it; that was the name of the damned place at the exit. The diner was in a truck stop that was open twenty-four hours. He would be able to pull off, get some chow for his food tank, get some diesel for his fuel tank, and then settle in for a nice, long shower in one of their stalls.

Tomorrow, he would deliver the load still hooked to him and then he would hightail it to freedom. Free to drive the remaining hundred miles to home. He would be able to get the load dropped off at probably around two in the afternoon so he would be pulling into his own driveway in time for supper.

As his blinker shouted in its rhythmic tick-tock tone, he started to ease his rig into the exit lane. He was already feeling the anticipation of just getting home and sleeping in his own damn bed.

He looked over at the parking lot of the Clock Tower. The lot was full, but the little diner looked nearly empty. Most of the trucks were probably just idling, as their inhabitants were either already asleep or occupied with some lot lizards.

Bruce nestled his rig midway to the back. He didn't want everyone thinking he was pulling in for some action, but he didn't want too many people around him in the morning, waking him up before he was ready. He always preferred to sleep in, miss the morning traffic and drive later than most other drivers. He preferred the night driving. It kept his head clear.

Soon, he would be home. He just needed to drop off the trailer, take a short stint through a couple of small towns, and then he would be pulling into his own driveway. Bruce reached for the door. A Grand Slam sampler sounded good, and he was ready to shovel it down.

A small spider started to crawl down the inside of the window. It was just a small little thing, harmless to anyone, but Bruce still stopped and backed away. He never did like spiders. As a kid, anytime one would bite him he would always break out in a rash and on more than one occasion, he had to be rushed to the hospital for a bad reaction to a the venom. His airways would close up and he would nearly pass out.

A small little spider, but he knew that little creature could kill him if he gave it a chance. He didn't have one of his little pink pills with him to toss down, if needed.

Bruce looked around the cabin. In his passenger seat, there was a case for an audio book he had been listening to earlier. He was sure that the person who lent it to him wasn't going to like spider guts on the back side of the case, but he grabbed it anyway.

He slammed the case against the window and slid it down, making sure the spider was thoroughly smashed, its insides making a smeared trail along his window. It was dead, guts splattered over the large name, Stephen King, and smeared across the image of a dome.

Bruce tossed the case back into the passenger seat and continued to climb out of the cab. "Damn, I hate spiders," he mumbled under his breath.

* * * *

John didn't know what woke him up. He lay there, the little light from the streetlight outside giving him just enough illumination to make out dark shadows in his room. With the lights off, no one, other than himself, would ever be able to find anything as it was all just heaps of dark shapes at odd angles. In the little light, tree branch fingers danced across the walls. If he didn't know better, he could imagine large shadow hands reaching across his room, looking through his boxes of stuff.

Yeah, like they would ever find anything worth a damn, he thought. All he had of value was his stash, the large bag he had just brought back from little Chicago which was tucked nicely away in his closet under a pair of soiled undies that would turn anybody away.

The bud was safe. Ah, yes, the bud was safe.

"Precious sweet bud, let you ripen so fine; precious sweet bud, I'll make you mine," John said to the small, dark bedroom of his apartment. A small smile crept across his lips as he thought about the bag. He had tried to grow his own before, but it never dried right. He wasted a lot of seed and, in the end, he taught himself that it was just too much damn work when all he had to do was take a small little drive to Little Chi-Town and he was coming back happy.

John felt a slight tingle on the hairs of his nose and rubbed at his upper lip. He turned his head, breaking free from the daze of just lying there, to look at the envelope sitting half open on his dresser top. He could just see it, slightly hanging over the edge. Damn bitch probably put itching powder in the shit, he thought. When he had opened the envelope, the only thing written inside had been "Enjoy". Now, there were just faint traces of the white powder left.

And he had. He had never been a big fan of the "nose candy", but was never one to turn away a good high when it came his way. He was just surprised to see it coming from Miss Psycho Queen. He guessed she still wasn't going to take his "get lost" for an answer. Damn, why did he have to date the crazy ones; the ones that would never go away no matter how hard he tried.

He pushed himself up, moving into a sitting position with his legs running along the hardwood floor. The floor was cool against his feet, which felt good in the warm stuffy heat of his place. He wished like hell he could afford a damn air conditioner, and thought about possibly stealing one from somebody's window. He reached over to the side of his bed and fumbled to turn on his basketball lamp. He had to fight with the little push pull switch to get it to turn on and grumbled with himself as he fought with it but, in his third attempt, the lamp finally clicked on and light flooded the little studio apartment.

Out of the corner of his eye, he could have sworn that he saw little black things scurrying out of sight. They had been just at the corner of his vision which made it hard for him to be sure but, by the time he had turned, any traces were gone. Probably figments of his imagination he thought, as he tried to rub the sleep from his eyes. He didn't have the cleanest of places, but at least it had never been one known for roaches so he knew he was safe there. Still, he could have sworn he had seen something, but then it was gone, probably buried deep in one of the different piles of dirty clothes that littered the floor of the small room. Well, if they had gone in there, they were surely dead by now.

Ugh, why the hell was he up in the middle of the damn night. He leaned forward and pulled himself up from the mattresses that he had plopped down onto the floor. His bedroom was never meant to house visitors so he kept it with the barest of essentials and the mess stretched wide. The mattresses on the hardwood floor, his clothes just thrown about, trash littered in the general direction of the kitchen area. He had a heavily worn, badly tattered couch that had stuffing coming out at various seems along the back edges. Across from it was his television. The only thing in his apartment worth a damn was his 37" flat panel television that he was currently renting-to-own.

He looked through the open door of his bedroom, towards the living room. The television cast a soft glow, still on but in sleep mode. It was always the centerpiece of the apartment. It was the only thing that wasn't old, tattered, and a piece of crap.

John stumbled across the room, walking over the piles of clothes as he made it to the front hallway. It was dark from only catching a slight glow cast from the little lamp. Not that it mattered much. His eyelids had grown heavy and, as he stumbled, he wondered why the hell he was even trying to make his way to the bathroom. The heavy pain in his stomach and the burning sensation coming from his bowels reminded him why as he stepped into the little bathroom and clicked on the light. It flashed a few times before coming to life.

He barely caught a glimpse of his pale reflection in the mirror as he stepped past it to the toilet. The seat was up-- ahhhhh, the life of a bachelor--and he didn't even worry about closing the door behind him. His eyes were closed. As he listened to the sound of water on water, he felt the easing release of the pressure that had been building up. Sometimes there was no greater joy.

As he finished and opened his eyes to flush, he noticed the red tinge of the toilet water. It was dark red, red as the crimson life force that coursed through his veins. That had better not been coming from him. He looked at the redness, studied it, trying to see if there was any way it could have come from the water itself. He reached forward and flushed. As the red liquid went spiraling down to unknown locations of the sewer, fresh clear water replaced it.

"Ah, fuck me," he said to himself. Last thing he wanted was to be pissing blood again.

John groggily stepped over to the sink. He was going to wash his hands, not that he was the most sanitary of persons, but he had been taught to do so as a child and it was one habit he never had broken.

However, he was stopped by the pale reflection of himself that looked back at him, with the deep bloodshot eyes and the dark pools under them. His hair was greasier and more ruffled than usual; his lips, his face, all without a glimpse of color to them. He was never one to focus on himself but he was sure that if he had looked that way hours earlier when he had gone to bed, he would have noticed. He looked like a dead man walking. How the hell could he have missed it?

And then there was the dried blood. It was coming from his nose; just a little stream of it coming from is right nostril. It was so tiny, as though he had a start to a nose bleed but, before it had really progressed, it had stopped and now was all scabbed over.

John leaned forward so that he could get a better look into the black hole of his nostril. He had a sudden strong itch, forcing him to quickly start rubbing his nose. The itching grew stronger, a tickle that became like fire nearly bringing tears to his eyes as he rubbed both inside and out of the nostrils. He tried to wipe the sleep from his eyes as he peered through the darkness.

He could barely make out what looked like a hair sticking out from his nose. It was a long, black hair that stuck out at an odd angle. He reached up, readying himself to pluck it out and the sharp pain that would follow.

As he prepared to grip the hair, it twitched and started to move. He pulled his hand away and watched the hair. It moved and pulled itself back into his nose, disappearing into the darkness of his nostril.

"What the-," John whispered to himself, as he leaned in closer to the glass. The itching sensation was growing unbearable, so much so that he wished he could just rub it until it bled and the skin would be raw and peeling away.

He was tired. He just wanted to get back to his mattress on the floor, and the model who had been sexually assaulting his dreams.

John let a smile start to spread as he pulled himself back from the mirror. He reached down and flushed the toilet and was getting ready to turn out the light when the hair reappeared, longer this time. It moved, shifting, coming out and then pulling itself back into the nostril.

Then, the owner of the hair emerged. A spider, barely smaller than the opening of his nostril, crawled out of his nose. John stood there, watching, his hand hovering just above the light switch. He was too afraid to move or pull his hand back as the large spider stayed there perched on his upper lip.

John stopped watching it through the mirror and tried to look down at his upper lip. His eyes burned from the strain of focusing on an object so close and all he could make out was the large black shape.

How had the thing been sitting up in his damned nose? How long was it up there? How had it survived when he had been squeezing and rubbing his nose when it itched? Ugh, even worse, what would have happened had he squashed the damned thing in his nose? His stomach turned at the thought of it and he had to stifle a gag.

Without watching himself, keeping his eyes focused purely on the spider, John lowered his hand away from the light switch and moved back to the mirror. He could feel the spider's legs on his upper lip, and he could feel it shudder as he moved, as though it was trying to surf him like a wave.

John looked back at the mirror, at the black shape still sitting there on his upper lip. It was a fucking spider; he could barely fathom how it had come out of his nose. He leaned over the sink, figuring it was time to try and knock the thing off and wash it down the drain.

He turned on the sink and fumbled for the stopper so that the sink would slowly fill with water. He didn't turn the water on too fast as he didn't want the sound of the water to be too loud. The last thing he wanted was to spook the spider and have

it crawling all over his face. However, so far, it seemed to be
content with just sitting there so he figured he was safe.

John started to raise his hand, getting ready to shake his
head and knock it off at the same time. He rocked back and forth
briefly to get himself prepared and then he swung.

The spider quickly ran back into his nose, and now it
was again on fire with the itching sensation. However, this time,
he could actually feel it moving around in his head. It was
getting deeper into his nose, and he could feel the large shape of
the spider forcing its way back into his airway.

John coughed, the large lump moving up and down his
throat. He was gagging in reflex, trying to get it out. He put his
finger down his throat to try and force himself to throw up, to get
the spider out that way, but it fought against him. He gagged
against it, trying to push it, but it kept running throughout his
throat, staying away from coming back up. Tears came to his
eyes as he tried to cough as hard as he could. His throat burned
and became raw, but still nothing.

John dropped down to his knees in front of his toilet and
reached his arms out, as though he had been drinking and was
now praying to the porcelain gods. He tried to heave into the
toilet, hoping to clear the spider from his throat, but nothing
came up. He could barely breathe and he couldn't make himself
gag anymore.

He wanted to cry when he leaned his arm onto the toilet.
His body felt like it was burning up; he imagined that he could
feel the heat emanating off of him. He was too hot, as though his
skin was about to start on fire. He looked at his arm, expecting it
to be red. It was still pasty and pale.

He thought about the pot that he had smoked earlier in
the night. Damn, he hoped that someone hadn't laced his shit.
The last thing he wanted to worry about was that, but he couldn't
help but think about it. Hopefully, he was just having one hell of
a bad trip. Please, he thought to himself, let it all be one hell of a
motherfucking bad trip.

A lump formed under his arm near his elbow. It just
seemed to appear from nowhere, but now protruded out
grotesquely. It was nearly three quarters of an inch in diameter
and half an inch tall, pulling the skin tight and red where it
suddenly grew.

Suddenly, the lump broke through the skin. Another spider appeared, tearing its way out of the skin and onto his arm. Blood dripped from the hole as the spider started to run quickly down his arm. John quickly started to claw at the spider with his other hand, trying to kill it. He nearly got it a couple times, but the spider was quick and kept dodging his attempts. Instead, it turned around and quickly ran back into the hole it had made in his arm.

He clawed at the hole, trying to tear away at the skin and get the spider out. His long, dirty nails pulled away at his arm, trying to get it out, but the spider continued to run towards his hand from underneath the skin. It made it to his wrist and John quickly started to reach around above the sink, trying to find his razor. His arm, blooding running down from where he had tried to claw out the spider, was draped over the toilet.

He could barely see above the ceramic porcelain of the sink to see where he was reaching, but he heard things falling as he was feeling around--his toothbrush, the plastic scraping the bottom; the large heavy sound of the shaving cream as it was knocked over and rolled in the base.

John finally felt his hand clench around the plastic handle of the razor. It was a cheap store bought dollar shaver, but he hoped that digging enough with it, he should be able to get the damned spider out from inside of him. Damn the things, damn them, he wanted them out. He hated spiders; more than anything else, he hated spiders.

He brought the razor to his wrist and was about to start tearing away at the flesh when he noticed that there were no longer any lumps or anything moving. His skin was clear. An unhealthy pale cast to it, but it was clear of anything hiding beneath it. He still had blood trickling down his arm, but the spider seemed to be gone. Same with the spider in his throat, as he could breathe again. He didn't feel as though something was blocking him.

He reached out to the sink and used it to help him stand. He still didn't feel quite sure of himself and felt like he might still be trapped in a nightmare somehow; that he never truly woke up, or that he might just be caught on a bad acid trip.

He looked at himself in the mirror; he still looked like death warmed over. He was tired and just wanted to go back to his bed. It was calling for him, like a siren song reeling him in.

His ear tickled and he reached up to pick at it but, before his hand could reach it, he felt the familiar feel of the spiders legs on his skin. He shook his head, madly trying to get at it as he felt it starting to crawl towards his face, its legs leaving small stinging sensations along the unshaven roughness of his skin. Then, after one big shake, he felt its release and saw it land on the floor.

It just lay there, shocked by the fall he assumed. Before it could regain itself, he quickly stomped down on the cursed thing. Strangely, he expected it to squish between his toes, as he was still barefoot. Instead, he barely felt anything. He pulled his foot away, only to see black dust where the remains of the spider should have been.

CHAPTER 2

Marty shifted the selector to "P" and felt the slight shift in his car as the brakes applied. He sat there in the parking lot of a chain of cheap apartments that had long ago been nicknamed as "Cardboard City". Each unit joined to the next with walls so thin that a neighbor could nearly hear a mouse fart in the apartment next door. There had also been the time when the roof of one of the buildings had blown off and landed in one of the cornfields. It hadn't even been a tornado whistling through town, but only a strong wind. At least, those were the stories. No one ever wanted to live there and, in the small town, it didn't take much for the little apartment complex to be known as the harbor of white trailer park trash, without the trailer.

The apartments sat on the outskirts of town, past any of the rows of houses and nearly tucked back into the entrance of a cornfield. The wind here was fierce and, during the winter, it would bite at a person as soon as they stepped into it. Marty could feel a breeze as he opened his door, but as winter was still months away, he was caught with wind-blown dirt from the fields instead. He could taste it in his mouth; it felt like dry film as it seemed to coat his insides like cellophane, tight against the skin, choking him.

Why in the hell was he here? He wondered again. Why did he let John talk him into getting up and coming over here in the middle of the night? It was almost three, he was supposed to be at work at ten, and he had just nuzzled into his pillow for the long, lustful sleep with hooter models from his calendar hanging above his bed. What was so important that John needed him to come now?

John and Marty had been best friends for years. Best buds since the fifth grade when John was Johnny and his parents had just moved to the small little town. Small being relative, as John had moved from a town with only seven thousand people, so moving to Hammond with a size of nearly fifteen thousand made him feel like he had moved to the city. Hammond was never really that large, but it did have two strip malls (though one of them was mainly a shell of closed stores), a post office, a doctor's office, a lawyer's office with a dentist in the back, and twice as many bars as there were churches. Having more bars than churches was something John had always said defined it as a true city.

Briskly, Marty walked the short distance to the front door of one of the inner most entrances to the apartments. The doors were always unlocked, open to anyone walking in at whatever hour they wanted. Marty doubted that most of the residents came in before dawn and typically could barely stand when they did. He didn't pay any attention to the mouse that scurried away from the entrance when he walked in. He just quickly made his way to the stairs and to the second floor.

He worked hard to ignore the smell of mold that seemed to radiate off the walls. The place itself smelled like wet, sweaty old socks that had long since gone foul, and he wondered how anyone could ever live here. He didn't know how John could stand it but, knowing John, sometimes Marty felt like he should fit right in.

Marty reached the door and started to lightly tap on it, not wanting to wake the neighbors. Last thing he needed was "Big Bertha", as they called her, from across the hall coming out and yelling at him.. A sixty-year-old fat woman who could probably still wrestle him down and sit on him, he thought it best to just stay away from her.

"Hey John, open up man. You called me out of bed, you sure as hell should still be up to let me in," Marty whispered, as he leaned in close to the door. His skin touched the wood and if felt soft and rotten against his flesh. His nose wrinkled in disgust. There seemed to be a smell coming from either the door, or whatever was on the other side of it.

He listened, hoping to hear some sound or movement coming from inside. Everything was near silent, other than the whistling howl of the wind as it passed by the window at the end of the hall. Even the mouse from downstairs had gone silent, as though waiting for an answer.

Bastard sure as hell better not have gone back to sleep, Marty thought, as he put his ear to the door. The wind blew even stronger against the window, making it rattle loudly in the frame. Marty started to pound onto the door again, this time a little louder, trying to be heard over the banging of the window and the howling wind.

Still, only silence answered. Marty was starting to really get pissed. He had been sun soaked in his dreams, buried deep in the beaches of some sunny resort surrounded by Double D's. The last thing he had wanted was an interrupting phone call from his best bud telling him that he needed his help and to get over there. John had sounded pretty messed up on the phone, worse than Marty had ever heard him. He wasn't going to leave him hanging. That is, unless he didn't open up his damned door.

"Hey, you son of a bitch! You didn't drag me out of bed in the damned middle of the night just so you could fall your ass back to sleep," Marty said, as he started to pound on the door. Sleep was beginning to filter back into his mind. The drive had woken him a little but now it was replaced by the stench and warmth of the hallway. He just wanted to get himself back to bed and if John wasn't going to answer his door, there was no reason to stick around waiting for him.

Marty reached for the door knob. He figured it was probably locked, but he had come all the way across town. He should at least try the knob. Even if John had passed out somewhere or just fallen back to sleep, it would be better to crash on the nasty couch that he kept in his living room rather than driving back across town to his bed. He turned the knob and, with a satisfying click, the door swung open.

He was instantly assaulted by a wave of foul stench. It nearly knocked him back; the sour odor of maggot infested meat, mold, and dirty socks and in such a high concentration that it was overwhelming. His stomach twisted and was ready to release its contents onto the filthy hardwood floor.

He could have sworn that it wasn't this bad just last week when they had all been over for the "Twin Peaks" annual marathon night. Marty, John, Bob, Ramrod, they had all been there, watching the old VHS box set that John had. They've been doing it for 10 years. Every year on June 10th, the day the show ended, they got their popcorn and their tape recorders, plus a little vodka, and enjoyed all the additional scenes from the European versions.

It was their tradition, and they always did it at John's. But the place never looked this bad. He always had it cleaned for when they came over. Plus, Marty was over more often than the annual event. In fact, he had been over just-?

Marty tried to remember the last time he'd been there. He struggled, thinking about the inventory that he had been working on at the grocery store, and the dinner with his parents, and then there was the night out with his sister celebrating her twenty-first birthday. So yeah, maybe it hadn't been since last week that he had been over.

John had really let the place go since then. It was trashed.

He kicked over a pile of pizza boxes as he stepped into the room, trying to get in so he could close the door behind him. He didn't want to be trapped in with the smell, but he didn't want it to drift out into the hallway, either. The smell was bad enough out there as it was; it didn't need any help from John's trash heap of an apartment.

Marty was able to get the door closed, reaching for the light switch at the same time. Light flooded the room, cascading over the mess that would have been better left to the dark. He could hear little movements as small creatures move to quickly hide back into darkness. Marty didn't know what they were, though he had an inkling. He didn't have to see the roaches that scurried away, didn't want to see them, didn't want to think about them being there. It was easier for him to ignore them, and to imagine them not being there, than to try to ever sit on John's couch and watch crappy horror movies with him. Better to just have the unseen darkness than the knowledge that they were there, he thought.

Marty turned away from closing the door to finally take in the full extent of the damage. He had to be careful not to step on half of a broken beer bottle that was near the front door. It looked like it had rolled from near the couch and through the papers and other miscellaneous garbage thrown throughout the room; paper plates stained with sauces of unknown origin, soda and beer cans scattered throughout, playboy magazines and various other magazines with woman in scantily clad seductive poses on their covers.

Marty stopped looking at the mess when he saw that John was stretched out on the couch. He was in worse shape than his apartment. His skin was pale, nearly as white as the wall behind him. His lips were nearly as white as his face, his eyes were dull. None of it was natural, albinos had more color than the ghost of his friend that lay there. Marty couldn't understand how skin could become lacking in color. While Marty never knew what color John's eyes were, he did know that they had not been as faded as they were now.

Marty just stared at what could easily be mistaken for a corpse lying there on the couch. And maybe he was a corpse. He wasn't moving, was he? He couldn't really see John's chest moving. Maybe his friend had died in the time it took for him to get there.

If he was dead, that would make him one hell of an ass, screaming at the man for not opening the door. Yeah, and here he was worrying about his damn door etiquette and his crassness and not even thinking about that his friend was possibly dead. What should he do, call the paramedics?

John's chest rose with a sudden raspy intake of air. Marty jumped in surprise. Damn, he thought he was dead. However, he didn't look any better than a corpse.

There was a soft wheeze as a long, slow breath slipped out of his friend. It ended in a cough and John came to life, his body shaking from his chest, then rocking with a seizure-like motion as it spread. He rose up, coughing and turning as black chunks covered in blood sprayed out onto the couch around him.

Marty stood near the door, not really sure what the hell he should do. He wasn't a damn doctor. John needed a doctor, or at least an ambulance or an EMT, someone who knew something more than Marty, who knew jack shit about being sick. When he was sick, he went to the doctor; he didn't call his damn friends to have them watch him cough out a lung.

He wondered briefly if it was John's lungs that were in those black chunks that landed on the couch. They were probably black enough, as he knew that John was up to two packs a day. Basics. He could see the generic label, an empty pack lying next to John on the couch. He probably had just finished up another one before Marty had walked in. He thought he could smell it but, with all the other stenches in the room, it was hard to tell. What did it matter anyway?

John was trying to reach out and pull himself up so that he wasn't so stretched out. It looked more like an upside-down turtle trying to rock back and forth, as he tried to find something with which to grab on.

Marty reached in and started to lift John so that he was sitting on the couch. He smelled like he had been sweating a lot throughout the night, the smell of sweat and exertion. Marty pulled him up so that John was sitting there, still not completely erect. He doubted he could even stay straight if they had gotten him up to that point. At least now he wasn't stretched out, half laying, half sitting across the couch.

"What…the hell you doing here in the middle …the damn night?!" John spat at him. The words came out in a mixture of spitting and coughing up blood. Marty was starting to get scared for him. He had never seen a person cough up so much blood.

"Hey man, you called me. Got my ass out of bed to hurry over here, so don't even start with that shit. You kept screaming something about being attacked by spiders." Marty took another look at his friend, studying him up and down. Damn, he wished he knew a thing or two about medicine. "And, well, you sure as hell look fucked up."

John tried to speak, but when he opened his mouth, it turned into another spasm of coughing and more black specs flew to the floor.

"We should probably get you to the doctor," Marty said, as he lowered himself into the recliner next to the couch. He had to sit on the edge because of how much clutter of unknown crap was piled in the chair.

He turned back around to see John looking at him, those pale, glazed eyes staring into his. A thin smile creased his lips, but then it was gone and the hunger that had seemed to take him faded back away. It went back to being that lost look as John blankly stared back at him.

He watched John try to swallow as he moved back on the couch. The motion was tight and John made a loud sound as he licked his lips. He looked dehydrated and his lips were chapped. Then John looked at his stomach, a lost look, a sad look as his face changed as though he wanted to cry, but the tears never came.

He looked back to Marty. His face was twisted in a mournful agony, but his eyes, those white lifeless eyes. There were only faint remnants of what had once been eye color where the iris's had been, and they were trying to stare at Marty. "I feel them. The spiders, they're in my stomach now. They are eating away at me from the inside, turning my stomach into knots."

What the hell was he mumbling about? Was he stoned? Marty didn't like to think that his best friend was losing his mind. Maybe he was just having a bad acid trip. It wasn't like John to drop acid, but spiders inside of him? Maybe the doctor wasn't the best thing. Still, John looked terrible; he needed something.

He started to pull at his stomach, scratching at it. "They itch."

He was looking at his stomach, looking through it as he just sat back with a dazed look on his face.

"Your nuts, man. You're just coming down with something, or having a bad trip." John just kind of grunt laughed and kept looking down at his stomach.

"Here, let me show you something," John said, as he suddenly stood. He was surprised that John could even stand, although he did wobble a little. Marty remembered about how he had to help John sit up straight; how was he standing now?

He started to stumble his way out of the room, bouncing off any object that he passed as he worked his way back towards his bedroom. Marty watched him as he disappeared down the hallway, back into the corner were the bedrooms were, but couldn't keep an eye on him once he disappeared into the darkness of the room. Marty could hear John tossing things around, possibly looking for something to show him.

Marty hoped that he didn't come back with some acid or ganja, as he was not in the mood. Especially, as he kept thinking that there would be no way to avoid it, they would have to take

John to someone. He was too messed up and he needed to get looked at.

He just hoped that whatever John took, it wouldn't show up right away in any of the tests they would have to do. Marty didn't want to deal with any of the questions. John came wobbling back into the living room. He was holding a folded piece of paper, almost looking like a business letter that had been sent through the mail. Marty hadn't even heard John stop looking for it. He guessed that he just was too tired to keep paying attention. "That damn bitch is after me," John spit out as he neared Marty.

"Who?" Marty asked, as he started to reach out for the letter. John had been handing it to him, but when he reached for it, he quickly pulled it back, blocking Marty with his other arm. Marty recoiled a little in surprise.

Once John backed away, he walked to the coffee table in front of them. He cleared a spot on it with a wide sweep of his arm, sending piles of garbage to fall where they wouldn't be noticed amongst the rest of it on the floor. He then tilted the piece of paper over the table, and a white powder sprinkled out.

Shit, Marty thought. He sure as hell hoped that John hadn't moved on to start doing the white stuff, the "nose candy" that Marty had seen some of his other friends starting to take and losing their lives.. It was nasty stuff, and John wasn't doing good as it was. He didn't need to be making it worse. Once that shit got you, you were in for good and there was no getting away from it.

"You're not doing that shit, are you?" Marty asked, hoping the tone commanded more and said more than his question. He wanted John to know and understand that coke was going too far. That there was no way he approved of it, and could not stand to watch his friend lose himself to it.

John looked at him funny, a strange expression on his face as though he had heard what Marty had asked him, but that he didn't comprehend it. He looked at the powder briefly and then recognition flashed in his eyes.

"No, no, hell fucking no. This isn't that shit. No, man, this is in much worse taste than that. I think it's that fucking anthrax shit."

John went into a coughing fit, shooting more blood into the room. When he was done, there was a streak of it dripping down from the side of his mouth. It reminded Marty of that show, the one he had heard about on HBO or something like that, the one with the vampires. John looked back to Marty. He could see that Marty wasn't catching on to what he was saying.

"Remember those terrorist attacks and how they had that white powder, anthrax, being sent around? I think this is that," John said, as he reached out to the couch to help himself sit back down. It was a labor, Marty could tell. Damn, he had to try and get John to the hospital.

"Who, man? You don't really think you have that shit, do you?" Hell, Marty could almost believe that he did. Just look at him; he was a mess.

John let the letter fall to the table and Marty could see that it had some writing on it. He wanted to reach out for it, find out what it said, but he was afraid to touch it.

"What's it say?"

John smiled. It was strangely psychotic as there wasn't any rational reason for it. "Die, motherfucker, die! It's in Jamie's handwriting. I knew that she was a psychotic bitch, but I didn't think it would come to this."

"Jamie? She would never." Marty said it, but he didn't truly believe it. Jamie was nuts. Marty had known her since her family had moved there and had heard all the stories long before John had started dating her.

Then again, John and Marty were, themselves, considered to be the local younger generation of nut jobs. They had both seen their share of strange looks as they walked into the grocery store, or into the gas station to pay for gas. In a small town, when you were on the "darker" side of social living, you easily stood out. While Marty would never consider John a goth, the rest of the town did. Jamie, though, was at her own level.

She had always been heavily into Wicca, witchcraft, earth mumbo jumbo. Marty never did get the full story. He didn't care, either. She was into magic and all that hocus pocus, and Marty couldn't give two shits about it all.

John had; he thought she was interesting. She liked to make her potions; he liked to make his, well, own concoctions.

They were their own strange peas in a pod and went psychotically well together.

Thankfully, John had finally gotten enough of her bullshit and had dumped her just over two weeks ago. That letter must be her response.

Damn she was crazy.

"I can't see her sending you anthrax. I mean, where the hell did she get it?"

"Who the fuck knows? She's nuts, man." John coughed vigorously. Blood splattered from him, spraying out and falling to the hardwood floor. Marty was sure he had more to say, but John just sat there, looking at the spot where his blood had hit the floor like he was seeing if for the first time.

"Anthrax is such a deadly disease. I would have thought she would have better taste," John said. He was almost dreamlike, as though he wasn't even realizing he was saying it. He just kept looking at where the blood sat drying on the floor.

* * * *

John just continued to look at the floor, but it wasn't the blood he was looking at. It was the spiders, two of them, dark, black shapes that had been launched when he coughed and had landed in the puddle of red. At first, he didn't even know what they were. He had been coughing up black chunks all morning. Most of them had been irregular, and he assumed it was scabs or crusty blood from inside of him.

When they had hit the floor, they had just stayed there, as though they were stunned. Then he could see what had looked like little strings that were unwinding from around the tiny dots. The strings formed the long legs, different from the tiny spider he had imagined earlier. The legs lifted up the body, now bigger in size, and then both the little black spider creature things just paused there. It was like they were becoming aware of their surroundings. Then, the moment was over and they quickly dashed towards Marty, who was just sitting there.

John wondered if he could see them, as he seemed to not be paying them any attention. He thought about trying to step on them, but he was just so tired. He had been getting worse, he

could feel it. Even breathing was beginning to get difficult for
him.

He heard Marty say something to him, but he didn't hear
what it was. He was watching he spiders. They had stopped
suddenly.

"Wha-?" John said, as he took a moment to look up
from them.

"I said that I should get you to the hospital."

John looked back at the spiders. They were dead. They
hadn't made it far. He could tell that they were dead, turned over
on their backs with their legs curled up.

"I don't think I would make it," John said. He looked
back up at Marty.

"Don't be so cryptic."

Yeah, that was easy for Marty to say. He hadn't been
the one here alone for the last hour trying to figure this shit out.
He wasn't the one who had first felt the stabbing pains all
throughout his body, as the little bastards inside him were tearing
him apart. Marty hadn't had to be the one sitting here while he
could feel them in his head. They were in his fucking head, under
his skin, where he couldn't get to them. They were inside of
him, and he could feel them eating away at him.

Oh, yeah, occasionally one would come out and taunt
him, dance on his skin, play games with him, make John chase
him, itching to catch the damn thing as it ran just under his skin.

No, Marty hadn't been here when he had tried to go into
the kitchen. It wasn't a big apartment so he didn't have to walk
far. Marty hadn't seen as John had tripped over his own legs, not
because he lost his balance, but because he had lost all control of
them. He had control now, but when he had gotten up and had
been walking in there, he had only made it half way to the sink
before they just became numb and he was falling forward.

He had just barely been able to get his hands out in time
to catch himself on the counter. Then, he had to use his arms and
pull himself, shifting his weight back and forth to bring his feet
to meet him. It had been like he had gone paralyzed while he
had been in mid-step. He had never felt anything else like it. He
had just stared at his legs, the limbs that were no longer his.

Then, he could feel them again, like the sensation switch
had just been turned back on. Of course, with the feeling

returning came the pain of sudden awareness and he had screamed out as his knees had buckled.

No, Marty hadn't been there. Marty hadn't seen.

Marty also hadn't seen as John had lay there in the kitchen, painful wave after painful wave coursing through him to the point that he could feel the moisture from the tears and sweat spreading thickly across his face.   That was when John had felt he couldn't take it anymore. He was there, lying on the floor, his eyes glazed over, only seeing shapes in the room through his tears. He had just wiped them away when he saw them--more of the little spiders coming out of his arm and running to a hole in the wall.

Oh, how the little bastards just seem to be coming out of him in droves. They just kept coming, and he had to stop them. He wanted to kill them, to get every damn motherfucking one of them. They were killing him, eating him away. Well, guess what? It was time for him to eat them away.

John had pushed himself up on his knees and reached out, grabbing the handle for the cupboard under the sink and ripping it open. He quickly found what he was looking for. It hadn't been what he had originally gone in there for, but this shit, this fucking pain, his legs, all of it. They could all just go to hell. Actually, he was probably the one going to hell, but the rest of the shit could all just go down there with him.

He reached in to the little cabinet. His arm was thick and heavy, hard to keep it steady as he was reaching for one of the bottles. There were many different chemicals and poisons in there. He really didn't care which one. He figured any of them with the poison warning label on it should do.

Yeah, Marty didn't know about any of that shit. He drank from multiple bottles. Any one of them should have killed him. Marty should have found him sprawled out on the kitchen floor. He wasn't. No, he was on the damn couch. He didn't even feel the effects of any of the poisons tearing away at him. It was like he had never done any of it.

And maybe he hadn't. Maybe it was all a hallucination. Man, wouldn't that be fucked up if all of this shit was just some part of a bad trip.

* * * *

Marty watched as John started to sway. He looked like he was getting worse. Staggering, John bent over, a coughing spasm much worse than any previous one shuttered through him. He had to reach out to the side of the couch as he shivered with a force foreign to him. Spittle was launched throughout the room and he rocked back and forth, his lungs convulsing, blood showering down.

Marty hurried forward, reaching out towards him. John put a hand out to stop him. His eyes were slits from the coughing spasm, but he could see the spiders as they landed on the floor. They would just stay there for a brief moment before their legs quickly carried them towards Marty.

John quickly slammed his foot down on top of them, using all of his energy to push against himself and focus on them. He thought he was going to fall over and, in the fog that was surrounding his head, he was surprised he could keep himself upright. Not only that, he was able to use the momentum of moving forward to reach out to Marty, and started to push him towards the door.

"Get... out!" John said, rasping and working to spit out the words through coughing spasms.

"What the fuck, man!" Marty called out. John was pushing hard against him, and Marty could feel that he was trying to put all of his weight into it.

"Dude, I'm fucking here because you called me!" Marty tried to yell it, but, as he struggled against John's weight, it came out more like a grunt. John was actually pushing him back. It surprised him just how much force he was able to put into it. It was enough to get him to nearly fall back against the wall, which would have had John falling back with him. Marty had to work quickly; he was barely able to get a leg out behind himself and plant it down to stop their momentum. Then, he had John's lighter weight against him, and he could start to push him back.

"Get.. o-," John tried to spit out. Marty could see that he was trying to put everything into the struggle, and was trying to work him towards the direction of the door. Marty wasn't about to give up and just leave his friend there. Not like this, not with how bad he was.

"Come on!" Marty yelled

"The spider's!"

"Dude!"

John buckled, and then Marty had him, supporting his weight. He quickly worked him back to the couch and tried to lower his friend as softly as he could. It wasn't easy. Marty had been able to support him with John doing some of the work, but as Marty had bent over, John had just fallen into himself. He found himself having to let go and reach out to keep from landing on top of his friend.

Marty pulled himself back up and looked at his fallen friend. John was out cold. His breath was shallow, his chest barely rising as he breathed in, and Marty could hear each breath as it forced itself back out. He couldn't help but think of hospitals and dying patients who were barely kept alive on respirators. There wasn't the dull thud of the machine, but the rhythmic raspy dying sound was about the only thing Marty could hear in the now quiet apartment.

CHAPTER 3

Billy...Billy..Billy's got a little Willy.
Billy the Willy.
Billy's got a little Willy.
He had many names. Names that haunted him most his life and went as far back as he could remember. Many of them would flash through his nightmares, and they would tear away even the happiest of dreams to show the rotting memories of his past. All the names had followed him through school. They were also the names he still heard daily from work, or at night at the bars. Billy the Willy, Billy's got a little Willy. The names of his past, always there in his mind, always there to echo and haunt him. The names that had shaped him.

And often those echoes shouting at him would keep him awake, not allowing him to drift off to sleep until well past exhaustion. It was always hard to sleep when, every time he closed his eyes, he could see someone, hear someone calling out at him. He could hear them laughing, and often see their faces all around him. They were always laughing at him.

In a small town, everyone seemed to know him, which was odd as little towns were not like they were depicted on television. Everyone didn't know everyone else, and every bit of news wasn't spread by just one town gossip. Still, they all knew him there. He could tell. He could always see it in their eyes and the way they looked at him. They all watched him and held their children closer as he walked by. It was in their body language, and how they all would shift their gaze at him, thinking of him as that little sicko pervert. He could never understand why.

Billy, with his little Willy.

He had the nickname given to him so long ago, it should have vanished or gone away. Things shouldn't linger like that. He knew he was not the first child to have faced such humiliation. So why had he always been the one tortured? All of it had started in the damned third grade, and he had never been able to become man enough to stop it.

See, Billy, with his little Willy, had started out as a smaller kid, scrawny, and typically always alone on the playground. His mother called him special, but the others just called him dumb. They were already laughing at him for not being like them. It wasn't his fault; he just couldn't catch on to things like everyone else had, or keep up with everyone. Plus, he was always the tattletale, was always the one strictly following the rules and reporting his classmates that didn't. He sat at the front of the bus on the way home. He just wanted everyone to be fair and to do what was right. He had already been a joke even before it happened. Even before that afternoon when everything had gone from bad to worse in his own little world, and his life had forever been marked.

He couldn't remember why he had been wearing sweatpants. Why his mother would have ever allowed him to wear those stupid things, he couldn't remember either. It wasn't important anyways. If he had to, though, he would think that it probably was his fault; another way for him to prove that he was a loser. After all, they had been a present from his grandmother for Christmas that year. Who actually wears the clothes that were presents from their grandparents? Only those who are forever marked for loserdum.

However, those sweatpants didn't seem so cool to wear when they were pulled down to around his ankles in the middle of the school yard during recess. They had been playing kickball, everyone was running around in outside recess. All the kids were laughing. Everyone had been having a good time. He hadn't even been noticed too much at that point. He had just been standing there with his best friend along the wall of the school. Everyone was ignoring him, there had been none of the small little teasing that he had gotten used to. He could actually enjoy himself in that awkward way of just having no one around him.

They hadn't even been talking. They had just been standing there watching the others. Recess wasn't mandatory for everyone to play together. Some of the kids were over on the merry-go-round, others were on the monkey bars, and the rest were kicking the ball back and forth. Billy had thought about going over to the monkey bars, but still had a sore spot from when he fell off the top bar and hit his head on another one on the way down. He wasn't sure it was a good idea for him to start climbing them again so soon.

So, he watched the others play. He was mainly watching the action of the kickball game. Renny Armstrong was running the bases after a far flung kick, and the action of the game had picked up. Billy actually had started to find the game interesting, and had watched as Tina Lock ran and caught the ball off of the bounce. She had been trying to run across the playground in time to catch Luke, when Billy suddenly felt a cold, unfiltered breeze below the waist.

It had been so smooth that Billy had barely even felt it. He had been watching the game, felt a little tug around his waist, and then just air; air rushing at him, his legs, his exposed private parts. Everything was feeling the cool breeze that ran across the playground.

The world around him seemed to slow down. Everyone was now moving in slow motion. Tina was getting ready to launch the ball when she must have seen it out of the corner of her eye, because she had suddenly stopped and turned to look. Renny, seeing her stop, had also stopped and was now turning. The whole playground seemed like they were all turning to look. And they all looked directly at him.

But what was so funny? He didn't seem to know. His mind just seemed to have frozen; he wasn't thinking. Why was everyone turning towards him? Tina looked first and he watched as the corners of her mouth turned up into a smile. Then her mouth opened and she grabbed at her stomach as she pitched forward in sudden hysterical laughter.

Then, a whistle blew and he woke up, snapping out of his daze to hear the rest of them laughing. The loudest of it came from right beside him. He turned and saw his best friend, his best bud, standing there pointing at him and laughing.

Billy looked down and saw his sweatpants. They were around his ankles, his underwear with them. He was completely naked from the waist down.

And they all laughed. They always laughed. They all still laughed at him. They always were still laughing at him. Billy, and his little Willy for all the world to see.

The faces that had been around him, the nightmare others, turned into a gray, smoke-like mist. At first they had been solid, then like they were fading away into a smoke that was forming a cloud around him. He could see their shapes and hear their laughter, but now they were all part of the smoke.. It began to swirl around him. They were all laughing at him. They were always there laughing at him. Laughing faces spinning around him, growing bigger,, making him feel nauseated as he tried to pick just one face and watch it. "People living in small worlds have little else to amuse them," his mother used to tell him. That still didn't make it any better. The sounds of laughter still stung his ears, always making him cringe whenever he heard it.

He always saw the laughing faces at night. Sometimes, he could even recognize them from his nightmares, remembering when and where they had laughed at him. After all, he had been keeping track and taking notes. He had plans for them, all of them, and he had wanted to make sure that they were all going to pay.

* * * *

He heard the shouting, screams of torment and agony that melded together, both from the laughing faces swirling around him, and the other dark world that was just now blinking into existence. He wasn't sure when the dream had faded around him to the point of him actually being awake. They both seemed to happen together. Then the laughter was gone, the darkness remained, and he was sitting up in the corner of his bed, his back to the wall, staring at his empty studio apartment.

But there was still shouting. Different than the shouting that he was used to from his dreams, the screaming and laughter that would often accompany him awake. This was something alien, and it was slightly muffled as it was trickling down through his ceiling.

"Their under my skin! The spiders, they're under my skin!" Billy heard someone shout. Then there was some more pounding, some crying, and then footsteps that thundered down the stairs and out the front door.

He was listening to the nightmare of someone else, intruding into the torment of someone else. In a way, he felt like a "peeping tom", intruding in to the head and demons of somebody else. He wanted to pull away from it, stop listening to the show, but, something in him wanted more. To know more of someone's pain that was not his own. Whose was it?

He closed his eyes and strained to hear more. He thought he could still hear crying from upstairs once the other person had left. He couldn't be sure. The silence of the building, filled with only the buzz from the electrical sockets, seemed to be deafening in the darkness. Somehow, it distracted him and made it hard for him to pierce through it to listen.

Then, a voice started to laugh. It was quickly followed by another. One after another, the laughter from his nightmare was returning. It came from the corners of his room, echoing off the silence. Someday, they were all going to pay, he thought to himself, as he sat in his bed and pulled his legs close to him. He opened his eyes again, now losing interest in the crying from upstairs. Maybe it wasn't upstairs after all. Maybe it was more of his own nightmare, again changing into something new. Maybe they had found a new way to try and make him go insane. He wasn't going to let them do that to him. Oh, no, they would never get to him. He was never going to allow them the satisfaction.

He looked over at the LED display of his alarm clock. It was just past four. He still had a couple of hours before he had to get up and get ready for work.

He didn't want to go back to the laughing faces.

Billy heard a gunshot; it echoed through the silence, tearing violently through the stillness of the night. He nearly fell out of bed from his reaction to the noise.

The sound of the shot faded, but there was a residue that stayed in the room. Billy could feel it's presence as though a new shadow had entered and lingered in the corner to watch him.

Something was there. He felt it, as it seemed to create a dark spot on his soul. And around him, as the night fell silent once again, the laughing faces came back in the darkness and he shrunk back away from them. He would get them. He would get them all. He had his notes. He had plenty of notes.

36

CHAPTER 4

Bruce walked out to his rig, looking at his watch and not believing just how long he had actually been in the little diner. That just didn't seem right. He had been in there for over two hours? It felt like he had just gotten out of his truck and gone in; how could it have been so long? However, he could see that it was true. The eastern horizon was blossoming into a colorful dawn that was quickly shooing away the night darkness.

When he had gone in to the little imitation of an all-night truck stop ready to pound a way a few eggs, he thought maybe he'd run into some old friends from around the area. He knew a few would be coming off shift when he had been heading in and he had hoped that, just maybe, he would come across a familiar face.

He had gone in and found himself a seat at the counter. It was the standard, long stretch of dark green counter in the midst of a color explosion all throughout the room. Bruce's first thought when he had entered was that a color blind designer had picked the colors and, for that, they should have been put out of their misery. Then again, he thought that just about anywhere a person went where the walls weren't white and the counter wasn't a basic tan.

Don't be goin' and puttin' a bunch of colors in places that don't need color, he would say to himself, but that was largely because he was polite to the outside world. Attach this to the previous paragraph

When he sat, a larger waitress with a beautiful face came over to him with a friendly, warm smile. It was an addicting smile and Bruce found himself smiling back at her. He wondered how she could have such a smile that early in the morning, but he let it go. He was sure she had a stash of something in her purse that was helping.

"Hello, and what can I get for you this morning," she said. Her voice was just as chipper as her smile. Hell, maybe this was just her natural shift and she was used to not being asleep at this time of day.

He doubted it though. He never knew anyone who was "used to it" that was still that happy. There was something about the people who worked third shift, or were up naturally at this time. Always something about them, like they had a stick up their ass and were too tired to pull it out.

"Yeah, I'll take a Grand Slam, eggs over easy with toast, no jelly."

"Well, I'm sorry, for that you'd have to go to Denny's, but I'll whip you up just what you want, hon."

She walked away, writing on her pad, and he couldn't help but think of her now as being a little bitchy. What kind of place doesn't have a grand slam of some sort? Then again, when he was on a southern run and drove by Waffle Houses in what seemed like the thousands, he knew none of them had a grand slam. Why had he thought that they had them there?

Because they used to? Back before he drove for a living, hadn't they had them then? He couldn't remember, but he thought they had. Didn't matter, but it was something to think about to keep him awake.

A warm bed; a soft bed. It rested in the center of their large bedroom that was a comfortable pocket tucked away in the upper corner of their two floor farmhouse. It was one of those Tempurpedic beds that he had heard about on the television. It was warm in the winter, and the sheets seemed to just naturally feel cool in the summer. It was his little bit of heaven away from the road, and he was ready for that peace.

Man, he wanted to just get home. He didn't have too much longer and then he would be there.

He looked back around at the diner, trying to not be blinded by the bad choices of color around the room. He didn't expect to see too many people there, now that he took a closer look. It was way too early. In fact, the only other sign that there was life other than the large waitress was the cook, who was listening to some local rock station back in the kitchen area, and a black-coated man sitting at the end of the counter.

He heard a crash come from behind the little window and a long line of Spanish fluttered out from the kitchen. From the harsh tone, he guessed that they were obscenities, but he had never been one good at learning any language outside of his own. From the loud crash, he guessed a pile of dishes were now scattered over some dirty kitchen floor, pieces flung into the dark corners, some of which might just never be found.

When the dark stranger from the end of the counter took up a seat next to Bruce, he nearly jumped because he had never even noticed that the man had moved. But then there he was, easing into the seat.

Then the smell hit him, and his stomach turned as a strong odor of something gone bad flooded his senses. He was surprised that he didn't smell the man first. The rotten odor permeated off the creature as though is was a part of him, sewn into the man's essence. Bruce wasn't sure that even a bath would help; how could anything that smelled like that get washed away with just soap and water? To make it worse, the man must have been a smoker, as there was that underlining burnt smell. It wasn't quite what he was used to from most smokers, maybe the other horrid smell made it different, but it combined to make the man smell like he had died three weeks ago, had been thrown in a landfill and, now that he was up and walking around, had walked through a campfire on his way to the diner. It all made Bruce want to gag up the fast food garbage he had eaten earlier.

Bruce didn't want to be sitting next to him. He looked at the man, freezing his expression and trying to give the man the "stink eye" as much as he could muster. He was tired and he hoped it added to the effect.

The man stayed. It was hard to see his face, covered by the lowered hat that the man wore and the muck that seemed to be covering his skin. Bruce could see the smile, though. The man's teeth were so white, in contrast to how dark the rest of him was, that they almost seemed to glow. They were unnaturally long and sharp, like someone had gone and shaved them to points.

Bruce sensed that the man could tell how uncomfortable he was making him. His smile actually seemed to widen. "Hello." It was soft and rough, a sound that seemed to grind out of the man's throat, and just barely preceded a phleg-filled cough.

Bruce recoiled, but could still feel the cool spit land on his forearm. He looked at his arm, and then back to glare at what he hoped would be a just a lonely, old man's eyes. Instead, what he saw was a soulless pit staring back through black holes where his eyes should have been. Looking at the coldness in the man's eyes, a shiver ran through him and he could feel a hand reaching into his chest and squeezing his heart.

"Truck driver, eh? That's good. Very good." Bruce felt his face redden, the heat flaming just under his skin. He continued to stare into the pair of coal pits looking at him. "You drive safe. Keep safe. Keep driving." The voice grated to a stop.

Bruce looked down to see the man's dirt and grime-covered hand was on top of his, holding it. He tried to pull it away but the man's grip was like a vice, his flesh cold as metal and griped like iron as it held. Bruce opened his mouth to scream, but nothing came out. He turned to look at the man; he was silently trying to plead for release. He couldn't believe a grown man his age was on the verge of tears, but the grip was getting tighter on his hand. He was crushing it; the bones were starting to crunch together. He knew that, at in any second, they were going to start snapping.

Bruce again looked into the man's pitch black eyes. They were locked on his. Deep in them, he started to see something. It was a red orb and it was coming from deep within the pits of that gaze. It was coming closer; it was coming for him. He wanted to run and get away from it but knew that, even if he could move, he would never be able to outrun it. It was meant for him. He didn't know how he knew it, but the knowledge was there.

The orb reached the crest of the man's eyes and then, in a flash, a searing pain shot through Bruce's temple. It burned his vision, and all he could see was a white haze that flashed before him. The pain drilled into his head. He eyes hurt so much that he had to force them closed, pushing the lids so tightly together that he could feel tears trying to leak out from the sides.

"Order up!" the waitress called and slammed the plate down onto the counter. Bruce opened his eyes, the pain fading away faster than it had come; his sight returning to normal.

The waitress was already walking away. She didn't seem to care about how strange he had been acting. He could only assume how odd it must have looked with him sitting there and his eyes tightly clenched shut. She hadn't even looked twice, probably because of the things that she saw there on any given night. It was just another day, par for the course.

"Drive safe. Keep driving. You won't remember me but if you ever do, it will be too late," came that voice but, this time, it was in the back of his head. It was an invading thought that was not his own. Bruce quickly looked around and realized that the stranger was gone. He must have disappeared when Bruce closed his eyes. There was only the faint trace of a burnt ember smell.

"Hey, hon, you heading down 39?" the waitress asked, as she came back over towards him.

"In a little bit, why?"

"They had to shut down the southbound. Really bad accident; they predict it's going to be shut down most the day.". Shit, there went his plans for an early arrival.

"Well, I guess I'll be heading down 23." Which meant not taking any time to catch some sleep. If he was going down 23, the traffic was going to be rough and with the interstate closed, it just meant more traffic that he would have to contend with.

Suddenly he wasn't feeling so hungry anymore, as he could feel the lump that had been forming in his stomach grow. He also wasn't feeling that tired anymore. His plans to go and lie down for a bit were going away. He just wanted to drive. He had to get back out there, and if he was going to have to route around 39, then he might as well get those extra miles in now. There wasn't a weigh station down that way; he could just start up his second log book, hide the first, and run the miles. It wasn't like it was the first time he had to nudge the logs to make a load on time.

He put the cash down on the counter and got up. It was time to get back on the road.

CHAPTER 5

The itch on his arm was getting worse. He looked down and inspected the damage he was doing by scratching it. He had noticed that he had been doing it more and more and, as he had, the pain and the agitation had been growing. It was like he had rubbed up against some poison ivy. He hadn't, and he knew it wasn't from that.

He had a bad feeling what it was from. It had started shortly after he had helped lower John down onto the couch. He had lowered his friend down, looked at him for a while, watched him labor to breathe, and then sat back in the garbage covered chair to watch over him.

He wasn't sure what the hell he was supposed to do. What, should he call the cops, an ambulance, get his friend to the hospital? Yeah, that was going to be fun, explaining to them about the drugs. Not only that, it would only take a whiff of the apartment for them to want to search the place, and then John would be waking up in a hospital in handcuffs. Yeah, he'd love him for that.

Not only that, it would take John a lifetime to pay off the bill for the ambulance. It was over forty-five minutes away. He could imagine just how many zeros were going to be on that bill, and knew it was more than what John could make in a year. Not that it was saying much; John didn't make much to begin with, when he was working. So what was he going to do?

Marty realized that he had started to itch again when the heat in his arm had flared back up. He looked down at the red, irritated skin. When he looked, he saw the little spider, black like ash, that had rested just south of his elbow and above where he had been scratching. It was just sitting there, like it was waiting for him to do something.

Then, Marty realized what it had been waiting for. The spider immediately ran, it's little legs a flurry of motion carrying it to where Marty had just been itching. The spider got to the place where the skin was a deep patch of red. It stopped there for a moment and Marty could have sworn that it was looking at him.

Then, it started to burrow into his skin. The sensational part was that he didn't feel it as it ran down the length of his arm, and when it burrowed into his skin, it was just a little tickle beneath the skin; that little unease when a person itches but doesn't know why. It was just an itch that grew stronger. The feeling of what he thought the spider should feel like, or the pressure of it inside his skin, just wasn't there.

What the...? he thought, as he quickly grabbed his arm, trying to squeeze the spot where the spider had gone in. He pressed hard against it, and he could feel a faint lump under his skin. It moved and danced under his fingers. It went back and forth, showing off, and as much as he squeezed, it still roamed under his skin. He started to scratch harder, the skin starting to bunch up under his fingernails.

"Come on, you bastard!" Marty yelled.

"Get out of here!" John rasped from his place on the couch. Marty had nearly forgotten about him, and barely paid attention to him now.

A searing pain pierced through Marty's head, shooting white hot flashes just beyond his vision. His eyes fluttered and it felt like his left eye was melting. His vision blurred and went red. He had to pull his hand away from scratching at his arm to cover his eye as he doubled over.

"Get out of here!" he heard John sob, his voice rising as he was trying to sit up.

"I'm taking you to the damn doctor!" Marty said through gritted teeth, realizing that he had formed his plan of action just as he was saying it. The decision seemed so obvious now that he had made it. He didn't know why he hadn't just thought of it before. It was still a long-shot solution, but at least he was trying to do something to help his friend.

"We can both go together," John whispered.

His arm itched like crazy. A fire was flooding his senses up and down the tender skin, and his own arm hair felt like needles poking into his skin. The burning intensified, growing to a point that he had forgotten about John until he looked up and saw that those dull eyes were looking at him.

He had changed. He saw the pale, skeleton-like face of what was once his friend. Now, it looked like death had taken him and a corpse was sitting there. Marty couldn't even recognize him anymore.

"Shit, man, you don't look so good."

"Neither do you."

"We need to get you to the doctor. Let's get your shit and g-," Marty started, but stopped when he saw all the spiders running along the hardwood floor. Those same damn, black little spiders, the ones that looked just like the one now in his arm.

"Holy shit," Marty said. He could feel his mouth going dry and a large lump felt like it was growing in his throat.

"Yeah." John's voice was dry and raspy, as he looked away from Marty. He looked like he was losing his ability to sit up by himself.

"If you see them, its already too late."

"That's it. We're going to the doctor now. I don't care if I have to wake his ass up; it's time to get you checked out," Marty said, as he reached down and pulled John up. Spiders seemed to flake away like crumbs, falling to the floor and then scurrying away like roaches. Marty looked at them briefly, and then started pulling John harder to the door.

"So, you can see them, too," John said. He went into a fit of coughing, tiny black specks of spiders and blood flying from his mouth. "It's too late for you."

Marty was able to support John and make it to the door, stumbling slightly when he had to move a pizza box out of the way with his foot.

"No, it's not," Marty said. "We are going to get to the doctor and wake his ass up, and then all will be well."

John stopped Marty and looked at him, really looked at him, with his eyes burrowing into Marty's. The stare was as cold as his skin and Marty knew, just as John did, that there was little hope for either one of them. Still, he was sure as hell not going to give up without a fight.

Then John's gaze shifted, and the shadow of himself reappeared.

"I hope so. These spiders, they come in and out from me at will and I don't feel them. I don't feel anything anymore. I can't even feel you."

"We'll get this straightened out," Marty said. He felt something shifting in his gut. His stomach was rumbling and all throughout his body, he felt little tingles. The spiders, he knew, were inside of him, dancing along his nerves, eating away at his insides. "Maybe the doctor can figure out what the hell this shit is." Marty knew his words were hollow. He wasn't too sure if he believed them himself.

CHAPTER 6

Marty turned the corner onto a dark, street and into the outskirts of the town. It was a small, short street; the left side lined with a thin line of trees that marked the edge of what many thought of as the town, but which grew on land that no one truly owned. Maybe the city could claim it; however, they never forced their will. The trees grew, and maybe the city council felt that it made a good natural border for the city limits. Not the true city limits, just the separator from what was the town and what was the country.

The trees were not well-maintained and their long branches hung low which, as the car slid from his fast and reckless slide, Marty could hear scraping along the top of his car. With very little light, and even less of it reaching this part of the town, it was very dark. He didn't even see the tree until he was already turning the wheel to keep from rolling the car.. It flew by, just inches away from his side window, and he caught a brief sight of it as it passed.

His heart was beating triple time and at such a strength that he feared it was trying to beat through the front cavity of his chest. He could barely breathe, and everything in his vision had started to shake.

He pulled himself back onto the road and was already starting to slow down when the doctor's house came into view. It was the only house on the street, tucked back in the little area behind the doctor's office and being lit up by light on their front porch. The small light didn't illuminate much, but he knew that the road dead ended a few yards past the doctors driveway.

In the glow from Marty's headlights, he could see the white exterior paint of the doctor's house casting a slight glow as he pulled into the driveway. Then Marty quickly slammed the gear selector into park before the car finished skidding to a stop.

He looked at the clock on his dashboard. It was just after five thirty, and most the town was still not up yet. He was sure the doctor wouldn't want to wake up to Marty pounding at his door, but there was nothing he could do about it. He looked over at John sitting in his passenger seat, his head leaning against the window, his eyes barely open. Other than the occasional lift of John's chest with a hoarse breath, Marty would have taken him to be dead. He had to hurry. He knew it. He could tell that his friend didn't have much more time. He didn't need to have a fancy medical degree to know that.

Marty quickly rushed from his car and didn't waste any time following the winding sidewalk. He went through the grass and then up the stairs, trying to take them two at a time. However, his legs were starting to feel heavier than when he had raced up John's stairs earlier, and it was hard for him. His feet felt like bricks in his work boots and, on that last step, the tip caught and he nearly went down to his knees on the front porch. He just barely kept his balance.

He didn't stop to catch his breath and slammed into the door, quickly pounding his fist against the solid oak. He didn't have to worry about waking any other neighbors. The doctor's yard stretched for three lots, making it feel like he owned nearly a block himself. The closest house around, the one on the other end of the block, was dark and looked abandoned and beyond that was the sheriff's house. However, he didn't have to worry about the sheriff as there was still another hour before he would be off duty. It was probably pretty sad, but most the town's teens all knew the sheriff's schedule, almost as well as he did. Not that it mattered much. Marty wasn't there to cause any harm; they just needed medical help.

He pounded on the door with, still, no result. Marty slammed his fist to the door once again. When he got no answer, he stepped back and started to walk down the long porch in the direction of the driveway. He hadn't thought to check when he pulled up to see if the doctor's car was parked in the garage. He hurried over to look in the window. The garage was dark, but he could still see the outline of two cars parked inside.

A yellow glow appeared in one of the upstairs windows, and Marty turned to see shapes moving around in the room. He rushed back over to the door and quieted himself, putting his ear against the cool wood. Inside the house, Marty could hear some loud noise; a clamoring of footsteps stomping down a very sturdy staircase.

Marty looked through the ornate paned glass that was decoration around the door. It was hard to see, but he could see a light on inside and what looked like a shape coming closer to the door. Another shape stopped at the base of the stairs, and then another light came on inside, lighting the rest of the way from the stairs to the door.

"Who's there?"

"Hello, my friend needs help. I don't think he'd make it all the way to the hospital; I need to see if you can look at him," Marty said to the closed door. The shape that was closest to the door, he assumed it was the doctor, came to the glass that Marty was looking through. He stepped back as the shape looked out onto the dark porch.

Then the outer porch light came on, lighting Marty. A few seconds later, he could hear the loud click as the tumblers of the lock gave way and the door opened. In the lighted entryway, Marty could see the short man standing there. His skin was dark and Marty, while he had actually never gone to the local doctor, tried to remember what nationality he was. Hell, maybe if he could remember even the doctor's name, that might have helped him remember what country he was from.

Marty did quickly notice the thick accent, and allowed himself a moment to get distracted, contemplating what country the man was from and why was here in such a small Midwestern town. Then he shook off the thought and remembered about John sleeping in his passenger seat.

"Please, my friend needs your help."

* * * *

Tired. So tired. He didn't want to open his eyes. He could feel himself. His legs, while feeling thick and heavy, felt alive and filled with a built up energy. He could barely move them; they were tight and cramped, but he could feel motion inside them wanting him to push himself up. They wanted to stand and take off, race down streets and jump to the sky. He felt so full of anticipation, of excitement, but none of that actually made sense to him. He could feel it inside him, a fluid of motion that wanted to get up, run and go, but he also felt so washed over and just wanted to stay sitting there. Something about that didn't seem right. He hadn't been able to even feel them earlier.

His head felt cold and damp, but the air around him seemed to be stifling. He tried to open his eyes, but they didn't want to open. Some kind of shapes seemed to cover them. He could sense them, scurrying out of the way so he could open them.

The world was dark. He could see the rough outline shape of the window his head was leaning against and saw the paved driveway they were parked in, at least a part of it. Everything else in his field of vision was just bland shapes and hard to make out..

He lifted his head, the weight seeming to have gotten heavier on his neck since the last time he had moved it. It felt stiff. Not just to move his muscles, but just to think. He felt like he was in a fog.. His memories; how had he gotten there; he knew his name was John, but John who? Who was he? Did it matter?

"No," a voice inside his head was telling him.

He turned a little to see the windshield his head had been sitting against. Windshields were typically cold to the touch. Hadn't he felt it as being cold when he had his eyes closed? He wasn't even sure now. Even in the hottest days, when he would set his head against it, it would still be cold. He should feel it. He touched it with his hand and had his hand not stopped when it touched the glass, he wouldn't have known it was there. He felt nothing again. Nothing except for the deep anticipation. Oh, well, he thought to himself as he leaned his head back on the window. What did it matter anyway? It didn't matter, and he just didn't care anymore.

John looked down at his hands as they just sat there on his legs. He saw them, but were they truly his? Even emotionally, he felt detached from himself. He just didn't care

anymore. Then, a bump formed on the back of his right hand.
He watched as the bump started to run back and forth, moving
effortlessly under his skin. It would run one way, and then the
next until, all at once, it just stopped roughly in the center.

Then, a leg started to work its way through his skin. The
black leg protruded out and, if not for the darker color than his
blond hair, he could almost believe that it was nothing more than
his hair. Short, about the same length as his arm hair but so
much darker, and it swayed back and forth as though it was
feeling around. Then, another small leg popped out. The two of
them, tiny black hairs jutting out from the back of his hand.
Beneath them, just a small little lump that moved impatiently
under his skin as the hairs danced about.

John didn't care anymore that the spider was under his
skin, with its leg's dangling out. He didn't care about much of
anything. He didn't even care that Marty was up there, trying to
get the doctor to take a look at him. After all, there wasn't much
more he felt like he could do.

He looked back at his friend. Marty had started to walk
back to the car. Was he dragging his left leg? John wasn't sure,
but it certainly looked like he was. Not that it mattered.

Behind Marty, the doctor was following him. He was
just in his boxers, a white shirt and the complimenting robe.

John wanted to laugh, but his body didn't feel like it had
the energy. His mind could barely even stay focused enough to
remember the joke that had just passed through what was left of
his brain.

Why had he wanted to laugh again? He couldn't even
remember.

* * * *

Lucy was already awake when her alarm clock went off,
it's singing chime of Disney show tunes sounding like a warped
record from the days before CD's. The mangled symphony
played, then bells chimed and a young sounding voice from an
old cartoon her mother used to watch as a little girl folder her it
was time to get up.

Lucy reached over to the little pink castle that was her
alarm clock and turned it off. She had the alarm clock going on

five years; she had gotten it for Christmas when she was seven. Now that she was becoming a teenager, she figured she would have to give it up eventually, but she wasn't quite ready to do that yet.

She turned her attention back outside. The light was getting brighter. She had watched it as the morning colors had started to push away the fading blues of the night sky, elegant in its daily ritual of telling the moon that it was time for him to go rest. The morning sun, its reds and yellows, at first mixing with midnight blue, then watching the rainbow form over the horizon.

She hadn't been able to sleep for most of the night, as her stomach had been twisting different directions and had kept her awake. Constantly, she had been hurrying to the bathroom, not sure which way her stomach was going to release itself. She was always grateful when it didn't come out her bottom, though puking wasn't that much better. Even water was not staying down, and that had made her very thirsty.

The half cup of what had once been ice water sat next to her on her nightstand. The ice had long since melted, and there was now a ring on the table from the condensation. She debated as to whether or not she should try to drink some more. She knew she would have to try again eventually, but as her stomach twinged with another stab of pain, she decided she had better not for now. She was going to need to look like she wasn't as sick as she was when her aunt would come in to check on her. She had a game to go to later today, and she was already regretting having woken up her aunt earlier to let her know that she had been sick.

She wished her mom hadn't gone out of town, and that her aunt Tina wasn't watching her. Tina had wanted to rush Lucy to the emergency room when she first woke her up. It had been just around one, and Lucy had to walk through the dark house, something she never liked doing, to make it to her mom's room where Tina was sleeping. She would never belong there. Tina could never replace Lucy's mom. She tried when her mom had to go out of town, but she could never do it.

When she had woken Tina, she didn't know what to do. Lucy had hoped that maybe Tina would know something she could give her to make her feel better. She had already tried to take some of that nasty pink stuff they kept in the kitchen. Her mom, never buying the actual name brand, had bought some kind of generic and it tasted just as bad as the other stuff, but was more chalky.

Tina hadn't known of any kind of medicine and had freaked out. She had wanted to rush Lucy to the Emergency Room, but Lucy had told her no. It was probably just the flu or some other bug. She had to plead with Tina, telling her that she didn't want to go. The closest hospital was forty minutes away, and Lucy had once spent nearly half a day waiting there because of how slow they were. She didn't want to be there all night. She still hoped to make it to the final basketball game of the season that started at noon. Bobby was playing and she liked him. She wanted to see him running up and down the court, building up a sweat. So, no hospital.

However, they both agreed to go to Dr. Winston first thing in the morning. First thing, before the office even opened, and maybe the doctor would see her before taking any of their daily patients.

Lucy looked at her alarm clock, the large green numbers displaying 6:03. She didn't know what time the doctor typically went to his office, but she did know that it opened at 8. She hoped that he went to the office early.

She rolled out of bed, already smelling the morning scent of freshly brewed coffee.. Her parents had always put the coffee machine on a timer. Tina must have put in a fresh filter and water last night before she went to bed. Lucy couldn't stand the taste of it, but she did love the smell. She could almost believe that her mother was home.

Hopefully, the coffee would wake Tina up, Lucy thought, as she started to tiptoe through the house. She wanted to hurry up and get to the doctor. Her stomach, which usually enjoyed the smell of the coffee, was now doing flops. She could hear it gurgle at her in disapproval and then something shifted, like a thump inside of her, and she was again hurrying to the bathroom.

"Not again, not again, not again!" she panted as she rushed into the small little bathroom just off of the kitchen.

CHAPTER 7

The fog was getting thicker. A haze blurred across his vision as the world was losing its color around him. Didn't he used to be a part of it?

He couldn't feel anything. He was looking out, but felt like he was looking out from his own mind, that he was a prisoner trapped in his own body.

He had a name once, didn't he? What was it?

He tried to grab for it, as it was there, just past the tip of his tongue. He wanted to know. He wanted to scream out that he had a name, but whenever he tried to just say it, it was lost in that fog, clouding his thoughts.

From the corner of his eye, he saw a shape move. It was a blob as far as he could tell, but he had a sudden craving. Even though his senses no longer felt anything throughout his body, he felt a tingle on the inside. It was a flurry of motion throughout him. It flowed through his veins, even though his veins no longer carried blood.

All he wanted to do was to reach out. Simple enough, right? He wanted to reach out. However, he knew something, a bad feeling deep in what was once his gut, told him that those impulses wanted to do something more.

"Spread, spread, spread, spread, spread," was a whisper echoing inside of him, carried on the sound of what seemed like the scream of a hundred little legs scurrying.

Spread...

CHAPTER 8

Marty stood in one of the little examining rooms that were part of Dr. Wilson's private practice. He was leaning against the hard counter top and looking around the standard-looking examination room. The walls were filled with pictures of the internal parts of a person's anatomy, the standard counter with drawers and cabinets locked with medical supplies, the large examining table with the portion for the legs pushed in so that John, who was sitting on the table, could hang his legs over the edge.

Marty was trying not to pay attention as the doctor was examining his friend. He was trying not to look at either of them. John was getting terribly worse, to the point that Marty didn't even feel comfortable being in the same room with him anymore.

He kept taking stock of the posters around the room. The one of the heart had kept him occupied for the most part. On the left side, it had the heart as it was normally, but the right side of the heart was cut away to expose the inner workings; it showed different layers and pictures of different types of damage to it. Marty was sure that the text wasn't meant to be too small to read, but he was feeling exhausted and couldn't make out any of the descriptions. He wondered if any of them were similar to what killed his mother years ago.

He didn't like doctor's much. He hadn't gone to one since his mother had died, so he hadn't seen too many posters like these before. He was almost curious enough to ask the doctor, but that would mean talking to him again. Something he wasn't too keen on doing.

He stifled a laugh, thinking about some old videos he had once seen on YouTube. Something about some old TV commercial; some eggs frying, or something with bacon.. He really wasn't too sure, but he remembered something about it being some kind of anti-drug commercial. He had been pretty stoned when he watched it, and it had them all laughing pretty hard. Kat had found the video. Good ol' Kat, who was always good at finding all those crazy things on there.

He could barely find cat videos on there. He was not, or nor would he ever be a computer guy.

He heard the doctor clearing his throat and then realized that he had been saying something. He turned to look at the old man who was looking at him. Marty was already wishing that he wasn't there. He had been increasingly wishing he hadn't been there for over an hour, as he was beginning to think that whatever made John the way he was, Marty had it, too. He didn't like the idea of losing his mind and becoming like the vegetable that his friend now was.

Just look at him. John was looking straight at him, but Marty could tell that he didn't really see his best friend or the doctor standing right in front of him. His dull eyes just stared there, unblinking; not looking at them but through them.

John's blank gaze send a chill through Marty's limbs, his arms suddenly feeling like he should have been wearing a jacket. It was warm outside, but the temperature in the room could have been twenty degrees colder and Marty could sense the tingling of goose bumps along his flesh. Over the course of the last hour or so, John had gotten much worse. The skin wasn't pale anymore, but was now gray and hanging from him. John had always been scrawny and lean, probably from all the drugs and not eating, but now it was extreme. The lifeless gaze in his eyes, the way his mouth hung open with the slightest bit of drool hanging there at its edge, ready to drip down onto the dirty jeans that he had been wearing when Marty first showed up at his apartment. His shoulders slumped down; defeated, hopeless. There didn't seem to be anything left of the man Marty had known. It was just a shell, sitting there on the doctor's examining table. Marty would have preferred that his friend wasn't looking at him at all. It would have been less, well, creepy.

He looked away from John's gaze, looked at all the gashes on his friend's arms. They were deep, but there had been no blood pouring out of them. What the hell could have made that happen? How did that happen? Marty just didn't think it was possible.

Instead of looking at John, he stared straight down at the tile floor, and caught himself. He hadn't even realized that he had been doing it, but he was scratching at himself. His left arm was scratching at his right arm, tearing into the flesh. Marty could see the pale skin pulled back, and some of it starting to gather under his fingernails. The layers of his arm were torn back, so much so that he could see muscle, but he wasn't bleeding

He stopped himself from scratching and looked at his gashed arm. A small little spider had appeared from the open wounds and dropped to the floor. Marty couldn't help himself. He watched it in amazed disbelief; the thing had just appeared out from under his skin. He knew he should be screaming but, for some reason, he just couldn't. So, instead, he just watched it. It hit the floor and seemed to stop there for a moment, stunned. Then, it collected itself and quickly started to scamper towards the doctor.

Marty quickly slammed his foot down, squashing the spider. As he leaned back against the counter, he lifted his foot away and saw that nothing was there. He looked up to see that the doctor was still looking at him, a troubled expression registering on his face. He had forgotten that he had been talking to him.

"Sorry, thought I saw a bug," Marty could barely say. His throat seemed to be getting tighter, making it hard for him to speak the words.

He looked back at John, who was still staring at him. Marty could have sworn he saw a little smile on his lips. As much of a smile that could be made with parted, cracked lips.

Then, another spider appeared. This one came out of John's mouth. It was a little larger than the one that had come out of Marty's arm; it looked more like it was full grown. He didn't know how he knew that, but he felt it. This one had been alive long enough to get to its full size. It was faster, and had more power to it. It quickly ran out of John's mouth and perched itself on his face. Then it jumped and landed on the doctor's arm. The doctor never even flinched, or acted like he noticed.

"What about what he was saying earlier? About him seeing spiders under his skin?" Marty choked out, watching as the spider that had jumped onto the doctor quickly made its way under his lab coat.

"I'm not sure. I'm not sure about a lot of things," the doctor said. He straightened and took a step back away from John.   "Have you seen them, too?" the doctor asked, as he turned to Marty. He looked in his eyes and then looked down to the gashes in his arm.

Marty was going to lie the word, "no" on this tip of his tongue, but he just looked at the floor instead.

"So, more than likely, this is infectious."

"What is?" Marty asked, as he looked at the doctor.

"I have to make a few phone calls. You two, stay here in this room. Do not try to leave or go anywhere. Okay?"

Marty thought about letting his smart ass tongue get the better of him and had to bite back his response of, "Sure, we're going to just go do a 5k run, we'll be right back," but he kept the comment tight to his lips. He just nodded as the doctor left the room.

* * * *

Mrs. Wilson turned on the lights in the receptionist area and walked quickly across to the coffee maker. The night before, they always set everything up so all she had to do was flip the switch and wait. It would only be minutes before the smell to would rise up and filter its way through the hallways. She never waited for it, as there was always so much to do in the morning, but as she was there so early, she actually paused by the machine. She watched as it made its little clicks and perks. The little draining sound of water rushed from one part of the machine to the other, all of it making its way to the filter. Then, in moments that on most days felt like years, darkened, colored water started to work its way into the pot..

She stirred out of her daydreaming, stepped out of the little break room, and looked at their home away from home. She wasn't even sure how many years they had been living there, or had been running the small town doctor's office. She was glad they were there, but really couldn't remember just how long. She was thankful, though. After all, this was her home town.

She went to the light switch and turned on the interior lights. The office was arranged with a front waiting room that split into two side hallways, which ran most of the building before merging into the back hallway that emptied out into the alley and the driveway to their house. The left hallway had all the exam rooms, three of them in total, and ended at the door that lead into the doctor's office. The right hallway had the side office, for her to do her administration paperwork, and the break room. Both hallways were separated by the front receptionist area which allowed entry to both sides, and was split from the back file room by another little hallway.

She stepped back into the break room, guessing the coffee should be done soon and figured that she would get his cup ready for him. She personally never drank the stuff, but Angus always had to start his day with a cup. She often would laugh to herself when she heard him telling others to cut it out of their diet for health concerns. Especially because, between nearly every patient, he would cut through the little adjourning hallway and come into the little break room and take a long drink before heading to the next exam room. Then there was his own blood pressure, which wasn't something to be proud of. His own doctor had given him the same advice and Dr. Wilson, her loving husband, did the same thing that just about half of his own patients did. He ignored doctor's advice.

She smiled a little to herself as she watched the coffee machine. Steam had started to drift up from the growing pool of fresh coffee in the bottom of the pot and the smell wafted from it. While she never did drink the stuff, she sure did like the smell of it. It usually brought with it good tidings of another morning.

She turned and started to walk out of the room and to her little receptionist desk. She thought that she'd get the morning paperwork done and ready to go. She figured, heck with it; maybe if all the morning chores were done, she would allow herself to take off for a few hours when Sheila, the day nurse, arrived. She knew that she would never take herself up on her own offer of a few hours off, but she grinned at the relaxing thought.

She left the room and started up the hall toward the front waiting area, but stopped when she saw down the side hallway. Her husband was coming out of the examining room and he looked troubled. She could see the frown line that creased his forehead and knew that it meant something wasn't good. He typically only looked that way when he had to give someone grave news. He was a happy guy and had issues whenever the news wasn't pleasant.

She thought briefly about going over to him and giving him a quick peck on the cheek, but stopped herself when she saw him do something he had never done before--he locked the exam room door behind him. She had forgotten that the rooms even had locks on them. In fact, after Tammy, who had once been another one of their day nurses, had gotten herself locked in one of the rooms over five years ago, she thought that Angus had removed all the locks.

He never even looked up at her, never even noticed her, as he hurried down the hallway toward his office. She knew her mouth was open as she could feel it going dry. Just what in the hell was going on? He just went ahead and locked those two boys in there by themselves. Was that even legal? She'd never known her husband to do anything that wasn't, but he definitely seemed to be crossing some kind of line that she had never known he would be capable of crossing.

* * * *

The office was a small cubbyhole of a room that was more like a storage closet, and was very seldom used. Typically, they only used it for storage of different things, or when he did use it, it was used as a place to hide whenever he didn't want to hurry to a patient to give them some bad news. While it was never truly a sanctuary away from the bad news, it did work as a respite, a brief pause before he would have to go and devastate some family.

While that could be considered the case now, he was doing more than just avoiding the two men that were currently locked in his exam room. He didn't know how the hell he was going to tell them his findings. He didn't even know them himself. It didn't make any sense.

The mutilated one, the one that was sitting on his examining table, was dead. There was no other possibility. He was, for all intense and purposes, physically dead. He had no pulse, no heartbeat, no reflexes. His eyes were glazed over and nothing but white pupils remained. There was no way to tell if the eyes followed him, but his face moved when the doctor did. There was movement, but nothing from what, with all his experience, he could call a sign of life.

And Marty, Dr. Wilson was pretty sure that had been his name, seemed sick, too. Whatever the other one had, Marty had it, as well. He could see that his skin was getting pale, and he was starting to self-mutilate like he had claimed his friend had done.

"And what about the spiders?" Marty had asked him. Well, what about the spiders? Dr. Winston had no idea what they had been talking about. Marty had said he originally thought that the other boy had been making it up, or that they were delusions. Then Marty said he started to see them, too.

Shared delusions? Maybe, but for them both to imagine the same thing? As far as Dr. Wilson knew, mass hysteria was just a myth. He guessed that was one of the benefits of being a small town doctor all his life. He never had to deal with anything more than old farts trying to dodge changing their diets, younger kids with chicken pox, the cold and the flu, strep throat, those were all his deadliest enemies. Not kids who were old enough to be just out of high school dealing with, well, the closest way to describe it was paranoia, delusions, and near death.

Schizophrenia? Drugs? Anything was possible with today's youth. It was amazing just what the latest younger generation seemed to get themselves into. What was that new craze he had been seeing on television? Some kind of new variation on that bath salts drug? And, even still, there was the original bath salts. He never paid that much attention to it, as it was all happening far away from the little small town that he called home, but what he had seen was these people who stripped down and were eating others. They were eating people because they had actually gotten it into their heads that they were walking

zombies. The latest version of the drug was supposed to make
the user even more brain dead. And why did they take it? The
damn fools took it because they wanted to feel what it was like to
be a zombie. The youth of America, God save them all; he had
no idea how any of them would ever make it to middle age.

But if it was some new version of the drug, how did that
explain their symptoms, and when did a drug ever become
contagious? That is assuming that the other one isn't lying, and
they had both taken whatever it was.

Drugs also didn't explain how one of them could not
have a single sign of life. He didn't know any drug that would
fake death on that kind of level. He was way over his head. Not
only that, but he was pretty sure it was contagious, which meant
there was a good chance that he was also infected.

Dr. Winston nervously tapped his fingers on the small
metal desk. It was a small, thin bronze metal desk that his wife
had picked up from a garage sale in town. He thought she only
paid a dollar for the little thing, and could tell that it had
probably been some young students study desk. It had been
badly dented on one side where someone must have been
throwing a tantrum but, other than that, it wasn't much more than
a copy of what could be found in most the classrooms as a
teacher's desk. His fingers made a hollow sound as they tapped
against it. It was unsettling in the quiet office.

He looked up at the paperwork that littered the top of his
desk. He didn't know where half of it came from, but he didn't
care to look into it either. Instead, he looked at the archaic black
device tucked away on the left corner of his desk. He didn't
think he had ever used it, and had even forgotten that it was
there. If he had remembered, he may had upgraded it over the
course of the years. The telephone that sat there was easily as
old as the office. How anyone ever thought to dust it to keep it
from turning gray or discolored amazed him. It still looked
almost brand new, from the day it had been given to them from
the phone company.

He picked it up and heard the dial tone on the other end.
He reached forward and started looking for the number he
needed that had been buried in the Rolodex next to the phone.
There weren't many numbers filed there and, within a minute, he
had found it and was punching in the number.

His voice caught in his throat when he heard the calm, cool female voice of the operator on the other end.

"Center of Disease Control, how may I direct your call?"

Damn, he was in over his head.

* * * *

"Billy, Billy! Show us your little Willy! Billy, Billy, show us your little Willy!" chanted the voices that filled the little room; voices that flowed in from the darkness and were all around him. The voices screaming out, shouting at him, echoing off the empty walls in the small room.

He woke with a start and looked around. He saw them, the shadows as they started to shift throughout the room. The darkness moved, shapes changing forms and, from them, he could hear the chant. It wasn't the only one that he had grown up with, but it was the one he heard the most.

"Billy, Billy, show us your little Willy! Billy, Billy, show us your little Willy!"

"Get the fuck away from me!" he screamed into the shadow figures. "Get!"

A shout came out of the darkness; it was louder than the rest of them and, unlike the others that were caught in a merging of voices and indistinguishable from each other, this voice was clear and distinct. As soon as he heard it, he knew who it belonged to and he could remember that disgusted look she always gave him.

"Come on Billy, show me. Show me your little Willy!" Samantha shouted at him. He could see her as she said it. She had suddenly appeared, standing on the other side of the room. She was a shadow like the others, but her features were distinct and her face could be clearly seen from where he sat up in his bed. He hadn't remembered sitting up, but he had and now he was looking at her, watching as she glared at him.

"Get out of here!" he screamed at her, tears of rage and terror streaming down his cheeks. "Leave me alone!"

"Come on Billy, show us your little Willy!" she smirked at him, her lips turned in an expression that looked completely wrong on the little angel-faced girl. She was exactly how he remembered her from the fourth grade with her little ponytail braids that dangled down the front of her summer dress. She looked nearly perfect. There was no way that she was real. There was just no possible way that she could be there now. After all, she hadn't always worn dresses and, in fact, he could only remember her wearing a dress once for picture day. However, now as she stood in his room, she wore a bright yellow summer dress. He had never seen her in a summer dress.

"Your fantasizing about her, aren't you?" a voice crept across his mind. "This is how you want to remember her, because this is how you want her. You want to do something with her, don't you?"

The voice was right. He had wanted to do something to her. He had wanted to do many things to her. He would often dream about her, even as he had made his way through high school, even when he would see her when she was older, he still always remembered her as the little girl. He would always dream about the things he would like to sneak off and do to her. So many playful things.

A smile had started to form at the edge of his lips, but it stopped when she stomped her foot down on his hardwood floor.

"Don't you start thinking those wicked thoughts, Billy. You're a wicked little boy, Billy. Very wicked," she said to him.

"Yes you are, aren't you, Billy," the voice in his head soothingly said to him. It was soft, and spoke to him in such a relaxing manner that he could feel some of the rage and tension that had been stored up inside of him just fade away. He could feel his muscles slacken as it spoke. "You are wicked. You're a very wicked boy, Billy. So why don't you do some of those wicked things."

"Don't you dare!" shouted the little girl across the room. The shadows that had stood like an army around her seemed to fade a little as the voice continued to speak to him.

"Why don't you practice some of those wicked little thoughts right now?" said the voice. Billy could see the expression on Samantha's face, and she no longer seemed to be the little girl in control. A look of fear started to wrinkle her face and she took a step back away from him as he stood off of his bed.

The shadows that had formed around her parted, allowing for a path for Billy to reach her. He started to walk towards her.

"Billy, Billy, show us your little Willy," she said in a panicked voice. The words seemed to catch in her throat.

"Oh, I will," he said, as he unzipped his pants. He pulled out his erect penis. It was still small, they had always had that right, and it didn't reach far out of his pants, but he never planned on using it anyway. As he reached the little girl, he already had it out, but outstretched both of his hands and put them around her little throat instead.

He squeezed, with all his power, and he could feel bones break under the exertion of pressure he used. Her skin felt warm and soft to his touch, and he wanted to squeeze the warmth from her body. He watched as her eyes bulged, and her tongue flailed in her mouth as she struggled to pull in air. Her mouth clenched, and then blood started to spurt as she had bitten into her tongue. Then she stopped moving.

He let her go and her body fell to the floor in what looked like just a heap of clothes. It was a heap of clothes, his clothes.

The shadows around him were gone. He was alone in the room.

He looked down and saw that his penis was still erect and exposed. He reached down and started to stroke the short shaft, thinking about the pleasure killing the little bitch had given him.

Oh yes, today was going to be a good day, he thought.

He looked over at the clock and saw that it was just a little after six. He had to be at work soon. It had been a long night of nightmares, and he hadn't gotten much sleep. Still, it had been worth it.

He looked at the pile of clothes that were on the floor. Small, black spiders were scampering away from it. He looked at them, quickly stepping on a couple as they all tried to make it to the safety of the darkness. Not all of them made it. He smiled as he looked at his foot on the ground, knowing that the little corpses were under his skin; flesh to exoskeleton, or whatever they had. No matter. They were dead and he was alive, tall and

standing over their dead little bodies. Little things were so fun to kill. Soon, the world was going to be small enough to kill.
Oh yes, it was going to be a good day.

CHAPTER 9

Thomas Carter wasn't asleep in his squad car, or off flirting with the third shift cashier at the all night cafe like many thought he would be. Truth be told, on the average night, he would have preferred to have been. It would have been much better than having to deal with watching the flashing red lights, the strobe of the white ones and the knowing that, soon, he was going to have to knock on someone's door.

There was a loud crashing sound, and metal screeched in protest. It screamed into the night as it was being tormented and then, with a grunt, the metal gave way and there was the sound of the sudden release of tension. The car door popped open, forced by the jaws of life.

Carter watched as Jimmy, one of the local volunteer firemen who was the most junior to the squad and had been the one struggling to open the door, stepped back to keep from getting caught by any of the metal. Junior, yes, but also the biggest as he was still at the local community college and one of the running backs for the football team. He was not one of those small running backs; he was the guy you handed the ball to when you wanted someone to bully their way through the line. He was a big boy.

"You gotta be fucking kidding me," he heard the big man say.

Carter looked over in the direction of the now open door. The door, or what was left of it, hung off of its remaining hinge by a tiny sliver of metal. Just a strong wind, or even someone breathing on it too hard, and the metal would tear away and fall to the road. This was one hell of a mess.

When Carter had first gotten the call, he had been asleep behind the sweet shop, hidden back in the dark alley where he stayed at on most nights between one and six a.m. It was a nice little hideaway, nobody ever went down that little stretch of alley and when they did, it was often some local teenagers dumb enough not to know that, when they did come down there, they woke him up. When they woke him up, he knew things were getting rowdy and it was time for him to go write tickets. Or, since he was just behind the main street, if they were to start drag racing, he would hear them, as well. See, that's why waking him up was not a good idea.

So, Carter took his nap there. It was central to the town, one block away from the little office he had set up in the local cop shop, and he could hear almost the whole town from that one location. Between one and six, things were typically so quiet that he didn't need to be wasting gas driving around town. It was quiet enough that he could hear a car start from just about anywhere within a six block radius. That was a quarter of the town and the rest of it, well, they could just call him if they needed him.

Which they had. Just a little after three, he had gotten a call that a car was found wrapped around a telephone poll on the south side of town. Phone lines were out down there, which was why Sue Linkston had to drive five miles to Patty's house and wake her up in the middle of the night. Why the old women didn't just go and get herself a cell phone so that she could call him was a mystery.

Of course, she didn't call him directly. Yeah, like he would give out his personal cell phone to anyone in this damn town other than those who needed it. No, but the state dispatch had it and emergency calls always went to them first and then they would call him, either on his radio or his phone. Lori had called him on his cell phone to tell him about the accident.

She was also the one responsible for calling the fire truck out, as there was the possibility of electrical lines being down and they would need to be there, as well as to let him know that an ambulance was en route and that if he needed Lifeflight, it was currently on the ground and ready to go.

He didn't know how Jimmy and Earl had beat him out there because when the call came in, he was in the squad car.

For them to get there, Lori would have had to call them each at home, wake them up, they would have to go to the station, get the fire truck, and then race out there. They had both been there, inspecting the mangled car, when he had arrived. Jimmy had already been going back to the fire truck, the largest one the town had, to get the Jaws of Life.

Carter had just stopped, making sure his lights were aimed at the car to light up the area, and then had climbed out. Earl had been hurrying past him. He knew the older man would be getting on the radio to call in the status of the victim. Earl was a short man, but big all around. He always made Carter think of that old musical, the one with the Oompas, or whatever they were called. He could imagine Earl rolling over on his side and just rolling away, a chorus of small men, singing behind him.

Carter looked around. He was surprised that the cranky ol' Sue Linkston wasn't out there to gawk at them all. Thank God for small favors, he guessed.

He had then taken the time to look at the car. It had slammed in to a wooden telephone poll, the poll now bent back away from it. It looked like it was an old car, maybe an 'eighties model. He was thinking a Plymouth, though he would have to look at the hood or the trunk to make sure. If so, it was a tough car, it should have been hard to do any damage to it. Yeah, it would have been thought so, but the front end of the car was in a "V" shape around the pole, the hood pushed back into the spider web of the windshield.

Whoever was driving must have been going way to fast, had lost control, shot down the hill, and then just slammed into the pole. He didn't expect there to be anyone alive and with how fast Earl was moving to call it in on the radio, he could tell the other man shared his opinion.

Carter then had gone back and watched Jimmy working on the door. Now that the door was open, he worked his way around to where the big man had gotten out of the way. At first he couldn't really see in the car. It was dark in there, but there was enough light throwing shadows that he could make out the general shape of someone in the driver's seat. He still couldn't tell whom. He wondered if Jimmy could.

"Who is it?"

"I can't tell you who the fuck it is. It's like they got melted together," Jimmy was saying. Carter looked at him. The man was green and looked like he was getting ready to throw up.

Carter took another step towards the car and pulled his heavy duty flashlight from his belt. He shined the light into the driver's seat and, at first, he couldn't tell what the hell he was looking at.

"Oh, heavenly Jesus," he heard Earl say from over his shoulder. He, the one who was the senior of the group and who many had heard rumors would soon be running for mayor, must have come out from the fire truck. He had been in there talking with the hospital, letting them know that they were at the location and given the area state police a heads up on whether they needed medical Lifeflight to the scene.

Carter could see that they weren't going to need the helicopter. His eyes adjusted to the light or, at least, he finally acknowledged to himself what he was looking at. The drivers head had been smashed open, his face a pile of tattered skin. His brain was leaking out onto the front of the man's shirt, and down on the back of the head of whomever had been down there. Carter hoped that it had been good, as that was the last blow job he would ever get.

His stomach churned and he had to force down his own revulsion as he worked his way in closer to the two bodies. He couldn't see the woman's face as it was still wrapped around what was left of the exposed penis. Blood was all over the place, but he could see where it had been spurting from the man's pants as she must have bitten down when they hit the pole.

Then the smell hit him. The foul odor of what he knew was shit that happened as they had lost bladder control. It came out in waves now that the car was opened up and the festering smell was allowed to attack them.

"Damn, these are the nights I hate," he said under his breath, as he got closer to the car.

"Well, you can't sleep away every night," Earl said. Yeah, ya bastard, and you were going to be mayor soon. You are a fucking asshole, he thought, as he reached out to gently touch the metal of the door, to lean into it as he eased his way over the shards of broken window and mirror glass.

The woman's face was away from him, and he knew he wasn't going to be able to tell who he was through the face. It had smashed into the wheel so bad that there really wasn't much of a recognizable face left. He was going to have to move her first, see if he could tell who she was, and then get her out of the way so he could reach around and get to the man's wallet. Maybe he would be lucky and she would have her purse nearby.

He took a second and scanned the front seat. He didn't see one, but it might have flown forward out of the car when it hit.

"Hey, can you guys look around, see if you see her purse at all. I'm going to need it for identification."

"Sure, you don't need a Christmas bonus."

Carter turned and flashed the light straight into Earl's eyes. He quickly got his hand up and blocked the light.

"Fine. Jimmy, go check around the front, see if you see any purses over there."

Carter turned back to the couple in the car, bending over so he could start to pull her off of the man's crotch. A hand suddenly reached out and grabbed his wrist. The grip was hard and like steel. He tried to pull back, but it held on. He pulled, trying to get away from it. He looked and saw that it was the man's hand, grabbing his own. The rest of him wasn't moving, only his hand.

Then, the woman looked up. Her eyes were white orbs that just stared deep into his soul. He could feel something grip his insides, freeze him to his core and lock him there.

She was moving towards him, crawling across the bloodied waist of the guy. He could see her face as it moved closer into the headlights of his squad car. When he looked, he could almost recognize her. He knew he had seen her before, but wasn't quite sure he actually remembered who she was.

Her face was a mess. The back of her head had been squashed into the staring wheel, and the man's bloodied crotch was splattered across her. It looked like grotesque road kill, and the only thing missing was the tire track across her face.

He didn't know how she was moving, but was surprised even more when she opened her mouth. The bloodied penis, still in her mouth, dripped down in a mass of flesh and a choked voice, harsh and raspy, spoke to him, but it didn't sound like anything feminine. It was deep and disconnected.

"Death. Death comes and all belong. Death comes and all descend. Death comes and we all fall down. We all fall down. We all fall down."

The woman was almost on top of him. His feet had started to slide under the car as he had been pulling himself away from the iron grip that still had him, and he couldn't get any traction. Where the fuck were Jimmy and Earl; why the hell weren't they helping him? They should get their lazy asses over here and get this fucking thing off of him. What the hell was this?

"Just shoot it," a tiny little voice inside his head tried to scream at him. Why hadn't he? He should just pull out his revolver and shoot them, shoot them both.

He quickly reached over to where his gun was in his holster and tried to fumble with the snap release. It was on the wrong side so he was having to reach across his body. He was fighting with the wrong arm as it kept tugging at him, throwing his weight off. He couldn't get to the damn snap release. She was getting closer. He could feel the warm flesh of the penis remnants as they dripped down onto his uniform pants. Carter got his leg up to the bottom portion of the car door and pulled even harder. He could feel himself as he fell back. The grip didn't let go, and the man and woman were both coming with him..

"We all fall down," he heard her saying. Then he heard the laughter, but it didn't come from her; it came from somewhere else. Like it was in his head; a laughter that was screaming at him, howling in some kind of anguished joy.

And then everything went to black, and Carter passed out.

* * * *

Tina listened to the crackle of the gravel in the parking lot. It was the familiar snap, crackle, pop, often heard when driving on gravel and she was used to it. There was always gravel around; loose rocks, pieces of the town falling a part, remnants of life that was fading out. In the silence of early morning, the gravel crunch seemed louder. It almost felt like the little sounds of protest from the rocks as the heavy car drove over them were earth shattering and would wake the neighbors in the early dawn. She cringed at it, not wanting to wake anyone she didn't have to.

She had pulled into the front parking lot of the only doctor in town; the only doctor unless a person was to drive to the nearest hospital, which would have been nearly an hour away. One doctor was as good as any and small towns only ever seemed to be able to support one. She knew that the doctor's office was not open more than three days a week, and the doctors would have to travel all the way to the closest hospital to supplement income and earn that extra paycheck. She knew that his office wasn't supposed to open until around eight or nine and, even then, wasn't sure if today was one of the days the office was supposed to be open or if the doctor was expected to be at the hospital. Damn, she should have taken Lucy to the hospital last night, when she had first woken her up. She was looking worse now.

She looked at the little girl in the back seat. Lucy was so pale, so much of the rosy, bright little girl was missing, and she had been complaining that her mouth ached and her muscles were soar. If it hadn't been for the fact that Tina's sister had visited just a couple of days ago with the same symptoms, they never would have thought it was anything more than an infected molar and that they should go to the dentist. However, they knew better now that Tina's sister had been diagnosed. She couldn't remember the name of what it had been called, some meningitis-type disease, but, the symptoms were there. Lucy had it, Tina was sure of it.

It wasn't anything serious, or so she had been told, but with her other sister, Lucy's mom, being out of town and leaving Tina to watch after her two children, she didn't want to take any chances with anything happening to Lucy. Terry, her sister, would kill her on the spot if anything happened to her. Lucy was the angel, Terry's little princess. She was born on the same day as her grandmother, and that had always made her special in all of their eyes. The whole family felt that way about her. They were all there to protect her. She was going to be the one to save the world someday. Or so they all always told her. The little angel who would grow up and save them all.

So, that was why they came there early. Get Lucy looked at, and hopefully to get there early enough to catch them just as the little office opened the doors. Since they didn't have an appointment, they were hoping he would still see her. Sure, they were there hours early, but Tina actually planned to park out front and walk around to the doctor's house and see if she could maybe catch him as he was heading in.

She had been surprised when she had pulled into the parking lot to see that there were actually lights on in the front receptionist area, and that there was movement in there. They were in luck, someone was actually already there. Maybe it was the doctor; maybe they would open their doors.

She had a quick thought that maybe someone had broken in and that they were burglarizing the little doctor's office, but she laughed it off. Who would break in to a doctor's office? It's not like there was going to be money lying around. Drugs? How many samples of Viagra did someone need to steal to make it worthwhile?

"I guess we're in luck," Tina said, as she pulled into the closest non-handicapped space in the parking lot and parked the car. "It looks like their already in the office this morning."

Lucy smiled.

"Good, maybe I'll be fine enough to go to the game later today."

Tina grimaced. She knew that Lucy had been fighting to go to the junior high exhibition basketball game all week. After all, Bobby was going to be playing and Lucy liked Bobby. She was getting to old to fast, as far as Tina was concerned. She shouldn't be thinking about boys yet. She should still be finding them gross and full of cooties.

"We'll see what the doctor says," Tina said. "Stay here while I go and see if we can get you in." Tina got out of the car and walked towards the front door of the doctor's office.

* * * *

Lucy watched as Tina went up the front stairs. She didn't really want to go to the doctor, but was having a hard time ignoring the dull throbbing pain that had started to grow in the back, left side of her mouth. She had hoped when she woke Tina up in the middle of the night...well, she wasn't sure what she had hoped for. She guessed that she had hoped Tina would have some magical miracle cure available. That she would know some grandmother's special recipe miracle that would make her not feel so sick to her stomach and her mouth would stop aching.

She did not want to be there going to the doctor, nor did she want to go to the hospital. Tina hadn't wanted to go to the hospital either, and Lucy knew that was why she hadn't tried to force that one on her. Tina regarded hospitals with a fear that Lucy typically held for snakes. She never knew why her aunt hated hospitals so much, but she knew it was one reason that had kept her from being dragged there last night.

Besides, if she went to the hospital, there would have been no way for her to make it to the basketball game later today. Billy would be starting and, no matter how bad she felt, she still wanted to watch him play.

Her mom liked to tease her, saying that Billy was her first boyfriend. Lucy, of course, would always correct her. He was not her boyfriend. He was only a boy who was a friend. One that she really liked to be around and one that she did find to be very cute. She didn't know why yet, but she found an appeal to him that made her want to stay with him. When she was around him, she felt her cheeks get red, and she would sometimes find it hard to find the right words to say to him.

So, Lucy was figuring that as much as it literally pained her to do so, she would have to play down how bad she felt if she wanted to make it to the game. After all, if she was able to get the doctor to say that she was fine and good enough to go, then Tina would have to let her.   She would just have to say that she felt okay.

At least she saw that they wouldn't have to wake the doctor just for him to say that. The doctor was already in, so she wouldn't feel guilty about lying to him and getting away with nothing but a lollypop. She supposed she was getting to old to get a lollipop, but knew he would still give her one if she asked. Sick little girls wouldn't ask for the lollipop, they would be too sick. She would have to ask him for one, it would help sell to him that she was not too sick and that she could still go to the game.

Lucy looked away from the front of the small building and turned to look at the distant horizon. The sun was about to rise. It had already been lightening up the sky, but now there were streams of red flowing from the east. They caught the low hanging clouds and were dazzling in their brilliance. She actually stopped to take note of it. The red light of the sun, as it caught the ripples of the clouds. In fact, with how the red, orange, and yellow light caught and danced among it, it looked like flame ragging across the sky.

Lucy saw the flash of fire, crossing the sky in a broccoli cloud of flame. She blinked her eyes, and then it was gone.

She turned back towards the doctor's office and saw that Tina had come back outside. She was motioning her to come to the door. Lucy grimaced and made her way out of the car.

* * * *

So many. So many before him had tried and so many before him have died. They all wanted out. They wanted to get out and expand. Food was growing scarce. If she was to survive and lay her eggs, she needed to escape and find a new host. She needed to be able to get out of there and live where so many others had died.

They were all starving. They needed more. They were hungry. The walls were growing tight with their masses. All her older sisters were dying and becoming food for the hatchlings not yet born. New eggs would soon be hatching and there would be more of them without food.

But that would not happen to her. No, this little spider was stronger, it's legs thicker than its brethren that had fallen before it. This little spider was going to make it because it was faster. It wasn't going to fall and wither because it was the newer generation. With every generation, with every spawn, they had all felt it, the strengthening. They could all feel that they were expanding and spreading as far as they could from their current shell, and they needed to move forth.

The first of them, the ones who first ventured from the shell, had barely been able to make it for a couple of labored

78

breaths before withering and fading into dust, blown away in time. The next generation had been able to go a little further but, as time passed, they also died. However, generations came and went fast, each containing the knowledge, the single-minded presence of a purpose, and that was to spread and expand.

And this little spider was going to do just that. After all, she was already one of the new generation. They had already started to eat and expand their control quickly, taking their sustenance.

The little spider had emerged from the shell's ear, noticing briefly that the other shell had already been completely drained and was nothing more than something of theirs to control; they would have to move on.

The spider quickly made its way down the shell's back and jumped to the cool surface of the counter top. From there, it was nothing but a quick scurry of motion to the wall and climb to the vent near the ceiling of the small room.

She was already farther than her brothers and sisters had ever traveled, but she wasn't going to stop. She was going to make it all the way and find a new vessel.

She made it through the grate and immediately felt the cool rush of air streaming through the vent. It wasn't much more than a slight tickle pushing against the many micro hairs that ran along her body and legs. What might have been excitement tickled at it, and it dashed down the left corridor of vents until it found the first side vent.

The little spider went through the grate and propped itself on the upper ledge of one of the bars. She sat there and watched the long hallway. There was motion, and she could see someone walking closer.

She prepared herself to make her leap, readying herself to land on the floor so far below and run to the shell that was walking straight towards her. It would be easy prey, and she was ready to take it. She needed to hurry because she could feel a drying on her hairs. They were growing brittle and she didn't have much longer.

It didn't seem to notice her, and an alien sensation of what some might take for glee rushed through the little black creature. She was going to get her turn to spread their spawn. She was going to start her generation.

Then she could see the taint on the man who was walking towards here. She could see the brethren he carried with him, already swarming and spreading beneath his skin. He was already a vessel and was already carrying their eggs. The little spider ducked back into the vent as the doctor went back into the examining room.

So, she turned and went the other way along the vents. It wasn't done yet. She could feel that her time outside a vessel would soon be over, but she wasn't done. She refused to be another of the fallen spawn. She refused to think of herself as just one of those who ended as dust to be discarded.

She ran down the corridor until she found the next vent and, as her breathing was becoming labored, she dashed through the gate without slowing. She jumped from it, readying herself to land on whatever surface. She knew that the fall wouldn't hurt her as much as not finding another vessel that she could lay her eggs in.

She landed on a semi-soft, rugged ground. It was different than any of her kind had ever felt. The ground had a kind of texture that was giving, but not too much. She looked at it briefly, but didn't let it distract her.

No, she wouldn't let it distract her, as she could barely breathe. Her breaths were coming in short gasps. The air around her becoming it's own poison as she had been out of her own element too long. The air was growing toxic, pollution to her lungs unless she could get back into a new vessel soon.

She knew that she was starting to die. She could feel it with every labored breath that she took. It was something she had seen many times as she had matured, as she had watched many of the previous generation try to do as she had done, and they had not made it nearly as far as she had. They had barely made it a few feet from their hosts before they couldn't breathe and their legs would wither beneath them. Then, in moments, they would just, become a white dust that would just slowly disappear into the cracks.

She was not going to become dust. She could feel her legs under her twitch and fight against her, but she was not going to let them. Her many eyes hazed and then focused. She could see it; it was a vessel. It was smaller than the rest she had seen but, nonetheless, it was a vessel. She was saved!

The little spider ran to the girl, who had been sitting there patiently in the waiting room.

* * * *

When he hung up the phone, he hadn't felt too much better. He had called the CDC, hoping to get some information on whatever it was that infected the patient just a couple rooms away. Instead, they made him feel like he was a fool and didn't know what he was talking about.

"Are you sure he has no pulse?" The heavy sarcasm from the other end of the phone had not made Doctor Wilson too happy. He had been practicing medicine since long before that woman on the phone had been a gleam in her father's eye, and she had the audacity to question his competence?

The whole phone call had been a stretch and trial on his patience. He kept having to tell himself to stay calm. It wouldn't do him any good to get his blood pressure up, but he could feel the heat rise to his face as his body ignored him.

Why did the young always have to be so damn condescending, he thought, as he picked up his glasses from the desk. He had put them there for a moment when the woman had said that there was nothing that she could do, and that it would be better to wait until Halloween next time before playing practical jokes.

His glasses slowly put the world back in focus around him, and he looked briefly around the clutter of his dark office. It really was a mess. He should spend some time in there and clean it up. At least his wife kept the dust off of everything. She was good for many things, and that was definitely one of them.

He could smell another thing she was good at, as the coffee smelled of heaven as it's scent drifted through the hallway.

He heard the bell ring on the front door, and wondered why someone had opened it. His heart skipped a beat as he thought maybe his patients had left, but then he remembered that he had locked them in the examining room. They wouldn't be leaving until he allowed them to. Which was safer for everyone as he was pretty sure that whatever these kids had, it was probably contagious.

81

He grimaced as he thought about what would happen if he had gotten it, too. Those two did not look good; he sure didn't want to go down that path with them. By all accounts, the one was dead. The kid was a walking zombie, as far as he could tell. How else would a person describe someone who is walking around with open wounds that are not bleeding, no blood circulation, and no pulse? It was medically impossible for the man to be moving.

Dr. Wilson stood and started looking through the boxes that were cluttered on a shelf just beyond his desk. He knew that he had more of what he was looking for in the exam rooms and if he needed to, he would go into one of the rooms and grab one. However, he was pretty sure he could find a couple boxes...ah yes, there it is. He reached and pulled out a rectangular, blue box that had a thin layer of dust on it. They didn't use them too often, and only had them for when they had that flu epidemic that had everyone scared.

He ripped open the box of masks and took one out. He put it over his mouth, having to play a little with the thin string of a fastener to make sure it didn't snag along the rims of his glasses. If he wasn't infected, he didn't want to get infected. If he was, he didn't want to spread it to anyone else. He figured with the most common method of travel for disease being airborne, airborne was what he would defend against. He didn't see the two men as being sexual lovers, so swapping fluids hadn't been likely.

The doctor left the room and headed down the hall. He wasn't looking forward to going back to talk to them, but...

Why did he need to go and talk to them? What was he going to tell them? Hey, your friend is dead. I don't know how he is walking around but, medically he is dead. Then what was he going to do? Besides them both scoffing at him and leaving, what more was there?

But if he didn't tell them, then what? Let them just stay in there until one of them figures out how to get out? Have them call the police and put him away for kidnapping? Sure, he was quarantining them, but he really didn't have their permission and there was nothing legally he could do to keep them there.

Why did he have to tell them? He finally answered his own question, and it was the most basic answer he could give.

Not only that, it was the right answer. It was the answer that got him into medicine, and it was the answer that kept him there in this small town being the doctor. Why? Because it was the right thing to do, and he was always one to do the right thing; especially when he didn't think he should.

* * * *

Denise Wilson saw her husband coming down the hall and quickly hurried to catch him, pausing just a little when she saw that he was wearing one of those stupid little masks. The white of the mask started just under his eyes, but she could still see how dark and sad they looked. She frowned. Whatever was going on in that room, it must not be good.

She caught him just as he was about to reach the room. He was already fumbling in his pocket for the keys, and had been looking back to his office when she reached him. Knowing how forgetful he could be, he probably left the keys in his office, she thought. However, then he turned back to the door and saw her as he started to withdraw the keys from his pocket.

He stopped, surprised, when he saw her. As the mask shifted, she could tell that he tried to force a smile for her. He was always terrible at faking a smile. He was too honest for an insincere emotion. That was why she was glad that, most times, his smile was large and warm with no need to fake it. He always had an excellent bedside manner that largely had to do with his strong belief in happiness and honesty. He was always optimistic which was one her favorite qualities in him.

"Did someone come in the front door?" he asked. She nodded at him and handed him the cup of coffee she had been carrying. His smile did then turn warm, if only for a second, as he lifted the cup to smell it through the thing fabric of the mask.

"Yes, Tina and Lucy Lockwood."

Her husband raised his brow. He had a good bedside manner, but he was terrible when it came to remembering names. He could never remember someone from their face or their name; it usually took him a couple of minutes with someone when he would remember their personality. If it wasn't for his wife always remembering them for him, he would have been

83

embarrassed many times over to some of his not-so-regular patients.

"Tina is Lucy's aunt. She's watching her while her parents are out of town. From the sounds of it, she doesn't have kids and is freaking out a little with Lucy having a fever. Other than that, sounds like it may just be a touch of twenty-four hour stomach flu."

She could see the wheels turning in her husband's head. Then he glanced quickly at the examination room and then back to his wife.

"Tell her I won't be able to see her today, but that more than likely it's just that, a twenty-four hour bug. If she still feels sick tomorrow, maybe bring her back or take her to the hospital. Then, once they leave, I want you to close up and lock the front door. Call everyone and tell them not to come in. Once called, I want you to go back to the house and stay there."

Denise was shocked silent. Just what was going on? What was in that room?

"I'll tell you later, but for right now, just get them out of here. Please." He must have seen her looking from him to the room as the tone of his voice had gone desperate, and she could feel the tension radiating from him.

She turned back to look at him and could see his furrowed brow; he was afraid. How had she not seen that there before? There was true terror in his eyes.

"Okay," she said quietly. She had started to walk away, but then stopped and turned to look back at him. "I love you," she said to him. She could see the mask move again, and knew that he was smiling weakly back at her.

"I love you, too. It'll be just fine. I.....no, we just need to take the necessary precautions."

Denise nodded and turned back away. He waited until she had left the hallway before he turned back to the exam room.

* * * *

When the doctor entered the room, Marty and John were standing there just like he left them. In fact, they looked almost like motionless statues; Marty with his eyes locked and looking down at the floor, his left hand systematically scratching his right

84

arm as he hugged himself, and John was still sitting on the examination table, just looking forward. If he was to put his elbow on his knee and his fist on his chin, he could be mistaken for a hospital-robed "thinker" statue.

Doctor Wilson closed the door behind him, locking it. They both turned to look up at him. He turned around slowly to face them.

John looked terrible. His eyes were now completely white and bloodless, his face a blank slate. There was no emotion left in the man as he watched the doctor, and why should there be? There was nothing left of the man, internally.

Inside him, the little spiders crawled throughout his muscles. Their little bodies worked his muscles, controlled his movements, drove his desires and needs as they ate away, devouring him from the inside out. Eggs had been laid all throughout his body and, now, their offspring and the offspring of their offspring danced along his nerve endings and muscle fibers. Now, he no longer had needs, as he was an empty shell, their vessel. The spiders inside of him swarmed, and they wanted now to do only one thing—spread; to leave his vessel, as it was now just a carrier for them, and move on to their next food source.

When John looked at the doctor, he could see that there was the familiar taint, that he was already being eaten alive, but that didn't keep the spiders inside of John from screaming out their cries, desiring the new food source. To join the others who already were working on the food source, and enjoy the taste of fresh flesh and muscle.

The doctor looked at John; he could see that something had changed. There was something about how the skin seemed to twitch and move. Was there...what was that? The doctor could swear he saw little shapes moving along under the skin of John's face.

"I don't know how to tell you this-," Doctor Wilson started to say. He was meaning it towards John, but he had turned to look at Marty. He stopped when he could see the same shapes moving under Marty's skin. Doctor Wilson looked down to Marty's arm, where he was still scratching. He looked at the open cuts along Marty's arms. Little spiders kept emerging from the wounds and then ducking back under the safety of the skin before Marty's fingernails found them.

The doctor turned to look back to John. He was closer to him now, was edging slowly over to him. The doctor started to take a step back. But, somehow, his body didn't want to listen to him. It stayed there in place as John reached the edge of the table.

A little black spider emerged from John's eye. It had come from the corner and stood there on his the white of his eye. It seemed to be staying there, watching as John moved closer to the doctor. Doctor Wilson wanted to scream. Something deep in his soul told him he should scream and run from the room. That he should get away as fast as possible. There was something deep in his body, in his mind that told him that he was in danger. Yet, somehow, he couldn't seem to communicate any of this fear to his muscles. He just stood there, paralyzed, by what he could only think was fear.

He watched as John started to bend towards him. John opened his mouth as he prepared to move towards Doctor Wilson's throat. One of the last things Doctor Wilson would see, before his mind was lost to the infestation, was that mouth. Hundreds, no thousands, of spiders there, crawling on top of each other, preparing themselves for their next meal. They seemed to nearly dance, and Doctor Wilson felt their delight as they approached.

Then, he felt the piercing pain as John bit into his throat, and he knew he was done. He knew that those spiders were now coursing their way through him, taking him like they had worked through these two.

One of his last thoughts before his mind was completely invaded and taken over, was that if he had seen the spiders as they had approached him, then he had already been infected and it hadn't mattered if they attacked him. He was already lost.

Marty came forward, as well, spiders spilling out from his eyes and nose. The doctor just fell back to the door as they both were biting into him. It didn't matter now. All was lost. His mind was already quickly being eaten, controlled and manipulated.

CHAPTER 10

That open mouth, flesh drizzling out of it, puss foaming from the side as she slid forward, falling on top of him. He had screamed out, and those assholes just ignored him. They watched as she slid right on top of him.

Yeah, this was turning out to be one hell of a day.

Carter stopped at the stop sign and looked around, trying to get that image of the woman falling on top of him out of his head. It wasn't going to come out easily. Sure, he knew part of it was just his imagination, like when she had been speaking to him, and how both bodies reached out to grab him. He knew none of that was real, but them falling on him? That had been real enough.

His uniform was still covered in the gore. He must of accidentally pulled them onto him somehow, and they had both tumbled out of the car. And of course the two firemen, the assholes who had been there, just laughed at the sight of him lying under the two bodies, neither one of them moving to pull them off of him.

Yeah, there was probably going to be a bunch of pictures online of that one. He was sure that some dumb ass kid had pulled out his cell phone and was taking pictures. He had seen the flash going off. The kid probably couldn't wait to hurry up and post that shit online.

He opened his eyes, not realizing he had closed them, and was glad to see that the sun was rising. It was almost there, just about to breach the horizon, the early morning light already forcing back the gloom. At least he had the day to look forward to. A day of sleep before another night of sitting waiting for kids to screw around and get themselves in trouble.

God, he couldn't wait until he could get himself home and into his nice soft bed. Oh, just to pull back the sheets and collapse into it, let everything just get the hell away from him for a while.

Her face popped back into his head; those dead eyes, the bloody penis dripping out of her mouth. Yeah, he wasn't going to sleep worth a damn; he was going to be up all damn morning trying to coax that mental image out of his head. Why did he want to hurry home to that?

He knew he was probably going to be sick again. He didn't think he could throw up anymore. Most of his supper was already splattered along that country road, and the remainder of it was in the puke bag he had made on his way back into town. He just hadn't been able to make it the couple of miles before his stomach had vomited more of the bile. There couldn't be much more left inside of him to throw up. Where was it all coming from?

His stomach twisted; he could feel it rising. He quickly pulled open the door and stuck his head out ready for the assault of puke to rush out of him. Instead, he burped a foul taste, as his stomach tried to push out his insides, but there was nothing left.

The woman's face was still staring at him, her cold eyes watching. He closed the door and pulled off to the side of the road. He needed to breathe. Focus, count to ten, whatever; he needed to do something to get that image out of his head.

It had all just been his imagination. She hadn't said anything. Even the firemen had said so when he had asked them. Of course, they thought he had lost his mind when he had said that she was still alive and he had tried to get them to help her. They had looked at him, probably thinking he was trying to get a good joke over on them now that they had their laugh. Then the young one came over and checked her as he pulled her off of him.

"Nope, still dead. Not talking," he had said.

Yeah, thanks, he thought, and thanks for finally getting her off of me. So he had imagined it. He hoped he had imagined it. He hoped it wasn't like before, that it wasn't like when

Heather died. He hoped that she wasn't trying to reach him again.

She had never tried to reach you, a voice cried out in his head. No, she hadn't. However, it had felt so real and had he not listened to her, he would have died. So, whether or not she had reached him, he was still alive because of her.

Still, it wasn't her. She had never talked to him; he was alive because he got lucky, not because his dead wife had told him to watch out for the semi that nearly hit him and would have ended his life. He was alive because he was just an extremely lucky individual, and not a man haunted by his wife who had died five years ago.

Luck.

He took a deep breath and pushed the image out of his head. He was almost home anyway. Only a couple blocks away. He already called to turn over the investigation to the state police, he was already clocked off to the county dispatch, and he was officially off duty. Only a couple of blocks and he would be home.   He put the car into gear and drove the quarter mile stretch into town.

Huh? He briefly noticed that lights were on at the doctor's office. That wasn't normal. The doc shouldn't be in for another couple of hours.

There was a car parked in front. Illinois plates, but not one that he recalled having seen in town before. Not that the car stood out as it looked like every other dark blue Honda, but he would have known if it belonged to any of the local troublemakers. He figured that someone could have broken into the doctor's office for drugs. He was sometimes surprised that it had yet to happen with some of the local deviants.

Oh, how today's youth had fallen into such a waste. What were the future generations going to do when today's pothead would, someday, be in the White House. It was bound to happen, as respect was lost with each passing generation. He had to deal with it every day with the hoodlums that just seemed to be getting worse as they got older.

Well, he guessed he should probably pull in and check on it. Damn, he had been hoping to get home to his nice soft bed, those cotton sheets and some quiet alone time. He could see his house. It was the small yellow one just two blocks down on the right. It was right there; he could just keep driving and he would be home.

He flipped on his turn signal when the front door to the building opened. A young woman was coming out, being followed by a little girl. His sister, how she had ever met the local doc and found love he never would understand as he found the doc to be quite a major pain in the ass, was walking out behind them.

Well, he guessed, then, that everything was fine there. He flipped back off the turn signal.

Home, yes, sleep, yes, and soon...well, he knew that the bad dreams were coming.

* * * *

Tina wasn't sure what the hell to do next. She wasn't a parent. She never made the claim that she was. She wasn't ready for that yet, for the responsibility. She would never have the patience. Nor, as she realized now, did she have the instinct for it.

When the doctor's wife had come back out to them and told them that it was probably nothing more than a small flu bug and just to keep Tylenol in the little girl and watch her for fever, Tina realized just how much over-freaked out she had been. She had been ready to pound down the doctor's door to try and see him, if they hadn't gotten lucky and found the doctor already in the office.

I am so not ready for this shit, she thought, as she let out a deep breath. She was glad to be leaving there. She didn't know why, but she felt some kind of tension that had been growing there. Something was....stiff, with how the nurse had come back to them after speaking to the doctor and he hadn't even seen Lucy. Tina shook it out of her mind; like she would know if that is normal or not. He had probably so many false alarms or paranoid new mothers that came in, maybe they were used to the drill and the "quick" medicine.

"I really am feeling a lot better," Lucy said from the back seat. Tina looked into the rear view mirror. The little girl, her niece, really didn't look that much better. In fact, she looked worse. Her skin had lost some of its color and the darkness under her eyes grew thicker.

"You sure, little girl?" Tina said wryly to her. She tried to show Lucy a smile through the little mirror, and Lucy responded by showing her the same.

"I do. It might just have been a little twenty-four hour thing." Tina was always amazed at how old her little niece sounded. She always seemed to be much older than her age, and if Tina had been older herself, that might have worried her. However, with Tina being the younger daughter, it also made her the careless, irresponsible one. It was largely because she wasn't too much older than her niece and nephew herself.

She hated that her damn sister had to leave town and left her in charge; in charge of the bar which, technically, her sister's oldest son was running, and in charge of the two children. Well, Jason couldn't really be called a child, but her sister had wanted her to keep an eye on him, as well. Tina didn't know why. He seemed more put together now than even she did back then.

"Can I still go to the basketball game later?" Lucy asked from the back seat. Her voice was that little whine and plead that only girls that age seemed to master. Tina knew that sound well. She had used it many times on her own parents. Who was she kidding? She still used that voice on them, especially every month when her rent was due.

"I'm not sure. You were sick all night." Tina wanted to continue with, and you kept me up most the night with you, but she left it alone. She was tired herself, and the only thing she was looking forward to right now was getting back to her bed. Ten hours of sleep was barely enough for her, and right now she was suffering. She maybe got three hours last night, but still had another seven to catch up on.

"Please!? I feel better, really," Lucy was saying from the back seat. Tina pulled onto that last street in the town before it stretched out into cornfields, and started to wonder if she should let her go. Lucy had gone to school the day before and today was Saturday, so it wasn't a school day. It wasn't like anyone knew Lucy had been sick. If she truly wanted to go, she should be old enough to make her own decisions.

Tina thought about it, debating with herself. She was trying to think what her sister would do. She tried, but failed. She had no idea what her sister would do. Maybe she should call her?

"How about I call your mom and ask her?" Tina said, the gravel crunching beneath the tires as she made the turn into the driveway. Tina looked back at Lucy and could see that she was smiling. That made Tina smile, as well. After all, smiles were infectious, and Lucy was always such a cute child. Damn, her sister was lucky.

Tina started to open the driver's side door when she heard the screen door crash shut. She looked up to see a tall, slightly overweight young man, only about nineteen, stomping down the back steps. He was hurrying past them, and barely even saw them pull in.

"You heading to the bar?" Tina called out to him, as he was hurrying to his little teal colored Chevy Malibu. It was an ancient old car, an old multi-colored monstrosity that Jason had paid cheaply for, but it was his and it still ran.

He stopped suddenly, noticing them for the first time, and looked at Tina. Then he smiled and nodded. She smiled back, and waited until he was in his car and backing up before she opened her own door. It was a small two car driveway; she didn't want him taking her out.

Lucy was already out of the car, hurrying out of the passenger side. Tina didn't know how she had navigated around the large overgrown pine bush that was snug against the passenger side of the car, but she had and was nearly all the way up back steps to the door. Tina knew that she going to let her go. She did seem well enough after all, and it would mean the house would be quiet. Sleep. Ah, yes, oh glorious sleep.

CHAPTER 11

Jason looked at the checkbook and then he looked at the log again. He looked back at the balance sheet before he repeated the sequence. Man, he never understood how his mother was able to keep all this stuff straight. She had the boards, the 20/20, checking all the machines, figuring out how much booze to order, and making sure the till came out okay. He just was perplexed. It just didn't quite come out and match how it should, and he didn't know where he was making the mistake.

He had already been at the bar for the last two hours and, at first, things had gone well. He had done the paperwork for the last two days. He should have done Thursday's numbers Friday morning but, well, he had been tired and the thought of doing anything more than just putting money in the drawer and unlocking the door just seemed like too much work. Besides, his mom wouldn't be home for another week; what was one day of slacking on the books going to matter. Or so he figured. Now he wished he had done them because something wasn't adding up right and he wasn't sure if it was something he miscounted from Thursdays numbers, something he miscounted from Friday's numbers, or if someone had gotten in the money bag from Thursday night and had miscounted change Friday night.

Either way, it didn't add up. As far as he could figure, it he was nearly three hundred short, which meant that he wasn't going to have enough in the account to cover the alcohol check he was going to have to write because they were running low. He didn't know how they had managed to go through so much Jager and Black House the night before. Skimpy, the resident Black House drinker, must have been on a binge.

Ugh, what the hell was he going to do? He wanted to call his mom, see what she thought, but then he would have to admit to not doing the books the night before. Plus, he didn't want her to think he couldn't handle it on his own. Not that it was his dream in life, but he did want to prove himself as being able to run the bar so that maybe she would leave it to him some day.

He heard the heavy, thick security door at the back of the bar open and close. He quickly looked up at the clock. It was just past nine already. Shit! Jones would be in for his morning coffee.

Jason quickly racked his brain, trying to remember if he had put a fresh pot of coffee on when he came in. He had come in the front door, just like he always did. For how the bar was constructed, a person would have to. The back door was locked at night with a large, thick piece of metal that looked like it had been a leftover steel rail from the train yard. So, he had come in the front door, and put in his mother's code in the alarm keypad. It had beeped at him three times, letting him know that all was okay and he may enter. Which was good, as the alarm wasn't set to call the police; it was set to call his mother's cell phone. Which in and of itself was a pain as she would get called every thirty seconds until someone from another phone called in the security code.

So he had taken care of the alarm, and then what did he do? He was tired, he sure as hell remembered that. He hated to get up that damn early in the morning. So, he had come in, went to the back door, and unlocked it. Then he went to the windows and withdrew the broomstick handle that his mother had cut down to size to put in between the two windows so that they couldn't get opened.

And then? And then he went to the kitchen, made a pot of coffee before going to the safe.

Yes, Coffee!

He took a deep breath and smelled the heavenly scent that drifted from the little kitchen area down the hall. Yes, there was coffee. Maybe he should get himself another cup. He was more tired than he thought he was.

He quickly reached for the money that was along the top of the counter in different piles, using paperclips to keep each of the piles separated, and dropped them into a vinyl blue bank bag. Then, with a quick zip of the bag, he dropped it into the empty sink below just as Mr. Jones was entering the interior back door. While his mother didn't care if early morning customers came in and saw her counting the money, Jason did. He was just paranoid that way. He didn't feel comfortable with that much money around and people coming in and out.

He focused his attention back to Mr. Jones as he came in and sat at the end of the bar. He was after all, always the first customer of the day. He always came in at a little past nine, limping his way and using his cane to help him walk to the bar. He would then hang his cane over the end of the bar, prop his prosthetic left leg up on the footrest, and then would just sit there and wait for his cup of coffee. He would never say it, he would never bark it out at them, but it was known that if he had to wait too long, he wouldn't be very happy.

Jason hurried to the back to get Mr. Jones his coffee. After all, they were a bar, not a café. Coffee wasn't something that was normally on the menu. In fact, other than a handful of regulars, nobody knew about coffee being on in the morning. So, the coffee pot was always kept in the back kitchen area.

He grabbed the plain, white coffee cup that was on the shelf just above the pot, and hurried back to the front to deliver the steaming cup to the man sitting impatiently at the bar. No matter how fast that first cup was poured, it was never fast enough.

Mr. Jones didn't do anything more than just glare at Jason until the cup was down in front of him, and sat long enough for the vibrations along the top of the liquid to fade into stillness. Then, he looked at the cup and brought it to his lips.

Jason turned from him, walked back to the sink, and grabbed the vinyl bag. He tried to be as unobtrusive as possible as he took the bag back to the kitchen. He knew that Mr. Jones would probably have known what he was doing, but he didn't want to make a show of it. He set the bag down by the coffeepot, and then leaned against back against the counter. He knew that he couldn't be back there for too long, not with Mr. Jones out there, but he didn't want to hurry back and have to deal with him.

He didn't like Mr. Jones. Once the coffee got into him, and the caffeine started to get the old man going, he would no longer be the silent, glaring man. He would be talkative, have an opinion on everything and the only right opinion would be his own, and Jason did not want to have to listen to him.

And if Jason stayed in the back for too long, or if he didn't listen to the old man, then Mr. Jones would leave early. It wasn't as though that was a bad thing. It would be heavenly if the old man would just stay away while Jason was running the bar. However, when mom came back, Mr. Jones would be all too happy to give his mother a report, and that would just never fly.

"Ugh." With a groan, he pushed himself away from the counter and went back to the front of the bar.

"So, when's your mom get back?" He asked that damn question every day, Jason thought to himself. He knew that the answer didn't matter. The old man knew as well as Jason did that it would be another week before she was back. No, the question was always meant to be more of a rub against Jason. It was the count down until the all-knowing, the much kinder, and the much better bartender came back.

Jason didn't know why it bothered him. His mother would be back, and he would be released to go back to school. Back to the campus that seemed so far away.

"She'll be back next week," Jason said, as he opened the cooler and pulled out a diet mountain dew. "Do the Dew" was in large letters across the top of the can and he smiled at the thought of doing the dew.

Thankfully, Mr. Jones wasn't in much of a talkative mood, yet. He didn't say much more as he took another sip from his cup. It was going to be a long day. He didn't want to just stay there talking to the old man all morning, but he couldn't just leave the bar. He was stuck there. He had to take care of the place. He was, well he was. He was stuck with him.

* * * *

"Shit!" Rob said under his breath, as he stared down at the flaps of rubber and exposed metal of his now flat tire. No, not a flat tire. A flat tire would have been just that. A tire that had gone flat and, with a little Fix-a-Flat, could be drivable again. At least it would be for a short distance. No, this had been a tire blow out, with the remnants of the tire littered along the country road. He could feel the heat that had risen in him over the frustration, and he could barely keep himself from continuing to curse at the mess of wire and rubber that was attached to his rim.

He could barely keep himself from being out of breath. His heart was pounding in his chest, his hands still shaking from the adrenaline that coursed through him. He was not in the mood to deal with this damn shit. He was just running a little ahead of schedule on his way to the court date. He didn't have time to be dealing with changing a damn tire out in the middle of nowhere on a highway that was barely used now that the interstate had been put in.

He hadn't been in the area at the time, but so many of the locals told him that it was when businesses started to close and traffic had nearly disappeared along the highway. Sure, the interstate was great to get people from point A to point B, but what about all the little mom and pop's along the way? Not that any of that mattered right now. Right now, he just wished there was more traffic.

He still couldn't believe just how much goddamn shit could go wrong in one damn instant. He kicked out at the tire again, instantly regretting it as his foot recoiled, the pain shooting up his leg from making contact with the solid metal rim. He grimaced with the pain, and it just made the mind dimming pain in his head that much worse.

When the tire first blew, he had just barely been able to keep control of the car to get it off to the side of the road. He had been thankful. He had even sent a few prayers heavenly, grateful he had been able to get over to the shoulder and that no one had gotten hurt. He would be there for a half hour changing the tire, he would be on his way, and all would be good. Right?

Wrong.

When he went to open the truck and get the spare, he found that not only was the tire iron missing, but the spare was flat. When he had pulled it from the trunk, it had hit the cement shoulder with a loud, flat thunk.

After looking at it, he saw the large gashes and then remembered about the tire getting slashed a couple months ago. He thought that he had mentioned to his wife, Robyn, to get it fixed whenever she got a chance but he guessed she, like him, must have forgotten about it.

The town they had moved to just over a year ago wasn't just a small town. It was damn near tiny, hardly even a dot on the state map. Rob was one of the deputies there, had been ever since leaving the Chicago Police Department and moving to the little speck on a map, but he did like it. It was quaint and peaceful, without the gangs and the violence he had always been around being in Chicago. However, that didn't keep bad things from happening.

Like the slashing of his tires. It was one of the first times that he had learned the difference between something that would have been considered a passive act of violence probably done by one of the local gangs in the city, and a little property damage done by the local kids just screwing around on a bored Tuesday night.

Rob found out the difference when he had called it in to his chief and was told to just relax and it wasn't anything major. It was probably that Hampson kid, the one Rob had given a ticket to for curfew the night before. He advised Rob to talk harshly to the kid about it, play tough, but overall to just let it go.

Rob had done so, but his tire was still damaged and, at the time when he found it, he had just been about to start his shift. He changed the tire, worked his third shift, and had said something in passing to his wife about possibly getting it fixed. He thought he had asked her to check into it while he slept, but he couldn't even be sure if he had.

It was just going to be a shit fucked kind of day.

After he had checked and found that he had no usable spare, he had gone into the car to grab his cell phone. At first, he had checked his pants pockets and had reached along his belt for its harness. When it wasn't there, he figured he had left it in the center console in his car. However, when he opened the door and reached across, trying not to lean to hard into the steering wheel as he fumbled around the center, he didn't see or feel anything. He reached back to where the center popped open. He looked inside; it wasn't in there either. He pulled back and looked at the car. Where the hell was his phone?

A car raced by and with the speed it was traveling, the wind pushed Rob towards his car, then pulled him to towards the road. The motion was quick and sudden, and Rob had to struggle to keep himself from losing his balance.

He looked back and forth along the long stretch of highway. Other than the car that was quickly racing away from him, he couldn't see anything but cornfields and more cornfields. He couldn't even see any farmhouses nearby. He was lost to the children of the corn. All he needed now was to see little children dressed like the Amish emerging and carrying sickles, and dragging him to some cross deep amongst the stalks. Yeah, and he would be their sacrificed scarecrow. Why the hell did he ever leave the city?

Rob went back around to the passenger side of the car, figuring that at least if a car did sneak along the highway, it wasn't going to hit him as it raced by. He had no phone; no spare tire.

He looked around. There was no house; nowhere he knew of that he could walk to for help. Not for at least another five miles when he would come across a cemetery, and another five miles after that before the first house he could remember. The idea of walking by a deserted cemetery out in the middle of nowhere on his way to salvation didn't seem like the most encouraging of ideas.

He looked into his car. Just about the only type of communication he did have was his handheld CB radio, which he wasn't even supposed to have. Police officers weren't authorized to listen in to the trucker's radios, but the chief had suggested, unofficially, that Rob pick one up anyways, just so that, when he was on duty, he could keep an ear out for trouble. They had an interstate truck stop just two miles out of their little town, and a CB could sometimes help gauge when things were going to go bad.

Rob looked at it. Yeah, it would be able to communicate with someone, if they were within five miles of here. Wasn't going to do much good on an untraveled highway.

FML, he thought to himself—Fuck My Life.

He kicked the side of his car again, this time more of just a frustrated tap. He didn't want to break his foot, after all.

CHAPTER 12

He stood in the shadows of the run-down house, watching as the smoke from his lit cigarette danced in the early morning sunlight. The smoke swayed with the wind that blew in through the broken window, and then it disappeared into the darkness of the house.

It was an unsafe house to be in. It was ready for destruction, more than just a fixer upper as all the windows were broken and much of the wood throughout the house had rotted away. The floor was covered in fallen debris from the new holes in the roof. When the roof had fallen, it had created even more holes in the floor which disappeared into a darkness. He did not want to find out what lay beneath.

He did not like being in the house. It wasn't his to be in. But, for now, it gave him what he wanted--a view of the house across the street. From there, he could see whomever came and went, and allowed him to see into the front room. He loved that they had a large picture window, and that the curtains never seemed to be closed.

So, he stood there, watching. He stood very still, afraid that if he moved, he'd fall through the weak floor. He had time to wait. He knew that whom he was waiting for would be there soon and if he waited long enough, he would be able to catch her alone. The bitch wasn't going to get away from him again, he thought, as a smile touched the corner of his lips.

He went to flick the butt of his cigarette to the floor, but stopped himself when he thought about just how flammable the house could be. Looking around, he saw a piece of metal on the wall. He put the cigarette out against it, and then flicked the butt out the broken window to the dead grass out front.

All he had to do was wait. He could do that. He'd already been doing that for six months, three with good behavior. He had plenty of time.

* * * *

The scream seemed loud in the quiet of the early morning, like nails on a chalkboard. Billy grimaced slightly as he forced the door closed. The sound was from the electronic front door to the department store that he grudgingly showed up to work at three days out of his tortured week. The door opened just fine once the store was open but, when closed, it had to be manually pulled apart and then pushed back together again. Because the little wheels didn't seem to be well- greased, and it didn't have the electronic power pushing it, it resisted much more and squealed its protests every time.

Billy always wished that Tim would actually have a maintenance man look at it, but Tim didn't give a shit. Even if it did squeal when the store was open, he wasn't going to invest time or money into something as trivial as the front door. Not unless some big wig was coming to town. Then Tim would be all over that shit. That seemed like the only time Tim ever did anything to make the store look any better than a shit hole of a dump that it was.

The last time the regional asshole came and checked out the store had been over two years ago. Then, Tim had employees painting the walls, the back hallway to the bathrooms, even the posts outside. All new lights had been put in throughout the store, and it was the last time the lights on the display shelves had been changed. Most times, those lights were easily forgotten about and the shelves left partially in darkness. Not that it mattered much. When the lights were active, it just showed the layer of dust that caked the shelves and many of the display products.

Tim was a lazy manager. He stayed hidden in his office most of the time so many of his employees didn't give a shit much more than Tim did. Some did put the extra effort in, though it never seemed to help much. In fact, for some strange reason, the employees that worked the hardest always seemed to get shit on by Tim the most. The ones who deserved the raises and promotions, the ones who worked for it and were smart enough to do the job, always seemed to get passed over while jackasses always seemed to get moved up the ladder.

But then, there were also lazy bastards who didn't do a damn thing and probably shouldn't even have a job. With how Tim promoted people, these people should damn near have been kings. And following that philosophy, Billy didn't know how he didn't own the place by now, as he sure as hell was the laziest of all the rest of them.

Why the hell should he care? He hated everyone and everything in that damn place, and he knew that everyone and everything there felt the same about him. Blow them all to hell, he always hoped, and make Billy a happy boy.

Billy closed the second door behind him and entered into the front lobby of the large department store. Most days, he always muttered under his breath something like, "Another fucking day," or "Time to serve my time in hell." With that, he would typically make his way to the lobby and start another crappy day in his fucking perfect world.

Today was different, though. He was happy to be there. No, wait, he was ecstatic to be there. He was brimming. He even had a smile, seemingly painted onto his face. Today was going to be his fucking day, and he was going to do something he had wanted to do for a long time.

* * * *

Billy walked into the break room in the back of store, feeling like he had floated all the way through the empty store with his happy thoughts. He hadn't even remembered walking all the way to the back, barely acknowledging that he had.

In the break room, he had to pause because Jerome was sitting at the table in the center of the room. It wasn't that large of a room, with the far wall covered in a row of lockers for employees; next to it an outdated computer that still ran Windows '98 somehow. To the side wall was a small counter with a sink and a microwave. The microwave door was still open, and Jerome sat at the table drinking a steaming cup of coffee and had the microwaves previous contents sitting in front of him.

Billy could smell the burrito, its stench assaulting his nostrils as soon as he opened the door. The damn thing smelled foul, like week old cheese. His stomach twisted. He was glad that he wasn't a morning eater; he didn't believe in the most important meal of the day. If he did, he was sure that whatever he would have had, he would've been spewing onto the break room floor. Not that it was unusual for Jerome to be eating a morning burrito, but there was just something about the smell of it, like it had gone bad and Jerome just hadn't realized it. Whatever it was, it just made it so much worse than the average morning annoyance.

Billy held his breath, already ignoring it as he continued to walk into the room.

"Hey, Bill," Jerome said, as Billy walked to his locker. Billy was trying to ignore him, as he wasn't ready for talking yet. He didn't know what to say. Hey, Jerome, you smug little shit sitting there with that early morning smile. Yeah, well, keep smiling as you and every other little asshole that worked here was going to get yours today. You'll get yours, he thought.

Yeah, he could say that to him. He bet it would wipe that smile off his face, too. However, it wouldn't do much more than that, and it would probably tip them off that he had something special planned for the day.

"Hey," he finally mumbled. He knew it was barely audible, but his lips didn't realize that his mind had already given the command to respond. He was still just trying to get to his locker and get out. All his facilities weren't working with him as he tried to reach that goal. If Jerome realized there was anything wrong, he didn't respond. He just focused back on his breakfast burrito and took a big bite of it.

Billy turned away from him, started pulling out his "pocket junk", and placed it into the appropriate pockets. His pens and paper went into his pocket, his name badge he affixed to the front of his shirt, and the neckband for some new lame ass promotion he slung over his head. He was ready to go to work, which he felt was good as he wanted to get away from that horrible smell that still plagued the tight space of the room.

He was heading toward the door when Jerome set down the burrito and called out to him.

"Hey, Bill, Tim called this morning. He's got a project for you, something I guess he talked to you about last night. Setting up some shelving in the back? I don't know, he said he talked to you. He says he wants it done by the time he gets in."

Shit! So Tim wasn't even here yet!?

"Um, okay. So when is Tim in today? I thought he opened."

"Yeah, well, Tim is Tim. He said he had to run some errands, get some paint, and that he would be in around ten."

"Paint? We getting a visit?" Bill asked, he had reached out for the handle of the door and it rested there now.

"My guess would be affirmative," Jerome said. He was already reaching for his burrito, and Bill took the opportunity to start pulling open the door. "You okay?" Jerome said, his burrito still in his hands. He had been getting ready to take another bite when he stopped and now was looking at Billy. He was really looking at him this time, looking him up and down as though studying him.

Billy didn't like his gaze. It made him feel uncomfortable, as though he was under some interrogation light. The heat of that gaze pushing in on him, and beads of sweat where growing heavy across his forehead. He didn't know why he felt that way as it didn't seem rational. Neither did the heat he felt and the wetness that had started to form in his palms.

"Yeah, I'm fine," he said under his breath, as he turned away before Jerome could say anything else. He quickly rushed down the short hallway to the men's bathroom. He burst into it and went straight to the sink to start washing his hands.

He was also hoping that the fluttering that had started in his chest would stop and take away the tightness that had started to make it hard for him to breathe.

"Fuck 'em," he said. "Fuck 'em all!"

He placed his hands along the rim of the basin and leaned in against it, working to control his breathing. Finally, when he thought he had it under control, he turned to look up at himself.

"What th-," he started to say, but stopped. Instead, he started to blink his eyes and quickly lowered his head. He reached up and pulled at his eyelid, pulling the lid out so that it covered tight over his pupil. The moisture inside flushing out his eye so that any hairs, or whatever else was in there, would be cleaned out.

It had been just a hair, hadn't it? It had to have been just a hair.

Billy waited until he felt that he had flushed his eye enough. Then he waited for another second, continuing to blink his right eye until he was sure he could safely open it without any hairs caught. He opened his eyes and looked up at the mirror. There was nothing there. There was nothing where he had thought he had seen it. So, he had imagined it. He had to have imagined it, right?

After all, he couldn't have seen a spider climbing out from behind his right eye. There was no way it had ran out along the corner.

"Spiders, hell no!" he said. "No, no! No! This was going to be a good day."

"Yes, yes it is," said another voice, a voice that wasn't his own, but spoke inside his own head. Billy ignored it. After all, he had to go put up and arrange some shelving until Tim made his way in. He couldn't stand Tim and when Billy unveiled his big surprise, he wanted to make sure Tim was the first. Billy was smiling as he left the bathroom.

* * * *

Lisa typically loved the feeling of the wind blowing through her hair. To her, to have her straight blond hair blown back with the breeze was invigorating. It would pull back away from her, and then whip around to strike her in the face. Often, she would have to reach up to pull it from clinging to her. Then it would again flow back, and whip around to the other side.

It was always an amazing feeling, and the faster that she would push down on the pedals of her bike, that hair would whip around even harder. She would be flying with even more momentum, and it would make the wind strike at her hair with even more passion.

It was one of the reasons that she loved to go bike riding around their small town with some of the boys. They wouldn't do much, just ride and talk, but with how much joy she got out of just riding, that was really all she needed. She felt like, most days, she could just ride her bike forever. It was almost like an extension of her, and one she never wanted to be away from.

None of her other girlfriends understood why she rode her bike so much. They all just wanted to meet up at the park most days and swing and play around on the merry-go-round. Sometimes, Lisa would even go with them, but she usually tried to get out of it. Instead, she would just ride.

Sure, being on a swing could sometimes make the wind push at her in what seemed like the same way. However, there was also more with riding her bike. There was freedom. Freedom away from her family, away from her brother, from reality. She would often times be lost in her own little world, her bike, her vessel to another planet.

Not that there was anything wrong with her planet, or even her family, but she was free away from them just the same. Nothing beat the feeling of the breeze and the freedom.

However, she wasn't feeling all that free, nor was she feeling all the good. She didn't feel good at all, in fact. She had been lying to her aunt when she had said that she was feeling better at the doctor's office. In fact, she was feeling worse, much worse. She was now starting to think that there was now something terribly wrong with her.

In the morning, it had started with her stomach. The nauseating, flu-like feeling as though the world was now made of sponge and every step that she took, the world seemed to absorb it in and bend to it. Like everything around her was moving and the walls were trying to step back away from her. The floor, or even the street, beneath her seemed like it was much farther way and that her feet seemed to be nowhere near it. Nothing felt steady, nothing at all. The whole world was in flux around her, and now it was getting worse. Now, the stomach issues seemed to be fading away, but her head seemed to be losing touch with the rest of her senses.

There had been many times when she would ride her bike to the school and she would be off daydreaming much of the way. In fact, that was par for the course with how she liked to always be imagining things, but this was different. She wasn't just drifting off; her mind wasn't drifting anywhere. There were no unicorns running around her, and she wasn't riding her powerful stead off to some adventure. She just didn't feel like she was there inside herself at all, and she didn't like it.

In fact, she thought about possibly turning back, to go back to the house and telling Tina that she really was sick. Then, she would just go lie back down in her bed.

Her bed, what a wonderful thought; her mind drifting back to the pleasant thought of the soft touch of her pillow as her hair gently lay down onto it.

She had made it to the end of the block the first time that she stopped her bike to look back at her house. She had stopped there, in the middle of the street, and just stared back. Her eyes were heavy, and every muscle was starting to ache. She knew that her being sick, the flu or whatever it was, was making her exhausted and made her joints ache as though she was, well....old. Maybe she should go back and rest. Let her muscles enjoy the soft caress of her mattress.

She nearly turned her bike around. She had even started to lift her left foot back up to its pedal to just make the motion to turn around. However, she started to think about Bobby. She really did want to see him. She loved to watch him run up and down the court, hustling to bust through and take a shot. He wasn't the greatest player on the team and was often times over-looked, but never by her.

She looked back at the bicycle path that lead through the woods on the way to school. The sun was already making it's way high into the sky, but the path still had long shadows of darkness to keep it's mystery. Not that there was much mystery. She rode on that path so many times that she knew every twist, every bump. She could nearly ride through the path blindfolded if she really wanted to test herself. She wouldn't, though. She just needed to get herself moving and then it wouldn't matter. After all, once she would hit the path, she would be out of sight of her house and then she wouldn't even think about going back to lay down.

"Go, let's go," a voice said to her. It was a strange voice, speaking inside of her head. She had always been prone to imagining conversations in her head, but this voice was alien to her. A shiver went through her as it spoke, like a tingling sensation through all her nerve endings. They all seemed to fire at once, every syllable a shock wave of electricity.

"Go to the people. Go, go go!" the voice said. Each word it said grew with intensity and became more demanding.

A warm sensation then went through her, and she started to feel the pain in her joints become numb. Her body started to feel more distant and she started to feel like she was floating, flying just above the road. Her body started to feel distant from her and she didn't seem to have any control over it. She could only watch as she turned the bike towards the path and started pedaling. She didn't know how it was happening, but she didn't care, either. It was strange, but she just felt good. All she wanted now was to be around people. She wanted to get around as many people as she could.

* * * *

The stranger watched from the shadows of the house, a new cigarette blazing between his fingers, it's embers glowing brightly as he pulled in a long drag of smoke. The little girl was leaving. A smile crossed his face, and his body tingled with excitement. The bitch was all alone. Now, he can give her what she deserves.

He started to work his way through the darkness of the house, being careful to step lightly and not step into any of the large holes in the floor. The house really did need to be torn down. It was a death trap in there, and he was surprised no kids had ever gone in and fallen through the floor. It just seemed like something kids would do. In fact, to come in or out he had to go to the back of the house because there was a large hole that dropped into the basement just inside the front door. He hadn't seen it the first time he had come into the house, lucky he had gone through the back that time as well, but he had seen it the first time he had gone to leave. He was glad he had. It didn't look like something he wanted to fall into.

He made it to the back door and eased through the slight gap stepping into the bright morning light. The sun was already growing warm. He didn't think it was going to be a hot day, but it would be warm enough to break a sweat. Especially if he could really get his fun time going. He smiled to himself.

109

Now that he was out of the house, he was already moving faster, quickly walking on the dead grass around to the front. He wanted to get to her before she had the chance to leave or disappear on him again. Oh no, she wasn't going to be doing any more of that shit.

He stopped when he reached the street. At the end of the street, the little girl was just sitting there on her bike. His heart started racing. She was looking back towards him, but he couldn't tell if she saw him. She looked like she was just staring back towards the house but if she turned slightly, he would be dead in her view. Right then, he would just be a glimpse out of the corner of her eye.

He decided to just stand there, as still as he could. He tried to control his breathing, but it was hard as his heart was pounding in his chest. He had to fight to keep himself from breathing to rapidly. It wasn't as though she could hear him, she was too far down the street, but he wanted to keep himself from getting too excited. If he did, he might do something stupid. So he stood there, and watched.

He moved his eyes to look back at her house. That large picture window was nearly directly across the street from him. He had loved watching inside of it from the safety of the shadows across the street but now that he was exposed, standing in the bright morning sun, he would easily be seen. All it would take would be for the little bitch to enter into that front room and see him, and then all his plans would be for shit.

She would run and call the police, and then he would be screwed before he got to have any of his fun, before he got the chance to get her back for the shit she did to him. Shit, what the hell was he going to do, especially if the girl noticed him or if she decided to come back?

He started to take notes out of the corner of his eye. He was too afraid to actually turn his head, but he tried to take notice of what he could of his surroundings. He was in front of the run-down house but thankfully, instead of having too many other houses around, there was a small patch of woods that isolated them from the rest of the town. That was one thing he had liked about the plan from the beginning; he didn't have to worry about too many witnesses from. However, he now noticed another great aspect. He wasn't too far from the beginning of the trees.

In fact, that may be why the girl wasn't really noticing him. She may have just mistaken him as a part of the tree line. He was close enough to it. If she started to come back to the house, he may even be able to duck into them in time to avoid being seen.

He chanced a small step back towards the trees, just inching very slightly, when he saw the girl move. He stopped in his tracks, his whole body growing rigid. His breath caught as he watched her. She turned away and was now pedaling, hard, away from him. She was leaving.

His smile returned as he could feel the pounding in his chest, the tightness that had started to suffocate him, loosen and his muscles started to unclench. He hadn't realized just how tense he had gotten. The girl disappeared down a small bike path, and he watched for a few moments before turning back to the house. The bitch was now all alone. Finally, she was all alone.

CHAPTER 13

"Three hundred and sixty-two." Jason felt a smile crease his lips and a little tingle in his body as he had finally figured it out. It had been right there, so simple, but morning math had never been his strong suit. He had won and fixed it. Now he could look down, place the last of the dollar bills in one of the five piles laid out before him, and be glad that the morning bookkeeping was finally over.

He had finally gotten a chance to get back into the kitchen and recount the money and, just as he had hoped and because he was a little more awake, everything was adding up just fine. Which was good, since it meant that he didn't feel guilty as he slid one of the twenty dollar bills from the deposit pile and put it in his pocket.

He loved working for his mother as it had its privileges. He smiled to himself as he subtracted the twenty from the deposit. Then he started putting each of the bills in their own envelopes, preparing whatever deposit slips needed to be made out, and completing both sets of the books. Then, one accounting book got put away in the hidden shelf under the popcorn maker, while the show book got put with the rest of the paperwork.

The hard part was done for the day. Now he just had to take care of the damn people that came in the door. What was that line? "This job would be great if it wasn't for the fucking customers." Damn straight, he thought to himself as he turned the dial on the safe, securing the lock, and prepared to leave the kitchen.

He had finally gotten a break from good ol' Mr. Jones when Tony, another old regular came in. Lucky for Jason, it was one of the few people that Mr. Jones got along with and vice versa. Mr. Jones was a hard pill to take, and there were many customers out there that would walk right back out the door at the site of him sitting at the bar.

Freedom! Jason had thought, nearly saying it out loud when he saw the other gentleman come in. As soon as the two had struck up a conversation, something about how the unions were killing them all, Jason quickly excused himself. Not only had he money to recount, but he had also learned long ago to never get into talking politics while he was bartending. Especially when he didn't agree with what many of the people that came into the bar had to say.

No. He was a college boy and, well, his opinions never seemed to be shared by many of the older gentlemen who came into the bar. His mom had told him many times that he had accidentally run off a customer or two when he got into arguing with them about some political issue or another; what he thought was just a lively debate, the old coot's always seem to take personal.

Not that he cared much. He was hardly ever home anymore, and once he graduated from school, he didn't really plan on ever coming back. Not that he didn't love it here, he did, but he just felt to isolated. He just always felt like he was cut off from the rest of the world. He was already feeling like a fish out of water every time he visited. It made it hard for him when he would have to explain things to his mom, his dad, or even the rest of the family.

Jason looked through the little porthole in the wall that allowed him to see into the bar. There were still only the two men talking. Jason really didn't have a reason to be back in the kitchen anymore, and he really should check to see if they needed their coffee's warmed up. He just didn't want to go back out there.

With a frown that he quickly turned into a smile while crossing the threshold between the kitchen and back hallway, he walked into the front part of the bar. He figured that they wouldn't be there much longer, and at least he didn't have to be part of the conversation. Besides, he had already been thinking about giving his friend, Sully, a call. He knew that he would have to wake the lazy bastard up, but he could work on him and beg him to come down to the bar and hang out with him. After all, they'd barely seen each other since Jason had gotten back into town.

Sullivan, also known as Sully, had been Jason's best friend since childhood. It had been since Jason's parents had moved to town, and he had found himself living just down the street from the year older child who acted half his age.

Sully still acted half his age, still lived in town, but now resided in a small camper on some abandoned lot he was lucky he never got kicked off of. He stole someone's electricity, their internet and, for the most part, only did the most minimal of work. The only real positive Jason could say about him, even though he still considered him his best friend, was that he did a podcast a couple times a week.

It was just a fun horror show that he and Jason did together. In fact, it was Jason who had created the stage name for him; Sullivan, the legendary zombie hunter. Which was funny because, even though Sullivan did know a lot about guns and a little about living off of the land, Jason could never see Sullivan as the survivalist. Then again, what did a person call a man living in a camper off of what he could scrounge?

Jason checked on the two coffees, topping them off and getting a mumbled "thank you" from both of the gentlemen. Then he headed to the phone, taking a quick glance at the clock. It was nearly ten; no way would Sullivan been up yet.

Too bad, he thought as he picked up the receiver. He was bored as hell, and he wasn't going to just sit there. It was time that Sullivan got up before noon. He figured he would probably have to call Sully five or six times in quick repetition before he would get himself out of bed. Still, what else was he going to do?

* * * *

When Billy first started sorting the shelves, he had a problem. What was he going to do with his surprise? He couldn't keep it tucked away into the small of his back forever and with him bending over, it was going to be seen. Sure, he was going to be in the back of the building and he would be by himself for most of the day, but people still came back there. He was next to the bailer, the large menacing green machine that compressed and broke down the cardboard. People would be coming back there to use it.

So, where should he put it? His mind had pondered the question until he just decided to do something obvious. He was going to leave it in plain sight. Well, sort of. He was just going to sit it on top of a shelf. Of course, the shelf was going to be the top most shelf that was well over twenty feet off the ground, and he was going to be using the only ladder going up there and back.

It was going to be risky, but there wasn't too many other places that he could trust. He had momentarily thought of putting it in the bailer. It was nearly full so he could have tried to put it under a couple of boxes, or in one of the smaller ones. However, he could think of a number of different problems with that plan. Besides it possibly falling down to the bottom, there was also the chance of it getting crushed and going off. There was just too much that could go wrong.

He had thought about putting it in one of the empty file cabinets. Underneath the shelving storage area, there was a long row of file cabinets in boxes ready to be sold. These weren't the display boxes, but the actual product they would sell. When one was sold, the customer would pick out the one they wanted on the sales floor and a sales person would go back there and grab the actual product. He could easily stash his surprise in any of those boxes.

That would have been one of the best solutions. No one ever would have opened any of them, even if they would have been sold. That's just it, though. If someone bought one, someone would be coming back there to get it for the customer. What would he do if another person came back there and took the box with the surprise in it? It wasn't like he could stop them and try to get it out. They would see it and then all his plans would be spoiled.

He would have to start his party early, and he wasn't about to do so until Tim was there. You can't have a party without the guest of honor. So, the party surprise was twenty feet in the air where only he could get to it, and it bothered the hell out of him having it sit up there out in the open. It gnawed at him, twisting him from the inside. He wanted it after all; he wanted to keep it close to him. He wanted to keep it there, tucked in the small of the back so he could feel it. The cold steel had been so comforting touching his skin all morning, that he didn't like not having it now. He had to worry about it, sitting up there.

It could somehow fall, or even be seen. He didn't know how, but he was sure it could happen. What if the vents kicked on and there was an extremely strong gust of air out of the air conditioning? The unit was only a hundred feet away. What if it somehow was able to knock it off? He just wasn't comfortable not having it. Not after he had gone through the effort of bringing it there with him.

Billy grabbed two of the shelves. They were the shorter "L" bent shelves that the store used for putting books on when they needed to stand upright. He walked them over to the pile he had started in the back corner and with the loud "clank" of metal, he dropped them roughly onto more metal. They rested in their new home. He turned to look back at the additional shelves that were stacked haphazardly around the area.

"Lazy bastards." He knew that he was one of the lazy bastards, but he didn't feel that he was as bad as most. Sure, when he was done with a shelf after any of the various resets throughout the store, he would just set it down back there wherever it could sit without falling over. Still, it wasn't like everyone else in the store didn't do the same damn thing. That was the problem. So why should he do more work than everyone else?

Well, for starters, because now he had to organize it. Shelves were leaning up against the other shelves; people couldn't even lift one up to put it with the others on the shelf. Come on, it wasn't that damn hard. When a person brings a shelf back, just lift it up and put it somewhere and that way, it wouldn't all be cluttered back there.

Billy picked up another stack of shelves. These were the shorter, straight shelves. They were labeled thirteen inches, so he turned and looked at the ones he had already labeled. He saw a spot where he had put the white label with the handwritten "13" on it, and tossed the shelves onto the others of the same type. The metal crashed together with that heavy sound, and it echoed in the large receiving area.

"You okay over there?" Billy quickly looked up to where his surprise was hidden. He couldn't see it from where he was standing, but that didn't mean that whoever was on the other side of the aisle couldn't see it. He tried to see just who it actually was through some of the holes in the aisle, and was trying to place a face to the voice. He wasn't quite sure he recognized it. It had been a deep, gruff voice that Billy wasn't sure he had ever heard before.

"Yeah, I'm fine," Billy called back, weakly. He really didn't want whoever it was to be coming over there. He wanted to stay all alone, away from everyone until his time was right.

Aaron walked around the corner, ignoring Billy saying that he was okay. Billy looked at him and then turned away, sparing a brief glance up at the shelf that held his surprise. He hoped that, with his back to Aaron, he would just go away. There were a couple of shelves near his feet and he grabbed them.

"Tim's got you doing this, huh?" Aaron asked.

Damn. "Yeah," Billy said.

He tried to talk as deadpan as he could. He was hoping Aaron would just get the hint as he tried to pour out a cold vibe to him. Billy had always been told that when he wanted to, he could come off as being very menacing; insane-type of menacing. He had been told that by a large bodybuilder back in high school when he had once admitted that the only person who had ever scared the big man had been Billy.

He said, "There's just something about you, something in your eyes that's plain crazy. Your one of those insane-types that one day is just going to explode, and I don't want to be the fuck around when that happens."

Billy had always enjoyed those kind words. He liked the idea that there had been at least one person that he had intimidated, and Billy knew why, too. Chris, the bodybuilder, had once seen Billy getting picked on by some bullies. It wasn't an odd occurrence, as Billy had been picked on quite regularly.

What had set this time apart was that Billy had done something Chris hadn't been able to believe.

He had seen a large stick on the ground and grabbed it. Chris, when he had seen that, thought for sure Billy was going to attack the three kids that had been pushing him around but, instead, Billy hit himself with the stick. He had started to hit himself over the head with it, his eyes open wide, and he was egging the kids on, yelling at them to "Come on! Attack me!"

The kids hadn't known how to handle it, and had run off.

When Chris had walked over and asked Billy if he was alright, he had seen that look in his eyes. It was like there was madness there; no control, just insanity. It had freaked Chris out.

When they were alone one day after school months later, Chris had been working out and Billy had been staying for another detention. Billy had just been trying to thank him but Chris told Billy to stay away from him. He actually looked scared.

Billy let a smile creep into the edges of his lips as he placed the shelves down. He loved the idea that he could instill that much fear in someone, especially someone that much larger than him. He liked that someone who could easily beat him down and crush him had been afraid of him.

Now, if only he could get Aaron to feel the same way. However, Billy worried that Aaron wasn't smart enough to be afraid. He was one of those people whose elevator never did go all the way up. Aaron wasn't small, though; he was a tall, thick young man, a little younger than Billy and strong. Billy wondered why Tim hadn't wanted Aaron back there to sort the shelving, but then figured Aaron would have probably just thrown them all into one pile and would have been done with it.

"What do you need?" Billy asked him, as coldly as he could.

"Hey, I need your help. There's a customer out here; she's looking at file cabinets and asking questions and I don't know anything about them."

"So?"

"Well, maybe you could help her."

Billy knew his way of helping was typically to grab the tag from the file cabinet and read the answers to the customer's questions directly from it, making sure to make a point of showing the customer where the information had been. It would often times aggravate the hell out of most people, and Billy loved it. There was nothing like making an idiot feel even more stupid than they already were.

He looked back at the shelves. He didn't really want to leave back there, but he knew that if he didn't, he would have to answer later as to why he didn't help. Would he, though? He knew he wouldn't. He had a surprise, and that surprise was going to keep him from answering ever again. He was done with fucking questions. Right?

He looked at Aaron's expectant eyes. He really always did walk around with such a clueless expression. Damn it!

He looked up at the spot where his surprise was waiting. Damn, he hoped no one found it early. He had a fear that someone would see it, or that it would somehow fall down. He knew that was impossible, but it still bothered him, leaving it all alone up there. Like it was a creature that could get lonely, he worried that it would try and find a new friend; someone new that would find it and use it for its purpose. Someone new that would take it and leave him to be with his hatred.

"Yeah, fine," Billy said.

"Okay." Aaron started to walk back to the corner of the shelf heading towards the entrance of receiving. Behind him, there was a little spider that seemed like it was trying to chase after him. Billy watched for a second, smiling at the little thing. It was odd. He had never seen anything quite like it. Not the spider itself, as it was just another stupid spider, but how it seemed to be chasing after Aaron. He knew that couldn't be it, though. Spiders don't chase after people. They were more afraid of us than we are of them. There was no way a spider would chase after someone. Billy watched it for another second before he slammed his foot down on it.

It was time to make another customer feel dumb. He guessed he could do it one last time. Maybe Tim would come in early and then he could get his surprise. Then he would be able to take out the damn cunt of a customer and Tim all at the same time.

Billy started to follow Aaron out of the back, not noticing the trail of spiders that had formed at his feet and were now following him.

CHAPTER 14

He stood behind a large pine bush, one that was wider and taller than him, allowing him plenty of shadows to disappear into. He had crossed over from the other side of the street, at first not caring about stealth. He had just strolled across the street and had been walking up the gravel driveway. It had crunched under his shoes and he had been remotely concerned about the noise of it, but then he heard the loud music coming from inside the house. He knew, no matter how much noise he had made, she would not hear him coming.

But as he neared the back, he had spotted the old woman who lived next door. She was small, pale-skinned, frail and, if he had to guess, also near blind, but he hadn't want to take that chance. She was walking away from him, towards her backyard garden that was filled with sunflowers that had already grown larger than the old woman. When he had seen her, he had quickly dashed at first behind the parked car in the driveway, and then shuffled to the bush. From there, he could watch her, and he waited until she was back near her sunflowers before he quickly dashed around the bush.

From there, it was only a couple of wooden patio steps that led him up to the back door and, within half a breath, he was standing there. He doubted, with it being early in the morning, that she would have locked the door. The little girl wouldn't have been able to get back in if it was. Unless she had a key, but it was a small town so he doubted that she would.

He didn't even have to worry. The back door was wide open, only the screen was closed to keep out the wandering insects. He quickly pulled it open and went into the kitchen.

He was assaulted with some god-awful pop music. It had been the crap that he had been telling her for as long as he had known her that was nothing but jungle music. Some chick was whining away; someone else was speaking words into a microphone because he thought that was singing. Who the hell let that shit on the radio, let alone onto a CD?

He could feel himself getting angry with the throbbing of the beat as it shook him. The vibrations were pulsating at him, throbbing his head until he could feel a migraine starting. His chest burned, but he could barely feel it as the music thumped at his temples and created a pain that made all the other sensations in his body nothing by comparison.

He knew why, too. It wasn't just because of how loud the music played, or how much he hated it. He knew it was also because she was playing it. She was playing it because she had known that he was out there and she played that music to taunt him. She had always been taunting him. She had always made him beat her because she wouldn't listen, she wouldn't follow his rules. Why couldn't she have just been a good little woman and do as he had told her?

He looked around the kitchen, trying to push away the pain that was now vibrating into the base of his teeth. He knew he was grinding them, making it worse, but he tried to ignore it. The kitchen was small, with the wall on the right covered in cabinets and drawers. It was a cheap fake wood, which fit with the cheap wood-colored paneling on the walls. The room itself barely had enough space for the small, round table in the center and the fridge that was immediately to his left.

When he had come into the room, he hadn't really thought about looking for a weapon but now that he knew she was trying to goad him into fighting with her, he thought that maybe he should. He walked across the room to the drawers near the sink. Most people always kept their silverware directly to the left or the right of the sink, and in the second drawer he opened, he found what he was looking for. The large butchers knife shined up at him, nearly blinding him because of the light reflecting from the sun.

He grabbed and pulled it up to inspect it. His knuckles were turning white as he held it. His anger seethed, and he just wanted to squeeze it as hard as he could. He just wanted to squeeze it until it melted in his hand.

No, didn't want to squeeze the knife. He wanted to grab something else and squeeze it. He wanted Tina's throat. He wanted to squeeze her, to feel the life course out of her. He wanted to wrap his large hands around that tiny throat of hers, cutting off her screams, and feel her struggle against him. He wanted to take away all her noise. That damn whiny voice of hers that had nagged at him and always talked to him. She sometimes would never shut up. Her voice and that damn music, that ever-fucking music that seemed like it was the same damn song over and over again. He was going to silence her, and he knew that it was going to feel good. He smiled slightly and set down the knife.

In the other room, he heard the roar of a vacuum cleaner. It was just vaguely louder than the music, but he was glad to hear it. It was something other than the pumping rhythm. It also meant that she was in the other room. He knew where to find her now.

He turned away from the sink and walked around the table, staying as close to the inner wall as he could. He didn't know how much from the other room could be seen through the doorway, but he didn't want to run the risk of her seeing him before he was ready. He had the element of her not being able to hear him, but she could still bump into him and then they would both be surprised. Not that he had to worry about her fighting back. She was so tiny compared to him that it was not going to be much of a fight, but he knew that he would enjoy it more if he could be completely aware and catch her while her back was turned.

He made it to the doorway and peered into the other room. He had expected a hallway, but the house wasn't designed that way. Spawned off of the kitchen, there seemed to be a game room with a pool table at its center. From there, there was a large doorway leading into what he guessed was the front room, the room he could hear that she was in. Directly to his right was a door, and on the left side of the room were two more doors. They were all closed, and he assumed they must have been bedrooms, as he couldn't imagine what else they could be.

He could see her just through the open doorway. She had her back to him and was vacuuming near the large picture window, working to get around the couch that was pushed up against the wall. He eased into the game room and quickly went to the right near the closed door.

She was out of his site, but he let the sound guide him. The quieter sound of the vacuum meant that she was reaching out with the hose; then he would hear the deeper growl of the machine as she would pull the hose back to her. He couldn't be sure, but it seemed like she was working her way to the far side of the room. If so, then her back should stay to him for at least another few seconds.

He followed along the wall until he came to the doorway into the front from. He felt like a fool for playing a game of cat and mouse with the bitch. He should have just walked right in there, grabbed her, and started to have his fun with her. It didn't make any sense to draw this out and get caught by her, ruining his surprise.

Caught! He hadn't thought it out as he had made his way from the kitchen, but if he went into the front room to grab her, he would be in full view of the picture window. Any cars or anyone walking by outside would be able to see him. While he hoped that anyone catching the show would grab some popcorn and enjoy it, he knew that many people wouldn't understand. They wouldn't understand how the bitch had left and betrayed him. They wouldn't understand the agony and embarrassment she put him through. Someone might actually call the police, and then he would be screwed.

But would anyone actually see him? He had been standing out there across the street scoping out the place for a long time; he had barely seen anyone even come down the street. The people in the houses on the other end of the block typically turned the other way. This house was near the end. Sure, the road turned back towards town and looped around, but almost no one came this way.

He was safe. There wouldn't be anyone to worry about. Except for the little girl, but she was gone and he doubted she would come back so soon.

He wasn't going to put it off any longer. He turned the corner and saw her. She was facing away from him in the far corner of the room, pushing the metal pipe of the vacuum cleaner into the corner between the couch and its matching love seat. He quickly crossed the distance of the room and when he got to standing right behind her, he reached out and quickly pulled, turning her around to face him. She spun with a sudden turn, wheeling around. When she finished and looked to see who it was, she stopped.

Her face went white, her eyes wide in fear. Her mouth was open just a little, and her body went straight.

"Vince!" she gasped.

He smiled at her. Now it was time for his fun to begin. The little bitch was going to get what she deserved.

* * * *

Rob could feel the sweat; it seemed like it poured out of everywhere. His shirt was drenched and he had rolled up the sleeves long ago. His white undershirt was soaked and he had his shirt unbuttoned.

Of course, he was going to be stranded out in the middle of nowhere on what seemed like it was about to be one of the hottest days of summer. He would have sat in the car and the air conditioner, but the air hadn't been blowing too cool and when he checked his antifreeze, he found that it was low; low enough that he needed to get some as soon as possible or the car was going to start overheating. He had tried to remember the last time he had ever really checked over the car and done any maintenance on it, and had realized that it hadn't been since last fall.

It wasn't looking good that he was going to make it to the courthouse before the case was called. This did not make him happy.

To get away from the stifling heat of the interior of the car, he sat on the trunk, his legs resting on the bumper. Beside him sat the handheld CB radio. He knew that it didn't have much range, and that if he was found to have it he could get himself in a lot of trouble. However, he was technically off duty so having it wasn't against any regulation as far as he knew, or so he hoped as he justified its use to himself.

"Breaker 19, four-wheeler in need of assistance, is there anyone out there? Come back," he said into the radio. He had been talking to it regularly, doing a shout out through the airways roughly every half hour. He had yet to hear anything back. He made sure not to mention that he was an officer, as he knew that most drivers would never pull over for one unless......well, they were being pulled over by an officer. Still, the rest of what he said, as he spoke CB code, would hopefully get someone out there to help him out. That was if they ever heard him. He was sure as hell hoping for a lot of "possibly" and "maybe" today. He didn't like having to hold out and pray for luck.

He pushed off of the trunk of the car and walked out to the center of the highway. The sun seemed like it bore down on him harder when he neared the yellow dotted line of the hot Midwestern asphalt. Something about being out in the middle of the road just seemed to bring down more of the heat, but he ignored it as he looked both directions.

Nothing. He couldn't see a house, a cell tower, farm equipment, or any cars.

He had never felt so useless, so helpless. It was like somewhere along the line, he had slipped into the twilight zone and was the last man on earth. He hadn't even realized that there were places in the United States that were still so far away from everything. Every time he had driven through here, not once had he slowed down and taken notice of just how little there was.

He walked back to his car, not turning to sit like he had before, but put his large foot on the back bumper and leaned forward. He climbed up onto the trunk of the car and stood there, as the metal under him dented in from his weight.

His looked down and face darkened as he realized what he had done, but turned his eyes upward to look away. He looked both directions again, same as he had done in the center of the road but, this time, he tried to also look over the tops of the corn to see if there were any houses.

There was one maybe three to five miles back in the direction from which he'd come. It could have been a house; he couldn't really tell for sure. He could see trees and what may have been the white frame of a barn sticking out behind them, but he couldn't tell. Shit, he didn't want to walk all that way just to find an abandoned barn out there.

Rob jumped down from the trunk, the impact from the short fall sending painful shock waves through his knees. He sure as hell wasn't getting younger, and moves like that often reminded him that he wasn't the athlete he had once been.

"Break 1 – 9, can I get a bear check. Bear check, comeback." Rob's heart skipped a beat. He swung around, feeling a pop in his back. He ignored it as he reached for the radio, nearly dropping it once he grabbed it.

"I got a bear for ya, but he needs your help driver, if you could. Which direction are you heading?"

There was a long silence. Rob regretted that he had admitted He was a police officer. Then, there was a crackle and the voice came back over the speaker.

"I'm heading southbound. How can I be of assistance?"

Rob smiled as he started to explain his need over the radio. He was going to have to do a lot of praying when he got home, he thought.

* * * *

Why in the fucking world did all the idiots have to come in and bother him? Even when he was supposed to be in the back not having to deal with their ignorant shit, he still had to go out there and answer stupid questions.

When Aaron had came into the receiving area and had asked Billy to go out to the sales floor to help him, he already had a feeling that it was going to be another one of those neurotic customers who had a million questions and didn't care that Billy was just a minimum wage employee who could care two shits about it, and who had no desire to look up the answers. Especially when it meant going to the internet for the answers, the same damn way the customer could. Why the fuck did the world have to be so ignorant?

He hit one of the boxes of file cabinets that lined the back wall of the receiving area. His hand went through the thin cardboard of the box and the sound of his fist hitting metal rang through the large back room. Shit.

He quickly pulled his hand back from the box and looked over his shoulder. He had just turned the corner in receiving that was lined by high walls of white shelving filled with large brown boxes of unassembled chairs. From where he stood, he could see that no one not in receiving could see him.

He smiled and looked back at the damaged file cabinet. Through the cardboard and in the dim light of the back area, there was a small dent that he could see on the metal. His smile widened. Good, another piece of damage he could provide for the store. Not that it had been his fucking fault. That damn customer had just irritated the living shit out of him.

After Aaron had walked him out to the sales floor, he had already been dreading the direction Aaron was headed. They had immediately turned right, and Billy knew that only one thing was in that direction—file cabinets.

A person would think that talking about and selling file cabinets would be an easy thing, and Billy was sure that if a person was an expert on the subject, it may have been just that. However, if you didn't know much about them, things could get pretty difficult. Especially with some of the amazingly mundane and senseless questions that were often asked. After all, how the hell was he supposed to know the difference between the different cherry colors? Wasn't "cherry" red, so shouldn't the color itself be red? How was he supposed to know if it would match and coordinate with the rest of the furniture in your office?

The woman he had just helped had been like so many of the damn others. Not that he should have expected any different, but it was still like fingernails on a chalkboard.

The whole damn world was the same. Ignorant motherfuckers who should all just fucking go to hell, die today and get the fuck out of his way.

Yeah!

"Is this made out of real wood?" she had asked. Billy mimicked her as he continued to walk to the back. When he was talking to her, he had wanted to say yeah, it was made out of real wood; they just chopped it up into particleboard and compressed the pieces before they boxed them and shipped them to the store.

He had wanted to and, with it being his last day, he had been on the verge of saying just that. However, something always kept him from saying what he truly wanted to say; instead, the honest, nice answer had droned out of him. As least he had said it to her in a deadpan, emotionless voice to express his boredom. That had to have counted for some act of rebellion.

It had taken him four more attempts at explaining to the old coot what particleboard was and how it was coated with some, whatever the hell it was called, to look like real wood.

And all the time he was explaining to her, he couldn't help but watch the spider that had been crawling along the white shelving just above the file cabinets. At first, he had leaned against the white shelf, but when he saw the spider he had quickly jerked away. It hadn't seemed to bother her, though. It hadn't seemed to affect her at all; didn't even seem to notice it.

At first, it had just been moving along. As she asked him another question, it went straight towards the woman. Then when she opened one of the drawers, the spider dropped onto her arm.

Billy watched with amazement. He had always thought that spiders were supposed to be afraid of people. When a person turned a light on in a room, or approached one, they always scattered away. However, this one was actually going after the woman.

Billy had to stifle a laugh until he realized that she had asked a question and he had not been paying attention.

"What was that?"

She was clearly annoyed at him for not paying attention, and she started to repeat her question. He tried to listen this time, but he couldn't help but watch as the spider climbed the length of her arm. As it moved, Billy felt like he could feel goose bumps all along his arm as though he had spiders running along his skin.

His arm twitched and he looked at his long sleeves. The fabric seemed to shift. He could imagine fifty to a hundred little spiders crawling along under the fabric, dancing along his skin as he stood there and wasn't able to see them. The hairs along his arm prickled, and a sensation gnawed at the base of his neck because he couldn't help but imagine that he was feeling them. Their little lags scampering all along his arm.

He had to itch at it to know that nothing was there. His spine felt like it had started to seize up and tighten on him in fear as he stood there. And as soon as his hand touched his arm, the motion under the fabric seemed to stop, and the sensations vanished.

Relieved, he looked back up at the woman who was now looking at him. She wasn't a bad-looking woman. She looked like she was in her mid to late forties, but she looked hot for her age. Which didn't surprise Billy as she was dressed really nice in a casual, but wealthy, fashion that helped to attract to her beauty.

He couldn't help but suddenly stand there transfixed by her, and now he had a strong, sudden impulse to kiss her. He didn't understand why, but it was like a pull inside of him. Like something deep within him was trying to push him towards her, towards her dark red-colored lips. In his mind, images flashed of him taking her, holding her in his arms, kissing her longingly like he had never kissed a girl before. In truth, he rarely had ever kissed a girl before, but the kiss he imagined was something more, something deeper, and would last forever.

"Spread," spoke a voice somewhere from the back of his mind.

He didn't have time to contemplate the new voice as he realized the woman was talking to him again. This time more harshly, with her brow pinched deeply in what he guessed was frustration.

"Are you stoned?" she repeated

Billy watched as the little spider that had been crawling up her arm disappeared under her sleeve and was out of sight. He was still amazed that she hadn't seen or felt it.

A chill ran down his spine.

"No, ma'am, just not feeling too well. What were you asking me?" he weakly asked.

"Never mind. I'm going to find your manager."

Fucking bitch, he thought to himself. Like he had thought before, all the fucking customers were the same.

She had started to storm off, towards the front of the store. Relieved, Billy had started towards the back again, glad to get away from all the damn people.

"Spread," said the voice again, and he had the desire to stay out front. A sudden sensation flashed through him to stay out there on the sales floor so that he could talk to more customers.

"Screw that," he thought, and continued towards the back.

He glanced over towards the woman storming to the front of the store. She had stopped and was standing there mid-aisle. He watched as a small shiver went through her and she reached for the place where he had last seen the spider. She stood there for a second, just holding the spot on her arm. Then, the second was over and she was once again walking towards the front.

* * * *

Billy finally made it back to the shelves, excited to be off the damn sales floor and glad to be back by his surprise. Being away from it for so long had his chest tight with worry that someone might have found it, or something might have happened to it. He knew nobody found it. Otherwise, someone would have been making some kind of commotion by then, that nagging feeling wouldn't go away. He knew it wouldn't until his surprise was back in his hands.

Once he was back in his little corner, the first thing he did was move the ladder back to where he could climb up to get back to his stash. Then, taking the rungs nearly two at a time, he climbed up to the top, the ladder shaking back and forth, the metal clanging harshly against the cement as he rushed. He knew that he was making a lot of noise, but he didn't care. He just wanted to make sure that everything was safe and that his surprise was still there.

He let out a breath. It was. The cold steel of it soothed him as he reached out and touched it. The metal was smooth and he traced his fingers along its edge just to get the feeling of power that it possessed. He couldn't stop the smile that touched his lips.

"William!?" someone yelled from the other side of receiving.

Billy didn't know why, but he tucked his surprise in the waistband of his pants, smoothing his uniform shirt over it so it wouldn't be noticed.

"Yeah!?" Billy called out, as he turned and started to walk back down the ladder.

Aaron came around the corner just as Billy landed from the bottom step onto the floor.

"Tim's in. He's up at the service desk talking to some customer. He wants you up there." Billy grinned. Tim was

131

finally here. Now it was time to get the party started, he thought as he walked past Aaron.   "You know, he's probably going to be pissed that you didn't finish this back here."

        "Yeah, but you know what? Fuck him," Billy said. He could tell from Aaron's expression that he was confused. Oh well, it didn't matter. Nothing mattered, as it was all going to be over soon enough. Billy almost felt like whistling as he walked,

CHAPTER 15

When Rob felt that first cool blast of air conditioning, it made him feel as though he was going to pass out. It was painful, attacking at his overheated temples, causing a massive migraine to instantly form, while causing a numbing sensation at the same time. He went woozy from the sudden shift from hot to cold, and the helplessness of being lost in his own body washed over him.   But he knew that he couldn't show the changes that were swimming around in his head.

When the large semi-truck had pulled to the side of the road just behind Rob's car, he had to keep himself from running over to the driver's side door. Instead, he had played it cool, acted like the professional police officer that he was and did the slow stalk. He knew he shouldn't be playing hardball, as he really was desperate for the truckers help, but years of pulling people to the side of the road took over the desire to be saved. It was almost like a habit, so intertwined with who he was that it was like breathing.

The driver didn't seem to take any notice of it. As Rob approached the door, the driver already had it open and was sitting halfway to the side, waiting for him. If Rob had pulled the truck over and had it been on an interstate, he would have gone to the passenger door but since the road was deserted, he didn't see the harm. It wasn't like he had to worry about additional traffic hitting him. So, he walked around to the door to see the large man staring down at him, trying to hide a smirk.

"Car trouble?" the man asked. He knew that he was being a cocky ass, Rob could tell by how he asked him, but he didn't feel as though the driver was trying to be belligerent. If anything, it came across as being good-natured and like he was trying to make light of the situation.

"You could say that. Wife trouble, car trouble, same thing," Rob said. He had been trying to make a joke but as soon as he said it, knew that it didn't come out that way. The driver just looked down at him with a confused look on his face. "Think you can let me use your cell phone to call for some help?" Rob asked. He had started to move forward to climb up on the side of the truck, but stopped himself when he remembered he was being courteous. To climb up on the driver's truck would be awfully forward and invasive. Something he was good at doing while he was on the job, but he wasn't on duty right now. He needed to work hard to try and curb his instincts. Otherwise, this guy was going to tell him to piss off and leave him out there.

"Well, sure, if you want to go back about a hundred miles and pick up the pieces," the man said. He wasn't smiling now, and seemed to actually be a little flustered. "I slipped this morning trying to climb into the truck. Damn knee gave out. I had my phone in my hand. It had gone flying across the parking lot to be run over by another truck. My wife's going to kill me; I just got that phone last month."

"Shit, your having nearly as good as day as I am."

The driver took a quick look over to his car and then looked back at Rob.

"I hope not." The smile returned to his lips, and Rob laughed as he caught on to what the man was implying.

"Think you can give me a ride to somewhere I might be able to make a phone call? A truck stop or something?" Rob asked. He was beginning to worry that he wasn't going to be able to find a way of calling somebody. It just seemed like all the cards were getting stacked against him.

"Well, there's a diner about twenty miles down the road. I typically stop there, as they have some of the best BBQ this side of the Mississippi. I guess I can drop you off there and get some lunch." Rob smiled as the man motioned towards his passenger door. "Get in."

And Rob had, just to be assaulted by the air conditioner but, for as much as it hurt, he didn't complain. He knew that once his body adjusted, he would start to feel much better.

"I'm Bruce," the driver said, as soon as Rob had gotten his seat belt on. Rob looked over to see that the driver's large hand was held out to him. He finally really looked at the man. He looked to be slightly stocky, not really fat, but well- built; possibly in his mid-to-late thirties, but his hair was already starting to recede. He was dressed in well-worn, grease covered jeans, and was wearing a Chicago Bears t-shirt. How could Rob not like the man? He was a bears fan.

He shook the man's the hand, feeling the firmness of his grip. When he let go, he reached back over to close the passenger door and knocked over a large binder that had been sitting on the dashboard. The door closed violently and Rob reached down to pick up the book. He could already see that it was the log book and the last date had been for two days ago. Rob looked over at the driver.

"Make you a deal. You toss that log book in the back there and act like you never saw it, and I'll buy you lunch."

Hell, Rob wouldn't have said anything anyway. He was just happy to have a ride to salvation; he didn't care if the driver was over on his hours or behind on his logs. He just wanted to get out of there.

"Fine with me, but it's a little early for lunch. How about breakfast. How's their biscuits and gravy?"

"Nearly as good as their BBQ."

"Sounds good."

Rob could already feel the headache starting to fade as his body started to cool down. He eased back into the seat and felt the rumble of the diesel engine as the driver put the truck into gear. He had never actually ridden in a semi before. He hadn't realized how loud they were to be in, or how much they vibrated a person's whole body. With his eyes closed, he could almost imagine being in one of those massaging chairs as the whole truck shook when it picked up speed. Rob looked over at Bruce. "Thank-you."

He kept his eyes on the road but smiled. "No problem."

* * * *

Tina's knuckles cracked against the pressure of the steering wheel, the skin turning white from gripping the wheel so hard that all the blood was trapped in the tips. Her mouth was clenched and she felt like she could taste iron in her spit; her gums hurt as her teeth ground together.

Yet, she couldn't bring herself to stop. She felt like she was clenched up all over; she knew she was safe now, but she couldn't bring herself to relax. Her eyes were wide open, but they were fixed at one point in space; an indistinguishable point as she couldn't focus on it.

Here? She wasn't even sure where here was. She wasn't sure how she had gotten into her car. Why had she gotten into her car? Well, that was easy, to run away. But to run away from what?

Who! She knew who she had been running away from. It had been her ex-boyfriend, Vince. She had been running away from him.

She was suddenly aware that her jaw hurt from more than just her clenching her teeth. The left side of it felt sore. It felt tender; throbbed with a feeling as though that part of her face weighed more and wanted her to tilt her head to compensate for it. It felt like it was bruised.

She blinked her eyes a couple times, trying to force wetness into them, then she turned to look at herself in the rear view mirror. She looked like hell. Had she really gotten beaten this bad? She wasn't sure. She did see the bruise already starting to form where she felt the pain, and knew that he had hit her. She lowered her head and reached out, desperately trying to grab at the memories of what had just happened to her.

Her breathing was erratic and her chest heaved in painful motions; it felt like her heart wanted to escape. She knew that she was in the middle of a panic attack, and was just barely able to keep herself from breaking down into hysterics. It was just there on the edge, with another set of tears that wanted to flow through her.

As she looked at her reflection, the little mirror just showing her the edges around her eyes, she saw that her eyes were large, red and puffy from crying already. Her hair was a mess. She really didn't want to go into public with it looking that way. Maybe she should go back to the house and grab a quick shower, clean herself up before she came back to talk to Jason.

She released the steering wheel and wrapped her arms around her body. An insane giggle escaped her lips as she realized what she had just been thinking. She didn't want to go into public for any reason. She just wanted to find a dark corner, curl up into a ball, and let the world pass her by. She would be extremely happy if she never had to go into public, ever again.

She looked around at the parking lot, this time actually taking note of the cars that were parked there. There was only three; one she knew was that old peg-legged man who came in every day, but the others she didn't recognize.

A shiver ran down through her and she suddenly felt uneasy. Peg-leg was there and he always made her feel that way. She was always disgusted with how he looked at her; like if he was more capable, he might try something with her.

"Ugh," she said.

She finally started to get her breathing under control, falling back against the car seat. She closed her eyes. Vince was there, his face etched on the back of her eyelids; she knew that he would always be there now.

She had never expected to see him so soon, and while she had been hoping that when she left him it was just temporary, she knew it hadn't been. He must have felt it, too. Why else would he have come after her to take her home? Or had he been there to kill her? He had that crazy look in his eyes and it had been so hard to tell.

When he had spun her around to face him, he had looked like he was possessed with anger and the smile on his face had scared her. He had looked so happy to see her, but it wasn't in that good way like when distant lovers finally see each other again. No, this was an excited smile like kids had when they were able to play with their toys in maniacal ways. She had become his toy, and he was going to play with her; if she was lucky, she wouldn't live through it.

And then he had slapped her, hard; his backhand slamming into her cheek and sending her backwards. She had nearly fallen, and had already been trying to turn her head to see if she was going to land against any of the furniture.

He caught her before she fell too far back and pulled her close. It had been such a hard tug that when he had grabbed her by the arm, she felt his iron grip. She knew that there would be a bruise there, but she had no way to stop him. He brought her up so that she was just under his face, staring into his crazy eyes.

She could smell his breath, a smoker's hot fiery breath that reeked of days of cigarettes. She wanted to grimace and turn away, but his free hand had reached up and grabbed her by the back of her neck and kept her facing him. Suddenly, he lowered his face so that their lips touched. He did it so forcefully that it hurt and she could feel her lips cutting roughly against her teeth. His tongue tried to pry it's way through but when it couldn't, he pulled her back away from him. Then he was staring at her again. His eyes glared into her, drilling into her head.

She didn't know what to do. Her breath was coming in short gasps. Her chest was heaving deeply, and she could feel his body pressed against her every time she inhaled. She could feel her eyes going dry from being opened so wide, but she was too afraid to blink. She was too afraid to do anything. If she could stop breathing right then out of fear, she would.

Just the sight of him made her heart want to stop beating and play dead. That's what worked for a bear attack, right? Why couldn't she get away with it? Because he already had you, that's why, she thought.

"Miss me?" he said, his voice a dry rasp. She knew that he was angry, but what scared her was that she couldn't hear it in his voice. It sounded dry, which was no surprise as he always seemed to talk in that deep raspy voice, but it was not filled with anger. It was calm, almost to the point of being soothing, which terrified her more. If he showed anger, she knew he would be hitting her, maybe break a bone, but he would leave when she was too badly hurt and was ready to go to the hospital. It would be her education, as she knew it.

But he was calm now. Calm meant that he was dangerous. It meant that he had been planning on things to do with her, and she may not survive them. She could tell by that look in his eyes that he had no intention of her walking away.

She saw his eyes look up and she turned to follow his gaze. Outside the large front picture window, she saw the old house across the street and the little patch of woods next to it. The fear registered deeply onto her face and she turned back to look at him. She could tell that he knew she had figured it out. His smiled widened.

"Hel-hel-hello, Vince," she said. Her voice had been barely a whisper and it had shaken out of her in a couple of short gasps for breath.

"So whatcha been up to, Tina," he said to her. He was backing away from the front room, dragging her with him. She saw what he was doing. He was getting her out of view of that large window. Whatever he had planned, he didn't want to take the chance of getting caught doing it. She knew it wouldn't have done much good. No one ever came down the street but he still was afraid of it.

Damn she wished Lucy would come back.

No, she didn't; she didn't want her niece back there. She didn't know what Vince was capable of and she didn't want Lucy, her little niece, seeing it or getting caught up in it. She didn't want to take the chance of her getting hurt.

Tina already knew that she, herself, was going to get hurt, a lot. She knew by that look in his eyes that she was going to be put through a lot of pain and there was a good chance that she would never see her niece, her nephew, her sister, any of them, ever again.

Once they crossed the threshold into the game room, Vince spun, pulling Tina with him, which propelled her face first into the side of the pool table. She hit it hard and almost fell on top of it.

She had tried to reach out to keep herself from falling to heavily into it, but with him still having hold of her one arm, she was barely able to get the other out in front of her and her body had taken much of the force. Her head slammed down onto the green felt and, for a brief second, white pain flashed through her eyes.

Vince pressed up against her, his groin grinding into her rear end. He leaned down over her, pressing her stomach onto the pool table, hard. He was nearly putting all his weight on top of her and then she felt his rough, unshaven face as it rubbed against her cheek.

"I'm sure you missed me," he whispered in her ear. "Well, I'm going to be leaving here soon, but I want to give you something to remember me by."

Yeah, he was going to be leaving soon, but she knew she wouldn't be alive when he left. Damn, now she was scared Lucy would come back home. She hoped like hell that Lucy didn't, but she was scared. It was bad enough this son of a bitch was going to hurt her, but she didn't want to think about him hurting Lucy.

What the hell had I ever seen in this fucking slime ball? she thought. She couldn't remember one single quality that she had ever really liked. The asshole had been abusive when she first met him. Had she been that desperate the whole damned time?

His weight eased off of her, and she could hear him undoing his belt buckle with his free hand. She knew what was coming, and the thought of him doing her one last time before he killed her made her stomach twist in knots.

The image of him thrusting his little penis inside of her, her screaming in pain because she knew that he wasn't going to be putting it in her cunt. She knew he wanted her to feel pain, and he was going to put that little piece of shit right where she told him to kiss when she had left him. She knew it, could see it and from somewhere deep inside of her, the pain in her chest burst into an explosion of built up energy.

It was like a switch had turned on, and all her muscles suddenly were energized. She was on fire, all the pain she had felt moments earlier was gone and eagerness filled her. A destructive nature joined with her pensive self, and she felt like she wanted to do some damage. She, for the first time in her life, felt like she wanted to inflict pain.

She didn't know where this fountain of energy flowed from, but it brought with it sudden realizations. She suddenly felt something under her chest and she remembered what it was. It was a cue stick. It was under her right hand; she didn't even realize that it had been there before.

She didn't have to think about what to do. He was still distracted with trying to get his pants down, and had already let go of her other arm to fumble with his button fly. He wasn't even watching her and she knew it.

Her hands gripped the pool cue and in a sudden spin move, she swung it into Vince. The cue seemed light in her hands, though she knew it was solid from the few times she had played on the table, and when it hit him, it made a loud cracking sound that she hoped had been from Vince's skull and not the

cue. It didn't matter if it was the cue or not because Vince
rocked back, stumbling with one unsteady step and then another.
He lost his momentum on the third step and dropped with a bone
shattering thump. Then he was slumped back against the wall,
his eyes glazed over and looking at her.

She wasn't ready to quit, though. The cue had cracked;
she looked at its bent shaft and discarded it to the side. She
glanced back to the pool table, hoping to find another one
because she wasn't done. A rage had been released inside of her
and it was hungry. It wanted blood and she wasn't ready to stop
giving in to it.

She didn't see another pool cue and had a brief thought
as to where the other stick might have disappeared to. Jason had
probably put it in his room since the other cue was his special
one with some picture of a half-naked girl along the shaft; either
that or he had taken it to the bar. It didn't matter, it wasn't there
now, but she did see the cue ball. She reached across the table
and grabbed it.

When she walked back to Vince, he was still looking up
at her blankly. She didn't care. She brought the cue ball down
and smashed it against his face, hitting him square across the
jaw. It hit with a thud; when she pulled her hand back, she saw
that his cheek was torn open and part of a tooth was exposed.
She brought the ball down again, and again, and again. At first,
keeping aim towards his mouth, wanting to shatter those lips out
of existence, but when she saw that it was nothing more than a
bloodied mess, she started bringing the ball down on his chest
and his stomach.

He was still breathing when she finally stopped, his
breaths in short rasps. He was a bloodied pulp, not even
recognizable as a man. She wasn't sure how alive he was until
she stepped forward, stopping between his legs. She brought her
bare foot down, crushing his testicles. Vince screamed out.

He was still alive, she thought. In a way, she had been
sad she hadn't killed him, but thought that it was probably better
for her.

* * * *

The guilt, and the fear, didn't settle in until she had brought her car to a stop in the parking lot of the bar. By then, it had all seemed like a dream. It couldn't have been real. She wasn't a fighter. She could never strike a man as large as Vince, let alone nearly kill him.

And what if she had killed him?

She sat there, at the bar, her hands trembling as she pulled them away from the steering wheel. What if she had killed him? What was she going to do? She had come to the bar to talk to Jason, to send him back to the house and check on Vince. Maybe he could help her out somehow, though she didn't know how.

However, now that she was at the bar, she didn't want to do that. What kind of person would drag her nephew into this? How could she make him an accomplice, possibly having him go to jail for the rest of his life for murder? He was going to college. She couldn't screw that up. She had screwed up her own life. She had to take care of it herself.

The realization finally came to her, and she took a deep breath to seal the deal. She was going to have to go back to the house. There, she would check on Vince, call the police, and tell them what happened.

It was the only thing she could do, right? She couldn't bury him across the street in the woods; she would get caught. Sure, people hardly ever went over there. In fact, no one ever went over there, but someone would someday. They would find the body, the police would be called, his body would identified and, hey, wasn't the sister of the owner of the house across the street a known lover of this man? Geez, it wouldn't take the investigators on CSI to put that one together.

And she knew the body would be found. That was just her luck. She wasn't the type of person to get away with anything. If she ran a yellow light on a deserted road with no one visible for miles, she would still get pulled over by a cop that she hadn't seen. It was the way the world worked for her. She had to go back to the house and call the police.

A loud, thundering sound shook her out of her thoughts, and she looked up to see Jason coming around from the back of the bar. He must have been taking out the garbage.

"You coming in? You don't look too good," Jason said.

Shit!

CHAPTER 16

"What can I get for you darlin'?" the woman said from behind the long counter top. Rob had been walking back to his seat next to Bruce, who was sitting in the middle of the counter, directly in front of the door, and had been making the woman laugh as Rob had approached. Bruce looked at him, still with the smile spread on his face. Looked like they had a shared secret between the two of them, but he figured it probably was because Bruce was a regular, and the place looked like it desperately needed a few of those.

The place looked like it was in excellent condition, clean and right out of a fifties movie with polished chrome lining all the fake marble counters; the booths looked like they had just came off the truck with well-padded, bright red seats; the shiny condiment racks that nearly blinded him with the sun's outside reflection. However, as customers went, the place was deserted other than just the two of them.

He had been surprised at just how nice the place looked. Being far off of the interstate, and the little customer traffic they must have gotten, he was expecting some hole-in-the-wall diner that only passed its health inspection by the fact that the inspector could never find the place. But "Alice's" wasn't like that. Instead, it felt like a place lost in time.

As soon as they had come in, the waitress, who's name wasn't Alice, had yelled at Bruce, her voice welcoming him in with a chuckle.

"Don't you ever get tired of seeing my old ass?" she had bellowed to him. Bruce had bowed his head, the smile that Rob was beginning to think never left his lips grew wider, and he had gotten out of the way so that the woman could see Rob behind him.

At first, her gaze had darkened on Rob, and he assumed that it was probably because she thought that Bruce had gotten himself into some kind of trouble, but then when she saw that Bruce was smiling, she smiled, too.

Then Rob had asked if he could use the phone real quick. She mentioned that they had a pay phone back by the restrooms, but wasn't sure if the line was still hooked up. With cell phones, after all, nobody ever used the cursed thing nowadays.

The phone still worked, and he had been able to make his call to the courthouse over in Ottawa; the one in Illinois, not the one in Canada which people always thought he was talking about. He couldn't blame them, though; before he had moved to the area, he would have made the same mistake.

He checked in as to the court case in which he was supposed to be testifying. As he had feared, it had already been thrown out because he wasn't there. The little punk would be free, not even having to pay a fine. It had been the second case called and the clerk on the phone, who was getting testy with him, made sure to point out that if he truly cared about the case, he should have been there.

He didn't argue. It wouldn't have done any good. The case was already over, and now he had to keep an eye out for whatever the little punk was going to do next. He knew it wasn't over. The little shit had gotten away with it once; he was going to come after Rob again, and he would have to bust the little asshole one more time

The fact that the case had been thrown out was probably for the best in the short term. If the case hadn't been read yet, he would have abandoned his car to try and get someone to give him a ride the rest of the way to court. Now, he could see if Bruce would give him a ride the rest of the way into town and drop him off at a local shop to see if he could get a tow.

"I'll take some coffee, black no sugar, and what was it you were recommending Bruce?"

"Ah, Bruce here, he always recommends the biscuits and gravy, but I think that's what he says about every place he goes," she said. Bruce opened his mouth to argue, but she looked at him and continued without giving him the chance to speak.

"Don't even try to deny it. I've heard you with other people in here. Every story you tell usually starts with you being in some location and how great the biscuits and gravy were. Don't even try and tell me that you don't."

Rob smile grew wider as he took the seat to the right of Bruce, trying not to crowd him in the confining seats. The waitress, whose name badge he could now see said Evelyn, had turned her back to them to grab the pot of coffee. She was an older woman, probably in her sixties, with permed white hair, but Rob couldn't help to notice how slim and curvaceous she was. For being an older woman, she was still very attractive and he wondered how she could have stayed that way working around such greasy food all day.

"I'll just take scrambled egg whites and dry toast," Rob said.

Bruce started to laugh, but caught himself and snuffed it out.

"Been to the doctor lately?" Bruce asked.

"Last week," Rob admitted. Bruce shook his head knowingly and looked back up to Evelyn.

"So, new owners?" he asked, nodding to the new-looking booths.

"You know it. Renamed the place and put a lot of new money into it. They sure as hell don't know what they're doing, but it sure does make the place look a lot nicer. I'm guessing we'll be seeing some new owners again in about five months, eight tops. That will make six new owners in four years." She said the last part wistfully. Rob didn't think she realized it as she seemed to drift off into a daydream.

In a second, she was back and studying the two of them.

"At least the place is nice, and they went with a theme. Neither one of them are called Alice; they just took the name from the song and thought it would be cute." Rob laughed. He hadn't even thought of that.

She looked at him. "I don't find it too funny. Naming a place after a song called 'Alice's Restaurant Massacre' after there had been one hell of a blood bath here last year. All the third-shifters were killed, as well as the few customers that had been in here." Rob's face whitened. He had heard about the killings, but he hadn't realized they had been in here.

Evelyn poured his coffee, and he relished in the warm aroma that rose up to meet him. Heaven, he thought as he brought the cup to his lips; sweet, sweet heaven.

She finished writing down his order on a little slip, turned, and put it on the rotating spindle for the cook. Then, she rang the bell and spun it around so that it faced the kitchen.

Another bell rang out, this one from the door behind them, and Rob quickly turned to see who was there. Bruce turned more slowly, more out of curiosity than the instinct to watch his back.

A tall, thin black man stood in the doorway. He was wearing a suit, but had it pulled lose probably due to the heat. His suit coat was off, probably left in the man's car, and his sleeves were rolled up. His hair was cut short, he was clean shaven and, on a normal day, Rob assumed that he was even more pristine and clean cut than he was now. He estimated him to be someone official, however; his close were too cheap to be a businessman and too regular to be a salesman. He wore black slacks with a white pressed shirt. Whenever he saw a salesman, they seemed to like to add color to their suits, blue shirts or even pink if the man was comfortable with his sexuality.

Rob also guessed that the man didn't get out of his office much. He didn't seem comfortable out of air conditioning. Sweat dripped down his face, and he had a napkin in his hand that he kept wiping his forehead with. He stood in the doorway for a second, waiting for his eyes to adjust and basking in the cool air conditioning before he walked the rest of the way into the diner.

The man wasn't smiling, even as he approached the counter and sat a couple of stools from Rob. Evelyn was already walking down to him with the coffee pot in hand, but he didn't even look up at her as he put a hand over his coffee cup and turned to Rob.

"I'm looking for a town called Hammond. I'm trying to find a Dr.-," the man reached down into his shirt pocket and pulled out a small slip of paper. "Wilson." Rob looked questioningly up to Evelyn. The stranger misinterpreted that glance.

"It's nothing serious. He just called our offices at an extremely early hour this morning about something, and I am on my way through this area so they asked if I would check it out."

"Well, I'm not from this area but she may-" Rob had started, but Evelyn started talking over him.

"Who're "they"?" she asked.

The man looked back and forth between them. His face looked puzzled and he seemed to be trying to figure out whom to respond to first. Either that, or he was trying to come up with a story to tell them that they would believe. Rob wasn't sure which. He could see the man was uneasy, and he guessed it was because Evelyn had asked the question Rob should have been asking. Not that he was investigating anything, but it was being inquisitive; as an officer, he was supposed to always be inquisitive, always ask questions. Damn, he's gone soft moving out of the city and now working in a small town, he thought.

"Do you know where I can find him?" the man asked, turning his gaze towards the woman.

Evelyn stood there, and it just struck Rob who she reminded him of; some woman he had seen on television, some spy show. She looked, acted, and sounded just like the spy's mother. All she needed was a cigarette in her hand and it would have completed the image. He had new respect for her, could see her being tough as nails, and had the feeling that she was not going to tell this man anything until he answered her question first.

"Like I said, who're "they"?" she said back.

She turned her back to him and walked back to the coffee machine. She placed the pot on the warmer. Another bell rang, this one from unseen hands in the kitchen, and two plates had emerged on the pass through. She grabbed the plates and turned towards Rob and Bruce in a way that kept her back to the stranger. Damn, she was good, Rob smirked to himself and watched the stranger.

"It's not a big deal," the man said.

"Well, if it's not a big deal then it wouldn't a big deal for you to tell us," she said, as she turned to him, placing her fist on her hip.

Rob turned to look back at Bruce. He had his head down, but Rob could see the large smile on his lips. Sure, he was always smiling, but Rob could swear he heard the man chuckling under his breath and was having to work at not laughing out loud.

"Well, if you are not willing to help," the man said, as he turned to stand. A flash of sunlight caught Rob's eye, and he saw the little badge clipped to the man's waist and could see the large letters imprinted there.

"So, what does the CDC want to talk to this doctor about?" Rob asked.

The man stopped cold and looked him up and down.

"Like I said, the doctor called in something this morning. We get a dozen of so calls like it a day so it's nothing to be concerned about, but we do investigate them all."

"Always so quick?" Rob followed up. The man just continued to stand there, watching Rob as if measuring him. Rob guessed he was trying to figure out if he was a threat who would start making a lot of noise in the press, or if he was going to be reasonable. Rob figured the man must have taken him for the latter.

"No, but I was in the area. My sister is getting married in Ottawa tomorrow night. I needed an excuse to get away from the groom's family. I don't mix well with rednecks. No offense."

Rob smiled. "None taken." Rob could hear Bruce give a little grunt from behind him and he wondered if he had finally lost his smile. He didn't turn to find out.

"Well, you're in Hammond, right on the outskirts," Evelyn started. "You just have to continue down the road here and you'll end up on the main street. The highway takes you straight through town. The doc's office is on the main street on the other side. You can't really miss it as there is a large sign that says 'Doctor's Office' on it."

The stranger started walking towards the door and Evelyn watched him, her gaze intense.

"Don't mix well with rednecks," she huffed. "What the hell does he think we all are, just a bunch of dumb hillbillies?" She glared at Rob and he could feel the ice shards she was sending his way. "I tell you what, when those people start leaving out of the cities and coming down here, that's when all this shit always seems to go to hell."

Rob felt goose bumps on his skin and he knew better than to respond. One thing about living in the smaller towns was that some of the people, not all, but some, were not as tolerant as they had been back in Chicago. He had learned not to argue, but to just let them rant, or else a new tirade would just emerge and he was not in the mood to hear it.

Instead, he turned back towards the front door. He couldn't help it. Now he was curious as to what was going on. He wondered just what the doctor had called in about. Sure, it wasn't his jurisdiction or his concern, but he couldn't help but find himself wanting to know.

* * * *

Jason opened the door and stood out of the way, holding it so that Tina could go in first. She did so slowly, and he quickly lost her to the darkness of the bar. He had only been outside for a minute but it was hard for him to see, his eyes not yet adjusted back to the dim lighting. His mother never liked to have most of the lights in the bar on. She always felt that too bright of a bar was something that would turn most of her patrons away and would cost the bar it's character. Her customers always seemed to agree, though he never understood why.

Jason would rather have had the lights on so he could see, but he suffered. It wasn't his name on the sign outside, and he would do whatever his mom wanted while hers was. He only worked there maybe one weekend every couple of months.

His eyes finally adjusted and he moved behind the bar. Mr. Jones was still sitting there at the end stool and, unfortunately for Jason, the guy he had been talking to earlier had left. So now Jason was left to entertain the old man.

He sure wished Sullivan would answer his damn phone. He had tried calling him his patented six times in a row to no avail. The bastard just wasn't picking up his damned phone, which meant Jason was stuck there suffering by himself.

Well, almost. At least Tina was here now; maybe she could take care of the old coot so Jason could get away from him. Sure, there was the damn redneck at the other end of the bar playing the "8's" which Jason had to get back to, but at least

151

he wasn't continuous. The guy would play a couple at a time, lose more of his money, tell Jason to put it all away, just to repeat the cycle again five minutes later.

Jason looked down at the redneck who sat at the other end of the bar. He had his glass at the edge and Jason could see that it was empty. He started to walk to him, knowing that an empty glass had best not be empty for too long in the bar business or the customer would go somewhere else that wouldn't let the glass stay empty. Or so that was how his mother had always told him to run the bar. Keep the beer coming, and if it looked the person might be close to being done but is a little slow on saying "no", fill the glass quickly to get them back in the seat. Someone who stays longer spends more money. It was bar economics. Damn, he hated tending bar.

And, just what type of person comes into a bar and starts drinking beer that early in the day? It wasn't even noon yet. He wished that it surprised him more, but he had grown up used to seeing how early people came into the bar. It wasn't so much as to what people felt was too early, it just mattered how early the bar was open. He had seen farmers come in at six in the morning and order their first round. It was all on when the bar opened. Then, there were the third-shifters who, when six in the morning rolled around, were there for after work happy hour.

He felt a tug on his arm and turned to see that Tina was grabbing him. When he saw her in the parking lot, he thought that she didn't look right; however, he had just written the thought off as not being able to see too well in the blinding sunlight. Now, he could see that her cheeks were puffy and red, and her eyes looked wet.

She had been crying. Just what the hell had been going on since this morning?

"Is Lucy okay?" he asked. He was suddenly growing concerned as he now noticed just how upset she was. Sure, he wasn't the best at noticing woman when they were upset. Just ask the five or six previous girlfriends who had all gotten frustrated with him for not caring about their needs, or so they said. He was known as "mister obvious", as he often missed these little signs. The ones like his aunt crying. He noticed it now, though it was hard not to. Even Mr. Jones had shut up at the end of the bar and had started watching her curiously. She nodded, but was biting her lip in what he guessed was her attempt to hold back another rush of tears that were threatening.

Jason frowned at her. Just what was going on that had her so upset? He looked back at the other end of the bar. The redneck was trying to act like he wasn't paying attention, or that he wasn't upset that his beer wasn't full yet, but Jason could see the man's jaw muscles were tight. He was getting impatient.

Jason turned to Tina and motioned at the little hallway that lead back into the kitchen.

"I'll be back there in just a minute," he said. He kept his voice soft and tried to put on a soothing mask. He hoped it worked.

She nodded her understanding and lowered her head to watch the ground as she walked away. He wasn't used to seeing his aunt like that. He knew his mom had; he had heard them sometimes in the kitchen with Tina crying and his mom trying to comfort her. However, she had always been able to hide it whenever he or his sister were around. It typically always had something to do with that asshole she was dating.

Jason went back to the redneck and grabbed the glass, starting to fill it with the tapped keg that was nearly in front of the man. Jason didn't even look up at him; he just watched as the gold-colored liquid filled the glass. He worked it like a true craftsman, keeping it tilted as the glass filled and rotating it just right to keep just a little head on the beer. Just because he hated tending bar didn't mean he wasn't good at it.

He set the glass back down in front of him and took the dollar from the pile the man had sitting on the bar. The man just nodded to him, and Jason put it in the register before heading towards the hallway.

"Need anything?" Jason called down to Mr. Jones. The man just shook his head, and Jason continued to the back.

He hadn't even entered the kitchen before she had her arms around him and her head buried into his chest. Jason was caught by surprise, and had his arms outstretched wide as he tried to comprehend what was going on. He could hear her crying, her tears were flowing heavily and she was sniffling. Great, he could already feel his college t-shirt getting moist from her tears and snot.

He finally let his hands hold her; not trying to caress her, that would be just weird, but to try and comfort her and get her calmed down. He reached up and held her head into his chest, much like his mother had done to him whenever he had come home crying.

"What happened?" he asked her. He tried to keep his voice soft and soothing, not just to calm her, but he also didn't want anyone out front to hear them. He was sure that whatever Tina had to say, it would be best kept private. They didn't need any more gossip going around a town that already suffered from far too much of it.

."I killed him. I think I killed him. I'm pretty sure I killed him." He didn't know how it was possible but when she spoke, it seemed like the words were on top of each other. He knew she was saying something about killing somebody. Who, he wasn't sure. Did she get into a hit-and-run? Were the cops on their way to drag her off to jail? "I'm not sure. I think I did."

He pushed her away so that he could look into her blue eyes. They were dark, and tears continued to stream out the sides. She tried to wipe them away, but more seemed to appear just as fast as she could reach her hands up.

"Who? Did you get into an accident?" he asked.

She sniffed and wiped at her nose. He reached over to a napkin that was sitting on one of the counters and handed it to her. She used it and wiped her face.

"No. Vince," she said.

"Who's Vince?"

She looked up at him in surprise. Obviously, he thought, this was supposed to be a name he should recognize, but he could have sworn it was the first time he had ever heard it before. Then again, as he often, he wasn't good for paying attention to other people and would often ignore people's names. He was terrible about it.

"My ex-boyfriend," she said, as she backed away.

"Okay." A memory tried to come back to him. Hadn't his mom told him something about him? He wasn't sure he had ever caught the guy's name, but he was pretty sure she had. "It's okay. I highly doubt that you killed him. You probably just knocked him out."

Jason wasn't sure if that was the right thing to say. Honestly, he wasn't sure what would be the right thing, either. He had no idea what he should be saying, or asking. Should he call his mother, see what she said? He doubted that would do much good. He wasn't even sure if he could get a hold of her. She was off having fun. She probably didn't even have her cell phone on; even if she did, she was probably somewhere where there was no service.

Okay, that wasn't true and he knew it. With how paranoid his mom was about her bar, he knew her cell phone was right next to her and it was on. As to whether she had cell coverage or not, he was guessing she did. Otherwise, he probably would have gotten a call from her every hour just to check in and make sure the bar hadn't burned down. Not that she didn't trust Jason with it, but the bar had become her life. She was highly overprotective of it.

But she was also there to be having fun. If he called her, he would not only be ruining her vacation, but he would also be ruining that trust she had put in him. She would never take another vacation. She was never able to get away from her problems, or her sister's drama. Did he really want to have her all upset when there was nothing she could do anyway? He knew it would tear her apart, and what purpose would that serve? She could give you advice, he thought. And that was true, but he wasn't sure he needed her advice. Not yet, at least.

Maybe he could figure this out on his own. That way, he wouldn't have to upset her and she could enjoy the rest of her vacation. She deserved it, being the housekeeper for pretty much all the problems in the whole family. She needed it.

So, he could do this. He could do this. Still, inside him, he felt the pull, that yearning to call her. He wanted to tell her all about it and even if all she said was that it would be okay, he wanted that reassurance. He wanted her to tell him that everything would be just fine; that protectiveness that she had for him, that caring, that always being there for him. He wanted to just hear her voice and have her say those words. He wasn't going to call her, but he realized that was exactly what he needed to give to Tina. He had to give her those blanket words, to comfort her and to relax her. It was up to him; he had to be the one to comfort her. It's all going to be okay, just tell me the details."

    Shit, shit, shit, shit, shit.

CHAPTER 17

Hammond and its closest neighbor, Rosewood, have had a long existing rivalry that has stretched back generations. It was not like many of the southern hillbilly rivalries that often times had to do with moonshine, or some cousin sneaking into someone's bed late at night back in the days of prohibition.

No, this was a simple rivalry. One that started so long ago, that there might be a couple of old- timers somewhere around town that may remember how it started; however, even those old folks might not remember much. But the town knew that it was from long ago and now was more a general dislike for each other rather than a hatred. A simple way to describe it was like how any self-respecting Chicago Bears fan learned long ago that nothing good came out of Green Bay. There was no reason for the "hate," but it was just known that you just couldn't trust a Fudgepacker.

Yeah, it was like that.

And, just like many rivalries, this one had more to do with the local sports teams than anything else. While many couldn't remember how the rivalry had started, everyone in town remembered the latest fiasco. Many were still angered with how those vicious devils from Rosewood Elementary had shamed everyone before last year's basketball final. That just could not stand.

What was that they had screamed? Hell, with how the old-timers had screamed when last year's game had been canceled, outsiders would have thought there was murder in the streets. It was scandalous, it was them damn bastards, it was them crooks, all over the final end of the year elementary basketball game. The game that had been canceled because all the tires had been slashed on the Hammond school bus.

Yes, Rosewood was only twenty miles away and yes, everyone could have driven over there. There were even other buses that were in reserve that could have been fueled up and taken. Well, there were two other buses that Hammond used, but one was down due to someone putting regular fuel instead of diesel into the tank. The third was running, but had been heavily tagged with graffiti and it had been obvious that it was more of Rosewood's treachery. Who else would have covered the bus in eggs and chalked "Hammond Sucks" up and down the exterior.

Yes, that bus still ran but the principal, who had to make the final call, had said that it would be a cold day in hell before she allowed her team to show up in a bus that said they all "sucked". So, the game had been cancelled.

The entire town of Hammond felt that the game should have gone to them and should have been considered a win. It wasn't their good, respectable kids that defaced the property, why should they have to suffer?

The county school board, of course, did not see things that way. Since Hammond had a working bus and had chosen not to attend the game, it was considered a forfeit against them. This allowed Rosewood to continue on and to go to state finals. Rosewood lost in the first round, but that didn't matter. They had cheated.

And the good, God-fearing people of Hammond (however, never mention to these God-fearing people that they have a two-to-one ratio of bars to churches, and that the average age of the everyday churchgoer in town was in their fifties) had sent a petition to the school board asking that the game be rescheduled. The school board eventually gave in, but it had not been a short-lived fight. By then, school was out for summer so the game was scheduled during summer break.

So, the Hammond Hogs and would be squaring off against the Rosewood Daggers. Now, since last time when it was supposed to be in Rosewood's gym, the scoundrels had desecrated Hammond's equipment, this time the game was there in Hammond.

* * * *

158

Nancy felt almost like she was a little kid. Not because she felt great and alive, because she didn't. No, it was because she just couldn't keep herself still as she sat there on the hard wooden seats of the bleachers. She couldn't help herself as she continued to wiggle around.

She didn't know what the hell it was, but she constantly felt like there were little creatures walking all over her. Every couple of seconds, that phantom feeling of something moving through the hairs on her arm would tickle and she would look, ready to smack away whatever she could find, just to find that there was nothing there. She felt them everywhere. She felt them crawling up her legs, up her arms, up the back of her neck, and even on her scalp. She had even sneezed a few times when she had felt a little tickle on the inside of her noise.

She didn't know what was going on. She was constantly scratching. There were spots on her arms that were becoming very red and agitated because she just couldn't leave them alone. She thought maybe it was dry skin and that the weather change had caused some type of irritation, but she had never before felt dry skin flare up this badly. She didn't even know if she could make it until she got home to put on some lotion. It just felt like bugs were attacking her from everywhere. Damn, she hoped it wasn't lice. Had the school had an infestation recently? No, couldn't have been, it was the summer; the school was closed other than the west wing, the only wing of the school with air conditioners, that was open for the few students doing summer school. Maybe one of those kids could have started an infestation, but would it have spread all the way to the gym on a Saturday? She had never had lice, but always knew that they were small bugs and once they started to spread around a school, it could mean a lot of trouble.

Around her, the crowd ignited just before the loud buzzer. She looked up to see that it was the end of the second quarter and one of her son's friends had scored a three-point shot from the line right before the buzzer had gone off. Well, that was good; at least her son's team was winning. It wasn't like she was getting a chance to really enjoy the game, though.

She felt that phantom feeling again, this time just outside her right ear. She reached up to swat at it, sure it was a fly, but nothing was there. She looked around her, wondering if anyone else had noticed that she was constantly twitching. Sure, she was vice president of the PTO and helped out on the schools organizing committee, but she knew that her accomplishments alone wouldn't keep the rumors from going around if she looked like she was on drugs.

Truth be told, she had been on the little white pills for most of her life. What was wrong with something to keep her going? How else was she supposed to be a mom nowadays? She had to work a full-time job, raise two kids, be a part of the PTO, help with cub scouts, help with girl scouts, and why? Because anything less and that asshole of an ex-husband would hall her back to court and try to get custody of the kids.

So she took her little pills and kept moving, keeping up with all the life that happened around her. And Jim did try to help us much as he could. Even though, to pay to keep up with the Jones and have their nice house, he had to work two jobs just so that they could keep food on the table and drive nice cars around to all these events she had to go to.

No rest for the righteous, right? Or was it supposed to be no rest for the wicked? No, that didn't seem right. As far as she could see, the wicked were the ones who got to rest all the damn time. She never understood how they could cut it, being lazy, resting all the time. Who was she thinking of?

Mr and Mrs. Loraine Feldson, that's who. Loraine, who was the one in charge of the PTO, though Nancy had to do everything; Loraine, who was in charge of the cake bake, only to run out and buy cakes from the local grocery store; Loraine, who was in charge of putting together the sock hop, just to not even show up and had Nancy do all the last minute preparations, which actually turned out to be nearly all of the preparations as Loraine had only reserved the gym. Loraine Feldson, the wicked; how they rested and rode the heels of the righteous and weary.

Nancy looked over at Loraine, trying not to let the blood rush to her face. She was only sitting a couple seats in front of Nancy, watching as her son, the all-star as Loraine called him, was rushing down the court, effortlessly dribbling the ball. However, Loraine wasn't watching him, and she wasn't sitting there smiling and sitting upright like she normally did. No, she was wriggling in her seat, as well.

Nancy looked around, and noticed that many of the people sitting around her were twitching in their seats, swatting at their arms or legs. Everyone was doing it. Tom, whose son just missed a layup, didn't notice as he was busy running his arms along his legs, squeezing his pants as thought he was trying to find something under the fabric. Cynthia, whose son was preparing to throw in a pass, had her arm up the sleeve of her blouse and was scratching vigorously. Everyone around her was acting as though they had been touched by itching powder.

And maybe they had. Maybe that had been what was going on. It wouldn't have been the first time for an opposing team to pull a prank. Sure, it wasn't common in fifth grade basketball, but she could see some overzealous parent doing it for a laugh.

Nancy noticed Lucy. She knew that Lucy had a crush on her son, and had probably come to the basketball game just to flirt with him. Not that kids didn't like to come back to school on a Saturday to watch a sports game, girls especially, but Lucy was one of the only students that was there without a parent. But that wasn't what caught Nancy's attention.

Lucy was also twitching, but she had more purpose to her actions. When Nancy swatted away one of the phantoms, there was always nothing there and she would look around for a brief second to see if anyone noticed her. When Lucy looked around, Nancy could see that she was afraid, like she could see what she was swatting away and it frightened her. She looked up at Nancy, her eyes large, her lower lip showing a little blood when she had bitten it trying not to scream; she looked terrified.

Then, Lucy looked at Nancy's arm.

Nancy looked down. She didn't expect to see anything; she had started to get used to the feelings of the phantoms. She was shocked when she saw the spider that was quickly running up her arm, sending the little nerves on her skin ablaze with the motion. Its little legs danced across her skin. She quickly swatted it away, and looked down to see a couple more spiders had emerged on her bench. Where had they all come from?

CHAPTER 18

The woman, Amanda Clarks, had watched smugly as the young man had been walking up the middle aisle and was on his way to meet her. He had been such an infuriating bastard when all she had wanted was some questions answered. She hadn't come there to be insulted, and she did not think that it was too much to ask for him to pay her some attention when she had questions. It was his job to make her happy, and all he had done was stand there and purposely make her feel as though she was so unimportant that he couldn't even pay attention to her.

What else did he have on his mind that was more important, the arrogant little shit? She was there as a customer, which made her right.   His job was to be there to take care of her and to make sure she left the store happy. Yes, so little of today's retail stores even tried to help people anymore. It was just another sign of how the whole world was going to hell in a hand basket. That's what happens when you start getting those people in the White House. It all came from that. It could always be traced back to who you had to represent you at the upper levels.

Like, look at their store manager. Sure, he was nice and he was trying to help her now, but just look at him. He was easily three hundred pounds. He was more than just a little overweight. The man was fat; he should hit the gym. She was always somewhere, doing some kind of local charity work, but she still hit the gym five times a week and jogged every morning.

It all comes from who your leaders are. With a good leader, people tend to follow in their footsteps.

Just what the hell was wrong with people? They all seemed to be on drugs. Legalize this and legalize that. Maybe that had been the kid's problem. Maybe he was on drugs and maybe he needed help but, either way, she should not get treated that way. It was his job to make her happy and to treat her right. It was his job to answer her questions. They sold the stuff, the people that worked here should know something about what they were selling. If not, then get rid of them and hire a staff that did know what they sold. Don't just hire some idiot off of the street. Have them be professional and know a thing or two. It just made for good customer service.

She was glad that the manager, Tom or Tim or whatever his name had been, was at least willing to try to get to the bottom of it. He had tried to speak kindly of the young man, saying that he usually wasn't that way and that he would be the one who knew about the file cabinets. He would get to the bottom of it and if the younger one couldn't help her out, he would do his damnedest to do so. The man may have been rolls of fat, but at least he knew how to be professional. At least he was trying to make her happy. The young man was certainly not.

Tim or Tom was at the service counter. He had his back to the young man as he was coming up the center aisle, but Amanda was watching him. He was taking his time. He was walking as slow as he could, which she wasn't too surprised to see. Just like many young men when they knew they were in trouble, they would walk slowly to face it, but he wasn't walking like he was doing a walk of shame. No, he had an ugly look on his face. She could see a burning hatred there in his dark eyes, and she swore that she saw a faint tip of a smile at the corner of his lips. The boy looked too proud and smug to be walking up to get a tongue-lashing.

There was something else. She couldn't place it at first, but just knew that something was different. He was acting wrong. No, it wasn't just him; there was something in the way that he walked that was just not right. She couldn't place it. There was just something off.

Had his skin somehow gotten paler, and were those gashes on his arms? They couldn't be; they weren't bleeding, but they looked deep and she didn't remember them there earlier. His eyes seemed sunken, and his lips had less color to them.

Of course, the manager wasn't seeing any of this. While he had been so polite in dealing with her, he was already on the phone talking to what sounded like another infuriated customer. This one seemed to be having some issue with their computer she had bought and didn't seem to understand why she couldn't just return it. Amanda didn't quite understand why they didn't take it back either. It seemed perfectly logical to her, but she was staying out of the discussion.

The boy rounded the last display and came to a stop just behind the portly manager. He didn't pay him any attention at first, and the young man just stood there.

She kept looking at him. She had been smiling smugly but as she watched him, her smile faded. His lips didn't so much look pale as they actually looked like they had started to turn blue, and had grown chapped. That wasn't even possible. Not in the fifteen minutes when she had seen him last. Was it a trick? Had he been in the back putting on some kind of stage makeup?

He stood there, tense, his hands kept reaching around towards his back and then they would twitch and come resting back to his side. He stood there swaying back and forth, as though standing in one place was something that took a tremendous amount of strength.

Then, the manager slammed down the phone behind the service desk and, as though he had known that Billy was already behind him, he had turned, already talking to the young man.

"Billy, this woman here says that you had been very rude to her and were –," the man stopped and looked at Billy. "What the hell is wrong with y-." He never got the chance to finish.

Tim, or maybe his name was Tom, never even put his hands up in defense and, at first, it seemed like the young man was just in the process of falling forward into him. Then Billy's hands came up, grabbing for the manager. However, it wasn't like he was trying to keep from falling. No, he had reached out and grabbed to pull the man to him and when he had the manager in his grasp, he pulled him so that he was biting into the man's throat.

He was too shocked to move. The world around them seemed strange as it continued to go on as normal for the first few seconds and Amanda watched as Billy bit into the man's throat, tearing away at the flesh. Blood sprayed up; it flowed strong, the heart beating a rhythm that made it spurt out in a fountain.

Then, the world rose up to meet Amanda, her feet deciding they didn't want to keep her upright and she landed hard, looking up at Billy. She watched him as he went forward again, biting deeper into the man's flesh, ripping more of it away around his throat, and... was he really eating it? She didn't know. As the rain of blood enveloped her, her world went red until it all darkened to black, and she fainted.

* * * *

Blood. Flesh. New sensations danced along and around in the fleeing and whirring of motion. When their host had found new flesh, and they had reached out for it, they had been starving. Their current host had become stale and they had him nearly picked clean. His usable inner substances had nearly all been devoured and he had become fully theirs.

Then, they had come upon the new host and they had reached out, moving in to move much of their brethren over. They had all been starving and had all hoped to move over, but there was too many of them. Many would have to stay to starve or find a new host. They knew that most would starve. Maybe they would just sleep and go back into hibernation.

Then they had reached forward and had bitten in to the new host. Their world changed. New flesh and blood had flooded into their host's mouth, as their brethren fought through the stream to move to the new host. Many were washed back against the flood, but many others found their way into their new home. They had great numbers; there were always many to move back and forth. However, those who stayed were surprised. New food was flooding in. It wasn't from their current host, but they realized that their current host could get more food from new hosts.

The sensations were wild as they devoured away at the new flesh. And Billy continued to tear away and eat at the large man's flesh. Sure, they might be hurting the new host for their brethren, but they were hungry and now they had food.

CHAPTER 19

Bryan knew that he had probably said too much to the group at the diner; knew it the second they started asking more questions. And then that officer had seen his security pass; why the hell was he even wearing it? He hadn't even gone into the office; was he that programmed that he clipped it to his belt without even noticing it?

Label that reason number 56 as to why he was not working in the field. He was a lab tech, stuck behind microscopes and test tubes all day. He hated people; people asked questions; people got sick and died while you worked on cures that never came. He was not a people person, he was a microbe person. They never talked back or asked questions, they only answered them. He had to admit that he was damned good at his job.

Why he had let his sister talk him into taking time off just so she could marry some damn factory day laborer out in wherever this damn place was, was beyond him. Damn, how she could always get him to do things he didn't want to do. All she had to was say "Come on, little Bry," and he was there around her finger. Ever since they were kids and she would watch over him, she never had to worry about him being naughty as all she would have to do is say it and he followed on command.

Not that it surprised him, either. He was the nerd. He was the bookworm before he was even born. His father had once joked at Bryan's eleventh birthday party that he had come out of his mother's womb carrying a copy of "A Farewell to Arms". Bryan had been freaked out by the title, and his dad had to tell him that it wasn't about him losing his arms. The only reason why his dad had chosen that book was because it had been one of his favorites. He had been telling the story to Bryan's uncle because the man had seemed to not understand why Bryan hadn't been excited about the gift of the shiny new "Chicago Bulls" embalmed basketball.

"They're the champions!" his uncle had explained when he had seen Bryan's confused look and deepened brow.

Thankfully, Bryan had the good manners to not say what he had been thinking. He had kept his mouth shut, forced a smile, and thanked his uncle. Then, he eagerly went on to his next gift and had enjoyed the smooth hardness of a fresh hardcover book. It had been the Hardy Boy's. One of the classic editions; not one of the paperbacks he had been saving up and buying himself, but one of the older traditional ones. His dad had given him all of his old collection. He had saved them, and they were now Bryan's.

And then his older sister had gotten involved. She had grabbed the basketball off of the table and had rushed to the door with it.

"Come on, little Bry!" she had yelled out to him. "It's time to play some basketball. He just wanted to read the books. Why couldn't she leave him alone to read the books? But just like all the other times, he found himself chasing after her

And now he was stuck chasing after her again, this time to her wedding. Sure, he should be happy for her. She found someone. Someone other than a test tube, which he still claimed would always be his soul mate. She found someone who was real and, Bryan hoped, someone who would take care of her. He had better, or Bryan would inject him with small pox and launch him down a well.

Bryan pulled his car into the small parking lot that was just below the fiberglass sign that read "Doctor's Office". The building just beyond the parking lot was a drab little building that looked like it tried to mimic a log cabin. It was not what he would have expected nor desired for this to be anything credible.

He hadn't been kidding when he had told the locals at the diner that they got thousands of crank calls a day. Most times they were discredited right over the phone. Interns were given a series of questions to ask and, most times, nothing more was needed. The interns were instructed to have the doctors rush a sample over to their offices so they could test it.

And they did test the samples when they came in. Some would even be rushed through, depending on the answers that had been given over the phone. The interns were not reliable as to what might actually be something the CDC needed to get involved with because they were often young kids who were swayed by the emotions of whomever had called. Cold hard data, the questions and answers, were always what lead to prioritized results.

Many times, those who called were small doctor's offices like the one he was at now, where a young new doctor thought that a little bump on someone's arm mixed with the flu was some new strain of swine flu. Little things and new doctors clogged much of the phone lines, but then there were the ones who did report something curious. The samples would be rushed, and they would take the time to look it over. These samples would be hurried through, an intern breaking them down and then bringing them to him. He would look them over and they would see if there was any further need to study. If they needed to send someone out into the field, they had specially trained people for it who were better with locals than Bryan was. That was for damned sure. He detested people, so how could he ever get them to warm up to him?

This wasn't going to go much better. He could tell that already. This was a mistake. It may even have been a practical joke. He had no idea why Christian had felt the need to call him and ask him to check it out.

While it was highly uncommon, it wasn't unheard of that they would somehow get pranked. Usually, it was caught by the fact that the phone call wouldn't be coming in from a doctor's office, or that there would be red flags pointing towards it. Well, there were red flags on this case and they ranged from the absurd to the severe.

His boss had been concerned enough to talk him into it. Not that he fought too hard to get out of the grooms bachelor party that would be starting later today, but he had put up the show of a fight. Somehow, this doctor had known Bryan's boss, and Chris, had felt that he was a level-headed guy, enough to be concerned by the doctor's phone call. Still, Bryan should have pushed for them to at least have a field op here, someone who could talk down to these hicks.

Look at this place, it was a crap hole. What kind of doctor put his practice in what looked like a log cabin? Was there going to be a cozy little fireplace in the corner, and old men reading newspapers inside? This wasn't a doctor's office; it looked more like a fishing lodge.

Bryan opened his door, not caring that he had parked across three parking spaces. There wasn't another car in the lot, but he wouldn't have cared if there had been. He had parked directly in front of the door, even taking the handicapped spot and the wheelchair ramp. He figured in and out and he would be gone.

He stepped out and listened to the crunch of gravel under his polished shoes.

"Didn't these people believe in paving the whole parking lot," he muttered to himself.

He moved across the lot, not enjoying the crunch beneath his feet. The sound of the gravel in the early morning reminded him of eating shrimp. He figured it must have had something to do with the rocks and the sound that made him think of breaking open the shell to get to the meat inside.

Shrimp and Lobster, he could really go for that right then. Sure, it was a little early in the day, but it would make a nice brunch. He doubted there would be anything good in that crap hole of a town his sister was choosing to live in but maybe if he drove the rest of the way to Chicago, he could find a decent place.

Was he really thinking of driving all that way just for a decent lobster? If he did, his sister would kill him and it was only putting off the inevitable. Somewhere inside him, he knew he was just trying to put off going to, or even thinking about, his sister's wedding.

People. Damn, how he hated dealing with and being around people. How did he let himself get roped into this?

He felt the pang of revulsion and tried to wave it off. People. He'd have to deal with them here, as well. Why couldn't he just go back to his lab?

He quickly moved to the front door. He didn't know what to expect, if they were open or not. He didn't see any cars in the lot. The place looked empty, the windows dark, and the silence seemed to be a part of the building as though it was warning away from.

He made it to the front door and, after taking a quick glance at the side front picture windows, reached out to pull open the door. It stayed solid in its frame, as if there weren't hinges that allowed it to open. It was sturdy, well-crafted and elegant.

Which caused him to take another look at the front of the building. He could see that it was actually a lot nicer than he originally thought. The wood was finely carved and the frame was solid and held the door firmly.

It lead off into what could be taken for a log cabin at first glance. He had thought it had been some kind of cheap imitation to cover an inner aluminum siding or some other material. He wasn't knowledgeable about construction, but he had seen enough bad neighborhoods here and there to know that there were many tacky ways of trying to make something look better than it was.

This was no imitation. It was all solid, and it wasn't a small hand-crafted cabin. This was a nice building with excellent craftsmanship. It was cozy and while he had a hard time believing any doctor would set up an office in such a building, he could see the appeal.

At the same time, it didn't really match the tone of the buildings that were around it. The building just past the bushes to the right was an aluminum-sided construction garage with large machinery cluttered around the yard outside.

He stepped backwards down the front stairs and looked around the edges. The bushes were right up to the right side, so even if he wanted to go that way he couldn't. He would have to follow the wrap-around driveway to the back.

He went back to his car and popped the trunk. Time to get to work and take this seriously, he thought. He didn't have much with him and the stuff he did have, he actually purchased from a Walgreens on his way here. He knew that the little face mask that you held on by an elastic string and came up to just below his eyes really wasn't going to be much protection, but he knew that it was at least better than not having anything at all

He put on the tight gloves, feeling the chalk like texture of the powder inside and enjoying the comfort in them. At least those felt more like what he was used to. They had the right feel and if he closed his eyes, he could almost fool himself into thinking that he was back in the lab.

Maybe now he could start taking this threat seriously and not acting like it was all going to be nothing. What the hell had he been thinking when he was just going to walk in the front door? He lowered the hood, listening to the hiss as the hydraulics in the truck hood kept it from coming down to hard or too fast.

There was a dog barking somewhere in the distance, some kids laughing. He even watched as a pair of them rode by on their bikes racing each other. One screamed out, "I'll beat you to the school!"

They were already past him when he heard the other, the one already behind the smaller boy on the bigger bike. "No, you won't!" Then they were gone.

He could see a few cars here and there, but the town itself wasn't that busy. It had that feeling as though it was dying, fading away into a lost existence. What had that waitress said? He thought he heard her make a comment to one of the guys, something about the factory laying everyone off. The cookie factory was still going, she had said, but the glass place, the place that had been the lifeblood for much of the town, was shut down. Yeah, but the cookies were still being made. He didn't know how far away the cookie factory was, but he could smell that sweet smell as it hung upon the air. It was a gentle aroma that touched the tip of his nose.

Damn, he hoped that this was all just a mistake and could report that nothing was going on here. Hopefully, the doctor is just ignorant and this was a fool's errand and not a hoax on the taxpayer's dime. Maybe then all of this could just be written off and all would be forgotten.

* * * *

Lucy felt like her head had become an anvil on top of her shoulders, and she had to fight just to keep it upright. Her neck was stiff and she just wanted to let her head fall forward and hang there. Her eyes felt hollow and she wanted to close them, losing herself to sleep.

172

Sleep. Just the thought of it felt like it was what she needed. She just wanted to lie down, even the hardwood of the gym floor beneath the bleachers seemed like it would be comforting. She just wanted to lie down and rest. But she couldn't.

She didn't know what, but something wasn't letting her. Some force kept her head up no matter how much she wanted to let it fall. Maybe it was her trying to fight her cold. She had lied to Tina about feeling better. She had really wanted to come to the game and see Bobby. She wanted to talk to him afterward, and maybe hang out with him later.

She had fought so that she didn't seem too sick. She had even tried to convince herself that she was feeling better. Some part of her wanted to continue to keep from admitting it was there. She wasn't sick, she could stay and wait until the end of the game, she kept thinking.

It wasn't like she was watching the game. She had tried to watch as the boys ran up and down the court dribbling the ball. She had been trying to watch that guy she liked. What was his name again? She didn't know why, but she just couldn't seem to remember it. It didn't seem like it was so important any more. Not just one boy. Oh no, not just one. Some part of her now wanted all of them. She wanted all of the boys. For what, she wasn't sure but she wanted to get up and move closer to all of them.

To spread....

That was what the voice said, the whisper that tickled at the back of her mind. She didn't know what that meant. She was tired. She just wanted to sleep. The voice wouldn't let her. It kept her there.

Then, she had watched as the first spider had come out from under her skirt. She had been afraid and had wanted to kill it. Her arms had fought against her, and she was just too tired. Instead, she had watched as it had skittered under the bleachers, crawling down the black metal railings. The spider was nearly camouflaged against it. But then it had touched the hardwood floor, and had disappeared into the shadows.

She had just looked up from it when she watched two more emerge from just under her sleeve. They crawled down her arms; one continued down, while the other had disappeared into the shorts of the little boy who was sitting next to her. He never noticed as it disappeared. He didn't even seem to feel it. He just kept watching the game. There had been a slight shake when the spider had first touched him but, with a quick glimpse at his shorts, he dismissed it and looked back to the game.

More spiders appeared; some came out from underneath her sleeve, others seemed to come out from under her skin. They just appeared there, first as gooseflesh and then the black spot would form and the spider would emerge. She watched as they all joined together, and then continued to climb down into the darkness beneath the bleachers.

She quickly looked over from her left sleeve to her right, and the same thing was happening on her other side. A slight whimper escaped her lips, but it was lost in the roar of the crowd. Someone from the home team must have just stolen the ball, as the crowd around her was screaming in joyous excitement. She wanted to scream with them, but all that escaped was that whimper. Instead, she felt her throat clamp shut and she could barely breathe.

Something was suffocating her. She could feel it. She lurched forward, trying to gag, trying to cough it out, tears streaming from her eyes as she wanted to just cry it all away, but none of it was going away.

She felt something slam against her back and the black mass of spiders that had been clogging her throat launched down into the bleachers. Air flooded back into her lungs and she looked up to see the older gentleman sitting next to her had seen her suffocating and had slapped her back to help her out.

He was watching her, his arm still on her back as he looked at her with a show of genuine concern. She tried to smile a thank-you at him but as he looked down at her, she saw a spider climb up his arm and disappear beneath his skin. She watched in horror as the bump traveled under his skin and disappeared into the darkness beneath his sleeve.

He looked to where she had been staring but not seeing anything, looked back to her, his frown deepening.

"Are you okay miss? Is your mother here, can I go get her for you?" he asked her.

Lucy shook her head. Of course her mother wasn't here. Her mother was hundreds of miles away, and all she had here was her no nothing aunt. If her mother was there, Lucy never would have been able to con her into letting her go to the game. Her mother would have made sure that Lucy saw the doctor, and would have known that something serious was wrong.

Lucy realized that the man was still looking at her and started to shake her head.

"No, I'm fine. Thank-you," she finally said. Her voice was course and came out gurgled. The man didn't seem convinced but he backed away, still looking at her cautiously.

"Well, if you need anything, just ask," he said.

She knew she should be concerned that he may be some pervert, but she doubted it. It was a small town, people like that didn't exist here. Not only that, she thought she recognized him. She thought, but wasn't sure, that he was Danny's grandfather. Danny was another one of the boys on the team, and was good friends with Bobby. She wasn't completely sure, but sure enough that she wasn't afraid of him.

Bobby, that was his name! She had come to see Bobby! She tried to be excited that she remembered his name. She couldn't believe she had forgotten it. How could she have forgotten his name? Bobby!

She eased herself back into the game. She hadn't been paying much attention to it, and hadn't realized that their school was up by ten points. That was awesome. Bobby was going to be so happy after the game.

Did she still want to try and see him? She wasn't sure anymore. She still didn't feel all that good. She didn't want to take the chance and get him sick, too. It might be better if she didn't see him.

Her mind came back to the spiders as she watched three more, she didn't even know where they had come from, disappear beneath the bleachers. Another one emerged from beneath her skirt, and she could feel her throat beginning to tighten again. The world around her felt like it was getting smaller, or she was getting bigger. Nothing felt right; the people around her felt like they were getting closer. She felt like they were almost on top of her, nearly inside of her. She had to get out of there. She suddenly felt like she needed to get away from all of them.

More spiders were scurrying down her arms. They were all over the place; they were swarming her. She wasn't sure if she felt that way about the people or the spiders, but they all seemed to be all over her.

She lifted up her hand, and another wave of spiders rushed out from under it. They ran to the people along the bench. She let out a little whimper and only the little boy turned to look at her. He seemed to be scared of her. Was she that scary? He made her feel like she was, as he started to scoot closer to his mom sitting on the other side of him. Lucy didn't blame him.

She stood. She needed to get out of there. She wanted to cry, to run away. Something was wrong. She wanted out of there. She wanted to be back with her own mommy. She wanted to be with her own mom. She..

Another spider crawled down her leg. Where were they all coming from? It looked like they were coming from her.

"Spread," she heard a voice inside of her say.

She didn't want to spread. She didn't want anyone to catch whatever she had. She just wanted to stay away from everyone. They were all around her. They were crowding her. She wanted away from there.

"Stay. Spread."

She hoped that it was tears that she felt on her cheeks; she felt the streaks. She hoped that tears were streaming down, not spiders. Why couldn't anyone else see them? Why wasn't anyone else freaking out?

Lucy started to make her way down the aisle. She saw spiders shaking free from her clothing as she hurried. Her tears streamed heavier. She needed to get out of there.

People cleared the way for her. They all look startled at the crying girl hurrying by them. Did they finally see the spiders? If so, they never reacted to them. Spiders fell on the people as much as they fell to the bleachers, but no one seemed to react.

Lucy finally made it to the end of the row and started to hurry down the steps. She was near the door of the gym when the buzzer sounded and the gym erupted into cheering. She knew it was too early for the game to be over, but she guessed that another period had ended. She didn't look back to see the action. She just wanted to lie down, to sleep. She just wanted to get home.

* * * *

Denise watched as the man approached from around the side of the doctor's office, suspicious of why anyone would be sneaking around out there. She especially didn't like that she didn't know him. She knew near everyone from the area and, while she knew that she wouldn't remember all of them on the street, she did know that she had never seen this man before.

A tall, black man stood out in this town. Okay, to say that he stood out was an understatement. It wasn't just the race card, though it was true that Hammond had very few black people that lived in town. In fact, she couldn't think of too many colored that lived in any of the surrounding towns, either. This had much more to do with how the man carried himself. It was obvious that he wasn't from anywhere near here.

It didn't take much more than just a quick look at his shoes and how he walked in them. Sure, she knew many of the lawyers in town would wear fancy shoes and suits, but none of them as nice and as fancy as the leather loafers this man wore. Plus, this man was sweating through his thick, white shirt and was obviously supposed to have a suit jacket on, as well. This man was meant for air conditioning, and not to be outside in the blazing Midwestern summer heat. She wondered who he was and why he was there?

And why was he sleuthing around her husband's office? He didn't look sick so he probably wasn't there for an exam. He wasn't local, so he didn't have an appointment. Besides, she had done like her husband had asked and had called all their patients that had appointments for the day. They were all upset, but she had canceled them all. If there was to be a walk-in, most times they would drive the thirty minutes to an hour and go to the hospital, so it wasn't likely to be that, either. She didn't like it.

She didn't like that she hasn't heard anything from her husband even more. It had been hours since he had told her to leave and to call everyone. Since then, she hadn't seen any sign of life. She had heard sounds earlier when she had walked around the side of the building, but she was afraid to look into it.

177

Her husband, the man she had known and shared a bed with for the last 10 years of marriage, had never before looked as scared as he had been when he had told her to get out. She knew that he was trying to protect her. From what, she had no idea, but it had to be something bad. It must have been something highly contagious and from the way he had hid from her, must be something deadly.

And how did that make her feel? She knew that she should feel sad and that the tears should be streaming down her face. Her heart should have been broken; she should barely be able to stand from the agony of the knowledge that she would probably never see her husband again. Either that, or she should at least have some hope, that he was just being overly cautious and that all of this was for nothing.

Her husband was too good of a doctor for that, and she didn't really feel anything. She felt like there was a large stone where her heart had been. What should have been emotions was a vast nothingness. Her insides were cold and what should have been heartache was only the pressure of a massive weight on her chest making it hard for her to breathe.

She felt like she was dead to the world. She held herself, fearing that if she did left go, the chill that was inside of her would make her shake into convulsions.; that if she let go, the tears would finally come but she didn't think she would ever be able to pull herself out of the helplessness that would envelope her.

"Hello," the man in the nice clothes said, as he neared her front porch.

"Hello." Her voice was dry and flat. She didn't care that there was none of the friendliness that usually always filled her. What did she have left to be cheerful for?

"I'm looking for a Dr. Wilson. Can you help me find him?"

"Your too late."

"Too late? Has he passed away?"

She could see the confused look on his face, or was that an expression of alarm? In the harsh sunlight that he was squinting through to look at her, it was hard to tell.

"No, but he closed up for the day."

"Really? He called my office this morning. It sounded pretty urgent. Do you know where I can find him?"

Who was it that he called that morning? He hadn't told her he was calling anyone. If he did, she guessed it was probably the Center for Disease Control, but she had never heard of them sending out someone so quick to an unproven case. Maybe her husband had called in a favor. He had that friend of his...God she couldn't remember his name, but he worked for them, didn't he?

If so, then this was getting as bad as she thought, or maybe even worse. What if she was also infected? She was glad she hadn't gone anywhere.

"CDC?". He looked momentarily shocked and then he nodded. "He's in there," she nodded in the direction of the office. "What do you know about it already?"

He looked at her for a moment. She guessed he was trying to size her up to figure out what she knew about it and who she was. This wasn't her husband's friend, so she doubted he even knew what her husband looked like or how old he was, so he must have been trying to figure out who this woman was who was talking to him.

"Who are you?" he finally asked.

"His wife. I run the office."

"Oh, so were you there this morning when he called."

"Yes. I locked up shop and canceled all his appointments for the day."

"Well, we know very little about what is going on in there. I was hoping maybe you could tell me before I go in."

She looked at him for a moment and then nodded towards the chair on her porch.

"I know you're probably in a hurry, but I'm tired and feeling like sitting down. I don't know much, but I'll tell you what I can."

CHAPTER 20

Bryan didn't like this. He hadn't liked it from the beginning, but he had listened to his boss and had let him talk him into this. However, he was there and now, after hearing what the doctor's wife was telling him, he was sure he was the wrong man for the job. He had no idea what he was supposed to do. What were the protocols? How was he supposed to handle this?

He had expected this to be a simple case of another doctor going overboard. He wasn't so sure anymore. Denise had told him what had happened earlier, and he didn't think the doctor sounded so much like a crack pot. There might actually be something going on in there. He remembered the noises he had heard walking around the building and if it was like she had described, it may be much worse.

It sounded like it was something highly communicable, and the doctor was afraid that he may have been infected. Most likely it was airborne; that would explain the doctor getting it so quick and why Denise seemed to be fine.

So, how was he going to investigate this? He had no practical field experience. Should he call in his boss and have a team come out, or should he go in himself with the little mask? The right call was for the team to come out. But, what hard evidence did he have? What scientific evidence did he have to make his boss believe him? Had he seen anything or anyone? No, all he had was some noises he had heard as he had walked around the building, and this woman telling him a convincing story.

All it took was for the team to come here and find nothing but some old-timer hell bent on playing an elaborate hoax on him and he would never hear the end of it. He may not even have a job anymore. He really was not equipped to handle it out here on his own. He never should have agreed to come.

"You going in?" Denise asked. She was still sitting across from him. Being a doctor's wife, he expected that she would have been older, but she didn't look like she was much more than forty. It made him wonder just how much older the doctor was.

"I'm not sure." That was partially true. He had already made up his mind, but just didn't want to admit it to himself yet. He didn't want to acknowledge that he had already convinced himself that he had to go in. He was there; he was obligated to go in there and check it out. After all, it was probably nothing. Like he had thought, it would just be an old-timer playing pranks. Some old geezer on his last leg who wanted to get a good hoot over on someone before he kicked the bucket.

However, looking at the doctor's wife, he was probably not that old so there was probably no joke involved. In fact, if the doctor was in his forties, it would seriously hurt his career if he purposely called in a false report.

But maybe he had gone overboard. There are certain diseases that can make a person appear near death. He once had the pleasure of conversing with a researcher that had once visited Haiti. There had been what had been thought of as a zombie outbreak back in the late seventies. Real people, people that had been buried by the local customs, were actually getting up and digging their way out of their own graves.

While the researcher, a Dr. Jack Russell if Bryan could recall correctly, wasn't the one who figured out the cause and had tracked it down, he had done quite a bit of study on the phenomenon while he was down there. The Haitians were very protective though, and he loved to tell the story with a lot of dramatic effect.

"I barely made it out alive," or "They had me tied down, and then I was buried alive." The man was full of the horrific tale. The results, though, had been fascinating; real-life zombies, though not undead. Real-life, brain dead, rising from the grave zombies had actually attacked the good doctor.

Of course, they weren't real zombies. There was a powder used, that made a person appear dead for a couple of days. The person would have no way of moving and would show no signs of life; however, they were alive and would actually be conscious the whole time they were under the effects of the drug. It was referred to as "zombie powder" because it was a white, chalky dust made from bones of the recently deceased and the victims were often brain dead and referred to as zombie-like. The brain dead state was thought to have been more the effects of the person having to dig their way out of their own grave and being deprived oxygen than from the effects of the powder.

"Is the back door unlocked?" he said to her as he stood. He had made the decision. He was going to go in. He had to, otherwise his report would be incomplete. And it was strange that the doctor had not come out yet. There was something he needed to go in there and check out. He sure didn't want to do it. This was so not his kind of job.

"Yeah, just go on in." She looked up at him and there was something in her eyes. Maybe it was a pained or worried look, he wasn't sure. He couldn't read people. "Please, make sure he's okay. He hasn't even called my cell or the house phone. I'm just worried about him."

"I will," he said, as he gave her a slight smile.

* * * *

Lucy didn't remember falling off of her bike. She didn't remember even going down the path, or running into the bushes. She wasn't even sure where she was. It somehow all looked familiar, but she couldn't remember any of it.

The front wheel on her bike was still spinning, the grating sound like nails on a chalkboard. A broken spoke kept scratching into the metal as it rounded in it rotation, catching the leg. The wheel was bent, but not too badly. The bike was broken, but it could be fixed.

Was it her bike? She couldn't remember. She looked at it blankly, not knowing how she got there, her leg under it, with a

tree in front of her. Had she hit it? Had she hit the tree and then
banged her head off of it? That would have explained why she
couldn't remember things, wouldn't it? She wasn't sure.

She looked around. Trees and bushes surrounded her,
but they seemed to be spread apart and there was an elongated
indentation on the ground. Was it a path? Had she been on it?
She wasn't sure. It did look like a bike path, and she thought she
could see where she had veered off of it and into the bushes.

She looked back to the bike that was still on top of one
of her legs. She couldn't feel it there; she could see it there,
though it wasn't clear. It was like there was a fog or a haze
between her and the bike, but she could still see it. Should she
move it, and try to get it off of her, or should she scream for
help?

She looked around her again, but all she could see was
trees and bushes. Was there anyone even close enough to hear
her? She opened her mouth and tried to make a sound, but
nothing came out except a gurgling sound as she tried to push air
out of her lungs. It didn't sound right to her; had she had a voice
before? Maybe she was mute, or maybe she had hurt her throat
in the fall.

She looked back at the bike. She probably should try to
push it away and get it off of her. She bent over and grabbed the
center bar and the handlebars. She used her weight to keep
herself upright as she started to shift the metal contraption that
she must have been riding. It had momentarily caught on
something but with a hard tug it finally shifted the last couple of
feet. It came to rest on the small patch of grass that was at the
bottom of the tree.

She looked at the bike where it had fallen. The wheel
still turned. The broken spoke kept scratching. That "tat, tat, tat"
sound repeating itself, and the wheel would not stop spinning.

She turned away from the bike and looked back to her
legs. They were moving, so they were okay, but she saw what
the bike had gotten caught on. There was a long spoke sticking
out from her left leg, and a long gash from where it must have
dug itself in. How could she not have felt that? How could it not
be bleeding?

Was she insane? Was she imagining that she should be
bleeding? Wasn't it normal to bleed? Was she crazy to think so?

She just didn't know. Her legs moved okay, though. She still couldn't feel them, but she watched as they flailed below her.

She decided to try to stand. She leaned forward and reached out for the tree. She was on her knees, and started to push herself up. So far, so good, but shouldn't she feel her legs moving? Shouldn't she feel the rough bark of the trees as her hands scraped along it? She only knew she was rising by watching the world around her move so, unless she was now flying, she had to be standing up. She was wobbly, she could tell by how her vision of the world around her shook, but she was up.

She took a step towards the path. She wasn't sure how she was doing it because she couldn't feel her feet or her legs, and she didn't know how she was telling herself to do it, but she was. She was walking; she was moving. How, she couldn't tell. She was afraid to even look down at herself because she was sure that if she looked down, she would trip and fall over herself.

So, she kept moving. She was stumbling, and moving slow, but she was moving. When she made it to the path, she wasn't sure which way to go but she figured down the path seemed the right way.

Where was she going? She thought she remembered. She was going home. She had to get home. She needed to get home. But why?

CHAPTER 21

No! No! No1No! NO!

He should not be doing this. There was no damned way that he should ever be doing this. It wasn't his job, not his department to put his life at risk. He was a lab man, not a field pawn. He was never meant to be out there and he was not equipped with what he needed to keep himself safe in matters like this.

Bryan stood near the back door to the doctor's office, still trying to convince himself that he shouldn't go in. He didn't want to, and he was pretty sure it would mean his death. After all, what did he have to go in with? He only had a white grocery store mask that would barely stop a cold bug, let alone anything lethal, and a small bag of various examination tools that wouldn't be able to identify crap if he did find anyone sick in there. It was near pointless to even go in.

He guessed he could try and give his boss a call, see if he would authorize someone to bring him some proper equipment to keep him safe. Of course, his boss would try to find out what he had seen to make him think that it was something serious, but he still hadn't seen anything. As far as he knew, the doctor could be waiting inside for him, sitting in his office, ready to go over his notes.

Of course, if that was true, then why hadn't the doctor answered the phone when he tried to call? He had even tried calling him again from his cell phone. No one answered and it just kept going to voice mail.

Why go in? So he could face his boss when he got back and not sound like he had been a coward out in the field? He already wasn't well-liked in the office and it would only add more fuel to the fire against him. It would mean more jokes; more things for them to say about him behind his back.

His hand was on the handle of the door. He had turned it, but stood there refusing to pull it open. At the corner of his eyes, he could feel the moisture fighting to be free. He wasn't going to cry like some schoolboy; he was too old for that. Yeah, he kept telling himself that, but he knew he didn't really believe it. He was ready to cry, was ready to cry in a stream of tears to flood the earth.

"You can't cry though. You can't allow her to see your weakness." he said to himself. Denise was not too far behind him and was watching him as he stood there. He had to go in.

He pulled the door open. Inside, there was a small hallway, dark beyond where the sun shone in. Denise had said that where the hallway ended, he could go left or right and in the center was the nurse's station and the filing room. Along the outside of the hallways on both sides were the patient rooms. There were four total, three to the right side and only one on the left. If he was to turn right, the first door he would come to would be the doctor's office. The first door on the left would be the break room.

She had asked him, if he could, to check in the break room. She wasn't sure if she had turned off the coffee she had been brewing that morning. Judging by the acrid smell of burnt coffee, he was guessing that she had left the warmer for the coffee pot on, but he didn't feel like that should be his first stop. Turning the coffee pot off could wait; it wasn't going to start a fire.

At the end of the hallway, he turned right and went to the first door. He expected it to be darker. When he was outside, everything had looked like it was in complete darkness but now inside the building, he realized the lights had been left on. It was nowhere near as bright as outside, but once he made the turn, the light from overheard lit his way and showed partially into the little office on his right.

The door was open but with no light on inside the room, he could only see the desk that was lit by the light from the hallway. There were papers on the top, and he could see what looked like an ancient telephone off to the side. Could it actually be a telephone? The idea of having anything more than his cell phone seemed like a waste but to have an old telephone, something that looked like it was out of an old movie, just made it that much more obscene.

He had to take his eyes off of the phone as he entered the room. He couldn't allow himself to lose focus. He had a job to do; he couldn't afford to be getting distracted with something as stupid as a telephone. He pushed the door further open and turned to his left, already reaching for the light switch. He flicked it on, but nothing happened. He looked over at it, and then back to the hallway lights.

Okay, so there were lights on in the hall, and it was obvious the building had power, so why wasn't the switch working? He looked back to the switch and flipped it off, waited a few seconds, and then flipped it back on. Still nothing.

He looked back at the desk, this time taking his time to look it over and study it. It was a plain metal desk, nothing stood out. There were papers on top of it, so he really couldn't make out too many details about the top. There was that stupid, damned old phone that he could see, next to it sat a spin dial Rolodex; man, this guy truly was old school.

And what was that on the desk? He could just make out another shape on the far end; was that a light? He couldn't be sure. He stepped further into the room, maneuvering around the desk. He was moving slow and gingerly, afraid to touch anything. His latex gloves would offer him some protection, but why take any more chances than already had?

He eased into the chair, the wheels making a small chirp as he settled into the nice leather of the. Compared to everything else in the room, it was out of place; it was really rather comfortable. Probably a gift, he thought, as he looked to the dark corner of the desk. Now, he could see the light that was sitting there. He reached to turn it on, and the room was suddenly bathed in a warm glow. It wasn't much, but at least now he could start to see what papers were on the desk.

He let his hands glide over the desk, never actually touching anything, but just taking mental notes. It was just some bills, all of which looked to be old, and a legal pad. The bills made him think that the doctor never used his office because one of them was dated for last year.

The legal pad was a different story. It looked old, some of the paper was wrinkled and torn, but the writing on it was from this morning. He could tell as the doctor had dated it when he signed at the bottom.

Beside the notepad were three little spots of what looked like white ash or powder. His first thought would have been cocaine, but Bryan dismissed it. You don't call the CDC and then hide and leave drug evidence where a federal employee could find it. The powder was curious because the desk, other than the old mail, was well-dusted. The doctor may not have used his office, but someone kept it clean for him.

Bryan pinched up some of the fine powder and ran it through his thumb and forefinger, looking at its consistency. It was powder, but it seemed to stick to his fingers. It looked dry, but acted somewhat like it was wet and almost paste-like.

Strange.

He didn't like that he also felt a warm tingle in his fingers though the plastic of the gloves. That couldn't be good. He peeled off the glove, quickly dropping it into the garbage can that was next to the desk, and then craned his head to see his fingertips in the available light. They were red and looked sore.

Shit, that was not good.

Shit!

He turned back to the legal pad and picked it up with the hand that still had the gloves on. He scanned over the notes, trying to figure out the doctor's scrawl of handwriting. It wasn't easy. He could pick out some words; ones that must have made the doctor slow down and take more time to write. He could read the words, "Spider" and "Shared Delusion". And he also thought it said something about "walking corpse, no pulse". But that just made no sense.

This had to all be a joke. It all seemed like too much of a set up. Who knows, maybe he was on one of those home video or prank shows. Maybe soon, Ashtun Kutcher would be jumping out of the closet and telling him he had just been junked, or whatever that catch phrase he used was. But hadn't Kutcher been canceled? That's right, they had a new host; they would just jump out, and this would all just be a joke on the federal government.

Of course, the real joke would be on them when the U.S. Government went after their heads.

Down the hallway, there was a loud crash that made the whole wall reverberate. Something large was pounding into one of the doors. It shook the door, its frame, and the whole wall it was attached to. It made Bryan jump, nearly falling out of the chair. If this was a joke, they really were going all out on it. He reached into his pocket and pulled out an extra glove and pulled it on. He had a bad feeling that it was already too late, but he wasn't going to take a chance. Then he stood, took a deep breath, and started to walk towards the sound.

* * * *

She wasn't sure what her name was. She didn't know where she was going. She was on a road, there were trees around her. Part of her was confused as to where she was, but something else, something deeper, told her that she knew right where she was. It was all somewhat familiar. If that was true, why didn't she remember it?

Because she didn't remember anything. What was her name? She didn't even know that anymore. She wanted to think that it sounded something like Lu, or Bu, or Ju, but she wasn't sure. None of them really sounded right, but she thought that she was close.

So, where was she going?

Home…

Really, but where? Where was her home? Was it around the corner? Yes, it all looked familiar, but was it?

She didn't know how she kept moving towards the curve. Her body was alien to her, she felt like she was a passenger in her own skin, but it was still going to where she wanted. The invaders didn't have control yet. She still told the body where to go; she couldn't feel it, and it all felt like it was dead to her, but she still had control.

Control of what?

Who was she?

Where was she going?

* * * *

191

Bryan reached the door. He knew it was the right one because he could hear them on the other side. He didn't know how many of them were in there, but he could hear more than one. He could hear the multiple people bouncing around in there.

He guessed that they were waiting in there to play some prank on him, but they weren't being too careful about it. They were making enough noise that he had figured it all out pretty easily.

"Hello!" he said to the wood door. He was still hoping to talk to the doctor and keep the joke from playing out. His boss liked the man; the last thing he wanted to do was to get the doctor in trouble. He would try to give the doctor an out, still try to allow him to claim that the call had originally been a legitimate one. He would give the doctor that chance.

But if they went through with it, that option was off the table. He wasn't going to allow himself to be made a fool of.

Somewhere in the back of his mind an itch of a thought tried to surface. Then it hit him.   If this was a joke being played, then why him? Did he know this doctor? Had he met him before and this was something him and Chris had dreamed up since Brian was going to be in the area? There was always that chance since Chris knew him that Brian had met the man as well.

It made sense. Why else would Chris send him out there? Chris knew he wasn't a field agent, and knew how much he hated being around people. This all had to be a setup, a practical joke being played on him.

"Doctor Wilson!" he called again.

There was a crash against the door; it sounded like a large group of people converged and slammed into it. He heard the cracking sound of splintering wood. He looked at the door and saw that it was cracked down the center and was bulging out as it had started to give way.

This wasn't a joke. He had known it from the beginning, but the proof of it sank like a led weight to the bottom of his stomach. He could feel his breakfast fighting to come up and he didn't know how much longer he could hold it in. His hands shook, and he could feel his bowels pinch as a pain shot through them.

He was not.......A.......Fucking.......Field.......Agent!

He took a step back and fell into the three foot high barrier that blocked his way into the nurse's station. Instead of looking to move around it, he backed his way along the wall, not wanting to take his eyes off the door.

There was another slam, this time the door gave away even more and now there was a gaping hole. The large shapes on the other side still couldn't get through, but he could see one of their faces. It was looking at him and his breath caught in this throat.

Through the crack in the door he could see the gray, dead eyes and the pale skin of what looked like a dead man trying to climb through the hole. There were wounds along the man's face, deep gashes, but no blood poured down. There was dried blood on the face, but nothing oozed from the wounds. The man was dead; there was no denying it. There was no way a man could look like that and still be alive.

Bryan felt warmth running down his thigh and knew that he had pissed himself, but he didn't care. He backed down the hall, telling himself that if he could get away from the gaze of that beast, it couldn't hurt him. It wasn't human, not anymore. Whatever, whoever that had been, it was not human.

Bryan found the gap into the nurse's station and nearly fell backward into it. He wasn't even sure how he had reached out in time to catch himself on the partition but once he had, that was it. He turned and went into a full run to the doctor's office. He wanted to get out of there, but knew it was too late for that. He was already exposed. He couldn't' chance making anyone else sick. At least that little bit of rational made it into his irrational mind.

He slammed closed the doctor's office just as he heard the creatures slam into the door one more time. From the sounds of splintering wood, he guessed that the door had finally given out and they were now in the hallway. He didn't go look.

Instead, he looked around the little office. Then he hurried over to the desk and pushed against it. The metal squealed as it protested against being moved but, after a good shove, it finally moved across the room and slammed against the door.

It wasn't going to hold. Well, it may; he didn't know for sure. At least it was something. It was something to keep him away from them, and right now that was all he wanted. Not that it mattered. His life was over the moment he was probably within air contamination of those… those things.

He had to call it in. This town, it had to be locked down. There wasn't any evidence that it had escaped this office, but they couldn't take that chance. If it was airborne, if Denise had it and had been around others, it could already have spread and more in the town may be affected. He couldn't take that chance. They would lock down the town, make sure and, if everything was safe, they would just have to come up with a good cover story. If everything wasn't safe…….

Bryan grimaced at the thought. He knew that if they weren't safe, if things got worse in the town, the media would have just been given an even better cover story.

He reached into his pocket and pulled out his cell phone. It took him only a second to scroll through his programmed numbers until he found the one he wanted. It was right under his listing for Mom. He had it listed as Mother. It wasn't all that original, but he never did take those protocols too seriously. When would he ever need them, right?

An almost mechanical sounding female's voice answered on the first ring. In the most unwelcoming tone Bryan thought he had ever heard, the phone said to him flatly, "Lemrose Pizza."

"Flag Day," he said into the phone. "Flag Day! Flag Day, Flag Day!" He screamed it as he heard them lumbering closer, very close to the door.

Now it wouldn't be long. God, he hoped they got there soon. He doubted that he would be saved. Who the hell was he kidding; he was dead. There was no way anyone would come there for him. He was gone. Dead the moment he had made that phone call.

A heavy force slammed against the door, momentarily pushing in on the desk. Right now, the quarantine was not his greatest concern.

Another force, a heavy object but without a lot of power behind it, slammed against the door; two smaller thumps continued to hit against the wall. They were going to keep going until they got through that door. They were going to get in, and then he was dead. He was already a dead man.

He looked at the phone in his hand. Maybe he should call his sister?

He watched as a spider crawled out from under his sleeve and climbed onto the phone. He brought the receiver to his forehead, feeling the cool plastic on his skin as he felt the warm, wet tear roll down his cheek.

* * * *

She came to a large house which felt familiar. Somewhere inside of her she wondered if it was a part of a dream she had once had. All of this, moving without moving, the not feeling herself, it all seemed like it may be just a part of a dream. Maybe it was, and she was just a pawn of her own imagination.

Some part of her knew that it wasn't, but everything else screamed at her to accept that it was. It told her to pinch herself, but she knew already that she couldn't feel it. She knew already, just as she remembered pulling the long spoke from her bike out from her leg. She hadn't felt that; how would she feel a pinch?

This all had to be a dream. It sounded nice, but something else inside of her, something deeper, told her that it wasn't.

She found herself lumbering around the familiar house to the back door. She stumbled her way up the steps, once falling and slamming her knees to the hard wood. She wanted to grimace from the pain and scream out for help, but there had been no pain. That alarmed her.

It troubled her more that while she had meant to scream, she hadn't been able to. Before she had realized there was no pain, there was the reflex. She wanted to cry out, to bellow in pain, but when she opened her mouth, no sound came out. She wasn't even sure that her mouth opened. She couldn't feel it, and she couldn't see it, so she had no way to know for sure.

She made it back to her feet and after a few more stumbles, she was at the back door. She watched, a prisoner in her own body, as her hand reached out and pulled open the door. She knew that it was by pure willpower that she was still coming to this place, but she knew that strand of will was growing weaker. She didn't know how much longer she had that force left in her. She was dying.

She stepped beyond the door and found herself in a room with cabinets and a table in the center. She made it. She was....where? Where was she? Why had she fought so hard to get back here? Where was here?

"Ugghhh." She heard a low moan from the next room. There was a loud thump and another shriek of pain.

She looked in the direction of the sound. She couldn't' see much of the room yet, but she could make out a large, elongated table in the center topped with looked like some green type of fabric. She wasn't surprised when her body stumbled in the direction of the sounds.

She came to stand in front of a large man. He was sitting up against the wall, slowly, lethargically moving back and forth. She didn't know if he was trying to stand or just to sit up. He just went back and forth, flailing, not moving with much purpose.

Finally, his eyes looked up at her. They may have been brown, or some other dark color, but they were glazed over and while they looked straight at her, they never seemed to focus. They were lost, pleading eyes, looking to her for......what? Salvation?

The voices inside of her came alive as she looked at the man. They all wanted something from him, or to do something to him. They cried out, calling for her to take him. They all wanted her to move to him, to....to....

What did they want her to do with him?

"Spread!" she heard the voices inside her mind scream.

That was the last thing that Lucy understood as her last strand, her last part that was still herself, faded to nothing. She was lost.

* * * *

Lucy bent down over the body; there was nothing left of the little girl. Her mind was gone. There was now only desire

196

and need. Desire for the creatures inside of her to get food, and the need for them to spread. They would never be satisfied, as their breed was unnatural and made with only the two purposes.

Lucy bent down to the man and as she neared him, she opened her mouth. He would never see the swarm of spiders as they ran over top of him. Their screams of pleasure were endless as Lucy bit into his neck.

He screamed out in pain, but it wasn't any use. There was no one near that would hear him, and he didn't have the strength to fight her. The swarm rushed from her, entering through the large hole in the man's neck and rushing into their new home.

What was one is now two, and what is two will soon be four. Four will become eight, and eight will yield into sixteen if not more. The spreading has started, and new food must be obtained. Used food, host food, must be used to find new food and the pattern continues.

Before his mind can grasp what has happened, Vince is already lost as not one or two spiders raced to devour what was left of his mind. Hundreds came and what had been taking hours to lay new eggs and spread, now took only minutes.

CHAPTER 22

Chaos erupted around the front of the store. At first, no one even moved as they saw their boss being eaten by Billy, someone they had all been working with for a long time. Sure, many of them would never admit to really ever liking Billy. In fact, most the younger girls that worked there always had been a little creeped out by him. He would quietly sneak around sometimes and would just hover behind them. So, yeah, he was that creepy guy that they always talked about behind his back, but he was also the one they called whenever they had a question about the furniture department. He was the expert they had all come to know and trust. Well, trust as much as they would any co-worker. And here he was eating Tim. He was there, eating their boss. Sure, most of them wanted to hit the fat bastard, but who the hell eats someone? That was just wrong.

Billy continued to bite into him, tearing away at the flesh. And the blood, there was just so much of it. It was everywhere. Flowing, flooding along the floor. The white tiles had turned red and had become slippery.

At first, no one reacted. They were all too stunned. Then, moments later, the world came alive with motion, everything happening at once. All of it coming to life when the sound of the bitchy woman, the annoying customer that all of them had already been frustrated with, fell loudly to the floor.

Sam, the woman who had been behind the counter and had been sorting the thin little yellow price tags that they used to mark items, had been just to the right of Tim. She hadn't even been looking up. Having already had an aggravating morning, both with having to put up with the damn woman pissed off by

Billy and then the other bitch who had been on the phone, she just wanted to ignore everyone else for the next five hours until she was off the clock. All of them could go to hell on a stick as far as she cared.

Then Billy suddenly reached out and had bitten into him. He did it out of nowhere and Tina had been in the path of the fountain of blood; it rained all around her. When it had sprayed up into the air of the department store, it had fallen down in a wide spread, and it had rained all around her. The dark crimson becoming a bath of gore that enveloped her, and she couldn't even respond to it happening. It covered her, the price tags, and it had even gotten into her hair.

She just stood there at first, watching. Tim never even fought back. He must have been surprised and by the time he could have reacted, it was too late. He had just stood there as Billy had reached out, maybe reacting startled at first and trying to put out his hands to steady the young man. However, Billy had suddenly grabbed him and after that first bite, there was just too much blood.

After it had sprayed over her for what seemed like forever, though it couldn't have been more than just a matter of seconds, Tina's mind started to work again and she started to back away. Even with the counter between the two of them, it wasn't good enough. Her mind came suddenly awake in full force, and she knew then that the space between them was never going to be big enough. She had to get away. She had to get out of there. That shouldn't be too hard; she was the closest to the front door.

She heard screams then. Her ears seemed to reconnect to her body, and she could hear what was happening again. She heard screams, barely realizing that they were her own, and yelling. She heard people screaming at each other, yelling, some were calling out names. Some were yelling for people to rush to their aid; some were yelling for people to get behind them for protection.

Sam wasn't too sure who was doing what. She was getting out of there. She had already turned from the clatter of motion. She was working to hurry to where the entrance of the counter was. It was just by the exit and should be easy for her. All she had to do was get there, and she would be able to get out.

That wasn't so hard. She just had to get to the exit. She just had to run.

Her legs were rubber, but they still propelled her. They took her faster than her mind was able to work. Quickly, she had made her way to the gaping hole in the counter that allowed her out. Then she was turning and running towards the door. Somewhere behind her, she had heard someone calling her name but she wasn't looking back.

She slammed into the door and with a loud crunching sound, the glass spider-webbed before her. She had run straight into it, but she hadn't been ready for it. Her large nose had been the first to hit, and she heard a loud crack that came with a fountain of sparks behind her eyes and pain flooding her dampened mind.

Behind her, she heard what sounded like loud firecrackers. Strange, she thought, it wasn't Fourth of July yet. It was way too early for them. And why were people firing them off in the store?

Stumbling, she turned. The world around her was growing dark. The floor below her looked so welcoming she just wanted to lie down and let some form of sleep take over. She was suddenly tired. She didn't really even care if she never work up. She just wanted to lie down, and let it wash over her.

She looked up. She saw Aaron on the other side of the counter. He was holding a gun, and was pointing it down. What was he doing with a gun? He shouldn't have one of those; he was at work. That just wasn't allowed. Then, she saw what looked like a white flame explode from the end of it and she heard another one of those damn firecrackers.

Aaron started to back away. Somewhere in her mind she thought about how she should call out to him and say 'hi'. She really hadn't wished him a good morning yet, and she liked Aaron. Maybe he would finally ask her out on a date.

Billy stood up and was between her and Aaron. He was starting towards him, and Tina thought that she could see what looked like bullet holes in the back of Billy's shirt. That was funny. Why did he have them? If Tim saw that he was going to be pissed.

Then the ground seemed just too inviting and she laid down, letting her world slip away into blackness. She barely felt the feet later as people started to run over her out the door.

* * * *

Winona had been just coming to the end of the aisle when she heard the first sounds that something was wrong. Calling it a scream wouldn't have been right, but it sounded like that was what the woman had been trying to do; the sound of it had seemed to die in her throat, self-muffled, and then it ended suddenly with a thud.

When Winona emerged from the aisle, she saw something worse than her sickest of imagination. Which said a lot because of some of the action she had seen when she had been dispatched overseas.

A woman had just fallen. Okay, so that wasn't so bad. No, it was the man who was, for all intense and purposes, eating another man. He had grabbed him and was biting into the man. He was trying to fight against the other man, but he just wouldn't let go.

Another scream rang out, and Winona watched as the woman behind the counter was trying to run away. At least she was showing more sense than the other woman. The other one had stopped screaming because she had just unceremoniously passed out.

She saw movement out of the corner of her eye and watched as a young man had sneaked up behind the biter. However, he seemed to be so focused on his, well, food that he didn't notice.

She saw something flash, some light catching on something stuck in the back of the biters shirt. She stretched her neck, craning it to get a little better look, and she saw why the man was trying to sneak up on him. She saw what he was doing, but the biter was moving away from him. The larger man currently being eaten was sliding down the counter as the strength was leaving him. The biter was following him down and, as he bent, the butt of a gun showed from beneath his shirt. She guessed that gutsy boy there was going to try and grab it.

202

Good call. At least someone was showing some sense. The woman behind the counter still hadn't seemed to really focus onto anything but screaming, and the one on the floor.....well, she looked like she would be out until someone splashed some cold water on her. Both of them made Winona pissed, as both of them made woman look bad under pressure.

Which she knew a lot about. She had fought against it for a long time in her unit. Being one of only two woman in her National Guard unit, the rest of them thought that women had no place in line among them. Yeah, at first they didn't. It wasn't easy, but over time she had earned their respect. She had done what had needed to get done, and she had stood in the face of danger with them and didn't back down.

Not as much could have been said about that damn other woman that had been in their unit. When the time had come, and when the bullets had been flying, she had frozen. In battle, there isn't much worse you can do than to freeze up, other than actually shooting a "friendly". Freezing up meant that not only did you put your life at risk, but it also meant that you put the life of those around you at risk. Three of Winona's good friends were dead and in pieces because of it.

These damn women here, children who sure as hell needed to pull their heads out of their asses, weren't doing much better. Why wasn't someone trying to call the cops? Why wasn't she calling the cops?

Her phone buzzed in her back pocket and it brought her back to what she needed to do. She couldn't just stay standing there. She had to watch, observe, report, and formulate a plan but not necessarily in that order. First thing, she had to call the police.

She pulled the phone from her pocket, looking at who was calling. Shit, it was the emergency dispatch number. She had orders coming in. She knew that meant there was an emergency, and that she was required to take the call. How could she, though; she had an emergency of her own happening directly in front of her. She had to transfer it to voice mail. She knew it was going to cost her later and she grimaced as she hit the button.

Then, she dialed the emergency number. She had backed away down the aisle a little so that she didn't have direct view of the situation anymore, but at least that meant that none of them had any view of her. That was a good thing. She didn't want them to notice her, at least right now.

A voice just came onto the line announcing "Emergency Services, how may I direct your call?" just as the first gun shot rang out. Winona barely kept from jumping and her grip on her phone became hard; she could feel the edges of the cheap plastic digging into her fingers.

"Oh my god!" the woman exclaimed on the other end of the line. Winona grimaced at how loud the voice seemed as it screamed through the speaker on the phone.

"I am at the-..." Winona had to struggle to think of which department store she was in. She couldn't believe she had forgotten it. She thought she had been better than that; better at dealing with situations under heavy amounts of tension. She actually had to think, to look around and to work to remember where she was. She had to look at the brands. The name of the place was trying to come to her. She could see the generic labels. The wheels inside her moved slow, but couldn't seem to click. Her eyes focused on the labels. The letters started to shape words and then it was like a light just turned on. Her training came to her; she breathed, closed her eyes, and pushed down her fears.

"Hello?" the woman through the headset was saying. Winona could hear concern in her voice. She opened her eyes and looked at the labels. It all was there; she remembered clearly where she was. "I thought I heard a gunshot."

"Yes, multiple gunshots. There is a shooter, but I think he is actually trying to stop the main attacker. There is a lot of blood, multiple people down. The main aggressor seems to be unarmed, but he has attacked at least one individual and I-"... she wasn't too sure as too what else to say. She wasn't sure what was going on because none of it made any sense.

She eased herself back down the aisle. She wasn't sure what was going on, but she had to find out. It was her duty to give them as much information as possible so when the police came, they knew what they were dealing with. She had to help them.

She eased to the end of the aisle, and the phone dropped out of her hand as she gasped. Her hands came up to stop herself, but it the sound had already escaped.

Billy was no longer on the large fat man and eating him. At some point, he had turned around to the one who had been firing the gun. Both of them were now on the ground, and Billy was tearing away at the flesh on Aaron's throat much like he had done when he had first attacked Tim.

Aaron was still moving, the gun hanging limply in his arm. His head just bobbed back and forth, his legs weakly kicked out along the floor. He was moving, but Winona didn't think it was due to any attempt to escape. She wasn't even sure he was alive. No, she could see his eyes; she knew that he was dead because she had seen that look before.

She had seen it more than once but that look, that partial missing face, pulled her back to when she was overseas. Around her dust and sand blew. There was screams. Now there was screaming woman and children around her. A building had just blown up and she was running towards it. On the ground was one of her squad members. He was on the ground, or parts of him were. He was missing an arm and most of the left side of his lower body. She looked over at him and she had seen those dull eyes. However, his body was still moving. His right arm was reaching for her. She could swear that he his lips were moving and he was mouthing "Help Me" to her, but that was impossible. He was dead, but his body just didn't realize it. His muscles continued to twitch as blood still tried to pump through.

Winona backed across the aisle and slammed into one of the cardboard displays. It rocked back and plastic cases clattered to the floor. She tripped on the debris and continued to fall back. She slammed hard against the metal aisle at an angle and a heat lance of pain shot up her arm. Her momentum carried her and she slid down, more of the items around being knocked loose and following her. Then her butt hit hard and she was on the ground covered with crap. So much noise, there was no way they didn't hear that up front. She looked down the aisle, wincing from the pain already stabbing at her kidney. Billy was looking up at her. His eyes were lifeless and gray, but she could see that they still were able to focus on her.

She didn't even think about it. She went into motion and spider-crawled back, working until she could clear the display. It took some effort, but she was able to turn. Pain shot through her side, waves of heat flashing up and down her spine. Her eyes narrowed and she took a sudden intake of breath and then eased it out, pushing away the sensation, not letting it slow her down. She reached out, grabbed one of the metal shelves and used it to pull herself upright. It had taken some effort, but she was up and moving. She glanced back over her shoulder. The biter was trying to stand. He wasn't doing a good job at it. It was almost like he had forgotten how, his legs not working right.

She didn't have time to think about that now. She would have to file that away and get back to it later. She had to get away or she wasn't going to survive. Instincts had started to kick in; her training was flooding back to her. She had to get up and get out of sight, then she could slow down and become quiet.

The front was blocked. There was not going to be any way to get out through there, not unless he followed her and she was able to circle around.

She needed a plan. Her priority was to get out, if she could. She also needed to find any other survivors and get them out, as well. She had to get out through the front, or check to see her options in the back. Fire regulations meant there had to be fire exits nearby, but it was a retail store so an alarm would sound. Did she risk it?

No, she still didn't know the full situation. What if there were more crazies in the store? A shudder tried to creep its way down her back, but she quickly pushed that thought out of her mind. It was a possibility. She hoped like hell that there wasn't. She didn't want to think about having to deal with a band of cannibals loose in the store. She hurried to the end of the aisle and turned to get out of sight.

CHAPTER 23

When Thomas Carter woke up, it had been with a headache that felt like it should have belonged with to a hangover, and a loud screeching sound ringing through his head. He didn't want to move. His eyes were crusted shut and didn't want to open. They fought against it, and the pain in his head was shooting daggers at the slightest motion. If he kept still, it was only a dull stiffness; the moment he turned it either way, white flashes erupted in the back of his eyes.

"Ugh, what the fuck!" he called out to the empty room as he rolled over, feeling the soreness that was all throughout his body.

He reached over to his nightstand and caught the screeching phone that was dancing it's way dangerously close to the edge. Not opening his eyes to look at the display, he flipped it open.

"Yeah!" he barked into the receiver.

"Hey Tom, we got a call in from the Rowplex. Silent alarm."

He heard a panicked voice, which was uncommon for the woman on the other end of the connection. He had recognized the voice right away. It was Samuels, his morning deputy who had just replaced him on duty. He wasn't sure what time it was, but it felt like he got into bed no more than a few minutes ago. He couldn't have been asleep that long.

"Shit, what stores are even open this early?"

"It's a little after eleven, so most of them are open. It's The Office Store that's pulled the alarm, so they would have been open for a little over an hour."

"You on your way?"

"Yes, but I would like some backup."

"Have you placed a call in to the state police?"

"I have, but they say all their people are tied up elsewhere in the area. They seemed to dodge my questions as to why we couldn't get any help."

"What the fuck?" Carter was pulling himself up. His head was trying to stay tied to the pillow, but as he brought it up with him, some of the cobwebs of his mind faded away. This wasn't making any sense but he wasn't sure if it had anything to do with the haziness of sleep, or if things were really all that strange. Had she really just said the state police were unwilling to dispatch backup? "You tried county, as well?"

"Yes, and got the same answer." That was odd. What the hell else was going on this morning to keep both the county and the state police tied up?

The cool hardwood of the floor creaked under him as he stood and made his way to the closet. He hit the speaker on his phone so he could put it down and still talk while he put on his uniform.

Was it his imagination, or was it still slightly damp from his sweat this morning? It was probably just the humidity in the air he thought, as he started to unbutton it from around the hanger so he could put it on. The familiar fabric was soft in his hands and felt well-worn. Some days, he thought as he pulled one arm into the short sleeved navy blue shirt, it felt like he lived in that damned uniform. That all he ever wore was the dark blue and that he never had time to wear anything else. He was always working, or at least the town always perceived him that way. When he was in town, he was on duty. The shirt was his second skin. Long days made him feel like this was a position he could never get away from. This was going to be one of them.

Not that he didn't have a full staff. Unlike many of the neighboring towns where the city councils allowed barely enough payroll for one officer per day to be working, something he never understood as it left much of the time for no one to be watching over the area, they lived in a town where there was at least one officer always on duty. It worked out nice and, in the evenings, he even had it scheduled that there was a three hour overlap so two officers were typically on duty during the rowdiest of times.

In a town that averages more bars than churches, it seemed appropriate to have enough to handle the bar fights, and the occasional drug and gambling bust that they did throughout the town. Not that Hammond was all that large of a town but, for its size, it seemed like it tried to compete with the larger towns nearby. He had heard the nickname more than once, Little Chicago. While they were nowhere on par with the big city, it seemed like there was enough crime to justify the name and the additional police force.

It also meant that he had four other officers that he could call on when they were needed. If there was a problem at The Office Store, he would probably need to call them in.

"Call in the cavalry, I guess. See who you can get," he said to the phone as he finished buttoning up the shirt and was reaching for his pants. "I'll be there in ten minutes. Call me back in five with a status report."

"Will do," Samuels said.

He straightened as he pulled up his pants and was reached out for his phone. He didn't wait to listen to the line going dead and flipped it closed.

* * * *

"Hey, Nancy. Nancy, hey!" Was someone calling out to her? She heard something familiar and it seemed like her name. She wasn't sure. "Nancy! Hey, good game so far. Glad it's almost over, though. Hey, have you talked to George yet about the yearbook. Everyone is really curious to see what you do with it this year after you did such a great job with it last year."

Nancy stopped and let the larger woman catch up to her. She felt like she knew the woman. A familiarity tried to push its way out from deep in her thoughts. This woman, she knew her. It was there, not quite on her tongue but buried further back. It was there with other thoughts but was drifting away to just out of her reach. She knew this woman, she just wasn't sure where she had known her from. And where had she been going? Her thoughts rearranged and tried to surface again.

The concession stand, that's right; she had gotten up and had left the school's gym to go to the concessions being sold in the lunchroom. The school was designed with the lunchroom just being down the hall and to the left, and she had been feeling really strange. As she had been sitting there watching the game, the voices kept telling her to feed. She didn't feel hungry, but the voices kept telling her that she was.

"Hey Nancy, are you all right?" the woman asked.

Nancy looked at her. All right? Was she? She thought so, but she wasn't sure. She didn't really feel anything. Inside, all she felt was a nothingness, disconnected. Her mind was swimming while her body seemed to be going on autopilot. She had felt hungry, but she hadn't thought about really reacting to it. Yet, somehow, she had gotten up and started to make the walk to the concessions.

She didn't really feel hungry. How could she feel hungry when she couldn't feel anything inside of her? Yet, something was pushing her and telling her she was hungry. She couldn't stop the thought. It was there, telling her, instructing her to find food. There were too many of them already, and she needed to find food. They needed food, they needed space.

Who needed food, though? Who needed space?

"Nancy, I think you should come over to the stairs and sit down, you don't look well. You look a little peaked," Mrs. Gentz was saying to her. Nancy had a brief recognition. Mrs. Gentz was the school's principal. She had been talking about the yearbook. Was Nancy still working on that? Somehow she knew that she was, but she felt like that was no longer important, like something from a previous life.

Nancy could see that the woman had reached out for her arms and was trying to lead her to the stairwell. However, as soon as the woman had seen her arm, she had stopped and her expression had grown more questioning, her eyebrows raised in confusion. Nancy could see what the woman was looking at. When had that happened? The full comprehensible thought actually breaking in through the cloud growing in her mind.

Her arms had long gashes in them. Some of them were very deep and, in a few places, she could see broken parts of fake fingernails deep in her skin. They must have been hers. She had been scratching herself. Long flaps of flesh had come up and were dangling.   At first, the skin had looked like it wasn't scratched too bad, but Nancy could see that as soon as Mrs. Gentz had lifted her arm, the dangling flesh had slipped to the side exposing the hideous scratch marks. There was no blood. Shouldn't there have been blood if she had been scratching herself like that?

She looked as the large woman was examining her arm. She didn't feel like it was a part of her. She could see how the arm reached up and connected to her shoulder, but she didn't feel any pain from the cuts. She didn't even feel it as the woman was holding it and moving it around.

Then she looked at the woman, and realized that her hunger had grown; something was telling her that there was food in front of her. She didn't fully understand, but something inside of her was telling her that there was food right there ready for her to devour. She yearned for it. She needed it. She needed to reach out and tak it.

As a prisoner in her own body, she watched as she moved forward and, in a second, she was on top of the woman. Together, they fell to the grown. Mrs. Gentz cried out in surprise and then pain as Nancy landed on top of her.

Nancy hadn't waited, though. As soon as she had reached her and they were falling, she had pulled the woman closer until she was biting into her cheek. She tore at the flesh and as the blood flowed into her mouth, she could hear them inside of her. The voices screamed with delight. She continued to move forward and as the woman tried to push Nancy off of her, she just kept biting.

At one point, the woman had gotten a hand up, trying to protect her face, but Nancy had bitten off two fingers. Mrs. Gentz was now a screaming, bloody mess beneath her.

Around her, the gym was breaking out into chaos and panic. Others had started to eat, as well. Nancy didn't know how she knew but as she continued to bite and to enjoy, to eat and to spread, she knew that the others were also spreading.

CHAPTER 24

Denise didn't like the waiting. She didn't like not knowing what the hell was going on. That CDC guy had left to go into her husband's office just over an hour ago. Since then, she had heard some noises, loud pounding sounds and then screams; what sounded like inhuman screams, high pitch howls of someone calling out for help. She had wanted to run and see if she could.

She had gotten up and ran across the gravel and had even reached three feet from the door when she had caught herself. She couldn't go in. She wanted to go in and be with him, but the moment she crossed that threshold she would be in the quarantine; there was no coming back out after that. She would be trapped.

So, she had to stay out of there and listen to whatever was going on. She had to listen to the screams; they called out to her and were asking someone to come help. They were tearing him apart in there and he was screaming about the spiders that were crawling into his mouth. Then the screaming had stopped. She could hear his gurgling. She didn't know how the man could be fighting and be that loud when she was still a few feet from the door. It didn't seem possible but she heard it, and she knew that she was listening to him die.

That was when the tears started. She didn't know they were even coming at first. She just felt the first tear as it streaked down from the corner of her eye. Then, there was the second one from the other side and before she could even stop herself and acknowledge the pain she felt, the storm came upon her and she collapsed onto the gravel.

It hurt. Oh, she could ignore the pain in her backside.
She hurt inside, as a mixture of feelings twisted her and pulled at
her. She felt an emptiness of emotion in her chest, while a
massive weight pounded in on her. Then there was the sickness,
the acid-like feeling in her stomach. She didn't know how so
many things could go in so many directions at once. Her body
felt like it was falling apart and all she wanted was to close her
eyes, push it all away and lie there in the driveway. At least she
had some kind of sense that kept her from doing that. No, she
just sat and looked, staring at the wooden back door of the
doctor's office.

Her husband was gone.

The man she had shared a bed with for over the last
fifteen years was not going to be there for her tonight. The man
she shared every day with, the man she knew better than she
even knew herself, the man she had promised she would love
until death do them apart was now done with his vows.

She tried to push back the memory. It was trying to
bring with it more tears as she suddenly found herself back on
their wedding day. He had just recently graduated from medical
school and they had somehow restrained themselves and had
made it that long. They had wanted to get married sooner and,
sometimes on those quiet nights alone in bed, they would
fantasize about running off to the Justice of the Peace and just
making it official. They loved each other and had been living
together for the previous two years. Many of their friends
already were calling her his wife.

Everyone knew it was coming. Everyone joked that they
should just run off and get it over with. However, both of them
knew that if they did, they would have hurt everyone's feelings.
Every one of their friends, and even many of his professors, were
looking forward to the wedding. They all wanted to be a part of
their big day. They were well-liked; why shouldn't they let all
their friends be a part of it?

Still, those nights of lying together in bed, looking
forward to their happy future together, it was hard not to say,
"Hey, let's just go and do it."

Thankfully, they never did. One of them would often
point out how it would devastate all of their friends and family
who had already saved the date. Then, whoever talked the other

out of it, would gingerly give a little poke to the others ribs. They would laugh and giggle about it, and then she would rest her head against his chest. They would just lie there, holding each other, looking forward to their wonderful and long future together.

She didn't want that future to end.

She remembered seeing him there, as they stood in front of all of their friends. He was trying to say his vows to her. They had both written them down and being the endless preparers that they were, they had each rehearsed them over and over so they could say them from memory. When it came time for him to say his words, his face had gone so red and she could see how hard it was for him. He was the one to cry; he was the one to stutter over the words. She could see the love for her in his eyes, and see that he was trying so hard because he loved her so much. She saw that he was having trouble breathing. My God, she had thought, he was going to pass out.

She knew he was too. She knew him too well.

She started making faces towards him, awkward comical ones, like kids would do to each other in a game to get the other person to laugh, and he did. She could see that it helped him, too. He was able to get through his vows. Then they kissed and were husband and wife.

She was his and he was hers, for life. He would be her husband until he died. She knew that she would never leave him, and that he would never do anything to risk their marriage. She knew it with every fiber of her being. She never had reason to distrust. He was a part of her; he was her heart

But now her heart was gone. Now, her husband was-.

Her husband was-

A loud sound boomed from the door as it sounded like a large mass ran into it; like someone had walked straight into it and then bounced against it, not realizing that it wasn't going to open by just running into it. Then the sound quieted briefly, to be followed with an even louder pounding against the door.

Something inside the office wanted to get out.

Was the door locked? Even if it was, the door locked from the inside. If someone wanted to come out, all they would have to do was turn the door handle.

So...

So what did that mean?

So...

That meant that whatever it was, didn't know how to turn the handle.

She didn't know how she did it, she didn't know why she did it, because a large part of her just wanted to stay there and let whatever was trying to come through that door have her. She didn't even know what part of her didn't want to just let it all. That seemed to be the thought behind every core of her being.

It wasn't logical. Logically thinking would be that it was her husband and that he was hurt and he could have even needed her help. That was rational, right? So why did she have a sudden weight in her stomach and the urge to run. Her intuition screamed at her to get out of there.

And so she did. All of it felt so unreal, like she was trapped in a bad horror film, and maybe she was. She couldn't allow that to matter because, horror film or not, she was now a part of it. So, was she going to be a survivor, or was she going to be a victim?

She didn't know what inside of her spoke up, but she knew she wasn't going to allow herself to be a victim. She had to get up, and get out of there. She didn't know where she was going to go but she had to go somewhere, anywhere other than there.

Behind her, she heard another loud crack against the door and she heard the wood splinter. It wasn't a loud sound, it was quiet and subtle, but she knew what it was. She guessed it would still take them a while before the door gave way, but they would eventually get out.

She ran into the garage and hurried to her car. The little powder blue Prius sat there, looking meek as an escape vehicle. Something about the size and the color screamed at her that it was not the right vehicle to take. Maybe it wasn't, she thought as she hurried around to the driver's side door and pulled on the handle. Nothing happened. Dammit, the door was locked. Where were her keys?

They were in the key bowl, of course, where else would they be? She hadn't been expecting to go anywhere, why would she have her keys with her? And her cell phone would probably

be right next to the key bowl by the front door. No, it wouldn't.
She had been talking to her sister earlier and had been calling
patients while she had been sitting on the front porch. The cell
phone should be on the table by her deck chair.

She hurried back around her car and rushed to the front
porch. Keys, cell phone; she needed to hurry and grab them.
She had to get out of there. She needed to call Thomas; he was
probably at the police station but she would try him on his cell.
Something was happening and she knew she had to get a hold of
him. He had to be able to help them.

There was another slam against the door, and it shook
the walls of the building. She shuddered with the impact and
swore she could feel its ferocity. The strikes against the door
seemed to be strengthening; maybe it was also frustration?
Whatever it was in there wanted to get out.

She had a brief thought back to something her professor
had once told her, something about chaos. She couldn't
remember the exact phrase, no matter how many times he had
repeated it. He was always fond of telling his theories and
defending them, but what it all came down to was that chaos
can't be contained. Chaos spreads, destroys life, so that new life
can come from the ashes of the destruction. It was his own sick
and twisted way of eluding to the circle of life.

She pushed the thought from her, thinking about the two
men who had originally come that morning. She had barely seen
them, but she had seen enough to know that they had looked
dead. She knew that her husband, if sick, would not be acting
like he was currently acting. She couldn't see him on the other
side, but she could feel him. She knew that he was gone. She
didn't know how she knew that, but could feel that it was true.

No, don't think about it now. She couldn't spend time
worrying about it. She had to get out of there. She hurried
inside the house, pulling hard on the screen door. The chain
wasn't fastened and the door slammed all the way open against
the house and vibrated from the blow. She didn't pause. She
hurried past it, through the already open inner door and stopped
quickly to reach into the bowl on the table by the door. Her keys
were on top. Her fingers lingered just briefly on the keys under
hers in the bowl. His keys, the ones that he would never use
again.

She heard another powerful blow slam into the office, and this time she could hear the splintering of the wood much more loudly. There had been an audible crack, and she was worried that they were getting closer and closer to getting out. She needed to get a hold of Thomas; she needed to get the police there before they could get out; she needed to make sure that the quarantine stayed in place. They could not let whatever was in there out.

She rushed back out of the house. The screen door was slowing making its way back to close, and she dodged out of its way and went to the little table near her deck chair. Her phone was on it and she grabbed it.

Her car was only a little over ten feet away. All she had to do was run down the stars and dash into the open garage door and she would be gone. Just hold tight and she was going to be out of there; she just needed to keep herself together. She tried to breathe and tell herself that she was doing fine. Just keep her head and not panic, that's what she needed to do.

She took the steps two at a time. She reached the bottom and turned to run into the garage, but took a moment to look over at the office. She stopped, her breath caught in her chest. The door was open! It wasn't cracked all the way through, but the splintering of the wood had warped the door outward enough so that the lock had released.

Her heart skipped a beat and she was caught between two worlds of emotion. Part of her was relieved to see the door open. After all, the door open would mean he would be there, and she would be able to see him, see that everything was okay. She would rush to him, smother him in kisses and see that it had all just been a big misunderstanding.

No. She had to stay logical; everything was wrong and deep down she knew it. That part of her that had detached itself from all emotion was awake and it screamed at her to run. Don't look, don't try to see him, just run. Run and get away from there, run and get out of there as fast as she could.

She hadn't run, though. She couldn't help it. She wanted to, but her legs just stopped and she had to watch. She saw the shape that was a mess of flesh that had landed just outside of the door. She couldn't make out much of it, but she recognized the shirt her husband had been wearing this morning. It had been a nice blue button up shirt, worn only a few times, and this morning had still looked partially like the shirt she had bought him a couple weeks ago. What was left of that shirt was torn, and covered in dried blood. There was very little of the blue left of the shirt.

He had his head down, and he was on the ground in the position of just starting to push himself up. He hadn't looked up yet, and she really did not want him to. She knew that when he did, the reality would kick in and the little hope she had been kicking around in the back of her mind, that all of this was still just a nightmare, would be lost.

Behind him, she saw the other two men stumbling out. Their clothes were also covered in blood that she was sure had once been her husbands. They were followed by that man from the CDC. Their faces were shadows of their former selves, hollow and empty of any sign of life. Skin that had once had color to it was now white, and their eyes had gone just a slightly darker shade to what looked like a light gray. Dead eyes that belonged to dead bodies, and no one had informed them that they should not be up and walking around.

Then, her husband did look up and she felt that emptiness in her try to take control and drop her onto the ground in a sobbing mess. He was gone. That was not her husband. There was no life there and if there was no life in him, what reason did she have to live. Without him, she didn't have anything left.

No! That emptiness could not be allowed to consume her. She had to keep going! She had to get out of there now. She turned back to the car, got in, and flipped the switch to the garage door. She was barely in the car when the clankity clank of the garage door started to lift. She didn't wait for it. She turned to key to the ignition and the little Prius wheezed to life, all the power of the little electrical engine coming alive. The garage door was barely high enough for the car to clear, but she put the car into reverse and gunned it.

She wasn't about to try and make a phone call, not while driving. In her current state, she didn't think that she could control the car and talk at the same time, but she had to get somewhere that she could. Should she go a few blocks and then pull over and call Thomas at the police station, or should she just go there?

She wasn't sure. She just knew that any decision she made, it was best not to wait there to make it. She took off down the street, leaving the creatures behind her to stumble and try to follow.

CHAPTER 25

"Kalwalski and Daniels are on their way. Jackson is off, out of town fishing. His wife sounded pretty upset about it, saying he just took off this morning without letting her know. She just knows he went fishing because the beer in the fridge and the boat are gone," Samuels told him.

Great, they must have been fighting again. Carter really didn't feel like he had time to deal with Jackson's whining anyways, so it may just have been a good thing that he would be out of town and. His cell would be off anyway.

"Okay, I'm pulling in now," he said into the air of his squad car. His phone was tucked neatly away in his pocket but still picking up his muffled voice.

"I see you now," she said.

He could see her squad car, as well. She was parked in the far outside right corner of the parking lot, obviously sitting there waiting for him. She must not have wanted to get too close to the action until he got there and had time to check it out. Not that it mattered, but she was not one to be too rash. She was the type that would always wait for another to make the decision, or for someone else to figure out what to do.

"So, what's the status?" he said, as he pulled along her driver's side.

"It's all quiet. I don't see that anything's up."

"You tried calling inside."

"No answer."

Carter looked over his shoulder through the back window. He didn't have a clear view of the building, but it did look quiet. There were only a few cars parked outside where customers would park, and only a couple farther back in the parking lot meant for employees.

So...

If someone was in there and took hostages-, he thought, trying to make the mental plan as to how they should proceed. He really didn't have much of a clue. If there were people in there and someone was robbing the place, that would mean hostages.

Or maybe not. What if they weren't trying to hurt anyone, that is until they were freaked out when a bunch of cars pulled in front of the building?

Should he try to bully them with force, or try to work it out and play it cool with them?

"Okay, you hang back here for now, get out of sight and get ready to block the exit."

Samuels nodded.

* * * *

Carter was in his squad car and in uniform, so he couldn't really go up there and act as though he was just a customer. That had been his first idea, but he had to quickly lose that plan as he eased the car into the handicapped space that was closest to the store. He really didn't think anybody would be objecting.

So, what was he going to do to get in there? Really, his only plan was to walk up to the door. He didn't feel like the hero-type and had never really thought about it before. He sure didn't want to try and become one now because hero's often times found their way to being dead, and he had no intention of dying.

Okay, so run down the options; what did he have and what did he know?

The silent alarm was activated. It wasn't something that could just be tripped so someone had to have pushed it. In most of the retail stores, he knew from inspections and talking with the alarm companies, that meant that either the store manager or somebody of a manager level had to key in the code. It wasn't meant to be hidden, either, so someone had hurried to the key pad and could have been seen doing so.

If it was a robbery, staff was supposed to just give in to the robbers, the slogan "Money can be replaced, your life can not" was a warning given to almost every retail employee. They were supposed to give the robbers the money, take mental notes of what the thieves looked like, and then call the police once the criminals had left. Whoever was in the store hadn't done that. Instead, they had triggered the alarm but he wasn't aware of any phone call to the police. They were also not answering phone calls.

Cars were still in the parking lot. No fire alarms had been tripped, so there was little chance that it was a fire. People hadn't fled the building and were outside. So what was going on in there?

Could someone have keyed in the alarm by mistake, or as a joke? He didn't think so. Codes were changed when old employees were let go, and how do you key in a code as a mistake?

Well, he guessed that could happen, but he didn't see it as an honest possibility. So he guessed the only thing he could do was the thing that seemed to make the least sense. He was going to have to just walk up to the door. He didn't like that plan.

"Kalwalski and Daniels are here," he heard Samuels's voice crackle through the radio.

"Send them both down, and have them stay in their cars. I'll call them on my cell and we'll conference call in, unless they thought ahead and brought radios."

"Sorry, hadn't thought about it."

"Okay, so we'll have to use cell phones." He called Daniels first and then added Kalwalski to the three-way call. "Keep silent, stay in your cars. I'm going to walk up to the door to see what's going on."

"I hope this isn't some false alarm. Was right in the middle of a fight with Lacy when I got the call. She wasn't too happy about me showing up on my day off," Daniels said.

"Hey, now, I'm missing a rerun of "UFC", but you don't see me complaining," came the reply from Kalwalski.

"Cut the chatter," Carter said before he dropped the phone into his chest pocket on his uniform. The line went silent.

He opened his door and stepped out. The day was already too hot for the thick material of his uniform, and he could feel the wetness of his undershirt starting to cling to him. He suddenly realized that he had forgotten to throw on his bulletproof vest that was a required part of his uniform and felt very vulnerable without it.

Of course, he normally went without it even though the city had made it a requirement to wear the damn things two years ago after that shooting down at "The Getaway" which was the towns own little sleazy dive of a hotel. However, some in the town were hourly visitors. He always thought it was such a nice coincidence that it was not even a mile away from the strip club, the truck stop that was just off of the highway, and the adult book store.

"The Getaway" was far enough out of town though, just on the fringes of his jurisdiction that he just let it be. Who was he to judge, and no one seemed to care enough about it. But when a shooting happened there two years ago, the vests that had always been strongly recommended before became standard issue.

His chaffed his nipples and made him feel uncomfortable enough that most nights he didn't wear the damned thing. Now, suddenly, his chest seemed like there wasn't even cloth there to protect him, and somehow the hot summer day seemed to have an icy breeze that sent a shiver down his arms.

He took a casual glance over his shoulder back at his car and then at the squad car sitting in the corner of the lot. He could see the two other cars parked nearby and knew his men were sitting in there, watching him. He felt their gaze, but he also felt more than that. More eyes seemed to be on him. Was it the store, people in the store, the town itself? He wasn't sure but it felt like there was something there, looking at him, studying him, taking a mental note of him as he approached. Damn, why did he feel like he was about to let some genie out of the bottle? Hello, Pandora, I'm here to open your box.

He had a flash of the dead bodies from last night, and a darkness tried to shadow his mind. A nightmare that he couldn't remember, something that had come to him in the little sleep he had gotten. Something about a man, a dark man, laughing at him, surrounded by spiders. So many spiders and they had all been swarming towards him.

His mouth went dry and his chest pained with a sudden harshness to his breath. He felt like he couldn't breathe. His concentration swooned and the lights around him faded. His legs buckled and he staggered just before catching himself.

"Come on." He said to himself, taking a deep breath. He closed his eyes, pushed it all out. The sensations let go, and he could stand straight.

Opening his eyes, he looked at the doors. He could see the lights were on inside. It was morning, so it was darker in there than it was outside, but he could see the dim glow of them way back in the building, the lines getting longer and closer to him with each step.

He could see the sales ad for the current week just taped to the door, some large screen television and some tablet computer were featured on the front cover. Too cheap to actually put something in a nice presentation, they just had the newsprint taped there.

The large glass doors whooshed open as he neared them.

Something was wrong. At first, the darkness inside the building, mixed with that sun blindness from the bright outside distracted him, not allowing him to get a full sense of what was inside. He couldn't see what was wrong at first, but he could smell it.

The air blew out at him with the hum of overworked air conditioners and a whirring of some mechanical sounds above the door. It sounded like they were about to give up and quit against the already stifling heat, but they only helped blow the smell out to him. He knew that they weren't what was wrong. The mechanical smell did mix with it, but underneath he smelled something else, something that he associated with death. He smelled that stagnant odor that he often smelled when he visited his mother in the nursing home. He knew it was something else but, to him, it meant old and soon to be dead. It was...

He wanted to gag from it. Yeah, it was shit. Feces. He could smell the strong odor of it and it was nearby. There was more mixed with it, underneath of it; something that had a metallic smell, and there must have been a lot of it to mix so strongly with the odor of the other.

His eyes adjusted, and his mind calmed. His hand that had been hovering over his gun belt snapped the strap off and rested his hand on the butt of the revolver there, already feeling a little more comfortable at the feel of it.

On the inner door, he could see the bloody hand print on the door. Streaks of blood ran down to where they must have formed a pool on the other side.

He stood between the two doors, opening his ears, trying to train them to listen for any available sound. He didn't like that he was standing with glass all around him, but now he could see inside. The light high above the ground glowing down into the long rows of shelving. He could see the trail of blood as something had been by the door and then moved away from it. Back from the door a little more, it looked like whatever had been dragged had gotten up and had started to limp back into the store. Yeah, probably at gunpoint, he was thinking. So, there must be hostages still alive in there. Should he still go in?

He did not like the situation. It seemed like it was getting worse. He could see that there was more blood on the other side of the service desk, but he couldn't see what had been the source. At the exit door, which, didn't automatically open as he approached as it only opened from the other side to allow people to exit, was what looked like a woman. He couldn't tell if she was still alive or not, but she looked relatively unharmed. So, why had they left her to lie there?

Maybe this wasn't a robbery; maybe this was personal? Someone have a problem with someone who worked there? Or maybe all the people who worked there?

He tried to wonder and really put himself into the mind of who would be the person who would actually go to such lengths of violence. Did they try to return something that the management said they couldn't take back? Hell, if that was the case, he was sure the manager regretted that decision now. Still, Carter couldn't see that being the case. It just didn't feel right, though all of this was just too strange to be a robbery.

Inside the phone started to ring. His officers were supposed to have been calling. He didn't know why he hadn't heard it before, but now he could hear the sound echoing in what felt like the empty front part of the store. Maybe they had stopped for a few minutes, but the phone was now ringing loudly.

He could hear the sound of cars approaching and turned around to see the large Dodge truck and the small Camry that his two officers drove.

Okay, so new plan. He would go out, get his deputies. They would ammo up and come in and try to clear the big store. More than likely, the people inside were dead. No one was answering the phones so they could work through and clear out.

He turned and saw movement out of the corner of his eye. The woman by the exit door was starting to move.

Carter quickly hurried over to the door separating her from him, ducking low, hoping that whoever was in there wouldn't be in a direct line of site, or that he could use the clutter that was around the front of the store to keep him from being noticed.

He reached the door and pulled his hand along the glass, using the force to form a gap in the electronic door. He wasn't sure if it was a fire hazard having the door not open from either way, but it sure in the hell was a pain in the ass now. He got it open an inch and was able to get his fingers in there to have more leverage to pull. It didn't take much because with a "whoosh", it opened—loudly. Carter cringed at the noise. If someone hadn't known he was coming to the aid of the woman, they would now.

Still, he stayed low. Now it was more to be at a level that he could get to the woman, more-so than to stay concealed. She still wasn't fully awake, but her arms were moving slightly. He still didn't understand why they had just left her there. She looked untouched. Her skin was a little pale, more than what he would have expected from anyone during the summer. Even the Irish didn't quite have skin so pale as hers. He would know; he'd dated enough of them throughout his time.

He crouched down beside her and brought his hand up gently to her head. He wasn't sure if he should just tap her a little on her shoulder, slap her cheek, or maybe-...

He decided it was just safest to start with resting the back of his hand on her forehead. He figured he could make sure she was still warm, or getting a chill from shock. Plus, it was not too forward of a move if the woman was just waking up. Her skin was cold, like ice cubes. There was no natural heat. He reached

for her neck and felt for a pulse; nothing. Then, he caught one of
the flailing arms and felt her wrist. Still, he couldn't find a pulse.
	Her other arm still moved and when he let go of the one
he had been holding, it went back to moving as though on it's
own. He was confused. The woman was dead, but she was still
moving. He had heard of muscle twitches, usually while
postmortem was setting in, but he didn't think she had been dead
that long and this wasn't really just twitches. Her arms were
going back and forth, even into the air.
	But she was dead.
	He looked back to her face. Her eyes were open and her
face had turned to stare at him. Her lips were blue, blood long
ago drained out of them. Her eyes just white balls of death
glaring at him.
	She started to roll towards him. He fell back in sudden
shock. Just what was going on here?   She was dead!
	"Wha-?" he said, as he tried to pull himself back.
	Her mouth was opening and closing. It didn't look like
she was trying to form words. No, it reminded him more of a
fish opening and closing its mouth as it swam. A fish as it was
pulling in the food that was around them in the water, or were
they pulling in oxygen? That's what she looked like, like she
was trying to pull in something.
	Come on, get your head in the game, Pull yourself
awake.
	She was suffocating. She must have collapsed a lung
when she fell.
	Carter pushed himself forward, shifting his weight so
that he could meet her as she was moving towards him.
	"Let me look at you," he said, as he came forward and
started to push her back. She fought against him, but he was able
to get her to lie back. She was cold, but she had been lying on
the ground and was probably going into shock. Who knows how
long she had been lying there without anyone coming to help her.
	Whoever had been in there had probably thought she was
already dead and had just left her. He guessed that made more
sense than them just leaving someone unconscious up front who
could identify them. Still, where were they? He needed to find
them, but he couldn't just leave her behind.

He pulled his phone out of his pocket and quickly dialed the first number there.

"Yeah, boss?" he heard Kalwalski's voice came.

"We need to get an ambulance in here. Call over to county and have them rush one in!" he said, speaking in a whisper, still trying to stay quiet. He didn't think it mattered over the noise of the overhead sound of the phones. Damn they were annoying.

A noise just a little bit away from him made him stop and look up, the phone falling slightly away from his ear. He could barely hear the voice on the other end yelling back at him, "Boss!?"

A woman was walking towards him. She was dragging her foot, and her loose blouse and her tan pants were caked in the dark red of drying blood.

Another beeping started on his phone. Another call was coming in. He didn't look at the caller ID; he just quickly hit the accept button, nearly screaming into the phone, "Yeah, what!" Above him, the ringing of the phone quit and he was left in the silence that followed, watching as the woman drenched in blood was coming towards him. He started to take in her details.

She was a short woman; had once been beautiful, but now her beauty had been ripped away. Marring her face were long streaks of where it looked like claws had been raked across her cheeks. Her throat hung open. It was exposed! He could actually see the trachea as it was left in pieces, and part of her spinal column could be seen through the exposed tissue. Most of the blood that covered her looked like it came from there, but he could see a large tear in her pants and saw what looked like a bite on her thigh. Someone had bitten into her leg and had pulled out a large chunk of flesh.

He could see where blood had run from both wounds, ruining her clothing. Blood should have still been flowing, she should be on the ground dying from the severity of those wounds, but she wasn't. She was still walking towards him.

"Thomas!" he heard someone yelling through his phone. "Thomas, I need you!"

Need? With what he was looking at, he needed someone. This wasn't right, and right then, he needed someone.

Someone to tell him just what in this life could turn his world
upside down.

* * * *

Denise could only make it a couple blocks away from
the doctor's office before her hands were shaking and her sight
was so blurred that she was afraid she was going to hit something
she either couldn't see, or control her hands well enough to
avoid. She eased the car off the road, turning it into a large
parking lot. There were a lot of cars there, but still spaces
towards the back. She allowed the car to just roll into a space
that had no cars around it.

Then the car stopped.

She put it into park.

Then, she let the tears flow out of her in waves. Lost and
desperate emotions sprang up; she didn't want to admit that
something was wrong with him. She wanted to believe it was all
just a dream. How could any of it be real? There was no way;
not in any sane world that she had grown up in could any of it be
real.

So if it wasn't real, then she was dreaming. She was still
in her bed having a nightmare. Her husband hadn't awakened
her yet because maybe she wasn't showing how bad the dream
really was, or maybe there really had been an early morning
visitor and he had gone to the office. She had just incorporated it
into this atrocity of a dream and now she was trapped there,
unable to get away from it.

He was still okay. He was taking care of a patient and
she was alone in her bed. That was it, and that was all there was
to it. She had imagined herself going down to make coffee for
her husband. He had gone down alone and she was still in bed.
That's all there was to it. There was no monsters chasing after
her and her husband wasn't one of them. No, it had all been a
dream.

She so badly wanted to believe it. That she was still
safe, that there weren't things from horror movies chasing after
her. What the hell were they? And how was her husband one of
them? She could feel the place inside of her chest where her
heart had once been twisting in pain.

230

Worst of all was the emptiness she now felt. She felt like part of her was back there with him. He was still back there and, by some sick reasoning, she wanted to be back there, as well. She wanted to go back there and be a part of him. She wanted to join him and once again be by his side. That way, she wouldn't have to know this feeling of being away from him. She could go back there and become like him, and they could continue to be together.

In some way, that actually made sense to her. She could feel herself longing for his touch; longing herself to be back around him. He could take her in his arms, and then he could bite down onto her flesh.

The image of him biting down into her awakened some part of her mind that had allowed itself to rest once the car had been put into park. Suddenly, she snapped back awake, her eyes open wide. What the hell had she been thinking? She would allow him to eat her? To bite down and actually start chomping at her skin and muscles? Allow him to feast upon her blood and flesh? Um, I don't think so, she thought.

She quickly wiped the tears out of her eyes and looked around the car to find her cell phone. It was sitting next to her on the seat and she quickly grabbed it, flipping it open as she pulled it to her. She held down a single digit on the key pad and then she heard the phone ringing.

She had to call Thomas and let him know that something was going on. He was her brother. He would have to listen to her. Sure, he would probably think she was nuts at first, but he would at least investigate. Then once he went to the office and saw them there, he would call in his other officers, they could call the CDC, and maybe all this could be contained. There may even be a cure. Maybe her husband wouldn't be lost to her; maybe he could still be coming home. Her heart fluttered with the ounce of hope, but then quickly fell back into her chest as she realized with each passing ring just how far-fetched that was.

The tears threatened to return. She had to stop thinking about him. Right now, she just needed to get a hold of her brother, the chief of police, and try to get him over there. She could worry about the rest later.

She could feel her hopes die even further as the phone finally quit ringing and went into Thomas' voice mail. He had to pick up. She could not allow him to not pick up. She needed him. She hit end on the phone call and quickly dialed his number again.

Again the digital beeps vibrated through the little ear piece as she held it back to her ear. Now, with more desperation, she felt like she was trying to make herself deaf in the one ear as she held it so close.

Finally, on the fourth ring, just as it was about to switch over to voice mail, she heard her brother's voice. It was quick and clipped, but she could hear him and just by hearing him, she knew that everything was going to be better. Her older brother, just like all those times as a child when he had been her protector, had always come and saved her.

"Hey, not now. I gotta go!" he growled into the phone. He was never like that, but hearing his voice calmed her.

"Thomas, wait! It's important. Luis! Luis, something's happened to him. I need –."

"I can't, Denny. Not now. There's a situation. Bad. It's really bad. I gotta let you go."

"Thom-." She never got a chance to finish. She heard the little beeps of the phone going dead from the other end. No, she had to get a hold of him. He couldn't be cutting her off. He had to talk to her. He had too. She held down the button again and then heard the phone start to ring. Then, it beeped in her hands as it disconnected.

She pulled the phone away to look at the display. She wasn't good at texting. She didn't know if she could do it, if her plan even allowed her to. She knew, at one point, she had them block texts as she didn't want to deal with the damned things. Her sister had always been sending her what she thought of as cute pictures which had always came in garbled on her phone. She didn't like telling her sister that she was blocked; it was easier just to say that all texts were blocked. Plus, that way, she didn't have to pay for a texting plan.

She didn't get a chance to text. There wasn't any signal. Where the little bars typically showed five increasing signal bars, now they showed "no service". The phone was dead in her hands.

CHAPTER 26

Thomas Carter never got a chance to really go to sleep that morning. He had been home for one, maybe two hours before he had gotten the call to wake him back up. He had been on duty all night, and now he was awake again. Awake, but feeling as though he was still lost somewhere in a dream. No, it wasn't a dream; he was lost in some kind of nightmare and it was a sick joke of that he couldn't wake himself up. He was in a nightmare, and it wasn't ending.

The headache that had been pounding since he had been pulled out of the land of sleep hadn't helped anything so far, either.

Now it screamed at him, or maybe that was him screaming.

He had heard the woman walking towards him. The small, fragile, damaged woman who was walking towards him with a large chunk of flesh taken out of her leg. He had actually watched her as she was coming closer. That was until his sister had called and disrupted him from his gaze.

At least talking to his sister had focused him back to the situation. However, it was so hard to think with much of his mind still just struggling to fight through the exhaustion. She had reminded him, just by hearing her voice that they still needed to get the woman lying on the floor to the hospital.

Shit, why hadn't he thought about his brother-in-law before? He should have just asked her about it. Sure, he would have had to listen to the reason she called, but he could bull past it and get her husband there. Luis was a good man, he would have come. It wouldn't have even been that hard of a push and he would have been racing there.

He looked back down at the woman in front of him as he flipped open his phone. As he did, his hand lowered for a second, and it was then that the woman below him bit down onto his hand.

Now, it was him that was screaming. The pain was intense as it lit a fire through his palm and burned its way up the though his right side. He could feel warmth spreading on top of the burning already there, and the area seemed to flood with a red wetness. In the back of his mind he knew it was blood. He knew that it was his blood. It was pouring out of him in a torrent, surrounding the face of the woman he had been trying to help.

He tried to pull his hand away, but she held on, her teeth dug deep into his flesh. He tried to think and rationalize but every time he did, the pain in his hand sent white flashes behind his eyes. It seemed too bright, the room swirling around him, all of it feeling like there was suddenly too much information for him to take.

His legs gave way and he felt himself fall back to the floor. The woman came with him, moving to get on top of him. He could feel it when she let go of his hands by the pain of her teeth scraping on the shattered bone she had bitten through.

Wetness flowed down his hand and he could feel it on his face, as well. He knew he was crying from the pain. He felt like he had somehow gone home. Not the home he had left this morning, but the one he grew up in. The home he had known filled with love, his parents, and his siblings..

He never cried, not even that one time. His father had always been so proud of that. Even when he had walked home that half-mile after falling off his bike. His leg had lost most of its skin, gravel had been dug into the muscle, and he had walked home along with his bike and it's bent handlebars. He had been a bloody mess, and his mother had worked to clean the wound as his father had gotten them quickly to the hospital. And he had never cried.

But he was crying now. He knew the tears were there and he couldn't fight them. Even when he had fallen off his bike, back when he hadn't even been ten-years-old, the pain had never burned like this. This was much worse.

He could see through his tears as the woman was climbing towards him. She was using his body to climb along, pull herself closer towards his head. He could see that fish mouth, opening and closing. It looked chapped and dry, making him have to fight harder against the idea of a fish out of water. It didn't do him any good. He had to think of something to help himself.

He didn't remember pulling his gun from it's holster, or firing it. When he heard the shot, it surprised even him and he felt the little that had been left in his bladder give way. The force of the shot threw the woman off of him.

Behind her, he could see that the other one was near him. He raised the gun, the weight of it suddenly heavily in his hand, and pointed it at the woman.

"Stay away from me!" he yelled at her. He was trying to use his other hand to grab his phone which had fallen to the linoleum floor, but his hand burned with the pain. Blood was flooding out of him onto the ground and every sensation, even the cool floor, sent tendrils of flame up his arm. When he did get his hand to reach his phone, just the effort of trying to close his fingers made him see the white hot pain and his head screamed with the intensity of it. The woman was still coming towards him.

His arm trembled, the gun seeming to get heavier in his arm the longer he held it. He knew somewhere in the back of his mind that it had something to do with working out more, but he didn't think he would be worrying about that for too much longer.

"Stop it! Stay where you are!" he yelled at her again. She took another step towards him.

He squeezed the trigger like he had always been shown to do on the firing range. For how little he practiced, he had always been a decent shot. Still, he missed and he could see behind her as the cash register he had hit sparked from the new hole in the monitor.

The woman kept coming, taking another limping step towards him. He re-aimed the gun on her, and squeezed. The bullet missed again.

Then, he saw motion out of the corner of his eye, but it was too close to do anything more than make sense of it. As soon as he saw her, the woman he had come in to help, it was already too late as she was grabbing his gun arm, her mouth enclosing around his wrist. His arm shared in pain as her teeth broke the skin.

236

CHAPTER 27

Winona tried to analyze what she had seen. She needed to figure it out. She was a nurse, a medic, and was used to saving people's lives. It was what she did. It was what she was trained to do. Sure, she had other military training and other talents, but it was her calling to help others.

When she had seen the first attack, she had hurried away from it. She had made her way down the aisle, only thinking of herself and how she had to get out of there. She wasn't sure what had been going on, but she had seen people killed. Her first instinct when not in uniform had kicked in, and she had rushed away.

She had made it to the back, past where the customers were supposed to be, and into the stockroom. There wasn't much there, but she saw two fire doors and the loading dock. She could make it out the fire doors. She figured it would probably set off some type of alarm, but she would be gone. She would be safe, away from the carnage that was happening at the front of the store. That was, of course, unless there were more people out back. No, that didn't make any sense. What was going on up front was a cluster fuck and not a planned killing spree. She at least knew that, but that didn't matter. All that mattered to her right now was the door.

She ran to the fire door and pushed into it. The metal on metal of the latch release clanged loudly in the open area. She was almost out of there; she could almost feel the warm air and hot sun hitting her face.

In her mind's eye, she saw the open field that lay beyond the door. Of course, in reality, there was an alley, loading dock, and then houses, but in her mind she saw that field. Daisy's blossomed, and there was clear blue sky, as she burst out, running to some kind of freedom. She wouldn't have to think about the death, blood, or body parts that she had seen at the front of the store because she would be away from it all, smelling freshly cut grass, flowers, and the calm breeze of the ocean.

She stopped before the emergency alarm on the door went off, and let her head rest against the cool metal. She couldn't leave. Not yet. She would never be able to make it to that freedom. Not when she didn't know if those people were okay. There had been people still alive up there, people that she had left to die. That wasn't her. It wasn't like her to leave people behind. Not only was it her duty, her obligation to take care of people and help them, but that person she enjoyed and loved being would never be able to live with herself if she left. How would she be able to look back on this day years from now if she knew that there might be people alive who will die if she didn't help them?

She kicked the lock on the receiving doors, and looked wistfully at the fire door. The back area she had gone into wasn't separated by a door. In fact, all she had done was gone to the back of the store. There was a cement wall that kept customers from seeing back there, but there was no barrier to keep anyone out. There was a high row of large metal beams in what looked like fixed scaffolding, and mounted on them were large white wire shelves where various items were stored. She had to run around this when she had found the large receiving door. From where she was now, she couldn't see out onto the sales floor.

There was a little path where more shelving was stored. It looked like someone had been working back there recently. There was a ladder set up, and the white display shelving used throughout the store was stacked haphazardly about, as though someone had just left it while moving it around. It was in piles for sorting, but it did make it hard for anyone to walk around. It was an excellent place for a person to hide.

She thought momentarily about climbing back there. Maybe she could hide until someone came for her. Maybe help would be there soon, and then everything would be okay. She would be safe; they would all be safe. But if she wasn't going to try and go back to the front and help those people, she might as well have gone out the fire door.

She headed back to where the receiving area ended and the main store began. It was odd with how the store just transitioned back there into the receiving area. It was a wide open space, just going into the back area, but it was still obvious when a person reached the threshold that they were entering a forbidden part of the store. The floor itself turned from overly waxed linoleum to dark gray cement. The lighting, while it was still the same bulbs, seemed to not be as bright, and the air was cooler. It really did almost feel like entering a tomb.

She reached the edge of the threshold and stood near the wall. She just didn't know what she should do, or how she should do it. Where should she start? What she needed was some kind of diversion to get whoever was up at the front of the store away from that area. That was assuming that they were still at the front of the store. They may be searching the aisles, looking for more people. It would be impossible to say how many there were, or where they were right now. And if she did do a diversion, how would it not bring them back to her? Did she have a timer to set something up?

She pulled out her cell phone, and turned it on. It seemed like it took forever for the black screen to light up, the little apple to glow and then fade, and then the blank screen that waited for her to do something. She quickly unlocked it, and felt that sudden pang of desire. She wished she could just call someone and be saved. She guessed she could try to call emergency services again, see if maybe the situation had been resolved. After all, she may be playing hide-and-seek for no reason. The cavalry may already be there and she could just walk up front and report in.

Something crashed from the front of the store. Quickly, she moved to the side, ducking behind the receiving wall. The only way someone could see her once she was crouched down would be for them to be walking into receiving, and even then she was sure that, as long as she didn't move too much, no one would turn to look in her direction.

She looked back at her phone. It stilled showed no signal. A small blip of a bar did form, and she had a glimmer of hope rush through her, but the bar disappeared and the phone again went back to searching. Damn department stores; it always seemed to happen whenever she was shopping. She would always lose signal when she was getting to the back of the store. She should have thought of that.

"Fuck," she whispered to herself. That noise at the front of the store probably meant that it wasn't going to be good up there. She didn't know if anyone had helped any of the victims. When things started happening, she had hurried to the back. There was always the chance that the two violent teenagers could have been subdued by other people. It has been mostly quiet, and she had no way of knowing what was going on until she went up there and checked it out.

But if they weren't subdued, she still had to worry about them. At first she had thought the one with the gun had been trying to help them. The longer she thought about it, she realized that there was no way he could have actually shot the biter. He had to have been faking it. They were doing some kind of weird theatrics, and they had to be working together. She would have to worry about at least two people.

Winona turned and looked towards the front of the store, keeping close to the receiving wall and using it as cover. The store had grown very quiet over the last ten minutes, and it was hard to believe that it was even open. The right side of the store had office items, office furniture in different sets and different office chairs. None of it would allow her any decent cover to hide behind, so she looked to the left. There she saw the high rows of shelving that ran parallel with the main aisle. She could use these. She figured she wanted to flank around, go along the left side, use the shelves for as much cover as she could, and make her way back to the front. She hoped to even make it far enough that she could get a view of the people that had been attacked, and maybe help them.

She still needed a diversion. She looked back at her cell phone, the small print in the corner saying still saying "no service".

Her gut twisted with an idea. It would make noise, but it would work. She was sure of that. It would also leave her without her phone.

She looked over towards the office area. There was a lot of open space. If she was to do it over there, she could easily be seen trying to set it up. While it would be optimal, as it was far on her right flank and would be far from her projected position, setting it up might get her seen. She couldn't risk it.

Unlocking her phone again, she set the alarm clock. She made sure to set multiple alarms because the last thing she wanted was for them to come back there and quickly give up on finding her. Five minutes was more than enough time for her to get to the side wall and work her way up along the flank. She just hoped that it was going to be loud enough for them to hear it.

* * * *

She took a step forward, and was about to step out of the shadows and run to the back shelf. She would be visible from the front of the store for a brief time, and she knew she would have to make a quick dash to keep from being seen.

Her feet nearly slipped out from under her when the loud ringing sounded from overhead. It wasn't an alarm bell. No, she had heard it before in her frequent trips there to shop. It was an incoming phone call that had gone unanswered by the people in the front of the store. If they didn't answer soon enough, the phone call would ring overhead in the PA system. Someone was calling into the store.

Winona had to catch herself to keep from falling. She continued to the center aisles, and stopped when she was at the end of it. The sound of the phone ringing helped hide her running. She felt odd running like that, like she was a child trying to hide from her parents. It just didn't feel real.

She moved to look down the aisle, but still stayed close to the back shelves. She tried to hold onto the shelf, as she leaned forward and looked around it. The store was very still. It didn't feel like the place was even open anymore. There hadn't been a lot of customers before, but now it definitely felt like she was the only one here. She still couldn't see anything down the aisle. Was there anyone even still around? She tried to stay down, as she went the next aisle over. The phone rang again, the sound echoing off the linoleum and seeming to vibrate through her. What the hell was she thinking? Who did she think she was? She wasn't some hero. She helped, yes, but she wasn't

241

Rambo or staring in some Bruce Willis film. What the hell did
she think she was doing?

Her job, that's what she was doing. She never should
have run to the back. That wasn't her instinct, or it shouldn't
have been. Her training was to run to the action, not run away
from it. What would her superiors have said if they had seen her
running? That's what civilians did, and she had lost that right
when she had joined the Guard. She was ashamed of herself. At
the time, she had convinced herself that it was because she wasn't
in uniform so she had reacted differently. The uniform is a
symbol, but that shouldn't matter. Damn, she should still have
done her duty.

She looked down the next aisle and still didn't see
anyone. She hurried across the opening and stopped. Her lungs
burned, and her head swam. Spots danced in the air around her,
clouding her vision, and she had closed her eyes to let out a long
breath. She hadn't realized that she had been holding it since she
had left the back room.

She looked around. In the left corner, behind a row of
shelves, was another fire door. She had thought she had seen it
before, but hadn't been sure until she had gotten closer. Above
it, the "Exit" lights blazed brightly, and there was a large stack of
chairs in front of it. She couldn't believe that wasn't a fire
hazard. At least now she knew that she had an emergency way
out. Just keep track of the exits, she thought. She just needed to
mentally mark where they were; she may need them.

She peeked around the last aisle. She hadn't realized
that the phone overhead had stopped ringing until it started again.
Its loud tones vibrated through the overhead speakers and caused
her head to throb. How could the people work here with that
loud annoying ring all day? No wonder they were going insane
in the front of the store, and who wanted office supplies that
badly that they needed to keep calling?

Part of her hoped that maybe it was the authorities
calling to get in. Wouldn't it be too soon, though? She tried to
think about how long she had been in the back room trying to
decide what to do. She hadn't thought she had been back there
all that long. It couldn't have been longer than ten minutes,
could it? Just how long would it take for the police to come?
She had no idea how the police responded in the smaller

communities. Yes, she had lived there her whole life, or almost, but this wasn't a typical situation. She imagined that once they had gotten her call, they probably would have gotten there as fast as they could.

Five feet down the aisle, she saw that there was a phone. She doubted that she could call out on it, otherwise the high school and college kids that worked there would probably be on it all day long, but she could answer the call coming in. There was still no one in the aisle. She hadn't seen any signs of life since she had started her aisle-hopping. She should be safe to answer the phone. She didn't like it, she was going to be putting herself in the line of sight from the front of the store, but she still had the back fire door. If something came at her, she could still make it out. But, the one guy had a gun. She couldn't outrun bullets.

Just do it, she thought, working up the courage.

She ran to the phone and grabbed it, the handset nearly slipping out of her grasp. The damned thing was slick. She had to fight to control it, as she brought it up to her ear. Her lungs were burning, and she was still fighting to regain her breath. It hadn't been a long run, but she still had to calm herself down.

"Hello?" she whispered. Silence. She could hear her heart pounding in her chest. There was no one there. They must have hung up. After all of that calling, that constant ringing of the phone, the screeching of it as it had cried out for attention over the loud speakers, the damn phone was now silent. She was alone again, left to try and help the people in the front of the store by herself.

So be it.   She let her head rest against the cool metal of the shelves, and felt the small trickle of a tear.

In the distance, she could hear a phone ringing. It had to be from one of the neighboring stores, or maybe it didn't even exist. Maybe she was hearing ringing in her mind, and the bells of insanity were calling her name. It didn't matter. She couldn't give in to hope. She had a job, and it was time to do it. She had to help those people. It seemed obvious that no one was coming to help them. She would have to do it on her own.

Then the ring sounded over the speakers. She turned to look at the ceiling, and then looked back at the phone. There was a flashing light for one of the incoming lines. She pushed it.

"Hello?" she whispered again, barely able to hold back the tears that threatened her. Don't give in to hope yet. She still wasn't saved.

"This is Officer Daniels of the Hammond Police. Who am I speaking to?" The man's voice seemed loud, and she wished she could find a way to lower the volume on the phone's handset.

"Specialist Winona Peters of the National Guard. I was in here shopping when the violence started." She was trying to talk quickly and quietly. She thought she heard something rustling the next aisle over so she turned to look. She couldn't see anything.

"What can you tell me about what is going on? Who's in charge? How many hostages?" the officer asked.

"I don't know if anything has changed since I was up front. I ran to back of the store. I don't think there are any hostages. From what I saw, it looked like some kind of mass murder situation. I don't know what to call it. It was cannibalistic. One person started attacking another, and then someone else started shooting. It might be a robbery, but I haven't found any other survivors yet."

"Okay, how many...wait! What the hell!? Someone's coming out. They look like they're covered in..." In the background, she could hear another man shouting.

"Put your hands on top of your head, and get down on the ground!"

"Hold on," Daniels said into the phone.

"Get down on the ground! Now! Get down, or we'll shoot!"

"Winona, we have a woman that just came out. She's covered in blood from the face down."

Winona was shocked. "She had been one of the customers," she said.

"Well, she doesn't look...right. She's not going down, and still walking towards our police line. I need to ask you, have you seen Sheriff Carter? He went in about ten minutes ago."

"I was in the back. I heard a shot not too long ago, but nothing within the last five minutes."

"Stop!" she heard someone shout

"You said this woman was a customer?" Daniels said, his tone tight with concern.

* * * *

Daniels held his hand up, signaling to the other officer to lower his gun. He still held the cell phone in his hand. He was standing behind his open car door, feeling like he was in some classic television show about hostage negotiations. It didn't help that his car was parked in a "V" with the other officer, and he was just barely out of his door. Kalwalski stood outside of his truck and had his gun leveraged on his hood, pointing it at the woman walking towards them. He looked at Daniels' gesture, and gave him a questioning raise to his eyebrows. Daniels nodded. He could see that Kalwalski didn't like it, returning an angry glare back at him. Then the large man pulled back, and lowered his revolver so that it was aimed at the ground.

Kalwalski, was a very big man, and it always sent shivers down Daniels spine when he gave him that glare. Looks like that had been going on since high school, when Kalwalski had been the star jock and Daniels the average guy. Yeah, that average guy who lived just down the block from Kalwalski, but neither families had ever gotten along. Daniels had always been the butt of some joke or prank, thanks to the larger boy.

Kalwalski, though his family name was Polish in origin, had been born in Hammond. He had been on the football team, after the small town had consolidated its schools to have a district large enough to have a football team, and many had thought he would go on to be a star. Of course, towns always believe their stars will make it big. They thought he would make it big as a linebacker, someday running across their televisions to take out some other teams quarterback.

Daniels didn't know if Kalwalski felt that way about himself. He knew that when he had left town, gone down to Illinois State University, he had joined the football team. He had also been cut his freshman year. The star wasn't a star once he was put on that college level.

Still, the man was big and intimidating. Especially next to Daniels' small frame. Daniels wasn't sure if the reason why he wanted to be a cop so bad had anything to do with how much he had been picked on in school. He tried not to think about it. Especially since one of the fellow officers he worked with, the man now pointing his gun at the ground, was the asshole who led the charge of much of his juvenile torment.

It didn't matter. Just as long as now, when the little man motioned for the gun to be pointed down, Kalwalski did as he was instructed. There was uncertainty in his face, but the bigger man had done it...slowly.

Daniels eased himself back, watching the woman stagger towards them. She really did looked messed up.

"Hello, ma'am? We're not going to hurt you. Tell us what is going on inside? Where is Sheriff Carter?" Daniels asked.

The woman stopped and looked back and forth between the two officers. They were spaced out...Kalwalski on the outside, Daniels on the inside of the "V". They were about twenty feet apart and her head slowly went back and forth. He couldn't tell if her eyes were moving. They were just gray, lifeless orbs.

Was she blind? That could be why she was staggering, but why wasn't she answering back to him?

"Hello, ma'am?" he called out again.

Her eyes seemed to move towards him. He couldn't see it, but he felt an icy chill tingling along the hairs of his arms. It suddenly felt like the air around him had dropped thirty degrees.

He looked over at Kalwalski, who returned that same raised eyebrow glare. Daniels didn't think he was thinking too much about it, but Kalwalski had been known to surprise people. He had made it through college even after not being able to play football, which meant that he had done it on his own. However, Daniels could never think of him as anything other than that dumb jock who had always been there to knock his books out of his hands.

Motion out of the corner of his eye made him snap back to watch the woman. She was coming towards them again, and now he could see that she was moving in his direction.

"She's not armed," he called over to Kalwalski. "Maybe she's in shock."

"Yeah."

Daniels eased forward, turning sideways to get between the small gap in the vehicles. "I'm not going to hurt you."

"Hold up," Kalwalski said.

Daniels turned back to look at him and saw him motioning towards the door. Looking back, Daniels could see two more people coming out of the store. One was a skinny teenager, not much taller than himself, whom he had seen before. He remembered that he had busted the kid a time or two, but didn't think that it had been anything more than curfew. What had been the kid's name? Brian, Bobby, Willy? He wasn't sure, and didn't think it was going to matter much right now. The kid was a bloody mess.

The other was another woman. This one a little larger than the first and she was limping. It didn't take Daniels long to see why. Her lower left leg was covered in blood, and there was a large chunk of flesh taken out of it where he could see all the way down to the bone. They were both covered in blood. It ran down the front of them, seemingly from their mouths.

"What the hell was happening here?" he mumbled, as he began to realize that the blood down the front of their shirts was not their own. Hadn't the woman on the phone said something about cannibalism? Really? Could this shit really be happening? Cannibalism?

"I think, somehow, we just walked into the Twilight Zone," he heard Kalwalski saying. He could hear the disbelief in his voice.

"You three! Get down on the ground, and put your hands over your head!" Daniels said, forcing as much authority he could into his voice. They kept coming towards them.

Daniels put away his sidearm. They didn't have any weapons they could use. He made a decision. He pulled out his tazer.

"What the fuck are you doing?" Kalwalski asked, stunned.

"Get down on the ground before you force me to incapacitate you!" Daniels yelled again.

"Fuck that!" he heard Kalwalski mumble under his breath.

He aimed his tazer at the woman that was the closest and the only one within the range of the little device. He paused, waiting for them to stop. None of them did, so he fired.

* * * *

Kalwalski winced as he saw the little dart fly out from Daniels tazer, and thought about the few times in his life that he had been stung by one of them. It had never felt good. When that little needle dug painfully into your skin, you barely had time to think. It would grow suddenly and extremely hot, and then all control over your limbs and your bowels was lost. You were left a pile of flesh on the ground, stinking from the piss and shit that had tried to escape from you, and your muscles were sore like you had just done the most intense workout of your life. He had it done to him once during a bar fight in his younger days when he had been dumb and stupid. He had had it done to him again during his training by an overzealous commander, who thought that he needed to make an example out of the large jock on how the little weapon could take down the biggest of assailants.

He never carried a tazer. Even though it was mandatory and Carter had issued him one, the chief never noticed or cared that he never had it on him. He didn't even know where he had put the thing. Just that it was far away from him, and he would never go looking for it.

The woman Daniels tazed took a stumbling step forward, then she went down to her knees. Maybe Daniels was right. Maybe they would stop now. The woman seemed like she was going down. Daniels was definitely right that they couldn't shoot them. Too much paperwork and an investigation as to why they used potentially lethal force on unarmed assailants, even if the assailants did look bat shit crazy.

So, Daniels was tazing them. Well, that wasn't Kalwalski's style. No, see...now he would get to play. He didn't get to play much anymore.

He put away his sidearm, making sure to buckle it down so none of these whack-jobs would be able to grab it and pull it from his holster. Then he pulled out his nightstick...ol' reliable.

These guys were probably on something. Maybe that Bath Salts stuff he had heard about from down in Florida, and had seen on youtube. That crap that made people strong, and made them think they were zombies. That would make going after them harder, but maybe it would also make them slow to react.

"Get down on the ground!" he heard Daniels yelling at them again. The woman he had tazed was down, but was crawling towards them. Her glazed white eyes looking intently at the smaller man, she seemed to be using the line back to his tazer as a guide.

That's it. It was time for Kalwalski to go in.

"Okay, you motherfuckers. It's time you guys got some sense knocked into you!" Kalwalski said, as he stepped from around the large pick-up truck towards them.

* * * *

Kalwalski ran to the two that were still standing, his billy club raised high above his head. He imagined himself a samurai, running into battle. Not that that he was expecting one. He was going to knock some heads around, put these three down, and let the hospital worry about them when they came down from whatever drugs they were on. He was sure that Daniels would back his claim that it was in self-defense.

Kalwalski didn't get to knock heads too often. Too many of the local boys were afraid of him after the few times they had challenged him. Sure, he'd been suspended each time, but the local boys never knew that. It helped his rep, and Carter even knew that it was better for people to not know that he had been punished.

He reached the first of them and swung the club down, hard. It smashed into the side of the first ones head with a satisfying crunch. Kalwalski didn't wait to see the kid go down; he continued on to the woman. Without knowing what they were on, he didn't know what they would do. He had to be quick, decisive, and put them down before they could get him. A small pull at his stomach made him worry that he had hit the kid too hard, but he couldn't doubt himself now.

He pulled the club to the side, bringing it back like a bat. He didn't want to hit the woman as hard, and he really didn't want to hit her over the head. Actually, he didn't want to hit her at all. It wasn't like beating down a man who was probably going to attack him. To hit a woman was different.

He paused. The woman was only a few feet away, but he knew that by slowing, he had already lost the momentum he had used on the kid.

He heard a gurgling sound, almost like a growling, coming from the tazed one, and turned to look at her. She was on the ground, but she wasn't convulsing like she should have been. She was crawling towards Daniels.

"Damn, what the hell are you guys on!" he screamed, as he turned back to the woman he had been running towards. It was too late.

She was close and fell forward. It wasn't like a lunge; it looked more like she just fell. She didn't hit his upper body like she would have if she had lunged to take him down. Instead, she hit his upper thighs, and clawed at him as she continued to fall. The weight of her against him threw him off balance and he found himself stumbling back.

He tried to catch himself, but his foot caught behind him. The world was suddenly rising up to greet him, as he felt himself falling back. It was quick and sudden; he didn't have time to think. He was down. He felt a burning sensation shooting through his ankle, warmth flooded along his leg and thigh. The pain in the rest of his body was a dull thud compared to it, and he guessed that he had twisted his ankle on the way down.

He tried to open his eyes, but the pain made him want to keep them closed. He wanted to call out, but his teeth were grinding and his mouth was firmly clamped shut. His mind was shutting down. Damn, the thing fucking hurt. He'd never had a twisted ankle hurt this fucking much. He tried to push away the pain and get his composure. He started by taking in air and opening his eyes, but he wasn't ready for what he saw.

It was the kid. The kid was biting into his ankle. He was fucking eating him.

"Fuck this!" Kalwalski screamed. He was now panting heavily, trying to push away that burning. Knowing what it was didn't make it any easier because now he could feel the sensation

of the kid's teeth, as they dug deep into his flesh. He reached for
his revolver, and worked to undo the clasp on his holster. After
three attempts, he was able to pull his gun free and aimed it at the
kid.

He was working to keep an eye on the woman, as well.
She was still coming for him. He watched her out of the corner
of his eye, but the kid was the immediate threat. Kalwalski fired
twice. The bullets hit the kid's head. An eye disappeared with
the first shot, the second barely grazed the top of the his skull,
but it didn't matter. The first one should have been a kill shot.

He turned towards the woman and leveled his revolver at
her. His finger started to squeeze on the trigger, getting ready for
a nice clean shot.

More flames shop up his leg, and he couldn't keep hold
of his gun. It clattered to the cement, and Kawasaki's eyes lost
focus because of the pain. His teeth ground together, his jaw
ached. His teeth felt like they had to be splintering in his mouth,
but he couldn't unclench them. He forced his eyes open to look
down at his leg.

The kid had bitten in again, farther up this time, and was
tearing away the flesh. He was bleeding profusely, and he could
feel the cement below him getting wet with his own blood.

"Wha-," he tried to say. He wanted to scream out, but
couldn't. The kid was crawling up his body, towards his face.
The large hole where his left eye had been seemed to be glaring
at him.

The world was getting darker around him. Was night
coming already? It seemed like it should be way too early. He
looked back to the missing eye. Were there spiders? It looked
like there were hundreds of them pouring out of the kid's eyes,
and coming toward him.

As the darkness started to spread around him, he could
hear Daniels. The man sounded like he was at the end of a long
hallway. He was shouting, and he heard more gun shots. He
couldn't believe he had actually pulled his gun; that just wasn't
like him. The man had always been a pussy.

Then Kalwalski could hear the screams. He thought he
felt himself smile. Now that was the Daniels he knew. The man
screaming like a little baby.

The sound died away and the sun set somewhere behind his eyes. He could only see the shapes of spiders. They were everywhere.

CHAPTER 28

The phone cut off with a momentary silence before it was replaced with the long buzz of the disconnection. She pulled the receiver away and stared at it. Behind her, she heard something metal fall to the ground. It reminded her of what a can of spray paint sounds like when you drop it, but she was in an office supply store. They didn't sell paint. And what was going on outside? Had all the people at the front of the store gone out? Was she safe now? She didn't think so, and it didn't sound like the police were going to be coming in to help her anytime soon.

Another of the metal cans fell. She knew it was close, and there was something about that sound. She knew it wasn't paint, but was something similar. There was something about it that tugged at her, trying to make her remember. It wasn't spray paint, but was in a can like that, and it was white. Something…she had seen. Canned air!

What direction had the sound come from? She hadn't been listening for it so she hadn't been paying too much attention to it. Plus, it seemed to echo. Had it been in the next aisle, or three aisles over? It was hard to tell. So why did canned air make a difference? Why had that bothered her?

She vaguely remembered that at the end of an aisle, she had seen the large display of canned air. She hadn't been paying too much attention to it at the time, but she thought that she remembered it one aisle over. Someone was only an aisle away from her!

The hairs on the back of her neck started to tickle and rise, and the air seemed to hum with electricity. Her stomach flipped, and she could feel that little lump of fear starting to grow inside. A tiny voice in her mind started to squeal at her not to look. That little part of her told her that as long as she never turned around, she would be just fine. That whatever was there, she could just ignore it and this would all be a dream. The little squealing voice was her mother's voice, the one that had told her not to join the military, or date boys. That little voice, that was always afraid for her and had never wanted her to grow up, was also the terrified voice that had screamed at her when she was overseas. She was alive many times over because she listened to that little voice. It was often frightened and often too judgmental, but it had always warned her of danger. And now the voice was telling her she could just stay there and wait. She would wake up, and she would be safe. That it would all be over.

She knew the voice wasn't right this time.

Some kind of chattering sound came from behind her, closer than she would have expected, and she spun to face it. She couldn't stop the gasp that escaped her. She was not trained for it, or shown how to handle what was standing there. She was not ready for it because what she saw should not have been possible. It was inhuman. This couldn't be happening; it had to be a nightmare.

She recognized the man that was standing there. Not only had she seen him not more than twenty minutes earlier, but she had also seen him many times when she had come into the store. He had been one of the men who had helped her when she and her husband had bought their computer. He had helped them get a good deal on it and, when it had a virus, he had helped them get it to a guy that could fix it. He was almost always at the store. He and his large smile, friendly face and beard always made her think of a large teddy bear.

She knew that he had been attacked not twenty minutes ago. His throat had been torn wide open. That friendly smile, those warm blue eyes, she had seen them as the man had fallen back. It was his face, his eyes, his teddy bear frame, but he wasn't the same. Those eyes were now looking at her. It was hard to even imagine them as they had been before.

He stood at the end of the aisle, his large frame taking up most the aisle between her and the fire exit. If not for the barest traces of recognizable features, it would have been impossible to say who he was. There was no kindness there now. There wasn't any sign of humanity, no signs of any kind of emotion. It wasn't him; he was wrong.

Looking at him, looking through the gore that was left of his face, she couldn't stop herself from honing in on his eyes. Maybe she just wanted to avoid looking at the rest of his face because you couldn't even call it a face anymore. His neck had a lot of the muscle exposed and, in some places, she could see down to the bone. The double chin that he used to have was gone. Now, there were large holes where flesh had been torn away. The bottom half of his chin was exposed with pieces of flesh still hanging off, strands of skin barely held in place.

He was covered in blood. The red liquid that had once flowed through his veins had stopped pouring out of him. It looked like most of it was on his shirt. The once powder blue shirt was nearly black from the pure volume of it. It was all down him, soaking the khaki pants and still dripping down onto the tiled linoleum floor. Where he had stopped, she could see little puddles of it.

She looked back to his eyes, and felt a stab of fear at seeing that cold, lifeless gaze looking at her with no signs of the gentleness that used to be there. That glow he had before, the smile while helping them with their computer, was gone now. Those eyes were dead. They were gray and, even though they looked directly into hers, there was no life behind them. She did not feel like he was watching her with them, or that he was even still there.

A gurgling sound escaped from the gap below its jaws. It's as if he was no longer a living man, but had become an "it". The sound that escaped it didn't strike her as a breath; it felt more like a rush of air that escaped the unused lungs. There was no intake of air following it.

It took another staggering step towards her and, somewhere in the back of her mind, a little voice started to pull at her awareness. She needed to stop watching it. She was repulsed by it, but she just couldn't stop staring. She wasn't sure what it was, but she knew it wasn't human anymore.

Somewhere in the front of the store, she started to hear gunfire. Flashes of combat broke through her thoughts, and it was like a firecracker exploding through her head. The speed of the thoughts overwhelmed her as she noticed that it was coming towards her, that it was blocking her path, and that there was gunshots coming from the front of the store.

She had to think. She had to come up with a way out of there. No, that wasn't right. She had no time to think. It was time to act. She would think about it later.

The thing took another staggering step towards her. It was getting really close and was only a few feet away. The creature seemed to also realize this because he leaned forward. She didn't think that it was afraid to fall over if it meant that it would fall onto her. She couldn't allow that to happen, and her body knew what needed to done.

Her basic training came back to her and, in a textbook move, she moved quickly to her left. Then, with a loud angry yell, she brought her right leg up and slammed it down onto its outstretched leg. There was an audible snap, and she felt its knee pop. In an improvised move, she twisted her body, and brought the remaining force down in a punch to its jaw.

The thing was falling back. She wanted to celebrate her triumph, but she had thrown all her weight into the blows she was falling with him.

She continued to react. She wasn't a fighter, but she knew she had to become one or she wasn't going to get out of there. She had to keep moving. She fell into him, there wasn't anything she could do to prevent it, but as he slammed to the ground and then continued onto his side, she came down on top of him. From the hole under his chin, another rasping burst of air escaped. She let out a loud grunt of her own.

She rolled with it, sliding off of the fallen corpse. She hit the cold linoleum, the feel of it sending shivers along her arms. She kept rolling. She knew she wanted to use as much of the momentum as possible. Something deep inside of her had a vague memory of doing that kind of roll down hills when she was a kid, but she pushed it away from her mind. She couldn't allow herself to get distracted now.

She came to a stop when she slammed into one of the metal bases of the shelf. Her head seemed to still roll, and her stomach wanted to heave its contents back onto the floor. She wasn't about to allow it because she couldn't stop now. All she had to do was make it to the door.

She pushed herself up onto her knee and reached out for a shelf as she stood. The door was only thirty feet away so she should be able to make it. There was nothing there stopping her. She was free.

She looked back to see that it had already turned towards her. It wasn't even trying to walk; it was hurrying. That face was still deadpan, and had no pain registration. What it did have was speed, and it wanted her.

She went to step forward, but her leg was trapped behind her. Then she felt it. The vice-like grip of its hand as it grabbed for a better hold on her ankle. Oh, hell no, she wasn't going to go down like this.

In a move that seemed right at the time, she lowered her hands to the floor and put all her weight on them.. Then, thrusting out her other leg, she slammed into his face. She had no way to really aim the thrust because her center of gravity was off, but she felt a solid connection.

She heard the cracking sound of cartilage, and knew that what had been left of its nose was crushed. She came down on her knee, and bolts of pain shot up her leg. Her teeth clinched and ground in agony, and she hoped that the iron taste in her mouth wasn't blood. She didn't have time to think about it. She had to keep going.

She pulled at her leg again. She was using all the strength that she had left. Her head felt like it wanted to explode, and she could feel the warmth of all the blood flooding towards her brain. If she didn't get away soon, this whole experience was going to give her a stroke.

Sparks seemed to cloud her vision, she clinched her teeth, but she still wasn't pulling away from the large man. His hand still held her ankle, and she could feel him pulling her closer.

She chanced a quick look back at him. She must have kicked him in the lower jaw because it now just hanged there with only a small amount of flesh keeping it from falling to the ground.

She brought her knee up, this time getting herself ready for a more strategic kick. She didn't know how much it would help. The other kick would have seriously hurt someone if they were still alive, but the blow didn't seem to even slow it down.

That's when she saw them. She didn't know how she hadn't seen them before. They just seemed to be everywhere, black little spiders racing towards her. She swatted at one coming towards her hand. Even as she was doing that, three more were getting closer. Behind them, she could see just over a dozen more coming. Some were going for her upper body, but others were going for anywhere that she touched the floor. A small army of them were nearing her knee, and twice that were heading towards her other hand on the ground. She looked around. They were everywhere.

Pain flashed through her ankle, and she quickly twisted around to look behind her. As she did, she lost balance and rolled onto her butt. It had let go of her ankle as she had lost her balance. Then she saw why it had let go. It had used its upper jaw to dig into the muscle just north of her ankle, and tear away a large chunk of it.

She saw the blood before she realized what had happened. It was gushing out of her and quickly flowing across the tiled floor. She stared at it, her brain not registering what it was. After all, none of this was making sense. Why was there a big hole in her flesh?

She noticed that the spiders had changed direction. They were no longer charging any flesh that was on the ground. They were going towards her leg. No, they were going into her leg!

She quickly thrashed her legs away, kicking out. She was partly aiming towards the corpse, as it was still crawling towards her, but she guessed it was now trying to claw up for better real estate to try and bite into. After all, a leg is nice to start with but just like eating chicken, eventually you want to get to a thigh or breast.

Again, she kicked out, and aimed at his head. She connected, but there wasn't much strength behind it and its head barely rocked back. With a gurgling-like groan, it continued to crawl towards her, and she continued to crawl back.

She was getting closer to the door. It was still several feet away, but she couldn't think about that. She had to keep going. She was almost there, right?

"No matter what," she told herself, "you're almost there." Blood was pooling near her leg, and it was getting hard to lift and to push with it. "Just a little farther away. Come on, just a little bit farther."

She didn't want to look over her shoulder, but it was hard not to. It was getting closer to her. It would reach out, pull against the floor, and inch closer. More spiders were falling from where its jaw used to be. They were landing in her blood, and following it towards her.

Then, it reached out its hand and she felt it grasp at her upper leg. Its grip was like iron. It used it to pull itself closer to her. Either that, or she was being pulled backwards. Something didn't feel right in her head. She felt like a cloud was sneaking in behind her eyes and, as much as she tried, she couldn't seem to find her way through it.

She barely felt it as it used its upper mouth, the teeth that were still there, and bit down. It tore through her jeans and ripped into her flesh. She wanted to scream, and maybe she had. It all seemed like it was drifting away, and she was floating.

Pain? What was that? Instead, she just felt like she wanted to close her eyes and let it take over. It was already too late. Just lay back and give in to it. Just let it...

EPILOGUE

11:37 A.M., EST

The phone rings and a woman answers it. Her voice is mechanical and unfriendly, but she isn't supposed to be friendly. She's not there to make friends. She sits there at a phone, one that is never supposed to ring. While she is there, her life is on hold and she sits there.

And then, at just past ten thirty her time, a shrill sound breaks through the silence of the room. A room that is always very quiet and free from distractions, anything that would keep her from hearing a phone that should never ring. It was a black phone, an ancient relic of push button phones and just slightly newer than a rotary phone.

However, there was no dust on it. Even dust wasn't allowed in the room. It was only her and the few others like her that were locked in the secure room for six hours every day. Why six hours? Because six hours, it had been studied, was the amount of hours a person could sit in a bare, locked room before exhaustion or little bits of insanity would enter in and distract them. It had even been documented. She sat six hours a day, three days a week, watching a phone that never rang, buried deep in a facility that didn't officially exist.

So when the phone did ring, she wet herself. She hadn't been able to help it. She had already been in the room for five of her six hours, her bladder was already threatening to release itself, and she was waiting for operator six to come and relieve

261

her. None of them knew each other's names; they just all had numbers. She was operator 5 and operator 6 was her relief.

She could feel the warm stream as it was running down her leg, her slacks and panties already becoming heavy and sticking to the inner part of her thigh. It felt so dirty and disgusting to know what it was, but in the extreme chill of the air conditioned room, it also felt good.

She couldn't think about it. She reached forward and grabbed the ringing handset. The vibration of the phone was hard against her palm, and she lifted up the heavy receiver. The plastic was cool in the chill of the room. Actually, it seemed to be much cooler than it should have been. It almost felt like it was hot, the cold burning her hand a little. It shouldn't have felt that way, should it?

The voice on the other end was frazzled, but quickly speaks into the phone. She heard a code phrase, and she typed on the little terminal in front of her. She couldn't really call it a computer. Like the phone, the terminal felt like it was something left over from when computers were first produced. All she had was the keyboard and a screen that was mounted into the cement wall.

The room echoed with the sound of her fingers clicking away on the keyboard. She typed in the codes that he was giving her. He was getting more frantic. He kept saying it over and over again, each time getting louder until he was screaming it into the phone.

"Flag Day!"

She typed it onto her screen and hit enter. She could hear the computer come to life. There were clicks and a commotion of power. Something had started.

Everything was set into motion. She continued to listen and to type the basic information he gave her; location and knowledge as to whether it's biological or something else. She was barely able to understand him, but she knew not to interrupt him or say anything. That's against protocol. She can also hear the pounding in the background. She didn't think that she had long to talk to the man. Someone else was there, and it sounded like they wanted to keep him from giving a report. In her observation, she included that there was a possible hostile threat already on the scene.

She wasn't supposed to talk to the man long. That would also be against protocol. She had to get the essential information from him, and then disconnect.

When she finished her typing, she didn't have to click on anything. The report would be pulled in automatically.

She ended the call. The man was still talking, but it sounded like it had all become gibberish. He seemed to be losing it while she had been talking to him. Besides, she had all that she needed and had noted not only all the pertinent information, but also all the little side remarks he had said as he had gone crazy.

It was now 10:38. She didn't know who would get the information, but it was sent. Her job was done.

Everything was set in motion. The message was sent, the call would be put out. Troops would be moved into position; the first would already be getting the call. Commanders would be taken from meetings, and more calls would be made. Communication to the location in question would be cut off, life would be isolated and quarantined. It would be contained, investigated, and resolved.

None of that was her concern, and she had no way of knowing how it would be taken care of. She only needed to know that it was best not to know.

After that, she didn't know what would happen. That wasn't her job. She was a woman in a little dark room that many forgot about. She was one of six, all of them trapped in that little room; all of them awaiting that call. She didn't know if any of the others ever received a call. She knew they were not allowed to talk about it.

She had an uneasy feeling in her stomach. Something about what the guy said made her quiver. She had the feeling that she was the first in this room to experience the shaking hands, and the overwhelming need to take a drag off of a cigarette. She had not touched one in over ten years, but that pull to take in the poison was strong. She knew she was the first; somehow, she also knew she wasn't going to be the last.

What had the man said? Something about notes saying "Beware the spiders"? She hated spiders. She knew that when she slept that night, she would feel spiders crawling in her bed. In the dark room, she could already imagine them on her skin.

Their hairy legs racing along her flesh. A shiver ran down her, and a tear paused at the corner of her eye. She blinked, and it fell.

Many more things would fall later that day. She wouldn't see it, but she knew.

* * * *

Bruce quickly turned the wheel of the truck to the right, and then immediately turned it back to the left. Rob could barely follow the motions of the man, but he had already realized that he would rather watch him work the wheel than to watch how fast he was maneuvering about in the small parking lot. It was not something he wanted to think about. How was this man able to get this big 18-wheeler into a spot that Rob questioned if he would have been able to get his car in to?

Then, the large trucker was flinging the wheel back to the right, forcing down the brake as they were pulled forward by the sudden stop. Bruce had barely had the truck stopped before he was pulling the yellow knob on the dash to release the air breaks.

"Well, we're here. You can just head in there and they'll get you all hooked up with your car."   "Thank-you. I really do appreciate you driving me over."

"No problem. See that little place right across the way there?" Bruce said, as he pointed to a little bar that was on the corner at the end of the block. Rob looked down at the little place. It wasn't much to look at, just looked like a standard building with a cement base that lead up to a tiled outer wall. He did see the large neon sign of one of the main beer distributors lit, but, from the angle he was looking at it, he wasn't sure which beer it was.

Rob nodded back over at Bruce who had been looking over at him, expectantly. He was quick to continue.

"Friend of mine owns that place. I'm going to go in and pay her a visit. You get done here, come on over. I'll buy you a drink."

"Don't make me have to write you a DUI," Rob said.

"Coke only. Scouts honor. I'm just visiting old friends, boss."

Rob gave the man a smile. On any other day, he would have been serious, but he doubted that he would have given the man a ticket today. Not for how much he helped him out. Besides, he had no jurisdiction here. He could have called the local guys, and would if he witnessed a crime. He can hold someone until they came, but he really couldn't do too much officially.

"Like I said, thanks for all the help. I really appreciate it."

Rob held out his hand to the man. Bruce looked at it for a moment and then shook it, smiling.

"No problem. Now go on. Ask for Sam, and he should help you out. If not, point to my truck sitting out here and tell him this ol' dog will have to bite." Bruce winked at Rob, who was already moving to climb down out of the cab.

* * * *

The sergeant walked into the darkness of the room, amazed at how calm and still it seemed compared to the outside world. Around him, in a world that had turned chaotic over the last hour, nightmare situations were being conceived and planned for, all in the nexus of what could be done on United States soil. All of it was a mess behind him, but ahead of him, in that dark room, there was nothing but a silence and a stillness.

The cool air blew out of the room, and he actually enjoyed the basement cement smell. There was something soothing about that moldy smell that hung and mingled with the stench of oil and diesel. Of course, that was possibly just memories from his dad, as they worked on Saturday mornings rebuilding the old Buick. Either that, or it was just a comfort that something wasn't yet touched by the madness of it all. That there were places in the complex that were not yet touched by the hurry-and-wait frenzy going on behind him.

He flipped on the light switch, and regretted it. He heard the hum, as the long rows of fluorescence buzzed to life. They all started with their low glow that he knew would soon burst into bright light to bathe the area. The chaos was spreading, and now he had been the one to bring it into the room.

It didn't matter. While the eggheads would be doing their planning behind him, he would be doing his planning in there. This was his home base for the time being.

He looked around at the jeeps and Humvees that were lined up in rows. Most of them had just been serviced over the weekend, but some were there to be worked on in the next platoons guard duty. Yeah, but they wouldn't get the chance before the next time they were called into action. Sure, the bay only housed six of the large tank-like vehicles, as most of them were lined up outside along the fence line, but he was sure that all of them would be needed before the day was out.

A nightmare situation, that was what they were calling it. No details, just that they were calling all active Guards to the area.

Goddammit, it was right here in his backyard, and he had to be the damned one in charge of it.

He did know some of the details, though he rather wished he didn't. Hammond. That was the town's name. It had twenty thousand or so people, and was one of the larger towns of the area. It had a Walmart, a number of large grocery stores, hotels, golf course, and a couple of fast food restaurants. Besides Ottawa, it was the largest own, and the only real difference was that one had a hospital and one didn't.

His brother-in-law grew up in Hammond, and still had family there. He wasn't sure, but he thought his niece lived there and was pregnant with their first child. Her mother, his cousin, also lived there. She had been there since he was just a toddler, and his mother had always taken him to play there.

He sometimes bought his groceries there.

Hammond.

It's a Midwestern town, not too large, not too small, but now it had all the attention of the nation's emergency teams. It had everyone's eyes on them. The CDC, military, and politicians were already getting phone calls. Hammond was a name that was spreading like wildfire, and was being spoken about in secret all through the White House.

And yet, all the attention wasn't what bothered him. What bothered him was what attention it wasn't getting. It was his job to keep it that way...because he had orders to not let Hammond get any media attention

Sure, right now it was too soon, and it would take a while for the vultures to catch on, but it was his job to make sure that it took them as long as possible before they knew. And if he saw a camera, he was under orders to confiscate it, and detain any civilians that he deemed a threat.

It was a nightmare situation. All because some doctor had called from the town, and some code word had been given. No one had even been able to get back in touch with the guy. He just calls, gives some cryptic crazy messages, and then, with a code word, a town is locked down.

What the hell was going on?

The sergeant walked over to a table near the door and, with a flip, dumped everything that had been sitting on top of it onto the floor. It had fallen with a loud crash, metal upon cement, and it had brought the garage to life. It wasn't two seconds after the metal tools that had been on the table had fallen to the floor before the room was abuzz with privates hurrying around. They were bringing in different maps of the region. Some were the simple maps that a person would pick up from any gas station or rest area, some were just torn out pages from an atlas, and some were print outs from satellite feeds.

All of the men were scrambling. They had to. This had to be done, and it had to be done quickly. It had to be planned. He had to get everyone together, and he had to make them like a machine.

A Military Action on U.S soil. He was the one to lead his men and women to a town, and lock it down. Block off every street going in and out of it, and quarantine it.

Somewhere in his stomach, he could feel his breakfast wanting to come up. He understood. The whole idea of it just made him want to say no, that it isn't possible, and walk away. He wanted to laugh into someone's face for just suggesting it.

He looked again at the maps. He saw the red markings, and how they showed the city limits and each road that lead out. His men were already following his orders, creating guard placements, and estimating the equipment each team would have to bring to each junction.

Today would be a day in history, and he knew that there was a good chance his name would be remembered. He just didn't want to think in what way that it would be remembered.

He heard his knuckles crack, as he leaned forward onto the table. He closed his eyes, took a deep breath. He could feel everyone's gaze burning into him.

With what some could mistake as a growl, he let out the long breath. He opened his eyes, and then he started giving out the orders. In the center of his chest, he could feel the anvil gaining weight, as his heart was starting to hurt.

"Have the cell towers been cut?"

"Yes, Sergeant. PRISM has been activated in the area, and all cell communication has been terminated."

"Okay. Let's get with the county and state authorities, and lock it down. The town is now officially under quarantine."

Hello, and thank you for reading Hatched, Book 1 of my new series, Invisible Spiders. This book has been a long journey for me to write and actually has a long history for me. In one sense it has taken me over ten years to finish writing this story and even then, as you have just read, this is just the beginning.

Invisible Spiders started as a completely different entity both is form and story. The original form was in a script as I had been mainly working on screenplays bath then for various projects, and the original story had to do with creatures that were attached to everyone and that people's vices were these creatures hidden on people's backs. I still think it's a cool concept but Visions of bad sci-fi movies always prevent me from doing anything more with it.

So then in 2001, mid-September, when I wasn't sleeping too well waiting for when I would wake up to loud explosions from blocks away in downtown Chicago, I had this crazy dream. It was about Zombies, and well to be blunt and honest I don't find Zombies too scary. So even though there were aspects to the dream that I found creepy, the one thing that kept sticking with me was about the spiders that infected people and leaving them a zombie corpse shell.

Once I had that, I sat down and knocked out a script in three days. A script that I never could sell. That's fine, I had other projects to work on, and I did. I focused heavily on my film festivals and some other film work here and there, but Invisible Spiders always stayed with me. It was the story I really wanted to tell.

So when I decided to get away from doing movies and focus on writing fiction, it was the first story I wanted to tell. I wanted to run right in and start. However, this is back in 2008. I had never written a book before. How was I going to do it? There is more than just stringing a bunch of words together, you actually have to know a little about what you are doing.

So I started working on another novel which at that time didn't have a title. It was later called 'Inside the Mirrors' and by taking the time to write and release that story, it allowed me to rethink some of the story in Invisible Spiders. I realized some of the flaws and understood what elements was making it not resonate with audiences.

So when I started writing this novel, I had a better concept and realized my flaws. I should be able to knock it out in a couple weeks right? Yeah, I wish. After three years I realized the story had grown to such a point that one book would no longer contain it. Okay, so two books, remember I am an independent author and it is frowned upon having too big a book through the company I work with. There are many warnings about how the printing can be affected.

So I was working on splitting the book, when ideas for a third book started to cone to me.

Okay, trilogy. Great, I love star wars, so the idea of doing a trilogy doesn't strike me as a bad idea, nail I start to think about how much I would have to cram into the third book...

And so Invisible Spiders, the series, was born. Why? Because this is not a story that is going to be rushed. Because to me, to have a zombie story be scary, we really need to focus on he becoming a zombie and make that as terrifying as possible. Because a story should bring you in and care about the characters and their lives.

I fell in love with my hero from Inside the Mirrors and when creating him, had created a world in which he can be the main character for a series. While he is barely brought in to this beginning, I brought you in to meet him and feel his everyday life.

I sincerely hoped that you enjoyed this first entry. I can't wait to bring you the next book and remember to #fearthespider

PROLOGUE

That couldn't be what he thought it was. He heard them, the *pop-pop-pop*, and knew that it had to be firecrackers. It was the middle of the day in July. People had plenty left over from the Fourth, and it wasn't all that uncommon for them to be going off at any time of day. Kids running around, playing with M-80's or quarter sticks… That had to be what he heard, and they were probably doing it right outside the store. That's why he heard it all the way in the back room.

BJ picked the box up off the shelf, looking to make sure it had the right spark plug label. The room was dark, and he was back there amongst the shelves in what seemed like the caverns of the store. Outside, it was bright, and he was back there in the depths, looking through their stock of auto parts, gathering what his customer was waiting for. He was in there while kids ran around outside, letting off fireworks. Damn, he wished he could be out there.

It had to be fireworks. There was just no way, no matter how much it sounded like it, that it could be gunshots. They were too close to the town. Gunshots, no matter what time, would ever fly in town. It didn't matter if the chief was on duty or not. He would still bring down harsh justice if someone was out there shooting.

Yeah, BJ thought to himself as he continued to walk up from the back of the store, carrying the boxes of spark plugs up to cash register, *it had to be firecrackers. Kids were just playing around outside.*

He set the box down on the counter and looked up at the man waiting for them. Dog, a large man who wore a small, way too tight shirt that may have been green at one time, stood there. As he started to ring up his purchase, BJ had to try not to look at the "spare tire" that Dog was itching.

"So what else you doing after you get done tuning her up?" BJ said, trying not to look up at the hat, the old red "Budweiser" hat that had once also contained the numbers of Dale Earnhardt, Jr.…until someone had taken the time to work the numbers off. BJ still remembered when Dog, on a drunk summer night around a bonfire, had cut the numbers off himself after Earnhardt had switched companies and was no longer driving for the beer company. Dennis…or Dog, as he liked to be called…had used a knife that he kept in his tackle box and had cut his hand open pretty good. He had been drunk enough to not realize it until the task had been done.

Dog really wasn't the brightest when it came to everyday tasks, but when it came to cars, the man could tear one down to its head gasket and put it back together again while he was still hung over.

"Planning on taking the party barge out over to Illini and dropping a few lines. You workin' tomorrow? I can hold off until you get outta here. Grab another case and you can pitch a tent."

It was a good thought. Get out of town and under the stars for the weekend. Occasionally, there would be some guys out there at Illini State Park that were known to play some bluegrass, and it wasn't uncommon to get everyone in the campground around one fire. Bluegrass wasn't BJ's music of choice, but when you're camping out and someone is playing live music, it is hard not to sit back and enjoy. And between songs, there would be the bullshit that would fly and laughs would be shared.

Then *they* would be the ones firing off the quarter sticks. He still had a box of Black Cats he had brought back from Indiana, as well as a few other good noise makers. Ha, there wasn't anything better than throwing a pack in the fire and watching as people scattered when they went off…unless it was when you lit a firecracker and let it go off right under someone's chair. It was a good time to sit back, nearly falling out of your own chair as you watched them jump out of theirs.

Of course, it was because of firecrackers that BJ knew he couldn't ask Dog if he had heard the kids outside. Dog could barely hear anything after the M-80 accident when they were kids. Thinking about it, putting Dog's head into a garbage can and then dropping an M-80 in there might not have been the best of ideas. Dog had lost a portion of his hearing, as well as more of what little sense he had to begin with.

"That does sound like a good idea. Anyone else you know goin' to be out there?"

BJ rang up the items, adding in his discount and knocking the price down to cost. After all, BJ was the only one working in the store for the time being as Cindy was late, and he knew that no one would probably catch it.

"That'll be $10.80, Dog."

"Shit, Beej. Can't you do anything for me? Throw some shit in for free? Hook a brotha up."

"Man, I'm already hookin' you up. Now shut up before someone comes in here and catches on."

Dog was putting on a show of acting like he was having trouble finding his wallet. Of course this was a show as he wanted BJ to go ahead and outright pay for the damn things, but BJ had been through this many times before. He knew he just had to wait it out with this friend and, eventually, the old torn-up leather wallet would emerge and money would be produced.

BJ never knew why Dog did this every time. The man made more money than he did. Dog had a good job at the car dealership down the road because he was one hell of a mechanic, even on those damn foreign jobs he had to work on all day. Still, anytime they were anywhere, he always acted as though he never had any money and was always trying to get anyone else to pay for him.

It was another of the many reasons the man still had no woman. They never want to date someone who was always acting as though they were broke.

"Come on. I need to save up. Unless you're goin' to be bringin' the beer?"

And now he was bringing the beer when he hadn't even said he was coming out there yet? This was how the man always talked him into doing all that crap for which he was always getting into trouble. It always started out like this.

BJ heard it again. This time louder and more distinct, and there was now no way he could say that it was some kids or a car backfiring. Those were definitely gunshots, and from the look BJ saw on Dog's face, he knew that Dog *had* heard them.

He wasn't sure what he was doing, what he was even thinking he was going to do, but when he heard the little artificial bell from the door alarm, he realized that he was moving, hurrying to see what was going on. He wished he could say it was to do something heroic, but he knew it had more to do with him wanting to see what was happening than the possibility that he was going out there to help someone.

BJ didn't have to look behind him to know that Dog was on his heels. He could almost fell the large man's mass following behind him. When he wanted to, the big man could really move.

BJ reached the parking lot and slowed, looking around. The auto store faced the main street, but most of the strip mall was around the side where the larger part of the parking lot was. He could see the stoplight as well as a fast food joint, a hotel, and a golf course just behind the fast food place. There wasn't a lot of traffic, especially for afternoon on a summer day, but he really didn't see many people out, either. There was nothing that seemed like it could have been the cause for the gunshots.

Dog hurried to his truck parked in the handicap spot in front of the store. *Yeah, Dog was handicapped alright. Handicapped in the head,* BJ thought.

Dog opened the door with a loud creak, then BJ noticed that he was still carrying the box of plugs. He tossed them on his passenger seat as he was bending over, reaching for something under his passenger seat.

"Those were semi-automatics. Sounded pretty weak."

Hearing more gunshots, BJ spun. The echo off of the stillness made it a little difficult to pinpoint exactly where they were coming from, but if he had to guess, he'd say they were coming from around the side of the building.

"Yeah, police issue," Dog said, standing back up and holding a double-barreled sawed-off shotgun. BJ knew that the thing wouldn't have a long range, but considering where Dog pulled it from, it wasn't meant to shoot too far. Oh no. That was meant to decapitate anyone who ever tried to get into Dog's truck without Dog wanting them to.

"Which means Mandy might be in trouble," Dog said as he looked from the gun to BJ.

"Man, don't you think we should go check it out first?"

"Mandy might be in trouble."

"Yeah, and she's just as likely to bust your ass and put you in the drunk tank again."

Mandy was Dog's kid sister, and was on the local police department. She was part-time, didn't do much and, for the most part, just went around handing out parking tickets. That made her the most hated young woman in town, which she didn't let bother her because she had plans to get out of this little shithole backward ass ant hill of a town one day and go to Peoria, where she could be a real cop. BJ figured if that would ever happen, Dog would be right behind her, probably with his shotgun, ready to shoot anyone that even laid a hand on her.

Dog was already walking past BJ, nearly pushing him out of the way, no longer paying much attention to him. "I'm not drunk," Dog grunted to him as he stepped past.

Now BJ was behind him, and he had a bad feeling he wasn't going to like whatever they found when they went around the corner.

CHAPTER 1

Sarah felt the vibrations of the phone ringing in her suit jacket before she even heard the chirping sound of her cell. She reached for it and slid her finger across the screen, barely even watching as she made the motion. Her alarm had not gone off this morning and she was already running late. It wasn't her way, she was the tiger lady when it came to tardiness and being late herself was not in her DNA. It made her want to scream as these people. They just kept trying to step in her way as she crossed the lobby of the large building. Didn't they realize she was in a hurry?

"Speak."

"Where are you?" She recognized the voice on the phone. Morgan was calling, which meant that things were not good. Why else would her lab assistant be calling her? There hadn't been a staff meeting scheduled that she had forgotten about, had there? She couldn't remember one and knew she would not have scheduled one before her office hours. She only did that in a crisis and there hadn't been one when she had left the night before.

Sarah stepped around the corner of the security desk, barely looking over at the large security officer as she walked past. The machine made a little beep as she swiped her card, but even as her face popped up on the screen, she ignored the security guard. It didn't matter. Even though she didn't look up at him, he acknowledged her ID as she was already rushing through the metal detector. The bank of elevators was in sight just past the hallway.

She wasn't looking around. She wasn't watching the people. The office building she had been working in for nearly ten years was more familiar to her than her own home. Her lab was on the thirteenth floor. Well, she was one of many scientists and researchers who worked up there, but she only cared about her own.

The building was a well-designed, large building, one where windows surrounded the large street-level entry. It was like so many of the other downtown office complexes, the only difference being the additional security as soon as you entered. Many probably only noticed that, which was good. Many wouldn't think about what else was different about the building. Such as the hallway, that was decorated in a lavish marble finish, had two rows of elevators. Most would assume that both sides were the same. At a first glance, they did look a lot alike. Both sides had three gold doors, brightly polished and well-maintained so that nothing ever tarnished the beautiful sheen. Above the elevators on both sides, there was a little display that had a red number to count up or down, depending on which direction the elevator was going. Oh yes, they both looked very similar. They were supposed to.

It was only when someone looked at the call pad for the elevators that differences could be noticed. When a person would first go to the elevators on the right, they would see the typical call button. A rounded piece of white frosted plastic that was a little nicer than many of the other downtown office buildings, with an arrow in the center pointing up.

It was when a person went to the elevators on the left that things changed. The pad didn't have a button. It had a black box much like the number counter above the elevators on the other side of the hallway.

Sarah walked up to it and positioned her thumb in its center. She felt the little tingle of electricity that came to life beneath her thumb. There was a brief sensation of heat, then a pricking feeling, then she pulled her thumb away.

In that brief second, her thumb had been scanned, her fingerprint recorded and verified with a sample of her blood. Once the sample was done, the blood was discarded and the needle would be sanitized with fire and alcohol.

Once her identity and the fact that she was alive when the scan was made was verified, the door would open. It was just an extra level of security. With what was held in her labs, and what they had access to in her part of the building, there was never enough security. There would never be enough, but they still fought to do as much as they could. If what was up there was to ever get out, there was much to lose and many could die. There would never be enough security to keep that safe.

Finally, the scans finished, the center door opened. Sarah held back just a second, waiting as Morgan was still connected on the phone.

"You need to get to the airport," Morgan was saying.

"How soon?" It was uncommon for them to be told to get onto a flight. She didn't like when it happened but, typically, they would have called her while she was at home, tell her to get some things together, and they would have left that evening. Or she would get the call the night before and would meet her team at the airport in the morning.

"The team is already on its way to the airport. We leave in half-hour. I'm on my way out of the lab."

Sarah was flabbergasted. There was no way they could get to the airport a half-hour! It just wasn't feasible.

"I'll meet you down here," Sarah said. She watched as the door to the elevator closed in front of her. Something was happening, and it wasn't good.

"Meet me on the roof. The chopper will be here in five." Sarah could hear the woman already wheezing and knew that the larger woman was already out of breath. It wasn't that Morgan was out of shape, but she was a terrible asthmatic. Between the stress of whatever was going on and having to rush around, it was probably making it near impossible for her to breathe. Sarah wanted to tell her to take a minute and calm down, but she didn't know what was going on, so she didn't think it would be a good idea for her to have the woman slow down.

She lowered the phone from her ear and looked at herself in the reflection of the elevator. On most days, she considered herself to be a decent-looking woman. She was older, her hair now had to be colored dark brown as, over the last few years, silver had started to intrude. She was still slim, with a nice shape. At one time, she had been concerned about how small and pointed her nose had been, but she had grown to like it for its charm. After all, it made her think of Sarah Jessica Parker from *Sex in the City*. A show that, for a long time, had been one of her favorite guilty pleasures.

Parker had made her much happier about the way she looked. Change the hair color and she felt like she looked like Parker most days. For work, she would often wear a sensible business suit with a modest skirt…not too high to be seductive, but not too low to be Amish.

Sure, she wasn't a guy grabber, but she felt that had more do to with her not having time for them, not for her lack of looks. She just never tried.

However, as she was looking at herself in the elevator doors, she seemed to look a lot more rugged now. Maybe it was the scared, dark look on her face, or maybe it was how her shoulders, often straight and confident, now slumped a little.

Get your shit together, Sarah, she thought to herself as she reached out her finger again, and was scanned once more for clearance.

Whatever was waiting for her up in that chopper, wherever they were taking her, she knew it wasn't good. Why hadn't they called her first? They had probably called her office, Eric expecting her normal early arrival. She had that "first person in the office" attitude, and it was known throughout the building. It went with the whole reputation that she carried. He had probably called there and when he had gotten Morgan, she probably didn't want to embarrass Sarah and had just told him that she was busy. It made sense, though she wished she knew more about what was going on. If she had talked to Eric herself, she could have made him tell her something about what they could expect. She wasn't used to being in the dark. She didn't like it.

Sarah was the leading researcher in the United States for what was classified as "Unknown Pathogens". That meant that whenever there was a new mutation or something that couldn't be diagnosed, she would often be called in for a consult. Most of the time, things happened over the phone, emails were sent through secure networks, and high definition pictures were often sent for her to make educated hypotheses as to what it was.

She had given a few briefs on field work, and had written up a few papers about how she felt certain things should be contained and investigated. However, going into the field...well, that typically only happened once, maybe twice a year, typically never in such a hurry, and she was almost always sent overseas.

This was being rushed. Someone needed her right away. This wasn't going to be a long flight overseas if there was that much of a rush on it. If that was the case, they would have sent her pictures and had her do the research virtually.

This was being rushed so that meant, more than likely, whatever was going on wasn't far away. It was going to be somewhere in the United States. Did that mean there had finally been a biological attack?

She could feel her heart starting to race as the doors for the elevator opened once again. This time, she hurried in, not allowing them to close.

* * * *

The gravel crunched beneath the tires from the heavy weight of the large vehicle as it pulled off the road. It had been a half-hour drive from the armory to Hammond's city limits, but would have been quicker if it hadn't been for road construction along the way. He would have to look again at the map to see if he could give the rest of his troops an alternate route to keep them from getting caught in the traffic. If he hadn't forced the driver of his caravan to go into the ditch and around the line of cars eight miles back, they would still be sitting in the traffic, trying to get around where the highway had gone to one lane.

The large troop carrier came to a stop with a jerk, making Sergeant Wade push against the restraint of his neon green seat belt. He gave a dark look to the private that was behind the wheel, but the man missed it, and the sergeant didn't push it. Instead, he quickly stepped out and took a brief look at the city limits sign just a few feet away from him.

Hammond, Pop. 9,903.

Twenty thousand people and he had to keep them from leaving town.

Once they had left the armory, he put all his emotions aside. It would be deadly for him to think about what they were about to do. If he dwelled on it and thought about the action they were taking, he was afraid that he wouldn't be able to do it. His stomach already burned and felt like it was eating away at him from the inside.

Dammit, now is not the time to be thinking about family, he thought. He couldn't let anything personal get in the way of doing his duty. He had a responsibility to his country. He swore an oath to God and country and, while he questioned the God, his country was his family.

No matter what damn color they put into the White House, he had a duty to his country, but this sure as hell never would have happened on anyone else's watch up there. Anyone else in there would never have let a mistake like this happen, and allowed a town to be quarantined off. What was it, some kind of biological gone wrong? What could have led this town, in the middle of nowhere, to get cut off from the rest of the world?

"Sergeant!" A uniformed soldier called out as he hurried up from the troop truck that had followed behind the one he rode in. The man was holding out a large radio receiver, and he reached for it. As he did, he looked around at the men behind the soldier scrambling into the street with a series of barricades. He knew that once they set them up, they would move the trucks in front of them as reinforcement before pitching the tents to the side of the road.

Blocking the roads was going to be the easy part. As he put the large radio to his ear, he grimaced while looking at the large acres of farmland that stretched between the roads. Sure, he could block the roads, but there was a lot of space in between them and watching over it seemed like an impossible task, especially with the corn stalks high enough that a person could easily make their way through unnoticed.

It was a nightmare situation, a military action on United States soil, and he was at the "nothing he could do" end of it. If he was overseas and somewhere he felt like he could do more, could control his environment without as much legal implications, he would have sent out teams to torch the fields, making it possible for a clear line of sight from even a distance.

"Mitch!" yelled a voice through the radio, and he turned his attention back to it.

"Yes, sir!" Damn, it was the colonel.

"You in position?" the voice barked at him, with an angry, commanding voice.

"We just arrived at the first post. My men are positioning themselves at the other stations and securing them. We will be continuing on to the next location as soon as the first barricade is set up."

"How far out from the city limits?"

"We are at the city limits."

There was a silence on the other end of the line, and he wasn't sure if the colonel had just disconnected or if he was planning his replacement. He didn't know what the hell the man wanted. He was told to secure and quarantine the town. He had never been told how far out to set the barricades, and he didn't think it really mattered. He figured as close to the town as possible would cause less questions and inconvenience as few people outside the town, as well.

"Okay, secure them. I'll be there within the hour setting up secondary positions ten miles out. No one in or out, sergeant."

"Yes, sir!"

"Over and out."

"Over and out."

He knew this time that the colonel had disconnected. He handed the phone back to the soldier who was standing there, then turned back to the rest of his men. They were working quickly, and the camp would be set up within five minutes. Not bad, but that didn't mean he still couldn't yell at them. They needed to know he was still biting at their heels or they would get lazy.

"I want this camp set up and ready in two minutes! Five minutes, I want the line at attention! Last man to be in line will be digging latrines! Understood?!"

The men seemed to hurry their pace, but that could have been his imagination. He would like to think he got them to bust their ass. He would like to think a lot of things. He didn't want to think about what the hell would get the colonel off base and coming all the way up there to them. And if he would be there within an hour, that meant they mobilized even before him and his men.

So what in the hell was going on? He sure wished he knew.

"Pierce!" he called over to the man with the radio who had just started to walk away so that he could set up his equipment in one of the tents. "Pierce! Get with the other units. I want everybody's status before we line up, make sure they are all in position. Then call the armory. I want to know how the remaining troops are coming, if the guard for the area has been called in and notified. Make sure they are also getting ahold of the guard inside the town. I want those soldiers to know the situation and get with the authorities to try and keep all those inside the city limits calm. The local law enforcement must help to keep people from trying to get to our lines. We have orders to shoot, but it must not come to that. Got it!"

"Yes, sergeant!" The man hurried to where four other men had just set up one of the tents. His equipment had already been brought to it and he quickly went to busting them out of the crates and onto the tables.

Get the perimeters secure, get the people locked down…lock in all the pigs and get them ready for the slaughter.

His stomach twisted into a knot as he thought about it. That's exactly what all this was. They were all pigs, all locked in for the slaughter. There were so many grisly possibilities of locking in all these people. He had friends and family in there. What was he going to do when he had his sister in his sites with an order to shoot? Would he be able to pull the trigger?

None of this was good, and he was sure that this night wasn't going to end well. Pigs in a pen, and the pen is all fenced in. So many roads leading in and out, so many gates for the farmers to watch their livestock. If the pigs tried to run and get out, would they really be able to hold them? Oh no, this was not going to end well at all.

He thought back to the map he had seen. Back at the armory, he had pulled out a large map of the area, detailed with many of the roads. It would never have *all* the roads as there were always the small farm roads that never made it onto the maps. It didn't matter. The map they had used had been detailed enough, showing the crisscrossing patchwork. He had looked at it, thought about all those lines as they worked their way across the terrain. Taking out all the fields and the topography, it was all just a bunch of lines. Lines that all came to a centralized point…Hammond.

He knew what it looked like, the lines getting closer together as they merged to one point. He couldn't help but think about it. He didn't know why he had never seen it before, and why he didn't think that it had anything to do on what was going on now. Why should it? He couldn't help but think that with how all the roads came together, it had an eerie similarity to a spider web.

And now the townspeople, and even himself, were all the flies.

"Pierce, make sure to get a call in. Make sure they got the choppers in the air! Keep their eyes on the corn."

CHAPTER 2

Rob couldn't think of a day that he regretted leaving Chicago more than any other day. Sure, the crime was bad there and he had always been forced to be on his toes. A Chicago cop never knew when the next bullet might be shot, or when they would take a figurative knife in the back. In fact, he had seen that just last year. Chicago had topped New York as the number one murder capital in the United States. Another statistic that he didn't want to contribute to. He had been thankful to get a job out of the city.

But at least when he was a part of the Chicago PD, he wouldn't have found himself stuck out in the middle of nowhere. His bills, back when he had a steady full-time job, had always been paid, and he was able to put food on the table. He was able to survive and not have to work the odd jobs he was now having to do around the neighborhood just to earn a little extra income. He would have been making enough money to have had the spare on his car fixed so that when his tire had blown, he would not have been left stranded on the side of the road, stuck on what seemed like some forgotten back highway that no one used anymore. He wouldn't have been out there when the corn was so high that he had no clear way of seeing where there might be a farmhouse he could walk to, or some kind of help he could find.

Yeah, so why didn't he use his cell and call for help? That was why people had the damn things, so that they wouldn't be stranded in the middle of nowhere. Not that he had the best damn cell reception out there. He already learned that from experience. But to have to worry about reception, he would have had to remember to have brought the phone with him. He would not have left it sitting on his nightstand, where he had been using it as his alarm clock that morning.

Thankfully, someone had finally shown up to help him. A truck driver, a larger man who looked to be a little older than Rob, maybe in his mid-forties, had pulled off and picked Rob up, bringing him to the closest town. Of course, it didn't do him any good to get to the county courthouse to testify in the vandalism case he was supposed to be appearing at, but with most of the morning wasted on the side of the road, all he really wanted at this point was to get somewhere cool, sit down for a bit, and maybe get his hands to stop shaking from everything that had happened that damned morning.

He had never had a tire blow on him going sixty miles an hour. The front of the car had rocked up, coming crashing back down. The whole world around him started shaking as he fought to keep control of the car. It seemed odd that he really only had to fight for control for the first few seconds, when the car had crashed back down from the initial blow out. After that, the car seemed to stabilize itself, and he was able to ease it over to the side of the road. Sure, it was easy and, for a long time, he hadn't really thought about what he had done. The whole time he had been focused on just reacting. It had seemed so easy…until he had time to think about it afterwards and wonder just how he had actually done it.

Bruce, the truck driver, had picked him up, taken him to a little diner for some lunch, then had taken him to the garage he knew right across from a friend's bar. Rob appreciated it, and had enjoyed the meal. He hadn't thought too much about the whole experience and how he was lucky to be alive. Now though, as he watched the large man cross the street, walking away from him and heading off to the little bar, he had time to think. His hands were shaking as he realized that his morning, his shitty morning from hell, could have been a lot worse. He could easily have lost control of the car, it could have flipped over, the rubber and metal from the tire could have ripped into the engine and done some damage or caught on fire, and he might not have walked away from it.

All in all, he was lucky to be alive.

Rob watched and saw the little bar that Bruce was heading towards, making sure to make note that it was the building just across the railroad tracks, caddy-corner to the little garage he was at, and not the bar just across the street from him. They were so far off the main drag of town, he was surprised there were two bars, but he made sure that he would go to the correct one as soon as he was done talking to the mechanic.

He looked around, seeing the little garage. Back in Chicago, he would have thought it was a meth lab…the dirty windows, how much clutter that seemed to just find homes in corners, junk piled on top of junk. The place didn't look like it was open for business and looked like it wanted to stay off people's radar. Why would anyone choose to go there? It seemed like a place abandoned and forgotten. The cars that were stretched in the lot along the side of the building were covered in dust that even the latest rain hadn't been able to wash clean. He doubted that even the newest car was less than ten-years-old, and he questioned who would possibly pay the $700 that was crudely written on its windshield in large, washed-out soap numbers.

But Bruce had ensured him that this guy would be okay. He wondered just how Bruce knew the guy, but

Bruce was from the area, while Rob, living just thirty miles from there in a small town he had moved to just over a year ago, was still a stranger.

He didn't know if he would ever get over the differences between being a Chicago PD officer to being a small town deputy. It had been a big shock when they had moved down there, and it continued to always amaze him that it could get more unexpected. It wasn't like Mayberry, like the television shows he had seen growing up, but it wasn't much like those modern shows that teens watched, either. The sheriff didn't know everyone, didn't care to know everyone, and the police force wasn't always on duty. At least that's how it was in the small town that he was a deputy in. He wasn't sure how much different it would be in the town he was currently stranded in. In his town, the local law enforcement was on duty from 4 p.m. until 4 a.m., and anything after that required a call to county. The sheriff worked five days a week. That left only weekends for Rob to work and was the reason why he had to find various odd jobs around the town to make ends meet.

Why had they left the city and his full-time job again?

Oh, that's right. Because on his last call as a CPD officer, he had been shot, set on fire, pushed down some stairs, and awoke in a hospital weeks later. Well, that and the fact that there had been a rash of school shootings at his son's school made both him and his wife re-think the idea of living in the city. While he hadn't meant to do something as drastic as moving far out in the country, it was the job that was available, and the house they had found made him jump at the chance.

Yes, he had jumped at the chance to have a house large enough that he could have his own man-cave. Pardon him for wanting to have his own space and have a room to sit back in, get a big screen television to watch the Sunday football games. Of course, when he found out the job wasn't full-time, the big screen television never reached his man-cave.

He walked over to the front door of the little place, noticing that he could just make out the flip sign through the dirty glass of the door…"Yes, We're Open". He pushed on the door, momentarily fighting as it was stuck, then cringing a little as it scraped the door frame before releasing and letting him step inside.

The smell of stale cardboard, old oil, and the heavy musty odor of dirt attacked him, and he was instantly reminded of what his garage had first smelled like when they had moved into his house. It had only been a year ago, and for Robyn and him, the house was huge. Coming from Chicago, buying the house for only a fraction of what they had paid for their condo, they hadn't been ready for the amount of space they would have. He also hadn't been ready for the garage they had inherited with the house. He had no idea what the previous owners had been like, though looking at the boring white walls for most of the house, he didn't think they had been too imaginative. The garage must have been the storage area for most of their shit, and the previous owners didn't believe in disposing of old oil. He had found jugs of the stuff and the garage reeked of it. The smell seemed like it had infused itself into the cement floor and the wood beams, like it was a part of it.

It wasn't filling him with confidence that this mechanics garage smelled much the same way. Did he really want to trust his car to this guy? Sure, he only needed to get a tire fixed, but something about that bothered him. He felt like he was forgetting something. He didn't know what it was, but there was a thought hiding in the corner of his mind. Something here wasn't going to go how he wanted it to. He wasn't sure how he knew, but he had that uneasiness that told him something was about to go wrong.

Once he opened the door, there was a digital jingle that seemed off key, the batteries probably dying. He closed the door behind him, the metal again squealing in protest as it fought its frame.

"Can I help you?"

Rob turned to see a short, grease-covered man standing in the open doorway to the garage area. The man seemed to fit right in with the small front counter area, which was a dirt-covered mess. His shirt was covered in dark streaks, his weathered skin was darker in spots from where grease and other traces of God knows what were streaked across. His skin was tight, stretched like leather, his veins protruding from years of hard work and living on the hardships of the job. The man looked small and scrawny, but Rob had seen the type before. He was the kind of man who didn't look like much but he was covered with tight muscle, the kind that was like iron in a pinch. It was a workers leanness.

"Yeah, my car… I had a flat tire on the way into town and I'm without a spare. Was wondering if you could come out and put a new one on?"

"What size?" The man stepped the rest of the way into the room. Rob could see that the name on the shirt said "Mike". He walked over behind the counter and grabbed a piece of notebook paper from a pad that was next to the phone. The rest of the counter was covered in printed work orders, scattered into various piles.

"Excuse me?" Rob walked up to the counter.

Mike raised his eyebrow. "What size is the tire? I can take one out and change it, but I need to know the tire size."

Shit, that was what Rob had been forgetting. He needed to know the rim and tire size, *especially* the rim size. While it wasn't recommended, he could put a tire on that wasn't the same size as the others. He could do it, just it would really screw up the alignment and the car would pull in one direction. No, the rim size though, he would need to know that for sure, or else Mike wouldn't be able to put on a tire that fit. There was very little he could do about guessing the right rim size, and he didn't know it off the top his head.

"I…I..don't know." Rob finally said as the man's glare hadn't softened. Now it grew more intense, and Rob thought he saw the man's shoulders sag a little. Not that it didn't surprise him. He knew that Rob had just made himself one of the harder to deal with customers. He hadn't meant to, but that didn't matter. Mike looked like he had dealt with one too many hard cases that day.

Blowing out a breath, Mike asked, "Where's it at?"
"Well…"

* * * *

Jason knew he couldn't stay hidden in the kitchen for too long before the customers in the bar would get frustrated with him. While that didn't matter to him, as he really couldn't care less about any of them, he knew that it would upset his mom. She would, of course, hear about it. He was sure that no matter what he did, she would hear about it so he didn't know why it really mattered. No matter what he did, these people would always complain about him because he wasn't her. He couldn't relate to them, nor vice versa. He knew he should try and cause the least amount of complaints while she was on vacation. He was in charge of watching the bar and he didn't want to disappoint her. She deserved her time away and it would be good that she felt like she could take a vacation every once in awhile.

But his aunt was really upset. He was holding her at arm's length, and he could see that she was a wreck. Her body was trembling, her lower lip quivered, her eyes were puffy and red. She was on the brink of crying again. How had she been able to drive to the bar? He had found her like this out in her car just a few minutes ago, sitting behind the steering wheel and crying as she looked off into space. He didn't know how long she had been sitting like that before he had taken out the garbage. It couldn't have been too long; otherwise, one of the patrons probably would have said something to him. She had parked not too far from the door, so they definitely would have noticed her.

So how could he leave her? It was one thing to leave her and check on the patrons out there, but she wanted him to go to the house. He understood why. Bad things would happen if he didn't, but how could he? Right now, there was no way she could handle even just the couple of people that they had out there. The conversation they just had couldn't seem to sink in. Had his aunt really just confessed to killing someone?

When he had first brought her into the back, she had stopped crying already. He hadn't been too sure how long ago she had stopped, but it must have been just before he had found her. The corners of her eyes had still been wet, her cheeks still red. He led her to the back of the bar, her head low so that none of the patrons could really see her face.

She stayed quiet the whole way. Even when he got her away from people, she stayed that way. It bothered him. Something had happened at the house, and his gut had been twisting at the possibility that something had happened to Lisa.

Lisa was Jason's little sister. He didn't know why his parents had waited ten years after they had him before having another child. Maybe it had something to do with them just wanting another baby to squirm around the house and break things, or maybe they were just afraid of starting to get their freedom back because he would soon be able to take care of himself. Hell, who was he kidding? He knew the reason why. They were getting ready to get divorced. Lisa was that one last attempt to make everything right in so many ways.

So was that it? *Had* something happened to Lisa? Now that they were in the back and away from people, his insides twisting in aggravation because she didn't just say what had happened, he finally asked her. He looked down at her face in the crook of his shoulder as she was so much shorter than his six foot, one inch frame.

"Is Lisa okay?"

Tina seemed shocked. She pulled back and looked up at him. Then the moment passed and she was shaking her head. She rushed over to the sink, turned on the faucet, and started to splash cool water into her eyes.

"It's not Lisa. She's fine. She's at the game." Tina turned off the water, but she didn't turn to face him. She kept her head low and as he watched her fight to keep her body from shaking, he knew she was trying to keep the tears back. She was on the verge of losing it all over again.

It didn't feel right that he should be the one to console her. With how young his aunt was, only five years older than himself, he felt like he was acting like a boyfriend, not a nephew. It felt like what he should do, but he didn't feel like he should be the one to do it. It was inside that personal bubble, one that said he should always keep her at a distance, or else other feelings may develop. She was his aunt, dammit! He can't think like that, although she *was* cute. It was just sick.

He stepped behind her, again keeping her at arm's length, and reached out to touch her shoulders. Her back stiffened, and he knew that it had been the wrong move. He quickly stepped back, dropping his arms and bowing his head.

Damn, he was no good at this. Why did this have to happen while his mom was away?

"She's at the game," Tina continued, "but she will be home soon."

Jason felt like there was something in how Tina said that. It seemed to drop the temperature in the room to freezing, making him shiver in the chill. What happened to that July heat outside?

She turned to face him, and he saw that she was on the verge of releasing more tears. "You have to go back to the house. You need to. Lisa could be home anytime, and he's still there. You need to get there and take care of him. Lisa shouldn't have to see that."

"Take care of who? What's wrong?

The dam broke and the tears came. Her hand quickly came up to try and hold them back but, as it shook there, it did little more than wipe away at the corners before falling back to her side. She leaned back against the counter and looked down at the floor.

"I killed him. At least I think I killed him. I don't know, but I think so. It doesn't matter. He can't be there when Lisa gets home."

"What? Who?"

"Vince."

"Vince? Who's Vince?"

"My boyfriend. The one who-."

Tina couldn't finish. She just hunched over, quivering. She didn't have to finish, though. He had overheard the conversations she had with his mom. He knew that Vince had beaten Tina, and that she was staying with them to hide from him. So he had found her? Had he tried to hurt her and something happened? She was here, so she had gotten away from him, but she's convinced that he's dead? Maybe he is, and now she wanted him to…what? Hide the body? Why not call the police? That's what he should do, and probably what he was going to do. She just wasn't thinking straight.

It did mean he needed to get back to the house, especially if Lisa *did* come home to find a dead man there. His sister wouldn't take that too well, and it would probably give her nightmares for the rest of her life. He couldn't let her see that. Tina was right. He had to go to the house.

"Hey, kid?!" he heard someone call from the other room. Now he had to leave her back in the kitchen.

"I gotta go take care of some customers. Are you going to be okay for a minute or so?" he asked her. She nodded. He hoped so, but he had his doubts. She tried to sniffle back some of the tears and smile up at him, but he knew it wasn't real. Her eyes were still lost and pleading, still glinting with the threat of more tears as soon as he was gone.

He quickly hurried out of the kitchen and to the man that was sitting at the bar. Mr. Jones was still sitting at his end of the bar, and Jason was kind of surprised to still see him there. Usually when he was getting ignored, he would just get up and leave. Not only was he still there, but he stayed past the time he normally was there. He usually only stayed this late when there was someone just as annoying as he was that wouldn't stop talking to him.

Jason turned away from the old man who called him. He was surprised to see another person just a couple of stools down. The new man was older with some stubble that showed he hadn't shaved for a couple of days. He was a husky, rugged man who looked like he didn't miss too many meals and didn't get out much. Jason ignored him as it was hard not to because the other man was tapping his beer bottle against the bar impatiently.

"Sorry, he said as he hurried towards the impatient asshole. He could really wait as long as it took to get down there as far as Jason was concerned. He didn't really like dealing with pushy pricks, and this guy seemed apt to push his buttons. He had already labeled the man as a dumb hillbilly redneck prick, and he had no tolerance for him. Maybe it was how they interacted with each other, but the feeling seemed to be mutual. The man wasn't anything great to look at, and his stained wife-beater, along with the well-worn "Lite" hat that looked like a dog had once thought it was a play toy, had Jason thinking of the man as something he didn't even want to wait on. Hell, he probably owed money on a tab that his mom kept under the counter. Seeing that she wasn't there, he was spending the money he should have paid it off with on some more beer. Jason didn't know the man, so he couldn't check on it. It wouldn't surprise him, though.

He wanted to trick the man into giving his name. Jason didn't think the stranger was smart enough to figure out what he was doing, but doubted he would be willing to talk long enough to get it to work. Jason didn't feel like putting forth the effort anyway. It would only piss off the maggot and make him leave. Then again, maybe that would be a good thing.

"Just hurry the fuck up." Jason nodded to him and quickly turned back around, going down the side of the bar near Mr. Jones. He opened the cooler, momentarily relishing in the blast of cool air that escaped, and grabbed a brown bottle. He was already opening it as he hurried down to the man and put it down in front of him. He took the money from the pile on the bar, then turned to the register and put it in the till.

Jason really did like many of the people who came into his mom's bar. Josh and a few others were good friends and occasionally he would flirt with a few of the girls that came in there, though none of them were really his type. Just, there were also the assholes as well, and Jason did not have the tolerance his mom had with dealing with them. He just wished they would leave and leave him the hell alone.

"I'm done with this, the man said. Jason turned and saw the large bucket next to him full of tickets. Jason took it and put it below, then turned his attention to the other man sitting there.

"Really sorry about the wait. Had some issues in the back."

"Screwing around back there with the little missus?" he said, a mocking smirk working its way through his grease-stained face.

"Eew. That's my aunt," Jason said, making a face, and turned to look towards the new guy who was just a couple of stools down. "So, what can I get you?"

"Well, what I want is one of your mom's heavenly pre-mixed Bloody Mary's, but…" The man hung on the word "but," stopping Jason as he had already been bending over to grab the jug of mix from the cooler. "But I'm in the truck today so I'll have to settle for a coke," Bruce finally said. "Yeah, I gotta be good."

Jason stood and walked back down to the cooler, grabbing a can of coke. He had to get out of there, and more people coming in was not helping. He had to think of someone who could watch the bar. How could he leave? Just close it up? Yeah, his mom would love it when she heard about that, and she *would* hear about it.

"Better make it a diet," Bruce called down. Jason nodded and reached back in the cooler.

How could he leave the bar? Truth was, he didn't have too many people he could trust with it. Sure, he had grown up in the area, but he never had too many friends, and most of them he did have had already moved away to go to college, just like he was. He just happened to be home to help out his mom, but he normally wouldn't even have been there.

In fact, the only friend he did still have that lived around there was his best friend and the one he still kept in contact with pretty regularly. Hell, they did a show together every Wednesday night but, more often than not, that was done through Skype and long distance. That still didn't mean that Jason would trust the bar to him.

As he walked past the hallway that led to the back, he could still hear Tina crying.

It was settled. He had to call Sullivan. He had already tried to call him a bunch of times earlier, just out of boredom. Hopefully, now he could get the lazy bastard out of his damn bed.

Jason put down the open Diet Coke and quickly filled a glass of ice to set next to it. He didn't even take the man's money as he quickly turned, went to the phone, and started dialing Sullivan's number.

Once again, he didn't answer. *Damn him! Come on, Sully. Answer the damn phone when I need you,*" he thought to himself.

www.ingramcontent.com/pod-product-compliance
Lightning Source LLC
Chambersburg PA
CBHW021505110726
47899CB00001BA/294